The Storm Within

A novel by
Darlene Deluca

Enjoy!

Darlene Deluca

Other titles by
Darlene Deluca

Unexpected Legacy

Meetings of Chance

To Mothers and Daughters,
especially my own

The Storm Within
All rights reserved. Copyright © 2013
by Darlene Deluca

ISBN: 1490379231
ISBN-13: 978-1490379234

The Storm Within

A
Women of Whitfield
novel

PROLOGUE

Claire shook the spray of liquid from her hand, laughing. "Jeez, take it easy. I didn't realize you'd already been drinking." She checked the glass for signs of damage before lifting it to her lips. Mary's toast carried liberal enthusiasm.

"In your honor, babe." Mary leaned forward. "Seriously, Claire. This is fabulous. You nailed it."

Claire grinned. "About time, too."

After months of wishy-washy deliberation, the Whitfield Library Board had finally agreed to launch a capital campaign to raise money for renovations. The improvements would bring the woefully inadequate children's section into the new century with computers and E-readers, reading nooks and a storytelling stage in a book-themed setting to inspire little minds and imaginations. Claire had spent an exhausting two years working on the project, building her case, researching ideas and putting together a proposal. She'd earned a toast.

"Did you see Jessup's face when you were making your presentation?" Mary asked, her laughter rising to a spirited cackle. "His tight little ass was all puckered and he was ready to bombard you with his usual roadblocks. Then, I swear the guy almost smiled." She slapped the table. "When he nodded, I knew he was hooked."

Claire had seen it all right. She'd damn-near fainted at the podium when he didn't ask a single question. "I don't know what kind of spell came over him, but I'm not gonna argue. Now all we need is money."

"No problem. It's time to turn on the charm, girlfriend. And if all else fails, there's always South Broadway. I hear Saturday nights are busy down there."

Claire smacked Mary's leg with her shoe. "Thanks for the vote of confidence."

She wouldn't be resorting to prostitution, but Claire knew some finagling and sucking up would be necessary. Raising this kind of cash wouldn't be easy.

It would take a lot of time, and she might have to call in a few favors. Still, she was determined to make it happen. She'd put the library project on hold while she helped bring Hospice services to the community. Letting people die with dignity had trumped giving them books to read. But with Hospice up and running, she wanted to move ahead with the library before something else got in the way. There was always something else.

"So, I guess the rest of my to-do list is going to the back burner," she told Mary. "Everything except the new deck. We're finally moving on that. Stan's got someone coming out to measure this week. I think he's kind of excited about it. Soon as it's done, we'll have you and Grant over."

"Just name the day. We're wide open until school starts up again."

Claire shook a pen at her. "Don't plan on me for school activities this year. I mean it. Do not volunteer me for anything. And I may miss a few book clubs. Can't imagine when I'll have time to read."

"Rather ironic, don't you think," Mary drawled. "Too busy building a library to read a book?"

Claire sputtered out a laugh. "Okay, okay. I'll try."

"You have to come to the next one, anyway, because it's your turn to bring goodies. No wait, maybe you're supposed to bring wine. I'll have to check the list."

"Oh, don't bother. I'll bring both. It's not like we can have too much of either. What I really ought to bring is a big bag of Depends. I swear I laughed so hard last time I almost peed my pants."

"Right there with you. Jane was in rare form that night."

"I haven't talked to her for a few days. Do you know if she got the motorcycle out of her kitchen sink?"

"Well, I haven't heard about any murders in town recently . . . and she did threaten lethal action."

"With good cause," Claire added, shaking her head.

The laughter died in her throat when she looked past Mary to see Stan striding toward them. What in the world was he doing here? In an instant, Claire's blood turned to ice. Her husband's face was tight and drawn, his eyes fearful.

There could be only one reason for that look, for him tracking her down like this. No. Oh, God. Claire bolted out of her chair with a strangled cry. "Something's happened."

He moved in close, his fingers closing around her arm.

Her heart pounded. "What?"

"It's Ben."

Chapter One

She looked at him, the man who'd been her husband for thirty-two years, and felt only disgust. No, not only. There was contempt, anger. Hatred?

"I don't love you anymore," he said, his voice stilted and unnatural, as if he were reading the line. "I've already seen an attorney. You'll get papers."

Though the words hit her like a punch in the gut, she refused to let him know it. Papers. A few pieces of paper full of formal 'whereases' and 'heretofores' wouldn't tell the real story – that he'd found someone younger and thinner, someone whose face and breasts hadn't yet suffered the effects of gravity. Bastard.

With shaking hands, she lit a cigarette, and exhaled in his direction. Through the haze, she regarded him with a cool stare.

"Then get out of my house."

"Claire—"

"*Get out.*"

He pushed back the chair, scraping it against the tiled floor. As usual. He could never move the chairs without that nerve-jarring scrape of metal against the surface. The beautiful designer tile they'd so painstakingly chosen – scratched and marred. Like everything else.

She didn't move until the door snapped shut behind him. Then she wandered into the living room and lay down on the sofa, her head resting against the arm. Fine. She could use a little peace and quiet. She closed her eyes, but the sound of the clock tick-tocking from its place on the wall grew loud and annoying. Had that thing been a wedding gift? It was plenty old enough, for sure. Reaching down, she pulled off a shoe and flung it in the direction of the clock. It hiccoughed. Then resumed its rhythmic beat.

Irritation flared, and she threw the other shoe fiercely at the face of the offending appliance. The needles bent, and the clock swayed against the wall, but again, the sound resumed.

"Why can't you give me some goddamned peace?" she screamed, getting up from the sofa. That clock had been in the same spot for years, its ticking and chirping telling her when to do this, when to do that every minute of every single day. In one fluid movement she yanked the clock from the wall and smashed it against the tile, finally silencing it as bits of wood and metal flew across the floor.

Claire saw Reggie, her fat tomcat, duck under the leather side chair. Briefly, she thought about coaxing him out. Reassuring him. But it required too much effort. Then again, she thought, maybe she could join him. Wouldn't it be nice to just duck and hide when shit came crashing down? Too bad she wouldn't fit under the chair.

With a deep drag on the cigarette clutched between her lips, she marched back to the sofa and flopped herself down. Why would she need to know what time it was? It didn't matter. She had nowhere to go. No schedule. No one to fix supper for. Nothing was required of her.

She was free.

Claire closed her eyes until warm ashes dropped onto her chest. With a start, she brushed the ashes away. She swung her feet to the carpet, and jabbed the butt of the cigarette against the glass dish on the coffee table, then padded into the kitchen for another. She withdrew one from its package, but changed her mind. Tossing it onto the table, she turned and headed for the cupboard instead, stopping to give the remains of the clock another quick shove with her foot as she passed it.

From the cupboard she selected a favorite wine glass, one of the good ones with the twisted blue stems. She filled it with Merlot and sipped, leaning against the counter.

Would he tell the childr– She stopped herself. Would he tell Elise? Or did he expect her to do it?

Elise would be sad, Claire supposed, but that was it. With two young children of her own, Elise wouldn't have time to worry about her parents' problems.

The bastard. He'd waited until Ben was gone. Ben would've hated him for it. He would've called him out. He would've looked after her. Ben. Oh, God.

She choked on a sip of wine, but took another drink, her shoulders shaking. Slowly, she slid down the smooth cherry cupboard until she hit the floor. She curled up, sobbing. What else could happen to her? Everything was gone.

"There!" She screamed into the silence. "That's it. You've taken everything. There's nothing left. Now leave me alone. Just leave me the hell alone."

**

She slept in Ben's room that night, surrounded by his memory, his things. Unable to think of anything else, she gazed at his mementos. School trophies stood solemnly on the shelves. His clothes hung in the closet. Photographs and posters sagged on the walls. The expensive speakers he'd wanted so badly for his music system collected dust on top of the dresser.

It'd been two years since the death of her beloved son. Two years since she'd died inside. She'd made no changes to his room. And she never would. This was Ben's room. His things. They belonged here. They belonged to her, and she loved them. She touched them, held them, smelled them. Would never part with them.

The hateful memento, the one stuffed inside a drawer, she couldn't part with either. Nor could she stand the sight of it. Her eyes shifted to the tall dresser across the room. Even thinking of it made her stomach clench, bile rise in her throat. They'd handed her the flag at the funeral as if it were a glorious thing – an adequate substitute for a strong, handsome, intelligent, kind flesh-and-blood young man. Full of pomp and circumstance, they'd carefully folded it with white-gloved hands, tucked and smoothed it, and presented it to her as if it were a priceless treasure.

She'd accepted it, as decorum required she must, but she'd wanted to smash the thing into the ground, to rip it to shreds.

Claire had survived that day the only way she could – on autopilot. A robot of good breeding with years of solid training in social graces and etiquette took over the task, while she, the mother Claire, remained shrouded in a frozen fog.

She'd done it then. She could do it again. Call in the robot. Go through the motions. Do the tasks required of her. Say the right things when someone extended sympathy or sent a card.

Stan told her she needed help – that she wasn't "handling it" well, wasn't coping. Wasn't getting over it. *Getting over it?*

"It's like you aren't even here anymore," he'd complained again and again.

He didn't understand that the day-to-day activities and responsibilities that filled her life were so inane, so inconsequential. Meaningless.

And so he'd turned to another woman. Presumably one who was alive, and not filled with pain and anger. A woman who felt something more than loss. A woman who could share his bed and not feel the absurdity and automation of it.

**

4

The call she expected came the following day. Almost evening. She couldn't explain why she'd waited for the phone to ring rather than making the call herself.

"Hello, Mother?"

"Yes, honey. How are you?"

"I'm fine. How are you?"

"Oh, fine. Have you heard from your dad?"

"Yes. He called this afternoon. Are you doing okay?"

"I suppose I feel a little tired today. It was a bit of a surprise, you know."

There was hesitation. A small silence.

"Was it? You didn't have any idea?"

"Of course not. I thought your father and I would grow old together. But, apparently, he made other plans. I found out last night."

Claire heard the deep intake of breath on the other end of the line.

"What are you going to do?" came the response, finally.

"Do? Well, there's really nothing I *can* do. He's already seen an attorney, and the ball is rolling, so to speak."

"No, I mean, on your own. Will you stay there? Get a job? What are you thinking?"

"Little too early to tell, honey. I don't know that I have to *do* anything. Other than hire a good lawyer."

"Well, I hope it doesn't get ugly."

"What's to get ugly? We divide our assets, and it's all done. We start over. Simple." She reached for a cigarette and lighter.

"Mom, it's never simple. What about all the property and the house, and your investments? What about Grandma?"

"Elise, I don't know about all that. That's what lawyers get paid for. I have no idea what he'll do about Grandma."

"Well, do you need anything? Do you want me to come down for a visit? Help you sort through anything?"

"Of course, I'd love for you to visit anytime. Do you have a free weekend?"

Another heavy sigh.

"I'm not sure. I'll look at my calendar. Maybe I could get away for an overnight. I'd have to bring the kids, though. And that's a lot of noise and commotion. You sure you're up for that?"

"Elise. I'd love to see them. Just let me know."

She inhaled deeply. If the children came, she'd have to go outside to smoke. Even in her own home, she wasn't permitted to smoke around her grandchildren.

"Okay, well, take care of yourself. Don't forget to eat."

Claire laughed at that. "Haven't thought much about it, but I'm sure I can manage to feed myself even if I don't have to get a meal on the table for anyone else."

It dawned on her that if her husband had died, she'd be inundated with casseroles and dishes from people all over town. But since he'd simply walked out on her, she was left. Alone.

She glanced at the wall where the clock used to be. Was it past dinnertime already? It didn't matter. She didn't feel like eating.

"Dad said you didn't really talk last night, so he wasn't sure if you were very upset."

Her thoughts snapped back to the call. "Oh, did he expect me to break down crying and screaming or beg him to stay?"

"I don't know. I just wanted to make sure you're okay."

"Well, when someone marches in and announces they no longer love you after you've borne and raised their children and picked up after them for over thirty years, it's a bit of a shock. I guess I'm not sure how I'm *supposed* to act."

"I don't know, Mom."

"You know he was cheating on me, don't you? There's another woman."

"No, he didn't say anything like that. He wanted me to check on you and make sure you're all right."

"Ah, so that you'll believe he's not the cheating liar he really is."

"Mom, I told you, I don't want this to get ugly, and I don't want to be caught in the middle of a he-said, she-said. I don't have the time or energy for it. I'm really sorry this is happening, but I can't take sides."

"I'm not asking you to." Claire knew her daughter better than that. Elise would watch from the sidelines. From both sides. She despised confrontation. There would be no support from her.

"I should probably get going, Mom. It's about suppertime. I'll check in with you in a couple of days and let you know if it looks like I'll have any free time."

"All right, then. My love to everyone."

She hung up, but kept her hand on the phone. Was Stan beginning to spread the word? Claire had stayed home, in and out of sleep all day. She hadn't told a soul. Telling would make it real. It would also make her the talk of the town. A hot news item. She shuddered, thinking of . . . the gossip. Whitfield could be a kind and generous community, but the fact remained, the higher the news dangled on the status ladder, the harder the fall, which made the news that much more captivating.

She took a deep breath. Better tell Mary. An ally she could count on.

Chapter Two

Mary's number was first on Claire's speed dial. Didn't that show the true nature of things. She punched it, and waited, the butterflies waging war inside her stomach.

"Well, it's about time," Mary said without so much as a hello. "I was just about ready to come over. Why haven't you answered your phone all day?"

"Guess I never heard it ring. Took a nap this afternoon."

"Yeah? Nice."

Yes. It was. She loved the oblivion sleep afforded her. When she could get it. Some days it was hard to come by. "You know I love a good nap."

"Don't we all."

Okay, Claire, she scolded herself. Enough of the idle chit-chat. Get to the point. She sucked in her breath. "I have some news."

"You do?"

Claire heard the concern, the hesitancy in her best friend's low voice. So she'd already heard.

"Stan and I are getting divorced. He's been cheating on me. Left last night."

"Oh, Jesus, Claire. I'm coming over right now."

"No, no. Hold your horses a minute."

"I'll be there in five."

Claire heard the click as Mary hung up. Well, what were friends for, after all? She tossed the phone aside and reached for a cigarette. And waited for Mary to arrive.

When their children were young, they'd lived next door, and had become close friends. Then, all they'd had to do was step outside to share a cup of coffee, borrow an egg, get a fashion opinion or vent about some annoyance of the day. When Grant built Mary her dream home ten years ago, they'd moved to the outskirts of town. Claire had cried over that. It hadn't changed her friendship with Mary, but it did take away the easy spontaneity.

Couldn't have been even five minutes. Claire hurried to the door at Mary's incessant knocking. When she opened it and stepped back, Mary barreled in and yanked her into a hug.

"Oh, Claire. I'm so sorry." Mary's chunky bracelets beat a rhythm against Claire's back.

She allowed it for a moment, then pulled away, making fake gagging sounds. "Hey, lady, you're choking me."

With a laugh, Mary disentangled then practically dragged Claire to the living room. They sat on the sofa, facing each other, Mary hanging onto Claire's hand.

"I can't believe it," Mary practically screeched. "After all this time. What is he thinking?"

Claire gave her a hard glare. "What are they ever thinking?"

"Well, I'd like to give him a swift kick in the ass for sure."

Claire laughed, and squeezed Mary's hand. "Be my guest. I've got some lovely pointed pumps you're welcome to borrow."

"No, no. I've got this covered. Cowboy boots. And I've got the perfect pair. Red with metal tips. They'd do nicely."

They hooted with a fit of laughter, then Mary turned somber eyes to Claire. "Are you okay?" she asked softly. "You'll be okay on your own?"

Claire sighed, and her fingers smoothed wrinkles on the sofa. "Guess I'll have to be. Don't see as I have any choice."

"What about money? Did you go to the bank today?"

She frowned at her friend. "What do you mean?"

"Did you close out your joint account and put everything in your name? Did you even check the balance?"

"No. I didn't leave the house today."

"Good God, Claire, you've got to make sure he hasn't cleaned you out."

Claire reeled as Mary's words sank in. Was she being a fool? Such a thing hadn't crossed her mind. And she'd just told Elise she didn't need to *do* anything. Apparently she did.

Mary's light hazel eyes widened, and she pushed her face within inches of Claire's. "Listen, first thing tomorrow morning, you get your butt down to the bank and make sure you get some money in your own name. Even if they won't let you close the joint account, take out as much as you can, and open a new account."

"Do you really think–"

"He's not on your side anymore, Claire. Don't forget that. You have to look out for yourself. I mean it."

Claire rubbed a hand over her face, as her eyes filled. "I can't believe this."

"I didn't want to believe it, either," Mary said with a heavy sigh.

Slowly, Claire raised her eyes to Mary's. "So you heard about it earlier?"

"Grocery store. Linda Brewster."

Claire shot off of the sofa. "How the hell did she hear about it?"

10

"Who knows. Maybe Stan's told people already."

"What did you say?"

"Told the hag I didn't appreciate her gossiping about my friend like that, of course. Then I high-tailed it to my car and called you as soon as I could without her seeing me."

With a wry smile, Claire shook her head. "Thanks, Mare, but you can't protect me from this. It's true. And it'll be the talk of the town."

Her cheeks flushed hot. She could fend for herself and call in the robot to handle the details of a divorce, but the gossip, the knowing stares, bothered her. She had a lot of friends in town, of course, but few people could resist news like this. It'd go viral in seconds. She and Stan were longtime residents. He was third generation. Even if they didn't actually know him, everyone knew *of* Stan.

"Maybe I should go somewhere for a while," Claire whispered, dropping back onto the sofa.

"Maybe you should. Take a vacation." Mary flailed her arms, the bracelets clanging again. "Get out of here for a couple of weeks. Go to the beach, whatever. I wish I could go with you."

Claire swiped at a tear that escaped. "Couldn't you? For a few days?"

Mary chewed her lip. "I'll look at the calendar, but don't count on it. Not with summer around the corner, and Jason's graduation."

Claire sat up. "Oh, I have to be here for that."

"No. You don't. Graduation ceremonies are tedious, even for those of us who are ecstatic as hell about the graduation."

"I don't know where I'd go."

"What about the lake house?"

"Maybe. It's a little early. We haven't opened it yet." It was the obvious thing to do. The house was hers, had been in her family for years. Stan had no claim to it. Thankfully.

11

"But first, you take care of the bank, girlfriend. I'll go with you. Eight o'clock tomorrow morning. I'll come by and pick you up."

**

Claire was up at five. Couldn't have slept more than a few hours all night. At seven, she finally got dressed and attempted to put herself together. It required some effort. She looked like a train wreck, as if overnight, some pendulum had swung back and forth under her eyes, carving deep circles under them. The rest of her face was pale and her eyes were bloodshot.

Thankfully her hair cooperated, and with just a blow dryer and curling brush, the coarse silver strands styled easily around her face. It was probably time to get to the salon. She'd grown tired of trying to keep up with coloring her hair, but insisted on keeping it in a stylish cut. Gray or not, it was her best feature.

She smoothed an extra glob of moisturizer over her face, then added make-up. And a little extra blush. Then stepped into heels. She downed the last swallow of coffee in her mug as Mary pulled into the drive.

Even though the bank had opened a small branch in the strip center close to the school, Claire preferred to go downtown. She loved the old deco-style building with its architectural details of stainless steel and sea-green glass. A few buildings in the downtown area, which covered roughly six square blocks, had been torn down and replaced over the years, but many still held their historical character and charm.

Charlie Fast, dubbed "Fast Charlie" by the townsfolk long accustomed to his presence at local establishments, stood outside the bank in his worn beige suit. He lifted his hat as Claire and Mary approached the entrance. "Mornin' fair ladies."

Claire's tense muscles managed a smile, but nothing more. Normally, she'd stop and chat, maybe inquire about Charlie's health and listen to a story about glory days when his arthritic hands had thrown footballs and caught baseballs with enviable precision. But now she just wanted to get inside and get this over with.

Hoping she looked more confident than she felt, Claire pulled open the heavy glass door to the First Trust Bank. A blast of arctic air hit her face. Walking into the bank was always like entering a cold storage freezer. For the first time in thirty years, she didn't mind.

With Mary beside her, Claire strode to the receptionist's desk. She explained what she needed, and waited while the girl stepped away. A moment later, the girl returned with George Sutton on her heels. Claire swallowed hard. She and Stan considered George and his wife part of their outer circle of friends. She started to extend a clammy palm to George, but to her relief, he leaned in and planted a quick kiss on her cheek instead.

"Hello, Claire. Come on back."

She turned to Mary. "Want to come, or stay here?"

"Up to you."

Claire jerked her head. "Come."

George raised his eyebrows when Mary settled into a chair beside Claire, but didn't comment. He cleared his throat.

"I heard the news, Claire. I sure am sorry."

Claire crossed her ankles and folded her hands together in her lap. "Thank you."

"What can I do for you this morning?"

She reached into her purse and drew out her savings book and checkbook. "I need to transfer money from these accounts into a new one."

When his eyes narrowed, she rushed on. "Now, here are the balances. If you could just verify these amounts . . ."

Claire held her breath and watched as George turned to his computer. Please, please let the money still be there. In her heart she couldn't imagine Stan being so hateful, but she'd never imagined him walking out on her, either.

Mary patted her arm.

"Looks like there was a withdrawal from one of the accounts yesterday," George said, his fingers tapping the computer keys.

Claire's stomach twisted. "Really?"

George's eyes met hers. "Five thousand out of the savings account."

Nearly dizzy with relief, Claire blew out her breath. "Okay, let's move everything else into a new account."

"Well, now, if you want to keep it open, you'll need to keep a couple thousand in there to avoid any fees."

"Oh, all right. That's fine." She pushed the savings record at him. So, this balance is correct, minus the five?"

George looked from the book to the computer, and shook his head. "Not quite. There've been a few other withdrawals."

Claire's face flamed as George turned his computer screen toward her. The glowing numbers shouted at her. Stan had been withdrawing money five thousand at a time for several months. Tears of anger and frustration welled in her eyes as she gritted her teeth. Why was he doing this to her? She hadn't done anything to deserve this. She wasn't the one screwing around.

"Fine," she ground out. "Move it. And everything in the checking account, too. Close them or do whatever you have to, but get my name off the old accounts." She damned sure didn't want to be responsible for any overdrafts if he started trying to spend the money.

Heavy silence wrapped around them as George prepared the papers. When he left the office to fetch a signature card, Claire let herself glance at Mary. At the sympathetic concern on her friend's face, Claire nearly lost it. She dabbed at her eyes and looked away.

14

"It's okay, isn't it?" Mary whispered. "You can get by until there's a settlement?"

Unable to speak as the cold reality of her situation sunk in, Claire nodded. Mentally, she prepared a to-do list. Shoot the bastard. Get a credit card in her name only. Change the locks on the door. Contact an attorney. Her head pounded as the list grew.

What else had Elise mentioned? A job? Oh, God, would she need a job? She'd dropped out of college when she got her M.R.S. Never finished the Journalism degree. Sure, she'd run fundraisers and food drives, but that was volunteer work. What kind of job could that get her? She excelled at folding towels and cooking dinner. Hysterical laughter bubbled inside her as she considered items for her resume.

Chapter Three

Claire glanced around the kitchen, and checked the counter again. No matches or lighters in sight. Then she opened all the drawers that would be within the kids' reach. Looked like the coast was clear.

With only a couple of minutes to spare, she scurried to the bathroom, then her bedroom. Oh, damn. Quickly, she scooped up the throw-away lighter from beside the television, and tossed it high inside her panty drawer.

Haha. She'd laugh about that one later. Back in the kitchen she downed a couple of pain tablets for the headache she knew would explode soon, and debated whether to set out a plate of cookies. She let that idea go when she heard a car door slam. Elise probably wouldn't approve anyway.

Claire glanced around to make sure Reggie was out of sight. Hopefully he'd have the sense to stay that way. She couldn't be sure how Andy would react to a cat. Opening the front door, she stepped onto the porch. Her granddaughter hugged her mother's side while Elise wrestled Andy out of his car seat.

"Helloooo," Claire called.

Olivia turned but stayed put. Leaning against the door to keep it open, Claire sighed. It always took the kids a while to warm up. She saw them so infrequently that they had to go through a getting-to-know-you period each visit. It was too bad. Claire had enjoyed

Olivia when she was a toddler, but the two years after Ben died were simply lost. She had to admit, she didn't know her grandchildren very well.

"Come on in," Claire shouted. "We can unload your things later. Olivia, come see Grammy."

When they finally made it to the porch, Claire knelt down, holding her arms out. Olivia allowed her a hug, but Andy held back, so Claire stood and ruffled his hair. Then she reach out and wrapped her arms briefly around Elise.

"Hello, sweetheart."

"Hey, Mom."

"I bet everyone needs the bathroom and something to drink," Claire said.

Elise laughed, and nudged Andy down the hall. "Exactly. Be right back."

Claire figured after a three-hour car ride, the kids were probably hungry and cranky, too. She'd let them settle in a bit. "I've put you all upstairs. Your old room and the guest room."

"Sure. That's fine, Mom. But the kids might just stay in my room with me. We'll see."

"Is the car unlocked? I can start bringing things in."

"Yes. That'd be great."

Happy to have something to do, Claire went out to the van and gathered up a couple of suitcases. Both of the kids had come in with small backpacks of their own.

"I need to get the cooler," Elise said, coming through the doorway. "I wouldn't let them have anything to drink in the car. Didn't want to keep stopping. Watch them for a sec, okay?"

While Elise finished unloading, Claire herded the kids to the backyard and hauled out the tub of toys she kept in the utility closet near the patio door. "Here we go. I bet we can find some things to do in here." She fished out a jump rope and a ball. She wiped the ball on her pant leg and tossed it into the yard toward Andy.

The swing set that used to be part of the backyard landscape had long ago been dismantled, and there was little for children to do. She supposed they could turn on the hose and run through the sprinkler if boredom set in. Early May, and temperatures were already soaring into the eighties. Looked like spring would be nothing but a blip on the calendar this year.

As she looked around, Claire realized the grass was long. Too long. With a heavy sigh, she sank into a chair. She'd have to find someone to take care of that now.

Elise joined them, with a couple of juice boxes in hand. She pulled out a chair across from Claire, and Claire could feel her daughter's eyes on her.

She pasted on a smile and turned. "They're getting so big," she said. The standard comment.

"Yeah. So glad to have Andy out of diapers now. Makes life a little easier."

"Yes. Is he doing better in his daycare?"

"Much. At least he doesn't cling to my leg when I drop him off in the mornings anymore. And no more biting incidents."

"Well, thank goodness for that."

"You look good," Elise said.

Claire let out a short laugh. "Didn't want to scare the kids, so I put on some make-up today."

"Have you talked to Dad?"

Claire couldn't control the rush of heat that hit her face at the mention of her husband. "Absolutely not. We communicate, if we have to, through the attorneys. That's the way they said it should be. He came over one day and took a few tools and some clothes. That's it." She'd had Mary over that day to avoid any unpleasantness. They'd lurked in the background, watching his every move, but said nothing. He was there less than thirty minutes.

"So you found a lawyer already?"

"Met with her last week. I like her. Annie works in her firm." Annie was Mary's oldest, a junior attorney specializing in estate planning. The lawyer she'd recommended, Lauren Armstrong, had a reputation for being a tough bitch, Mary had told Claire. Just what she needed. She liked the name, seemed appropriate for a kick-ass attorney. Claire refrained from passing that information along to her daughter.

Instead, she and Elise chatted about nothing of consequence until Olivia complained she was hot. Sweaty tendrils of hair stuck to her face and neck.

"It *is* getting a little warm," her mother said. "Let's go inside."

Claire moved toward the family room while Elise went to the kitchen.

"I need to get the cooler unloaded," Elise said.

"Sure. Whatever you need to do," Claire told her. "I'll watch the kids."

A moment later, Elise peered over the counter that separated the family room from the kitchen. "Mom, there's nothing in the refrigerator."

"Was there something you wanted?" Her daughter was very particular about what she fed her children, so Claire hadn't bothered to go to the grocery store. She would've bought all the wrong brands.

"No, but we'll need to eat. You need to eat."

"Oh, I thought we'd go out," Claire said.

"For every meal? Is that what you've been doing?"

"I'm not cooking gourmet meals for one, if that's what you mean." She was a damned good cook, too, whether it was a simple summer barbecue in the backyard or a lavish holiday spread for twenty. But cooking for one? Too much work. Too much waste.

Elise came around the corner, regarding her with a look that fell short of warm fuzzies. "I see you have plenty of wine."

Was that observation or mild accusation? There were two boxes of wine inside. "They were on special. Buy one, get the other half price." Claire said. "Would you like a glass? Help yourself." Who wouldn't get two?

Really. Were the contents of her refrigerator her daughter's business?

"Are you having people over?" Elise asked, not moving toward the cupboard for a glass.

Claire draped herself into a chair. "I have no plans. Mary stops by occasionally, of course. And other friends."

She patted the ruffled pink rump in front of her. The children had found her stash of crayons and coloring books, and were coloring at the coffee table.

At five, Olivia's personality seemed to be set. She was a quiet girl, rather serious. Cute, but not in a breathtaking way. She could be cuter if her mother would only take the time to fix her hair. Andy was three, and a handful, plain and simple. Typical boy. He had a mop of basic brown hair, and his round face still puffed with baby fat.

"I thought we'd go into Paxton for dinner," Claire said.

"Mom, really? You'd rather drive forty-five minutes than cook?"

"I thought it would give us something to do, and that way the kids would have some options. But if you'd rather, I can certainly go to the grocery store." She could never get it right. And it made Elise's visits more stressful than pleasant.

"No, it's fine," Elise said with a sigh. "But in that amount of time, Andy will probably fall asleep, and then when we wake him up, he'll be fussy."

"Well, why don't we just stay here for dinner, and maybe go in for some shopping tomorrow." She couldn't wait to buy Olivia some of the adorable shoes she'd seen at Halston's Boutique.

Elise laughed, moving into the room. "Mother, have you forgotten what it's like to shop with two kids, especially a three-year-old boy? I guarantee you, it won't be fun."

20

Claire's face went hot, and for an instant, she wanted to slap her daughter. How dare she? With supreme effort, she kept her hands in her lap. "Yes, Elise." She swallowed the lump constricting her throat. "I remember what it's like to have a three-year-old boy. And a twenty-three-year-old boy," she whispered.

Elise blushed, and touched Claire's arm. "I'm sorry, Mom. I didn't mean to– I wasn't referring to–"

Claire jumped up, avoiding her daughter's eyes. "What about spaghetti? I'm sure I could throw together some spaghetti. Would they eat that?"

"Sure. That'd be fine. But I'll still need to go to the store. We'll need fresh milk. Do you have any cereal?"

Claire leaned against the counter. "I don't know if it's anything they'll like. The thing is, the last time you were here I ended up throwing a lot of food away because it wasn't what the kids would eat." She'd bought two-percent last time, and the kids only drank whole milk. Or maybe it was the other way around. She could've called and made a list, but it seemed like so much effort. Besides, she'd been avoiding the grocery store. She never failed to see someone she knew there.

Elise joined her in the kitchen, opening one cupboard after another. Then she glanced around and back to Claire. She nodded toward the wall. "Where's the clock?"

"It broke."

"Broke? You sure it didn't just need a battery?"

"Of course I'm sure." Did she really seem that stupid to her daughter? "It came off of the wall and crashed onto the floor. Believe me, it's broken."

"Oh. Okay. Well, how 'bout if Olivia stays here with you, and I'll take Andy?"

"Perfect." Claire reached for her purse. "Here. Let me give you some money."

"No, Mother. That isn't necessary."

Claire fished out some bills, and shook them at Elise. "Take these. I mean it."

After they'd said goodbye to Elise and Andy, Claire turned to her granddaughter. "All righty, Miss Olivia, girl time. What would you like to do? We could mix up some cookies, or paint your toenails, or read some books. Any of those sound fun to you?"

Claire watched a shy smile light the girl's face.

"Yes."

"Yes, what? Which one sounds fun?"

"Painting toenails."

"Let's get to it, then." Claire took Olivia's hand and whisked her down the hall to the bathroom. She lifted a case out of the cupboard, set it on the counter, and began pulling out bottles of nail polish. "Let's see here . . . I have all kinds of colors for toenails. You choose the one you like best."

Olivia picked up several and shook them around while Claire waited. When Olivia looked up hesitantly, Claire gave her an encouraging smile.

"Is that the one?"

Olivia nodded.

Claire grinned. She'd chosen the brightest, hottest pink in the lot. "Okay, you shake it up really good," she told Olivia while she dumped the rest of them back into the case and put it away.

She turned on warm water, then lifted Olivia to the sink. "We need to get your feet clean before we put the polish on."

Olivia giggled as Claire scrubbed her feet, then began filing the toenails.

"Grammy, that tickles."

A pang of affection hit Claire, and she gave Olivia a quick squeeze. It really was too bad she didn't see her grandchildren more often. "I'm all done with that part. Now for the pretty part." She stretched Olivia's legs out on the counter, dried her feet, and began applying the color.

Olivia squealed.

"You like it?"

She nodded.

"Me, too. It's beautiful."

They were still in the bathroom when Elise and Andy arrived.

"Mom?" Elise called.

"Back here," Claire shouted over the hairdryer. She'd have to get the polish dried before she let Olivia down, or the paint job would be ruined in seconds, she knew.

"What are you do—"

"Look, Mommy. Grammy painted my toes. Aren't they pretty?"

Claire held her breath, hoping her daughter would see the happiness glowing on Olivia's face, and not squelch it.

"Yes, honey. They sure are," Elise said to her daughter before turning an exasperated glare on Claire. "Really, Mother. I don't want her to grow up thinking she has to paint herself to be pretty."

"Oh, Elise, it's okay to indulge every once in a while. Painted toenails aren't going to destroy her self image. They're just fun."

Shaking her head, Elise turned. "I'll put the groceries away," she muttered.

**

After supper, Elise put in a Disney movie for the kids then helped Claire clean up. Claire studied her for a moment. As usual, she'd pulled her striking dark hair into a ponytail. Elise had been blessed with beautiful thick hair, but no one knew it, because she never bothered to fix it. Hair had been a constant battle between the two of them when she was younger. She wore little to no make-up, which only accentuated her pale face. Thank goodness she had full lips. Claire was convinced they alone kept Elise from looking sickly.

"You look a little tired," Claire commented, sliding the last plate into the dishwasher. "Why don't you go put your feet up and have a glass of wine?"

"No. A glass of wine would put me to sleep."

Claire gave a short laugh. "That's the idea."

"No. I need to give the kids a bath. And I don't like to go to sleep before they do." She let out a loud sigh. "Olivia's been wanting to stay up later, and for some reason, Andy's been waking up at night. It's ridiculous."

"Well, for heaven's sake. No wonder you're exhausted. You can go to bed early tonight, and I'll stay up with Olivia."

At Elise's quick look, Claire added dryly, "Don't worry, I won't perm her hair or anything."

She poured two glasses of wine, and handed one to Elise. Then she opened a cupboard and took out the small bag in which she'd hidden her cigarettes and lighter. "I'm going outside for a few minutes."

She stopped in the mudroom and gave her arms and ankles a shot of bug spray, even though she hated the stuff, and stepped into the warm evening. The sun was just beginning to wane on the horizon. Claire lit a cigarette and settled into a cushioned chair, but not before noting the cushion had seen better days. She glanced around. Maybe a little patio spruce-up was in order. The deck they'd planned had never materialized, and the whole patio area looked old and dated.

As her eyes closed, a thought struck her. Would the patio furniture, or the patio, for that matter, be hers? What if Stan wanted the house? With a deep drag on the cigarette, she dismissed the thought. What woman would want to move into the ex-wife's home?

**

When she heard footsteps above her, Claire forced an eye open. Rolling over, she squinted at the clock. Seven thirty. Too damned early, but she was determined

24

to give Elise a morning off. Apparently her under-achieving husband didn't think to do the same. Claire swung her legs over the side of the bed and sat a moment, then gathered up her robe and shoved her feet into slippers.

She tiptoed upstairs and found both Olivia and Andy in with Elise. Claire put one finger over her mouth, and motioned to Olivia.

"Is your brother really asleep?" Claire whispered to Olivia.

The girl nodded.

Claire took her hand and led her out of the room, and quietly shut the door.

"Your mommy needs some extra rest this morning, so why don't you help me in the kitchen? We could mix up some pancakes. What do you think about that?"

Olivia nodded again.

"Coffee first, though," Claire said, reaching for the carafe. Together they prepared the pancake mixture, then she turned it over to Olivia for stirring, while she sliced some strawberries. Elise had certainly done a thorough job of grocery shopping, Claire realized. And probably spent way more money than she'd given her.

Claire glanced at the clock on the microwave. She'd give Elise until nine, then start cooking.

"All right, Miss Olivia, let's go outside for a few minutes until it's time for your mom to get up."

Claire grabbed the newspaper, and a few coloring books and crayons. Olivia seemed happy to sit quietly and color at the patio table. Elise was lucky – Olivia was a sweet compliant girl. For now, anyway.

"Mommy's tired all the time," Olivia said after a few minutes.

Claire's head snapped up at this bit of unsolicited information. How could she not be, working fulltime and managing two kids and a house?

"Are you a good helper at home, Olivia?" Claire asked.

Olivia nodded. "But Andy's not."

"No. He's too little. What about your daddy? Is he a good helper, too?"

"He takes out the trash."

Well, thank God for that, Claire thought.

"He doesn't like it when Mommy's tired. He says she does too much."

Yes, and whose fault was that? Claire straightened, and pulled off her reading glasses. Her glance darted toward the door, then she gave Olivia her undivided attention. She took a deep breath.

"What do you mean, Olivia? Does your dad get mad at your mommy? Does he yell or hit her? You need to tell me."

Olivia kept coloring for a moment, then she rested her arms on the table and leaned in. "He yells sometimes. But that's because of all the toys."

Claire blew out her breath. Her son-in-law was so dull she couldn't imagine him mustering the energy to yell, but could the slacker take his own shortcomings out on Elise? You never knew what went on behind closed doors. Then another thought struck. Could Elise be pregnant again? That would certainly raise the tension. How could they possibly afford or have time for another child?

Standing up, she ran a hand through Olivia's soft honey-brown hair. "Well, sweetie, it's about time for us to start those pancakes."

She let Olivia help set the table, then nudged her out of the way when she turned on the stove. "All right, this part is my job. You go wake up Mommy and Andy, okay?"

By the time the three of them appeared in the kitchen, Claire had scrambled some eggs, heated the syrup, and had a tall stack of perfectly browned pancakes ready to eat.

"Morning," she said, taking a mug out of the cupboard for Elise. "Coffee?"

26

"Please. Wow. You two have been busy in here."

Claire watched Elise peel Andy from around her waist and settle him in a chair.

"You got some extra sleep?"

"Yeah. Andy was up once, but went right back to sleep."

Claire handed her the coffee mug. "Good."

"Thanks, Mom. This is really nice. I haven't slept until nine in a long time."

"Why's that? Can't you sleep in on the weekends while Brian deals with the kids? Good heavens, you're working every day." Careful, she scolded herself. Elise would go on the defensive in a heartbeat. And she didn't want to let on that she knew what Olivia told her. The last thing she wanted was for her granddaughter to be punished.

Elise didn't meet her eyes, but took a seat at the table. "So's he, Mom. And he's coaching. And he brings home papers to grade on the weekends."

Claire felt her blood pressure rise. Elise was always making excuses for the man.

"Well, I have an idea for Christmas this year . . ." She stopped. Christmas? Where had that come from?

"Yeah?" Elise shot her a puzzled frown. "What's that?"

"Oh. Um, I was thinking maybe I'd hire you a housekeeper. Have someone come in once a week to help you out. Would you like that?"

She heard Elise's heavy sigh.

"I don't know, Mom. I don't really like the idea of having someone in the house. And neither does Brian."

"We don't have to decide today. Give it some thought." Claire resisted rolling her eyes. No pressure, she reminded herself. She took a long drink of coffee and changed the subject. "Now, what about our day? Everyone up for some shopping? I want to get Olivia these darling sandals I saw last week."

"Mom, are you sure you should be spending money right now? I mean, before the settlement? I don't want you to overspend. And Olivia doesn't need anything."

This time she couldn't help it. She rolled her eyes at her daughter. "It's not about needing. I have plenty of money, Elise, and I want to buy the kids a gift. That's what grandmas are for. And God knows I could use a little fun."

Oops. That last part slipped out. She intended to be on her best behavior this weekend and not unload any of her problems on Elise. Hadn't mentioned her lousy dad at all. Scooting back her chair, Claire picked up her plate, avoiding Elise's eyes.

**

Three hours and two bathroom stops later Olivia squealed with delight as she tried on the brightly striped and polka dot sandals with large fluffy flowers on top, and danced around the store.

Even Elise was grinning. "You're right. They're darling," she told Claire as the saleswoman rang up Olivia's choice – an eye-popping combination of yellow, orange and pink.

Claire handed the bag to Olivia. "A girl's gotta have cute shoes," she said, giving Olivia's shoulder a quick squeeze. "All right. We'd better get something for this big guy, too."

They wandered around the downtown shops, and Andy finally settled on a set of squirt guns in silly shapes – the only kind of gun Elise would allow. And only after a good deal of whining.

By the time they made it to the Gardenview Cafe, one of Claire's favorite places to eat, she was frazzled. Claire ordered the chop salad and a glass of Chardonnay. And ignored her daughter's pursed lips.

Andy couldn't make up his mind, so while the waitress was still working on getting the orders, Claire grabbed her purse and stood up. "I'm going outside for a minute," she whispered. She couldn't get there fast enough. Along the sidewalk, she found an empty bench with a lovely view of the flower-lined entrance to the retail square then lit a cigarette and leaned back, taking in the scenery.

With a population of close to fifty thousand, Paxton boasted a big mall with dozens of stores under one roof, handy in inclement weather, but Claire preferred the downtown square. The city did an excellent job of maintaining the quaint appeal of the area.

When she returned to the table, the kids had calmed down. Thankfully, the drinks had also arrived. She lifted her wine glass, just as a cough came over her. Setting the wine back down, she reached for water, but coughed for a good ten seconds, her eyes watering. So much for fresh air.

"Might be time to give those up," Elise said, shooting her a cool look.

Claire patted her chest. "Oh, my, I must be allergic to something in the air out there."

Elise rolled her eyes. "Come on, Mother. That has nothing to do with allergies and everything to do with cigarette smoke."

Claire picked up the wine glass. Irritation flashed through her, but she refused to ruin the day by getting into that argument. But apparently Elise was spoiling for a fight.

"And what's with all the drinking, Mom? Wine at lunch? Can you not make it through the day without a drink? Are you going to let me drive back to the house? Are there any other addictions I should know about? Have you taken up gambling, too?"

Claire ignored that last nasty comment. "Look, after all the whining of the past hour, I deserve a little wine of my own. One glass is not going to keep me from being able to drive, especially if we walk around some more. Now please, can we enjoy some lunch?"

She gave Elise a pointed look. "I think we're *all* getting a a little cranky."

Once their meal was delivered, they ate in exhausted silence, which Claire relished. Even the kids were busy eating. She sipped her wine and enjoyed the view of the beautifully landscaped courtyard on the other side of the window. Bright red geraniums mixed with ivy and yellow petunias cascaded over the planters. Maybe she'd plant a few flowers at the lake house. Maybe she'd be there long enough this year to keep some alive.

When the waitress came back, she cleared away plates and announced that the kids would get ice cream with their meals. "Chocolate or vanilla, you guys?" She looked from Andy to Olivia, and Claire could see Elise bristling because the woman hadn't asked her permission.

"Vanilla, please," Olivia said before her mother could object. Andy bobbed his head.

Elise said nothing, but drummed her fingers on the table. Thankfully, she chose not to fight that particular battle. But when the ice cream arrived, it was topped with whipped cream, covered in multi-colored candy sprinkles and included a small chocolate-chip cookie tucked along the side. Claire couldn't decide what was funnier – her daughter's aghast expression or her grandson's look of pure delight. The kid's eyes were as round as his open mouth, and his fists clenched as they shook with excitement.

When Elise started to speak, Claire rested a hand on her daughter's arm. "Let them have it, Elise. Oh, my, the look on Andy's face is priceless. Just enjoy their joy this time, okay?" She paused a moment, then added under her breath, "You never know how long you'll have them."

**

That night they ate dinner at the local pizza shop, then watched a silly movie and turned in early. Claire had wondered if Elise would insist on talking about the divorce, but she didn't say a word. And that was fine with Claire. After the others had gone upstairs, she poured herself a nightcap, grabbed her purse and a magazine, and headed for her bedroom. Damned if she wouldn't smoke in her own bedroom if she chose to.

She flipped through the magazine, but didn't stop to read any of it. Her mind kept drifting. For the most part, it had been a pleasant day. It'd been fun to watch her grandkids and treat them to little gifts and lunch. But tomorrow they'd leave again. And what would she do? Wash sheets and towels? Clean house?

She tossed the magazine on the floor, and massaged her temples. No. Those things could wait. She'd pack. Time for her to hit the road. She needed to get away. Unfortunately, it'd be a solo run this time. Mary couldn't go. *Her* husband still wanted her around. Maybe that was for the best. Claire sighed, as she turned out the lamp. Being by herself would give her time to think. Time to re-focus.

Breakfast the next morning was a much simpler affair of toast and cold cereal. Everyone seemed fine with it. Even Andy seemed quite content slurping up the milk in his bowl.

"I thought we might stop by and see Grandma before we leave," Elise said, turning raised eyebrows to Claire. "Have you talked to her recently?"

Pouring her second cup of coffee, Claire nearly sloshed it on the counter when Elise interrupted her thoughts. Claire hadn't seen or spoken to her mother-in-law since her son had announced he wanted a divorce, and walked out of the house. And one thing she didn't miss was the constant phone calls and dashing over to check on Harriet a couple of times a day. Chuckling inside, she wondered how Stan was managing that. Bet he was getting a hefty dose of reality.

The man had no idea how much of her time his mother had taken up.

"I haven't," Claire said, sipping her coffee. "But I'm not sure this is a good time to visit. I heard your dad moved her out of the house and into the manor. You might want to give her some time to get settled. She seemed a little disoriented the last time I saw her."

"Really? Hmm. I'd like to see her, but those kinds of places aren't generally receptive to kids. Do you think she has her own apartment?"

"Not sure. I can watch the kids if you want to run over there and check on her."

"Maybe I should."

Claire cleaned up the kitchen then took the kids outside. Twenty minutes later, Elise came around the back gate.

"That was fast," Claire said.

Elise shrugged. "Wasn't there. She is living there now, I guess, but they said a friend had picked her up for the day."

Claire frowned. "A friend? Not your dad?"

"That's what they said."

"Huh. Maybe JoAnn Carter picked her up. She still gets around pretty well."

"Well, anyway, I'd better get packed up. Olivia, Andy, you guys come upstairs and pick up all your things. We need to get ready to go. You want to see Daddy tonight, don't you?"

Before she could stop herself, Claire asked the question she'd been holding in. "Are you stopping by to see your dad before you leave?"

"Nope. I talked to him before we got here, and he said he wouldn't be around much this weekend."

Hmm. Claire didn't care to contemplate what the bastard was up to. While Elise was packing, Claire stretched out on the couch and closed her eyes. There was no time for a nap, of course, not until they left, but she needed just a few moments.

When she felt something brush across her forehead, she swatted and bolted upright. Olivia wailed, holding her cheek. Turning, Olivia ran toward the bedrooms as Elise hurried down the stairs.

"What's the matter?"

"I don't know," Claire told her. "I closed my eyes for a minute, and the next thing I know, Olivia is standing here crying."

"Grammy hit me," Olivia cried.

"What!" Elise exclaimed. "You *hit* her?"

"Of course not," Claire said. She reached out to Olivia. "What in the world are you talking about? I would never–" Oh. Perhaps she had. On accident.

"I was just waking her up with a kiss," Olivia whined tearfully.

"Oh, honey," Claire said. "You surprised me. I didn't know it was you. I'm so sorry."

"So you did hit her?"

Claire blew out her breath, and held up her hands. "I had closed my eyes, something brushed against my face, and I swatted. I thought it was a fly or a moth. I didn't know she was even in the room."

"I sent her to ask you for a plastic bag," Elise said. She looked down at Olivia. "Next time, don't wake Grammy up."

Olivia turned big, hurt eyes on Claire. "Mommy always says the nicest way to wake someone up is with a kiss. Like a princess."

Claire glanced at her daughter. Where had that come from?

She turned back to make amends with her granddaughter. "And you're absolutely right. That's very nice. It just surprised me, sweetie. I'm sorry. Come here and let me give you a hug."

Olivia took a couple of steps toward her, and Claire pulled her into a quick hug. "There now. It's all okay. Let me get that plastic bag."

She hurried to the kitchen. Good Lord, so much drama.

Chapter Four

Elise stopped folding the towel in her hands when Brian settled into a chair in the living room. They could never talk until the kids were in bed, and she was about to explode.

"I think this divorce could push Mom over the edge," Elise said.

Brian studied her a moment, then shrugged. "You never know. Maybe it'll be a wake-up call and she'll find something to do with herself."

Elise shook her head. "No, really. It looks like her new favorite pastime is drinking."

He leaned forward, a frown on his face. "Are you serious?"

"Yeah. She had two boxes of wine in the fridge. When I asked her about them she said they'd been on sale, buy one, get one or something. But I emptied the trash when we were packing up, and there were several bottles and an empty box in the bin. Plus, she had wine at lunch and wine at dinner." Unable to sit still, Elise stood and paced the room. "It was ridiculous. Seemed like she was either smoking or drinking the whole time."

"Was she acting drunk or out of it?"

Elise thought a moment. She hardly knew how to read her mother anymore. "Not really. She might be all right, but then she might be putting on a good act, too. You know, I thought she was starting to come around, then Dad hits her with this divorce. I understand there were problems, but I wish he'd given her a little more time."

"She shouldn't have let her hair go gray. Makes her look old. She hasn't aged as well as your dad."

"What? You think this is about her looks?" She stared at her husband.

"It's about their differences, babe. Remember that last church picture she showed us, even before Ben died? She thought it was a great picture, but I'm telling you, she looked ten years older than your dad. She got old. He didn't."

"Nice," Elise said, her voice tight. "Men can age. They can go bald and get a beer gut, but a woman has to jump through all kinds of hoops to maintain her looks. The old double standard." She yanked a towel out of the basket.

"That's not the only thing. Come on, El. You know your mom. How many times do you think they had sex in the last couple of years, huh? Probably zero. Your mom's been a zombie ever since Ben died."

She rounded on him then. "And why is that? Why did Ben's death affect Mom so much harder than it did Dad? Don't you think that's weird? Didn't he feel anything?"

"I'm sure he did. But I think in a way he was jealous of Ben. I mean, your mom practically worshipped the kid."

Elise shook her head. "I can't believe you're taking his side now."

Brian rose and squeezed her shoulders. "Look, hon, I'm not saying I agree with your dad. What he did to your mom was shitty, no question. I'm just saying I can see his side, too."

"So you think he's seeing someone else? He's been cheating on Mom?"

"Probably."

Tears stung her eyes. *Unbelievable.* Her entire life she'd thought she hailed from the all-American family.

36

They were so typical, so normal. Now they were imploding. "She has an attorney. Other than that, she didn't mention the divorce while we were there. Not sure whether it's acceptance or denial. If she's bottling this up, or drowning it in wine, sooner or later, she's going to melt down. All she's ever known is being a wife and mother. She doesn't know how to deal with all of this."

Brian pulled her into his arms. "Hey. Don't get upset. You can be there for your mom, but you can't take on her problems."

But what did "being there" for her mean? She had a full-time job and two kids. And no time to babysit her mother. Elise let her head rest on Brian's shoulder. "I hope she snaps out of it."

**

Claire stuffed the sheets and towels into the washing machine. She couldn't help herself. They could wash while she packed. Certainly wasn't something she'd look forward to coming home to.

She hadn't committed to a firm date for coming home. Her plan was to stay at least a couple of weeks, assuming that she didn't need to meet with her attorney. And Mary had called. There was a slight possibility she'd be able to meet Claire for a few days.

With so much uncertainty, Claire tossed a few extra clothes into her bags, including a black skirt, just in case. If Mary came down, they might want to go out, and she'd need nicer clothes.

The peal of the phone interrupted her thoughts. Distractedly, she picked it up.

"Hello?"

"Hello. This is Rachel Hollins calling from Coventry Manor. It's about Harriet Stapleton."

"Harriet? I'm afraid I'm not the right person to call anymore."

"I know that. But, well, we don't know who else to call."

"Have you called her son, Stan?"

"Yes. We haven't been able to locate him."

"You've called his office?"

"Yes. His secretary says he's out of town. He left instructions not to be bothered unless it was an emergency."

"Is it?"

"I don't think so. I think she's confused."

Aren't we all, Claire thought dryly. "What's the problem, exactly?"

"She's just kind of upset today, and . . . well, she's asking for you."

"Me?"

"Yes. Could you come?"

She had to be kidding. "You want me to come up there?"

"If you could."

Could she? Claire inhaled deeply on the cigarette in her mouth, letting the smoke out slowly as she processed the situation. Why should she go running up to the manor? Harriet was no longer her mother-in-law. She had no responsibilities there. Hell, the woman might not even know who she was. Stan's mother had been slipping in her memory lately, the onset of Alzheimer's the doctors said.

Claire had no obligation, but still, her conscience wouldn't stay out of it. "I'll be there in ten minutes," she said. It was the right thing to do.

Quickly, she hung up the phone, kicked off her fabric loafers and slipped into some sandals, then ran a brush through her hair. Make-up would take a tad longer, but she wasn't stepping foot outside without it. Not in this lifetime would she be seen looking like some tossed-off bit of garbage.

She rummaged through her jewelry cabinet for a little flash of color. Then she hooked a bright coral and pink necklace around her neck, and grabbed her purse.

In exactly ten minutes, Claire pulled into the parking lot of the Coventry Manor where her soon-to-be ex-husband had callously dumped his eighty-four-year-old mother.

She had no doubt Harriet was confused. How could she not be? It had all happened so fast, and without warning. In only a week's time, the poor woman was uprooted from her home and things, placed inside a tiny apartment, and surrounded by unfamiliar people. His own mother. Was there no end to the bastard's appalling behavior?

Claire approached the receptionist's desk, where a young woman she didn't recognize sat. "Hello, I'm here to see Harriet Stapleton."

"Yes, just a moment please."

She waited while the woman placed a call.

"Rachel will be right with you."

Claire wandered the lobby. It was similar to a hotel, with small pockets of seating areas. A few people milled about. A couple of elderly being pushed in wheelchairs.

When a woman approached her, Claire pasted on a smile.

"Claire?" she asked.

"Yes."

"I'm Rachel. Right this way please. Thank you so much for coming. I hope it wasn't too much trouble. Harriet is most anxious to see you."

Claire smiled and nodded, following Rachel as she chattered down the hallway.

She stopped at a door that was ajar, and gave a gentle tap before proceeding into the room. "Harriet? Mrs. Stapleton? Claire's here to see you."

The blank expression on Harriet's lined face turned to a frown. Then, to Claire's complete surprise, it crumpled, tears welling in her eyes.

Oh, dear God.

Harriet spread her arms and Claire moved forward, patting Harriet's back for several moments while the woman sobbed.

"Oh, Claire. What's he doing? What can he be thinking? He's just not right."

"Shhhh. Shhhh, Harriet. Calm down. It's okay." Taking Harriet's gnarled hand, Claire coaxed her toward the small sofa that divided the tiny suite. The stress had taken its toll, Claire saw. Harriet's eyes drooped. She seemed older, perhaps thinner.

"Here we go," Claire said. "Let's sit down a minute. Let me get you something to drink." She turned to Rachel, who still hovered behind.

"She has iced tea in her refrigerator, I think. I'll get it. Would you like some?"

"That would be lovely. Thank you," Claire said.

Rachel handed them each a glass then left the room. Made her escape, Claire thought.

She sat down beside Harriet. "Now, how are you doing, Harriet?" She glanced around the barebones room with its boring beige walls and brown furniture. There was a family portrait on the table, but not much else. Surely they could bring a few pillows and some personal items from her house. Make it feel more like home. Of course Stan would never think of that. For one spiteful instant she wished Elise had been able to see what her father had done.

"Looks like they've got you all set up here," Claire said, trying to sound positive without being false. "It's very nice."

She started in surprise when Harriet whirled on her. "You call this nice? Look at it. It's so small, I can hardly turn my ass around in it."

For the first time in weeks, Claire laughed out loud. Harriet had never minced words.

"Well, you're right. It's much smaller than your house, of course. But, you don't have to clean or cook. How great is that?"

"I like to cook," Harriet argued.

Proof that her mind was slipping for sure. Claire had delivered more meals than she could count in the past few years. If she hadn't delivered them, she prepared them, and invited Harriet over, which more recently also included going to fetch her.

With a sigh, she looked around the room again, and her gaze settled on Harriet's feet. The slippers she wore looked as if they'd once been pink, but had turned a grungy shade of gray. Her throat constricted with a pang of sympathy for her. To have to depend on a clueless man. Claire made a mental promise to bring Harriet some decent house shoes, if nothing else. She wondered if she could sneak into her house and bring a few things. She still had a key.

She pushed off from the sofa. *Stop, Claire. What is wrong with you? Do not meddle in this. It's not your place.*

"Harriet, why did you want to see me today? Is there something you need?"

"I want to go home."

Claire's stomach clenched. Dammit, she did not want to deal with this. There was nothing she could do. She tried to speak in a soothing voice. "Harriet, I'm very sorry, but I can't take you home. I don't know what's left over there, or even whether all the utilities are still on."

Harriet's eyes flashed. "He's sold it, hasn't he? It's mine. He can't sell everything."

A sense of dread filled Claire. Had Stan started clearing out the contents of the house? Probably not yet. That would qualify as news. She would've heard something if he'd held a sale.

"He's selling everything," Harriet wailed. "My jewelry. My car. *My* things. Says he has to, to pay my bills."

Harriet clenched a fist against her chest, and when she raised her eyes again, Claire saw confusion in them.

"What bills? I don't have any bills."

Oh, but she did. Claire knew that for sure. Stan had been taking care of his mother's finances for years. He had the Power of Attorney to do just about anything. Of course he'd sell her house and car, but her jewelry? Claire glanced at Harriet's hand. Her wedding ring was still there. But nothing on the other hand. Harriet had plenty of jewelry. A diamond cocktail ring, pearls, assorted precious gemstones. Her heart ached. Surely Stan wasn't liquidating his mother's personal possessions. Would he be so callous?

Fighting the wave of panic that rushed through her, Claire stayed a little while longer, and helped Harriet settle in front of the television. She patted her arm, then practically fled from the room, digging in her purse for her car keys and cigarettes.

Outside, she took a deep, shaky breath. If he'd treat his mother this way, what did that say about what lie ahead for her? Could Lauren Armstrong, bitch attorney, stand up to him?

Chapter Five

Feeling like a thief, Claire pulled her Acura into the driveway and glanced around. She saw no one, but it was Whitfield. There was almost certainly a neighbor somewhere down the street pushing back a lace curtain.

Claire's car was over there often enough, maybe no one would think anything of it if they saw her. She grabbed the empty shopping bags she'd brought with her, and opened the car door. With another check up and down the block, she hurried to the porch.

Her hands shook as she fumbled with the lock. *Come on, dammit.* She jiggled the key, and released her breath when the door swung open.

She surveyed the front room. Looked like it always did. *Ugh.* Smelled like it always did, too. Old and musty, and desperately in need of an open window. All the furniture was still there, anyway. Maybe Stan had made an idle threat. But if his mother was going to stay at the manor, there'd be no reason to keep the house.

She switched on the crystal lamp on the side table. That was one thing Harriet could use in her room at the manor, but there's no way it would fit in a shopping bag.

Instead, Claire snatched up two decorative pillows from the couch and shoved them into one of the bags. She gasped when she stepped into Harriet's bedroom. What a mess. Clothes were strewn across the bed, and spilled from open drawers. Good grief. Had it really been that difficult to gather up some clothes for her?

The closet door stood open, and Claire moved inside to inspect the contents. She selected a couple of pairs of shoes, and some scarves. From a plastic bag, she withdrew a black cotton sweater. If they blasted the air-conditioning over there, Harriet would need a few sweaters, even in the summer.

Harriet kept her good jewelry tucked deep inside the bottom drawer of her chest. Claire briefly thought about taking something for Elise and Olivia, but she wouldn't risk being accused of stealing. She resisted checking to see if the good stuff was still there. Besides, it would be no safer at the manor. With cleaning crews and visitors coming and going, valuable items could easily disappear. No. She'd take some favorite costume pieces. Maybe that would at least give Harriet the impression that she still had her belongings.

Claire sifted through the large box on the dressing table, trying to find the most versatile pieces.

"What in the living hell do you think you're doing?" Stan's voice boomed into the room.

Claire let out a short scream. She spun around, wincing as her hip connected with the dressing table, then leaned weakly against it, her heart pounding. "Oh, good grief. You scared me."

Stan crossed his arms, and glared at her. "What are you doing, Claire?"

Gathering her wits, she returned the stare. "Well, hello to you, too."

His jaw tightened. "What's going on?"

"I'm on a mission for your mother."

"What's that supposed to mean?"

"It means I got a call from the manor today. Your mother was upset and wanted to see me. I understand you couldn't be disturbed. And since you also couldn't be bothered to get some decent things for her to wear, and a few personal items from the house, I'm doing it for her. Really, Stan, didn't you think she might want to look like herself and have a few of her own things around her in that place? It's supposed to be a home, not a prison cell."

He had the grace to look guilty as he shifted his weight, but still his demeanor was less than cordial. "You don't need to worry about it."

Claire straightened and scooped several necklaces into the bag of clothes. "Don't be an ass. I've been doing errands for her for years. What's one more?" With more bravado than she felt, Claire dropped the bag at his feet. "Here. Take these things to her. It'll help your image."

Stan snorted. "My image?"

"Yeah. Right now, I'd say it stands as a royal J-E-R-K."

She pushed past him and out of the bedroom. He followed close behind.

"I want your key," he said, his voice an unpleasant growl.

Claire sucked in her breath. Well, that was that. She picked up her purse and removed the key to Harriet's house from her key ring. She slapped it down on the table beside the lamp. "Here you go. If you have any decency left at all, you'll take these bags to your mother, and this lamp, too.

"Oh, one other thing. Your mother says you're selling her jewelry. Perhaps you remember that you have a daughter and a granddaughter. They might like to have something of your mother's, as an heirloom – if you think you could spare it."

With that, Claire turned and hurried out the door. Her legs shook like china in an earthquake, but she managed to make it down the steps and to her car. She felt Stan's eyes on her the whole way. Good grief. Did he think she was stealing his mother's possessions? As if there were anything in that entire house she'd care to have.

Inside the car, she drew a shaky breath, unsure whether she had, in fact, accomplished her mission. There would be no second attempt, that was for sure.

**

The following day, Claire had just slammed the hatch on her car when she saw Mary's Ford Freestyle turn sharply onto the street. Her face automatically broke into a grin. Her friend's driving was often erratic, and sometimes downright frightening. Mary pulled into the drive, came to an abrupt stop, and climbed out of the car, waving a red gift bag in her hand like a matador.

"Oh, my gosh. I'm glad I caught you. I drove like a maniac to get here before you left." She shoved the red bag at Claire. "This should at least get you to the other side of town."

Claire took it, and peeked inside. Laughing, she shook her head. "Well, maybe." Inside was a book, plus all of her favorite road trip snacks . . . sunflower seeds, Tootsie Rolls, and gummy bears. Enough to get her to the lake house, and then some. She pulled out the book.

"That's the novel I was telling you about," Mary said. "Once you start it, you won't be able to put it down. I guarantee."

Claire nodded, but a sense of loneliness stole over her. With a deep breath, she shook it off. Time away, and alone, would be good for her. And relaxing on the deck with a good book was a luxury she didn't enjoy often enough.

"All right, then. You ready to head out?" Mary asked.

"Just need to get my purse, and Reggie. Come on in."

They wandered inside, and Claire picked up her things. "Actually, I'm making one quick stop."

Mary's eyebrows spiked as she lifted Reggie's carrier and poked a finger inside. "Where to?"

"The manor. I have a couple of things for Harriet."

"Harriet?"

"Uh-huh. Some candy and some new slippers. You should've seen what she was wearing when I was up there yesterday." Claire hadn't had time to run into Paxton, so she'd had to make do with Larson's Variety in town. But she found a pair of cute house shoes embroidered with flowers and sequins. Whether Harriet knew it or not, she'd love them.

Claire had combined them with a large box of jellybeans and had the whole package gift-wrapped. Her plan was to simply drop them at the manor as a surprise delivery, without a stop at Harriet's room.

Mary squeezed her arm. "You're nicer than you need to be, you know."

Claire shrugged. "I'd want someone to do the same for me."

Truth was, that's what she did – take a gift here, deliver a meal there, run an errand for someone. Seemed perfectly normal. And she needed a touch of normal in the face of the complete upheaval of her life.

∗∗

Claire stopped at the manor, and curiosity almost compelled her to go to Harriet's room and see if Stan had delivered the bags. She checked her watch. Already later than she'd planned to leave. Mary's visit had set her back a bit. She left the package with the receptionist instead. Like Stan said, she didn't need to worry about it anymore.

After that little detour, it took only a few minutes to get to open road. Claire set the cruise control, and settled into her seat. Not quite ready to be alone with her thoughts, she cranked up the music and listened to some classic soft rock.

The miles passed quickly, and she took only one break. As she neared the last retail area before her turnoff toward the lake, Claire debated whether to stop at the grocery store. Thirty minutes one way, it'd be a waste of time to get to the house then have to leave again. With resignation, she slowed and pulled into the parking lot.

"I won't be long," she murmured to Reggie as she lowered the back windows a couple of inches. He opened an eye at her voice, but closed it again and readjusted his head on his paws. "Guess you're not gonna miss me, huh?"

It took longer than it should have, though. Claire wandered the aisles and was uninspired. Nothing sounded good – except for everything in the snack and candy aisle. But then, she couldn't spend two weeks at the house without sufficient munchies. Groaning, she tossed in some pretzels and popcorn, then forced herself to pick up some fruit and veggies for a salad. The deli offered several pre-cooked options as well. She loaded them into the cart, picked up a bag of ice and made her way to the check-out line.

Standing in line, Claire couldn't help but notice that everyone else seemed to be stocking up for a party. It was only Tuesday, but their carts were full of twelve-packs, bottled water, and bags of charcoal for cookouts. Gearing up for fun times on the lake.

Stan had often complained that the house was in the most remote, sleepiest part of the lake. It was harder to get the boat in, harder to meet people and join the activities. Claire smiled, loading the groceries into her car. It was her favorite aspect of the lake house.

Another thirty minutes along winding roads that could be unnerving in the rain or dark, and she turned off of the blacktop onto a gravel road for the rest of the journey. Reggie stirred as the car bounced along the ruts, and gravel sprayed underneath them. Claire watched the road, but also took in the landscape. Pretty much the same, so far. Heavy woods, few houses. She craned her neck as she passed the Arnolds' place. Didn't appear to be anyone there, or at the Stauffers'. Apparently, she'd be the first one out – other than the

Richardsons, who lived there almost year-round. They'd torn down a quaint little bungalow a few years earlier and constructed a hulking monstrosity that loomed over the lake and looked completely out of place.

She sighed as *her* house came into view, the cheery façade welcoming her as it had for as long as she could remember. "Here we are, Reggie, babe," she sang out, opening the car door and stretching her cramped legs.

She'd given Nathan short notice about her early arrival, but he'd assured her that he could have everything taken care of, especially spraying for bugs. Sitting empty all winter long was like an open invitation to all kinds of spiders, bugs and creepy crawlers that Claire preferred not to encounter.

Nathan had been opening the house and helping to maintain the property for at least ten years. Claire trusted him, but she hadn't confided in him. He knew only that she was coming alone, which she'd done before, but not that Stan's days there were history. It was so awkward. But before his schedule filled for the summer, she'd have to let him know she'd need him more this year.

Considering her new situation, she looked at everything with a critical eye, worries of maintenance and money clouding her thoughts. She and Stan had always divided responsibilities neatly between traditional male and female domains. Claire had been in charge of cooking and entertaining. She wielded a spatula or corkscrew with skill. But a screwdriver or wrench? Forget it.

As she approached the porch, she noted that the asphalt driveway was more gray than black, and could use a coat of sealant. She'd have to start a list.

The front of the house looked fine, just a little dusty. With its white wood siding and bright blue shutters, the three-bedroom house had the feel of a cozy cottage. The shutters used to be red with wooden flower boxes underneath each of the front windows. Those were her mother's touch, and the look was reminiscent of a Holland travel brochure. Too cutesy for Claire, she'd painted the shutters cobalt blue when the house passed to her. Time, weather and neglect had done away with the flower boxes.

She unlocked the door, and dumped the first load in the middle of the floor, then went back to the car. After three more trips, she closed the door and locked it. Scraping her hair back from her face, she blew out a breath, and looked around. Everything seemed in order. And clean, but a little stuffy. She let Reggie out of the carrier, gave him a quick scratch under the chin, then began opening windows. She wandered into the kitchen, flipping on lights, then opened the door to the deck, and stepped outside.

The lake breeze whispered over her skin, and her heart gave a funny lurch as she surveyed the familiar surroundings. For a moment, she wondered whether the lake house offered escape or estrangement. Would she feel cut off out here by herself, now that she was truly alone?

Chapter Six

Just before dusk, Claire moved the car into the garage. She stifled a scream as something scurried out the door before it closed. A mouse, probably. Thank God it went that direction, she muttered. Hopefully it hadn't left any friends or relatives behind.

She switched on the overhead light and looked around at the years of history – and layers of dust – collected there. Fishing poles and bicycles lined one wall. She moved toward them, and ran her hand down the bright orange rod. Ben's pole. The one he'd wanted for his fourteenth birthday. They'd spent almost the whole summer at the lake that year. Had so much fun. She'd sat on the deck and watched as he fished from the dock. He'd turn and flash her a huge grin and a fist pump every time he got a bite. Leaning back against the car, she let the memory wash over her. Oh, how she missed her son's smile.

Her gaze meandered along the shelves in the garage. With a short laugh, and a lump in her throat, she reached over and lifted Ben's old slingshot. She held it to her chest and shook her head. They'd fought over that stupid thing. Unexpected memories slammed into her. She'd forgotten that the lake house would hold so many reminders of Ben. Such a perfect place for a boy growing up, though. The exploration, the chores, the boating and jet skis, the thrill of adventure that boys

51

were drawn to. She was so thankful now that they'd had the house, had given Ben such a rich childhood.

With quiet tears rolling down her cheeks, Claire switched off the light and stepped into the house.

So now what? She swiped the tears away, and leaned against the door. Here she was, with her own company, and nothing to do. Mary's book was an option, but Claire knew she wouldn't be able to concentrate. What she needed was a drink. Something to calm her nerves and numb her mind.

She poured a glass of wine, grabbed a sweater, and headed to the deck. Wrapped in the sweater, she sat on the steps for a few minutes and watched the sky turn from pink to a deep orange, the effect mirrored in the water as the sun set on the lake. But when she heard rustling behind her, she jumped up, her eyes darting around, searching the evening shadows of the yard. She saw nothing, and tried to convince herself it was nothing, but a sense of uneasiness set in.

"Get over it, Claire," she scolded. "You're a big girl, and you're on your own now. Better get used to it." Just the same, she picked up her glass, retreated inside the house, and turned on the television. She checked the locks on the doors, closed the windows, and pulled the curtains shut, then sank into one of her favorite chairs, an over-stuffed floral chintz in sunny yellow with green and blue accents. Those chairs were the only pieces of furniture with which she'd been allowed to have fun – a whimsical complement to the navy striped sofa and solid blue recliner.

At three in the morning, Claire woke to the sound of scratching at the back door. She shrugged on her robe and quietly hurried through the living room to the kitchen. Oh, no. Surely Reggie hadn't got out. She switched on a lamp and glanced around, and saw Reggie sound asleep on the sofa.

Thank goodness. She didn't need fleas and ticks inside the house. Pushing the curtain back, she peered outside. Then she banged on the door. She didn't see anything, but the noise stopped. Of course it could've been one of a dozen animals that lurked around the area, everything from a deer to a fox or a raccoon. Not a big deal.

Instead of going back to bed, though, she curled up in one of the stuffed chairs. At five, she gave up the notion of deep sleep, got up and got dressed. Maybe by afternoon her brain would shut off, and she could take a nap. She made a pot of strong coffee, then stepped onto the deck and inspected the screen door in the dim morning light. Definitely scratch marks. Looked like a small animal, probably an opossum.

The day loomed before her. Determined to do something, Claire opened the garage door. She found a few old gardening tools and a stack of clay pots. After she pulled on some work gloves, Claire gingerly lifted the top container, hoping nothing would slither, scurry or crawl out of it.

"Morning, Mrs. Stapleton. Can I help you with those?"

At the cheery greeting, Claire spun around. Nathan stood outside the garage, a friendly smile on his perpetually tanned face.

"Why, Nathan. Good morning. How are you?"

"Just fine, ma'am. You need me to bring those pots out for you?"

Claire brushed her hands across her jeans. "I'd love it if you could. Thought I might spruce up the deck a bit, plant a few flowers."

"Sure thing. Everything look all right inside?"

"Oh, Nathan, it's all great. Thank you so much."

"Not a problem. Maggie helped with the inside," he said as he lifted half of the pots and turned.

Maggie, Nathan's wife, often helped with cleaning and laundry while Nathan handled yard work and home repairs. "Well, tell her thanks and hello from me."

"Will do. Where would you like these?"

They walked around to the deck. "Anywhere here is fine. I'll need to fill them with dirt."

Nathan glanced around. "Let me do that for you. It'll just take a minute."

Claire laughed. The man certainly was eager to please. "I don't even have it yet. I'll pick some up when I get the flowers. Nathan, do you have time for a cup of coffee? I'd like to talk to you if you have a minute."

"Sure. That'd be great. Let me go ahead and get the rest of these."

Claire nodded, and went inside. She poured another cup of coffee, freshened her own, and dug her checkbook out of her purse. Maybe he stopped by this morning for more than a friendly visit.

Nathan stood at the bottom of the steps when she pushed through the doorway with the coffee.

"Come on up," she called, setting the mug on the table.

She pulled out a chair, and wondered where to start. She'd only told a few people about the divorce. Everyone else had heard through the grapevine, which in its own way turned out to be a blessing. At least she hadn't had to recount the ordeal over and over. It still sounded so unreal to her own ears. She supposed it would get easier in time. Would probably be easier than explaining that she'd raised two children, but now only had one.

With a heavy sigh, she launched in slowly. "Nathan, I know you do maintenance for several other homes out here. Are you extremely busy, or might you have time for a little more work this summer?"

"Oh, I can always fit in another job or two," Nathan said with an easy smile. "Is there something you need?"

Claire gripped her mug. "Well, yes, actually. You see, my husband and I are getting divorced, and I'll need someone to keep up with the mowing and repairs around the house. Do you think you could do that?"

54

Her throat constricted as she paused and took a sip of coffee, looking out over the lake for a moment before meeting Nathan's eyes.

Nathan rubbed a hand across his face, and sat back in his chair. "I sure am sorry to hear that, Mrs. Stapleton. Listen, I'll plan on doing the mowing, probably once a week or so, and you just let me know what else needs done. You've been a good client, and I'm happy to have the work."

Blinking back tears, Claire reached for the checkbook. A warm hand covered hers, and she looked up to find concerned eyes leveled at her. It was almost her undoing.

"You all right?"

She nodded, and offered a shaky smile. "Fine. Thank you. Now, what do I owe you for getting the house ready?"

"Two-fifty for the initial opening work."

Claire wrote the check for two hundred seventy five, and tore it from her checkbook.

"Now, Mrs. Stapleton, that's too much. You don't need—"

Holding up her hand, Claire shook her head. "It's a tip. I gave you short notice, and I appreciate you taking care of things."

"Well, you let me know when you get that dirt, and I'll swing by and load these pots for you."

"Absolutely not. That I'll do myself. I need a few odds and ends to keep me busy. But there's one more thing. Please stop calling me ma'am and Mrs. Stapleton. It's Claire. All right?"

He stood up and flashed her a smile. "I can't promise I won't forget now and then, but I'll try. You take care, and I'll check in with you later in the week. And just so you know, I drive along here several times a day. I'll keep an eye on the place."

"Thank you."

When he got to the bottom step, he turned back. "Mrs. Sta– I mean, Claire?"

"Yes?"

"Are you planning to keep the boat?"

Claire's gaze swiveled to the carport beside the garage. She hadn't given it any thought. But she sure as hell would not be keeping the boat.

"No. I don't think I will. Know anyone who's looking for a boat or some jet skis?"

"This early in the season, I bet it wouldn't be too hard to find a buyer," he said.

"Really? Could you ask around?"

"Sure."

A feeling of empowerment came over her, and she couldn't help but smile. Okay, so maybe it was also a tad bit spiteful, but, hey, she would never put that boat in the water again. It was just clutter, taking up space in her life. And she didn't give a damn whether Stan would want it or not. It was on her property. Too bad she hadn't thought to grab the title from the safe deposit box.

"Tell you what," she said, as an idea came to mind. "You find me a buyer and a good price, and you keep ten percent."

"Deal. I'll see what I can do."

It'd feel good to get rid of some baggage.

Chapter Seven

Claire started when the sharp peal of her phone jarred the morning stillness. She'd been watching the choppy waves on the lake, letting the constant rolling motion hypnotize her. Almost disoriented, it took her a moment to recognize the sound and find the phone. She picked up on the fourth ring.

"Hello?"

"Hey, you," Mary said. "How's life on the lake?"

Claire wandered back to the deck and picked up her coffee. She took a sip, and nearly spat it out. How long had it been sitting there? What was Mary saying? Life on the lake. Hmm. Sounded more exotic than it really was.

"It's quiet," Claire said, heading back to the kitchen. "How's the garden coming along?"

She rinsed the cold coffee down the drain and poured a fresh cup.

"Not as fast as I'd hoped. If everyone would leave me alone for five minutes, I might be able to get something accomplished."

"Sounds typical."

"Everything okay there? Nathan got it all taken care of?"

"Yeah. Everything's great."

"So, what are you doing? Getting some rest? You feel better?"

Sure. Four days into her 'get-away' and she was getting plenty of rest, but she was still so tired. Feeling better? Had she felt bad? No. Not really. She just felt . . . empty. Claire pushed the hair back from her face, and slumped into a chair at the table.

"I don't know, Mare. I'm not really doing much of anything."

"Well, what about freshening up the place? You said you might do some painting, plant some flowers. Maybe you should start a project."

Claire's eyes shifted to the empty flowerpots sitting near the deck.

"Claire. Talk to me. What's going on there? Are you all right?"

"I'm fine. Not sure this was such a great idea, though. I'm bored out of my mind."

"Well then *do* something, for heaven's sake. Did you start the book?"

"Not yet. Thought I might crack that open today."

"Have you gone to the biscuit place?"

Claire smiled at that. It was one of their favorite places. Just a little shack, but the proprietors of the Rise and Shine Café made the best cinnamon rolls she'd ever known – hot and gooey, with icing that oozed like lava over the sides. The cafe wasn't far, a mile and a half or so around the cove. She and Mary had walked there before. Made all that frosting justifiable.

"No. I'm waiting for you. Get your butt down here." There was a beat of silence before Mary answered.

"Claire, come on, you know I might not make it. Don't wait for me to have fun. Go enjoy yourself. Indulge a little."

"It's no fun by myself. What I really need is my best friend to come hang out with me."

Claire chewed her lip. She knew she wasn't being fair. Mary had too much going on. She had her own life, her own obligations. Her son was graduating from college. Claire choked back the tears that threatened. Thank God Mary had let her off the hook on that one. As much as she adored Jason, there was no way she could attend his graduation.

"Listen here, Toots," Mary said, exaggerated scolding in her tone. "I'm not one of your kids, so don't try that guilt-trip thing on me. The only trip I want to take is to the lake to see my friend."

Claire released her breath, silently thanking her friend for her good humor and not taking offense to the insensitive remark. She drew herself up and forced the whine out of her voice. "I know. But you don't have the time. You know what? I don't want you to think about it anymore. It's not the right time. I'll stay a few more days, through the weekend at least, then I'm heading home. We'll come later in the summer when we can enjoy it. Right now I'm not good company even for myself."

"Oh, pshaw. You're being too hard on yourself. Just try to enjoy the peace and quiet. Make yourself a big bowl of popcorn and have a chick flick marathon."

It sounded fun. And would eat up some time. There were plenty of movies she could enjoy watching over and over. Lots of movies that Stan would never sit through in a million years. So why was it so hard to find the energy to do it?

She forced a laugh. Then Cher's famous line from Moonstruck, 'Snap out of it!' came to mind, and she smiled for real. "Maybe I will."

"All right. Well, there's no exciting news from here. So you cozy up with a couple of oldies, but goodies, and I'll check in with you later."

"Sounds good. Bye."

Claire disconnected the call, took one sip of her coffee, and dumped the remaining liquid into the grass. Obviously not a coffee morning.

She puttered around the kitchen for a few minutes, then wandered through the house trying to find something to do. In the back bedroom she found temporary relief from the boredom. She yanked three photos off the wall, and snatched up another from the dresser. Two of them could simply be tossed – with pleasure. The other two required surgery.

Claire inspected the two photos, then retrieved her reading glasses and manicure scissors from her cosmetic bag. It would be a delicate operation. Stan stood on the edge of the group in the first one, so she'd start there. He was no longer part of her life, so why should he be taking up space in her family photos? Playing a phony role. She snipped him out, and replaced the empty spot with some trees from the other corner. Then she trimmed the entire photo and placed it in one of the smaller frames.

The second one took longer. Not only was Stan more central, but his hands were on Ben's shoulders. And Claire had to stop several times. She couldn't keep tears from blurring her vision as she gazed at her son's image. He must've been about twenty in that photo, almost a man, with a man's stance and square jaw. She ran her finger over the photo. He would've made a good husband, she mused. Any girl would've been lucky to have him.

With a felt tip pen, she dabbed at the photo, coloring in the dismembered fingers left on Ben's shirt. Luckily, he'd worn a black shirt that day. Then she tucked the photo back into the frame, and held up the finished product. Not too bad. With a sense of accomplishment, she hung the photos back on the wall. "A definite improvement," she told Reggie, curled up on the quilted bed in the one sliver of sunshine that peeked through the window.

Claire sat on the bed for a few minutes, then forced herself up. She sliced an apple and popped a bag of microwave popcorn for lunch, then she turned on the television and put a movie into the player. For ten minutes, she pushed every button on the TV and remote, trying to get the movie to play. "Come on, dammit!" She banged the remote against her palm. What was wrong with the stupid thing? On her hands and knees, she looked behind the unit, checked the wires, and rattled cords. But still, no movie.

Out of ideas, Claire conceded defeat. With an exasperated sigh, she dusted her hands on her capris, and dropped onto the sofa, drawing the popcorn bowl into her lap. She scooped up a handful of popcorn and shoved it into her mouth. Then washed it down with a big gulp of Chardonnay.

Halfway through the popcorn, she refilled her glass. As she watched the wine swirl, she debated whether to call Nathan about the movies. Damn technology. It was constantly making her feel like a fool. That was another thing that would probably cost her more money living on her own. Stan had actually been pretty good with electronic gadgets and computers. She glanced at her computer on the kitchen table. Maybe she could get the movies to play or download on it.

When she opened the laptop and powered up, her email account sprang to life. She gave it a quick scan, surprised to find an entire page of emails to be read. Junk, mostly. Online ads, and . . .

Her face warmed, and she caught her breath. There, about halfway down, a message from Lauren Armstrong. In the subject line: *Initial settlement proposal.* Claire gripped a chair and slammed her glass hard onto the table, fighting a wave of nausea. Already?

She slid into the chair, her hand hovering over the keypad. But she couldn't open the email. Wasn't ready for this. She pressed both hands to her face. So fast. He wanted to get away from her so badly. Couldn't wait to be rid of her.

She stared at the screen for several minutes, indecision immobilizing her. In a fog, she picked up her glass and downed the remaining wine.

Her life as she knew it was disappearing. That alone was hard enough to take in. But what would come next? Was this the beginning of a battle? Would he fight her? Cheat her? A dull throb started at the base of her neck, and she rolled her head side to side.

To calm her nerves, Claire refilled her glass. Then she paced the floor. Surely if it was bad, Lauren would've called her, she reasoned. Or flat-out rejected it. An email was probably a good sign.

When she couldn't stand it any longer, Claire perched rigidly on the edge of the chair in front of her computer and took a deep breath. Then opened the email.

The note from Lauren was reassuring. *No rush . . . Look over the details . . . We'll send a counter-offer.* Damn right. Claire opened the attachment, and scanned the document. *Blah, blah, blah, whereas the parties . . . blah, blah, blah.* The list was on the next-to-the-last page. Her stomach clenched. A lump-sum settlement or alimony. Half of the stocks. They'd each keep their cars and any personal possessions brought into the marriage or gift items. She smiled. No mention of the boat or anything at the lake house.

Okay so far, Claire thought. But Lauren already knew she wouldn't accept alimony payments. Claire had made that clear up front. She wanted a lump sum, no strings attached. No way would she wait for a check signed by the new missus to pay her bills every month the way Dana Gerard had to. So humiliating.

She read on. *Negotiable: property at 704 Mastin Road.* What? If neither party wanted the house, it would be sold and the proceeds divided equally. Claire's chest pounded. Sell the house and move? No. That was her home. She'd raised her kids there. Ben's room was there. She wasn't giving up her house. Stan could move. He could move to Paxton or Oakmont. It made sense. He had business dealings in both places.

The sentences began to blur, run together in her mind. She pushed back the chair, picked up her glass, and stepped onto the deck to catch her breath. The mid-afternoon sun was overcast with a few high clouds. A sunburn day. She looked out across the water and saw a couple of boats in the distance. People on the lake, with the breeze keeping them cool, would be especially vulnerable. She took a few sips of wine, but grimaced. She needed something cold, more refreshing.

Then she remembered the frozen margarita pops she'd discovered at the liquor store. The coolest thing – icy pops for grown-ups. She'd been hoping to share them with Mary, but that wasn't going to happen anytime soon. Inside, Claire pulled one out of the freezer and snipped the top off, then headed back to the deck. While she stretched out on the lounger, she let the lime-flavored icy shards melt in her mouth.

**

Claire rolled to her side, and flicked the hair back from her neck. She moistened her lips, but her tongue seemed thick inside her mouth. She swallowed hard, still floating in the semi-conscious state between sleep and awareness. It took a minute for the stickiness to register.

In one quick moment Claire realized she'd fallen asleep. She sat up, and wiped at the sticky spot on the side of her face. What in the world? When the foil wrapper from the margarita pop on the cushion beside her flashed in the sunlight, reality flooded in.

She glanced at her watch, and saw not only that it was five o'clock, but that the skin on either side of the round silver face was glowing pink. Groaning, she lifted the watch and saw the distinct outline, the contrast of white skin against red. *Stupid, stupid!* She knew better.

Claire stood up, but her head was foggy, and queasiness churned her stomach. She sat back down, and rested her head in her hands, waiting a few more minutes before making another attempt. Inside, she went straight to the bathroom and ran a washcloth under cool water. She patted her face then held the washcloth against her burned chest, which had taken the brunt of the sun's rays. In the mirror, she inspected her face. At least her moisturizer had sunscreen. Her nose didn't look too bad. The doctor had warned her against sunburn when he'd removed a spot from the side of her nose a few years ago.

"Note to self," she muttered. "Do not follow wine with margarita icy-pops." Not outside, anyway. She gingerly smoothed a thick layer of aloe gel over her raw skin then cranked up the air conditioning, and lay down on the bed, flat on her back. No covers touching her skin.

**

Claire woke to rumbling in her stomach and an aching soreness over her entire body. She lay awake for a moment wondering if she had the strength to get up and get dressed. But she was already dressed. Oh, no. Had she slept all night? The morning sun peeking through the window gave her the answer. She flopped back against her pillow. She'd planned to head to the Rise and Shine Café this morning. But rising didn't sound too appealing, and shining was out of the question. Still, she had to do something. She couldn't stand another day like yesterday.

After a few more minutes, and some nagging from Reggie, she swung her legs over the side of the bed and eased herself up. Testing the waters. So far, so good. She forced herself upright and stumbled to the kitchen to make coffee. While it brewed, she poured fresh food for Reggie then headed for the bathroom.

Careful to adjust the showerhead to a gentle sprinkle, she stepped inside and let the stream of tepid water soothe her aching skin. Several minutes later, she blotted her skin dry and applied another film of aloe gel before pulling on an apple green blouse and a pair of

64

khaki crop pants. Her stomach grumbled again, and it hit Claire that she'd completely skipped dinner last night. No wonder she felt woozy. At least she could justify the huge cinnamon roll in her future.

She slipped into her comfy flip-flops, poured coffee into a travel mug, and then climbed into the car.

At eight a.m. the road was deserted, so she drove slowly, meandering along, scanning the scenery, looking for both change and familiarity. A man she didn't recognize waved from his yard when she went past. She waved back, unsure whether she should know him.

Just ahead was the Rise and Shine Café. Claire was surprised to find no cars lining the road leading into the tiny parking lot. Until she turned in. She jerked the car to a sudden stop, her heart sinking as she took in the scene before her. No wonder there were no cars. No people. No noise. Only a charred shell of the shack remained. A piece of paper blew from one of the partly blackened posts that once held up the awning.

A deep sadness gnawed at her, and once again she felt as though she'd stumbled into someone else's life. She stepped out of the car and made her way across the dusty gravel lot, shaking her head. The damage was devastating, and the faint odor of fire still clung to the remaining structure. The happy aroma of fresh bread and cinnamon she'd been expecting – gone.

Her breath caught on a little choke. She supposed it was silly to be sentimental about something so trivial, but it touched Claire. More change. Another piece of her life vanished. She read the sign on the post. It thanked the patrons for many years of business and requested that they visit the new location. In town. *Oh, no.* Would they not rebuild? The café was an icon, part of the very fabric of lake life.

Claire rubbed a thumb across the post, black soot staining her skin. Then she wandered around the burned skeleton of the building.

"Did you not know?" a voice called out.

Claire's head snapped around, and she saw a frail-looking woman walking a small poodle heading toward her, teetering across the gravel.

"Hello," Claire called back. "No. I showed up this morning ready to gorge myself on a monster cinnamon roll. And I'm very disappointed. When did it happen?"

The older woman looked from Claire to the café. "Let me see. I'd say a couple of months now. Grease fire. Gone in a flash."

"Oh, how awful. I hope no one was hurt."

The woman shook head. "Was closing time. Only a few workers there. And Maggie, of course."

Claire knew Maggie, the owner. Always in a hurry, always rushing around, waiting on tables, greeting customers, hollering at the kitchen staff.

"So sad," Claire murmured. "So they aren't planning to rebuild?"

The woman shrugged. "Can't say for sure. They've already opened a new place."

"Oh, but in town. That won't be the same at all."

"Better for business, I suppose."

Claire looked at the woman and finally remembered her manners. She extended her hand. "I'm Claire Stapleton. I have a place a couple of miles down the road. Just before Richardson's."

The woman's eyebrows rose. "Really? How long have you been there?"

"Forever, it seems. My parents bought it in forty-seven."

The woman's eyes widened. "Well, I never. How little we know our neighbors anymore. I'm Lena Bishop. Very nice to meet you, Claire. I live right down the path here. I can't offer you a Rise and Shine cinnamon roll, but I've got fresh coffee if you'd care to have a cup. And some homemade muffins. You can leave your car here."

Claire hesitated a moment. Did she feel like socializing? If she went back to the house, what would

66

she do? She supposed she should get to know more people in the neighborhood if she was going to spend more time out there. Maybe some company would help get her out of the funk she'd been in ever since she arrived. Besides, she was already up and dressed. Might as well get some mileage out of that. And she needed food.

"That would be lovely. Let me grab my purse and lock up the car."

They started down the worn dirt path, and Claire had second thoughts. The dust and dirt would ruin her sandals. Not to mention they weren't the most practical shoes for tromping around the tall weeds and grasses. A snake could slither out anywhere.

Lena interrupted her thoughts. "Now, which house is yours, Claire?"

"It's a small one, right off of Sunset, white with blue shutters."

Lena stopped and turned, surprise on her face.

Claire nearly barreled into her.

"I used to know a woman who lived there," Lena said, walking forward again. "Let me think. What was her name? Caroline, I think."

At that, Claire stopped. "Caroline Bradshaw?"

The woman glanced back. "Why, yes. I think that's right. Did you buy from her family?"

"She was my mother. The house has been in the family since she and my dad bought it."

"Oh, that's wonderful." She beckoned toward a stone house with an old slate roof just ahead. "Here we are."

Claire climbed up the stairs and was surprised by the spacious great room with vaulted ceiling and golden hardwood floors that greeted her.

"This is beautiful," she said, taking in the elegant décor. Wow. Maybe she did need to spruce up her place after all.

"Thank you. We just had the floors redone last year. Every year we try to fix or update something."

Claire smiled. "I know what you mean. There's always a project that needs done."

"Here you go," Lena said, setting a large sunny yellow mug in front of Claire.

"Thank you." Claire sipped the coffee while Lena turned back to the kitchen. A few moments later, she set out plates and a tray of blueberry muffins. And Claire revised her earlier thought that Lena was frail. The woman was small, but wiry, and still had strength in her hands and arms.

"I know these are a poor substitute for the Rise and Shine, but maybe they'll take the edge off."

"They look wonderful." It was all Claire could do to keep from snatching one up and shoving it in her face.

Lena plopped down in a chair and removed the navy bandana that had covered most of her white curls. "Now, I want to hear all about your mother, and you."

"Well, Mother's been gone about ten years now. Complications from a stroke."

"Oh, I'm so sorry. I didn't know her well, but she was a lovely lady. Always friendly and welcoming."

"Yes. Thank you." Claire bit off a piece of muffin, trying to decide how much detail to share. How much did a casual neighbor really want to know?

"As for me, my life is a bit of a mess right now. I lost my son in Iraq two years ago, and my husband and I are in the process of a divorce." She blew out a breath and took a sip of coffee. There, she said it. Summed up the implosion of her world in one simple sentence.

When she finally looked over at Lena, sympathy radiated from the woman's face.

"How sad," she said softly. "I'm so sorry. Please forgive me for being nosy."

Claire shook her head, and the tears welled despite her efforts to prevent them. "No. It's fine. I've got to learn to say it without going to pieces."

They sat in silence for a moment, then Lena launched into the news of the area. Changes that had taken place in the past year. After about an hour, Claire stood to leave, and extended an invitation for Lena to visit.

"I'd love to, dear. Maybe next time you're here. You let me know."

Alone on the path back to the car, Claire's thoughts drifted again to her mother. She hadn't given her mom a single thought since Stan's departure. How odd. Her mother had been right. She caught her breath. Her mother had been *right* after all. She'd thought Stan and Claire were mismatched from the beginning. That he was too much a country boy for her. A country boy who wanted to elevate his place in the world, he put on airs. She'd told Claire that his need for status would lead him to compromise his standards when times were tough. And when times got tough, what had he done? Committed adultery. Cheated. Lied.

Stunned at the realization, Claire slowed her steps. She'd been so sure at the time that Stan was the one. Had ignored her mother's concern and warnings.

When she arrived at her car, Claire unlocked it, and sank into the leather seat. She turned the key, and cranked up the air conditioning. With her hands pressed to her temples, she let the cool air blast against her face.

Chapter Eight

On Sunday morning, Claire wiped down the kitchen counters and ran a quick broom over the floor. Normally, she'd bleach the surfaces, and vacuum the floor, leaving the place white-glove spotless. But this was the new normal. She could do as much or as little as she wanted. And she chose not to haul the vacuum sweeper out of the closet. No one else was coming to the house, so why bother?

It wasn't until she was clearing perishables out of the refrigerator, and nudged the box of wine over, that she realized the box felt empty. She lifted it out and shook it. Not enough to save. Hmm. Didn't seem like that had gone very far. If Mary had joined her, they'd have needed more. She tossed the box in the trash, and headed to the bedroom next.

She stuffed the used sheets and towels into a large trash bag, then pulled the car around. It was easier to load from the front porch than the garage. Just before taking off, she put in a quick call to Elise. For some reason she'd wanted to know when Claire was on the road.

"Hey, Mom."

"Hi. Just wanted to tell you I'm heading out in a few minutes."

"Oh, that's good. So you'll be home before dark."

Puzzled, Claire shook her head. She'd driven in the dark before.

70

"Yes. Probably close to five."

"So, did you have a good time?"

"Oh, it was nice. Good weather." The weather had been the one thing that had actually cooperated, Claire realized. Only a couple of light rain showers.

"Read any good books?"

Claire nearly choked. She'd opened Mary's book a couple of times. Gave it a chance. Truly, she did. But it didn't hold her interest. After a chapter or so, her mind kept wandering. She didn't care who was sleeping with whom, or who killed dear old Mrs. Millicent.

"Not really. It was low-key. Quiet." She let the robot take over while her thoughts drifted. "How are the kids?"

"Great. Maybe next time you head to the lake you can swing up here for a couple of days first."

"That would be nice."

"Did you meet anyone at the lake? Do anything fun?"

Fun. Somehow she'd missed the fun part. Why did everyone seem to think that going off by herself was going to be fun? "Oh, I met a lady who used to know Grandmother."

"Really? That's cool. You know, next time you should have a luncheon or a dinner party. Meet some people."

"Hmm. That's an idea. Hadn't thought of it. Maybe you could come down."

"You mean by myself?"

"Of course. You deserve a little get away."

"No time, Mom. Not sure we'll even make it out there this year. Let me know your schedule."

A schedule? Who was Elise kidding? Claire's summer yawned before her, a huge expanse of nothingness. "Elise, I don't have a schedule. Just let me know what works for you all, and I'll be sure to work around that. Mary and I would like to come out later."

"Sure."

71

Claire stood and went inside to gather up the remaining items for the car.

"All right. I better get going."

"Be careful, and I'll talk to you soon."

**

With only twenty minutes more to go, the reserve light on the gas gauge blinked on. Claire groaned, wishing she'd filled up halfway. She weighed her options. She could probably make it, but she'd rather arrive home with a tank full of gas than limp in on fumes. And there were a couple of stations close by. She pulled into the one on her side of the street. While the tank filled, she turned to wait in the car, and stifled a scream when a man stepped in front of her.

"Well, hello there, Claire. How are you?"

The man gave her a wide smile and lifted his ball cap. It took her a moment to recognize Ray Gleason from Oakmont. A friend of a friend. An acquaintance, actually. One for whom Stan had never cared.

"Oh, Ray. Hello. I'm just fine. How are you?"

"Can't complain, I guess." His gaze flickered to her car. "You heading home?"

"Yes. Couldn't quite make it all the way without gassing up."

He nodded, and braced himself against her car. "You know, I was thinking about you the other day."

What? Why in the world . . . Before she could respond, he continued.

"Yeah, I heard the news. And I'm thinking to myself, what kind of moron would give up a classy dame like Claire Stapleton? Only Stan. Gotta say, that man is out of his mind crazy."

Claire could've caught flies in her mouth for a full couple of seconds while she gaped at Ray. Then she shook her head, and forced a smile. She appreciated the compliment, and agreed with his assessment, but even to her rusty ears, that sounded suspiciously like a pick-up line.

"Thank you, Ray."

In the awkward silence, she busied herself by returning her credit card to her wallet and tucking it into her purse, instead of getting back inside her car.

Ray took a step forward, wiping his hands on his jeans. "He'll regret it one of these days, I guarantee it."

She sputtered out a little laugh, thankful when the gas shut off, sparing her any further comment.

"Let me get that for you," Ray said, moving toward the pump with a slow, lanky gait, like a man with time on his hands. He put the nozzle back in the holder and twisted the gas cap into place. Then he turned back to Claire, and shoved his hands in his pockets.

"Thank you so much–" she began.

"Say, Claire, have you had dinner yet? Would you like to run over to Bailey's and grab a burger?"

Of course she hadn't had dinner. It was only five o'clock. She was about to politely decline, but remembered there'd be no fresh food in her house. Did she want to head straight to the grocery store, central hub of gossip, the minute she breezed back into town? Not really. But then did she want to have dinner with Ray Gleason? She hardly knew the man, and Oakmont was only twenty minutes from home, after all. It was still possible she'd see someone she knew. Wouldn't that just set the rumor mill on fire?

It was tempting. And there was certainly no reason she shouldn't enjoy some company. Especially after ten days of solitude.

"You know, Ray, that's an excellent idea. I've been at the lake, and I'm not going to be the least bit interested in cooking or going out again once I get home. I'll meet you there."

Bailey's was only a couple of blocks away near Oakmont's downtown strip. Before going inside, Claire reached into the cooler in the backseat and added an ice cube to Reggie's water dish. "Here you go, big fella. We'll be home soon." She took another moment to apply fresh lipstick and fluff up her hair.

When Claire rounded the side of the building, Ray was standing outside waiting for her. He smiled and opened the door, ushering her inside. They found a vacant booth with a window view. Well, a window, anyway. Not much of a view. A small farming community, Oakmont was a town in decline. One out of three red-brick storefronts across the street had boards over the windows. A faded and sagging awning greeted customers across another.

Claire picked up her menu. It'd been a while since she'd eaten there.

"We don't have much," Ray said, "but there's not a better burger this side of the Mississippi."

Claire smiled. "I don't eat burgers often, tell you the truth," she said. "But you're right, these are the best." She ordered an iced tea and a Swiss burger then handed the menu to the waitress. Claire studied Ray while he gave his order. He wasn't a bad-looking man in spite of a receding hairline and weathered face. Those were standard equipment around there. His plaid shirt was a little tight across the shoulders, probably from a complete lack of interest in shopping for clothes. Again, nothing out of the ordinary. But there was something about him, maybe the way he jiggled his leg or kept clearing his throat, that gave Claire the feeling that Ray wasn't a man comfortable in his own skin.

"So heading home from the lake, huh?" he asked when the waitress had gone.

"Yes. Opening up the house there."

Ray's eyebrows rose. "Yeah? Table Rock?"

"Yes. My family's place."

"Nice. You share it with other folks, then?"

"Not really. My brother lives in Chicago and has no interest in it. My daughter and her family use it occasionally, but they're so busy. It's mostly me."

When their drinks arrived, Ray sat back, crossing one leg over the other out in the aisle. "What part of the lake?"

"Sunset Road. Off the beaten path."

"Uh-huh. So you been up there all by yourself?"

"Yes. I'm sure you can guess why. Hoping some of the talk has died down by now."

"Right. People around here do like to talk," he drawled with a shake of his head. "I imagine that news hit like an F-five tornado."

Exactly, she thought. Just like Dorothy, it had picked her up, spun her around and dumped her into a completely different world. One that didn't make sense. And she was pretty sure there were no magic shoes waiting to whisk her back to her former life. There was no going back.

Claire took a sip of tea, and forced herself back to the present. "So, Ray, tell me, what are you up to these days?"

He shrugged and took a swig of his beer before answering. "Little of this and that, you know. Doing some farming. Some car repairs."

Claire hadn't heard much about Ray in recent years. She knew, though, that his wife had left him, and that he'd taken over his parents' hardware business several years ago and run it into the ground – according to Stan. He'd tried to sell a little too late. Too many creditors, and not much value left by then, and he ended up simply closing down.

The waitress arrived with their dinner, and something else jogged in Claire's memory. She frowned. Hadn't Ray lost a son? How awful she couldn't remember the details. Her burger hovered in her hand for a moment. She wasn't sure she could take a bite without choking. She hadn't given Ray's son more than a passing thought when she'd heard about his death. Death was just another occurrence, a sad one, but devastating only when it touched you personally.

Claire looked across at Ray. The man had more than one reason to seem somewhat lost. She could relate to that. "Ray," she said softly, "tell me about your family."

"Aw. Not much to tell. Kids are all grown up. Everybody's moved away. Peggy's the closest over in Joplin."

"You lost a son, isn't that right? I'm sorry I don't remember his name."

A flash of pain crossed his face, but he covered it quickly, dabbing at his mouth with a napkin. "Been a long time, now," he said, then cleared his throat. "Cody. His name was Cody. No honor in his death, though, not like your boy." He let a French fry drop onto his plate. "Cody was drunk. Ran off the road and slammed into a grain elevator." He shook his head. "How stupid is that?"

Claire's stomach clenched. What in the world had possessed her to bring this up? Was she really interested in Ray's son, or did she have some narcissistic need to talk about Ben? Or did she want to see if he'd suffered the way she was. More than her son's father appeared to.

"I'm so sorry. I shouldn't have mentioned it."

He took another drink of his beer and his gaze met hers. "It gets easier with time, if that's what you're wondering," he said. "But it never goes away."

"I don't expect it to." Truth was, she didn't want it to. She wanted to remember her son. Wanted the rest of the world to remember him, too. She would not simply move on with her life as if he'd never existed.

"So, you staying in Whitfield?" Ray changed the subject.

"Yes."

"You got the house then?"

"Well, things aren't final yet, but I believe that's the way it will go."

"Big house."

76

"More stuff than I care to move."

He smiled and nodded. "Lot of upkeep, though."

"True. Every day it seems like there's something new to deal with. A leaky faucet or a toilet that runs on and on."

"Stan already take his things and leave you to deal with maintenance?"

Hmmm. She'd have to be careful. She didn't want any rumors running around that he'd left her a mess to deal with on top of divorcing her. Or that the house was falling down around her. "Not really. Since the divorce isn't final, he still has things in the house, and we're both still responsible for maintenance, I suppose."

Ray looked out the window a moment then turned back to her with a kind of smirk on his face that she didn't understand. "I bet he's got a lot of stuff, too. Stan Hotshot Stapleton. A man who likes to impress people with his stuff."

Claire's face warmed. Puts on airs, her mother had said. Was she the only one who'd never seen it? What about Mary? Claire folded her hands against the table and regarded Ray.

"Ray, is there some animosity between you and Stan? Did something happen I'm not aware of?"

Ray ran a hand over his jaw. "Aw. I shouldn't bother you with any of that. Ancient history, I suppose."

"Doesn't seem so ancient," Claire said mildly.

He eyed her for a moment before answering. "Turned my kid down flat one summer he was looking for work. Wouldn't even take his application."

Ray took another swig of beer, and Claire waited, certain there was more to the story. He looked past her as he spoke again.

"Stan was on the board at the bank the year they decided to foreclose on our building. My parents had been paying on that building for a long time. Only a few more years, and it would've been ours."

Claire vaguely recalled something about that now. For the most part, she didn't get involved in Stan's business dealings.

Ray leaned forward. "The man likes to throw his weight around, you know?"

Well, she supposed that was true. She knew Stan thought he was superior to Ray for some reason. Thought Ray was a slacker, a loser. Whatever. She sighed, and decided she didn't really give a damn.

Just then, the waitress brought the ticket and handed it right to Ray. Claire protested and reached for her wallet, but Ray held up his hand.

"I'm getting this, Claire. It was my invitation, remember?"

Apparently he wasn't so much of a slacker that he let a woman go Dutch for dinner. "Thank you, Ray. That's very nice of you."

She scooted out of the booth as Ray tossed some bills on the table.

"So, Claire," he said when they stepped outside. "You got those problems right now? The leaks and toilets?"

She gave a little laugh. "Yep. One of each."

Ray propped a hand on his hip. "Tell you what. Next time I'm passing through Whitfield, I'll stop by and see what I can do. Probably wouldn't take more than a few minutes."

"Oh, Ray, that's very thoughtful, but please don't go to the trouble. I'll have a handyman in town take care of it."

"Up to you. But the offer stands."

He walked her to her car. "Thanks for having dinner with me, Claire. I enjoyed it."

"Me too." She slipped into the car and gave him a wave. As she pulled her Acura onto the street, she saw Ray hop into an old Dodge that had seen better days. Large splotches of rust wove through the dirty gold to create a patchwork effect across the truck's back end. A few dents told not only of the truck's age and wear, but perhaps the owner's inability to afford cosmetic bodywork. Claire thought of Stan's truck. He never kept one more than three or four years. And didn't skimp on the bells and whistles. She'd bet Ray Gleason had noticed.

She made a quick stop at the liquor store at the edge of town – one she hadn't been to in a while. She browsed the short aisles and considered picking up something other than wine. What would be more refreshing, but also easy? Without a lot of mixing and messing around. She couldn't bring herself to buy more margarita pops just yet. Then she saw a stack of cards on the counter that offered a recipe for sangria. She slipped one into her purse. That's what she'd do. She could mix up a whole pitcher and keep it in the fridge. Perfect.

Of course that would require a trip to the grocery store.

**

The day was melting into evening when Claire turned onto Mastin Road. The first thing that hit her was that the pinks and purples of spring, present when she'd left for the lake, had already been replaced by the green shades of summer. The old clematis that wound through the trellis in front of the house for years had dropped all its petals and was a tangled mass between the evergreens on either side. Same for the cluster of redbuds to the side.

She pulled the car into the garage, and sat for a moment. Home sweet home, she thought wryly. She swung Reggie's carrier out of the car and unlocked the side door that led into the mudroom.

She'd turned up the thermostat when she left to save on electricity. Still, it seemed awfully warm inside. By the time she'd unloaded the car, her hair clung to her neck and face. This was not right. Claire marched down the hallway and peered at the thermostat. Ninety-three. "No wonder," she muttered. She dialed it down to sixty-five, hoping for a quick turnaround.

Thirty minutes later, she checked again. Ninety-one. She listened. No fan blowing. Dammit. She clipped her hair up and went outside to the air conditioning unit. It looked perfectly normal, of course, as she stared down at it. Just a box of gray metal. That in itself annoyed her. What right or reason did this heap of metal have for making her miserable? Claire had no idea what the problem was. The only thing she could tell for sure was that its usual dull hum was missing. No sound. No movement. No cooling. She glanced at her watch. Was it worth an emergency service call? Or could she suffer through one night with a couple of fans?

Claire headed to the storage room downstairs. She'd located the fans, and was pulling out the big box unit when she heard the phone ring. Turning quickly, she lost her balance and tangled with the cord. As she tumbled forward, she caught herself, but not before her chin connected with the cover grate of the fan.

She let out a sharp yelp, and dropped the fan on the tiled floor. Tears welled in her eyes, and she considered lying down right there on the cool floor of the basement. Maybe even throwing a tantrum. As appealing as that sounded, she picked up the phone with one hand, and gingerly touched the sore spot on her chin with the other.

"Hello?"

"Hey, you." Mary's cheery voice came on the line. "A nosy neighbor told me you were home."

"Nice." Claire checked her fingers, not surprised to find them stained with blood. She hurried to the bathroom for a tissue.

"Hey, you there?"

"Yes, yes, I'm here. I just busted my chin open."

"What? How'd you manage that?"

"Long story. But I'm standing here in the sweltering heat sweating and bleeding. How's that for a welcome home?"

"Oh, for heaven's sake. I'm coming over. I need to get out of here for a while, anyway."

"Don't come here. It's like a sauna, but no cucumber water or aromatherapy. According to the thermostat, it's ninety-one degrees in the house. No air conditioning."

"Oh, no."

"Oh, yeah."

"What about your chin? Do you need stitches?"

"No. It's fine. The bleeding's stopped."

"All right then, you come over here. Or we can run over to the diner. What do you think?"

"I think I'm wiped out, honestly."

The unexpected events of the day had thrown her off kilter. Earlier, she'd been looking forward to coming home, to talking to her best friend. And now she could hardly muster the energy to walk back upstairs. What was wrong with her?

"Oh, come on," Mary coaxed. "You've been at the lake for ten days. How can you possibly be tired? Tell you what, grab some jammies and a toothbrush, and come on over. You can stay in the guest room and call about the air conditioning tomorrow. Grant can go to bed, and you and I can stay up 'til all hours gabbing."

Claire considered. She had to admit, it didn't sound half-bad. She'd missed Mary's company at the lake. After a moment, she grinned. "Well, when you put it like that . . . I'll be right over."

Chapter Nine

While Ted from Best Heating and Cooling worked on the air conditioning, Claire sat under the ceiling fan in a sleeveless cotton blouse, and sifted through ten days of mail. Most of it went directly into the recycling bin, but a bright yellow envelope caught her attention. She picked it up and turned it over. She recognized Elise's handwriting, but the return address said Olivia Keaton.

Claire slit the envelope open and pulled out a small card with a giant sunflower colored on the front. Smiling, she opened the card. *"Dear Grammy, thank you for the cute shoes. I wear them all the time. My teacher likes them too. You are the best Grammy. Love, Olivia."*

Touched, Claire set the card on the table, wondering how much of the note Olivia had written herself. Didn't matter, she supposed. It was a nice gesture. And she was happy to know that Olivia was enjoying the shoes. She grinned at that. Oh, boy. Elise just might have a little fashionista on her hands. She wished she'd thought to have Elise take a picture of her and the kids when they were there. Or at least one of Claire and Olivia. Next time she'd have to remember that.

She opened a few other cards. A "thinking of you" from Dana. Maybe Claire would invite her over. Or invite a few gals for lunch. That'd be fun. Her thoughts drifted, mulling the possibilities. She could hold a girls night in. They could watch movies or play Bunco. Eat chocolate and drink sangria . . . maybe. Sounded fun, but fun took energy, and she was short on that these days.

Claire turned her attention back to the cards. There were a couple of funny ones. She laughed out loud at the one from Mary – it pictured a woman dressed to the nines, cocktail in hand, at an airline ticket counter requesting a ticket to send someone "non-stop to hell." If only it were that easy.

She set the card aside when Ted clattered in, his tool belt swinging from his hefty hips. She stood up, expecting him to address her, but he chugged through the living room and made for the thermostat in the hallway.

"All right, Mrs. Stapleton," he said a few minutes later. "You ought to be feeling some relief real soon now."

Thank God. She offered a polite smile. "Wonderful. Thank you. Let me get my checkbook."

"I'll figure up the damage for you."

Claire nodded and went to the kitchen to retrieve her purse. When she returned, Ted handed her a piece of paper. "If you could just sign here, ma'am."

She glanced at the total. Three hundred and forty. Could've been a lot worse. She signed her name, then wrote a check and handed it to him. "Thank you. I appreciate you coming out so quickly."

"Yes ma'am. You have a nice day, now."

Well, it was looking up. Except that she still needed to make a grocery store run. She thought about putting it off until she'd be in Paxton to meet with her attorney, but she couldn't make it quite that long. With a sigh, she resigned herself to the worst errand on the planet.

But as she poured iced tea into a plastic cup to take with her, an unwelcome thought took up residence. Why in the world did she want the house, want to stay in Whitfield if she couldn't even muster the courage to go to the grocery store?

She set the pitcher down, and leaned against the counter. She couldn't live like this – hiding, avoiding people. Since Stan had walked out, she'd isolated herself. Hadn't been to her regular activities or the library. Of course Elise had visited, and then Claire had left for the lake. There hadn't been a lot of opportunity.

Her thoughts went to the cards she'd received in the mail. They were proof that she had friends, people who cared about her here. There was no reason to be afraid of seeing people. She had nothing to be ashamed of.

She glanced at the blinking light on the answering machine. It said there were seventeen messages, but she hadn't played them back. Why not? A "classy dame," Ray Gleason had called her. Was she? Wouldn't a classy dame put on her best shoes and toss her hair to the wind, embrace her friends and smile with charm at her enemies? *Get real, Claire. You lost your husband, that's all. Happens to women every day.*

With renewed resolve, she picked up her purse and headed for her car.

There were maybe ten cars in the Meyers Market parking lot. Two-thirty on a Monday afternoon wasn't a heavy shopping time. Pasting what she hoped was a nonchalant look on her face, she climbed out of the Acura, and made her way to the sliding glass doors.

Inside, she yanked a cart out of the stack, and smiled at the cashier closest to the entrance. She'd start in the produce section like she always did. Just go about her regular routine. Yeah, for about a minute and a half – until Lisa Carter stepped from behind a display of salad toppings.

"Claire," she sang out, waving her hands. Her cart stopped inches from Claire's, and Lisa pulled Claire into a fierce lilac-scented hug. "How are you? Oh, my gosh. I've been thinking about you. Did you get my message? I want to take you to lunch."

"Hi, Lisa." Claire laughed as she disentangled herself from Lisa's death grip. "I'm sorry, I haven't had a chance to listen to messages since I got back from the lake yesterday. The AC went out, and it's been crazy."

Lisa leaned in, and lowered her voice. "You know we all think Stan is being a total ass. Even the men are talking about it. Jack just can't believe it."

Jack and Stan had gone to high school together. Two of the dozen or so who'd settled in their hometown. They were pretty good friends, so Claire knew there was a good chance they'd already heard from Stan. And that it would be hard for her to keep a friendship going with Lisa.

They talked for a couple of minutes, and Claire agreed to a lunch date. But before she could push her cart on down the aisle, another familiar face sidled up beside her.

"Hey, what is this? A party in produce?" Jane Wharton laughed and squeezed Claire's arm. "How you doing, Claire?"

She nodded again, but could feel tears threaten at the sympathy in Jane's eyes.

"You okay?" Jane asked softly.

"I'm fine, thanks. Just trying to get a few groceries. Haven't even made it half-way down one aisle yet."

"I'll walk with you."

"And I better scoot," Lisa said. "I'll see you gals later. Claire, we're on for lunch."

"Okay, if she gets lunch, I get coffee," Jane said. "What are you doing tomorrow morning? Want to invite me over?"

Claire couldn't help laughing. Maybe she should come to the grocery store every day. "Yes. Come for coffee tomorrow. But not before nine o'clock. God knows I need my beauty sleep."

"Bull. But, okay. Nine it is. I'll bring some muffins or something."

Claire stopped her cart to pick up some peaches and berries for the sangria. "See you in the morning."

Jane gave Claire's shoulder another squeeze then moved on down the aisle.

Thirty minutes later Claire left the store feeling more content than she had in weeks, but also rather silly for avoiding her friends in the first place.

**

At eight-thirty the next morning, Claire switched on the coffee pot then finished her hair and make-up, and found herself looking forward to spending an hour or so with Jane. Mary had brought her up to date on all the gossip that wasn't about Claire at her house Sunday night, but Jane would have new information. She worked part time in the school district office, and always heard interesting tidbits about life in Whitfield.

When her doorbell rang at nine, Claire thought she heard voices. Now what could that be about, and right when Jane was due to show up? Claire opened the door, and peeked around it. Her mouth dropped open. Jane, Mary and Dana stood on the porch, arms loaded down with flowers, bags, and trays of food. A party had just landed on her doorstep.

Tears stung Claire's eyes and immediately spilled onto her cheeks. With a lump in her throat, she backed away from the door and her friends barreled inside, circling around her, laughing and whooping.

For nearly two hours they laughed and talked. Talked about new aches and pains, kids and grandkids, and who'd heard what about whom. They remembered good times, and a sense of profound gratitude spread through Claire for these women who'd been through so many ups and downs with her. They'd been there for her when Ben had died, and here they were again, helping her pick up the shattered pieces of her life.

But even as she felt the bond of friendship circling her, she knew this intensity wouldn't last. After a while, everyone would go back to their own lives, just as they had after Ben's death. She couldn't impose on them to hold her up indefinitely.

After they'd switched from coffee to iced tea, and moved from the kitchen table to the living room, Jane pressed a bag into Claire's hands.

"Here, open this."

"Yes, ma'am." Claire drew out the tissue paper, then a bag of Jordan almonds, dark chocolate toffee, a hand-painted wine glass that toasted friendship, and a small box. She lifted the box and opened it. Inside was a round disk on a rubber stand. "No crisis too big or small," it said.

She glanced at Jane. "I give up. What the hell is it?"

"Push it," Jane told her.

Claire set it down on the table and pushed the center of the button. Red lights flashed on, and the shrill pre-recorded message screamed, "This is bullshit!"

All four of them shrieked with laughter. "Oh, my God, that's hilarious," Claire hooted, wiping her eyes. "A bullshit button – just what I needed."

As soon as their laughter subsided, Mary hit it again. And they laughed some more.

Then Dana reached over and took Claire's hand. "Speaking of bullshit, tell us where you're at with the divorce, hon. Are things moving along?"

Claire set her tea down and one by one, met her friends' eyes. "It's going incredibly fast. I go see my attorney next week to talk about a settlement. If we can negotiate that, it should only be another few weeks before it's final."

"Wow. That is fast."

"Which is a good thing," Jane added. "Just get it done so you can move on."

"So *he* can move on and get the hell out of your life," Mary said.

"That's right. It's the waiting that's worst. Limbo Land," Jane said. "Listen, you let us know the minute the word comes in, okay? I mean it."

Claire smiled. "You'll be the first to know. Only don't come for coffee."

"No," Dana said. "We'll bring booze."

**

Claire lit a cigarette and finally punched the button on the answering machine and listened to seventeen messages. One was from Lauren, but the others were all messages of support, people calling to check on her. Rev. Ansel had called twice. Claire sighed. She supposed she should call him, or go see him. He'd hound her if she didn't, but she had to admit she wasn't exactly feeling God's presence in her life right now. Hadn't for a while.

For many years, she and Stan were solid members of the church, participating, attending and tithing regularly. But after Ben died, it didn't make sense to her anymore.

The church was there for her. The people, anyway. But where was God? Was this part of the plan? Claire took a deep drag on her cigarette and leaned against the counter, amazed at how easy it was to go from feeling good surrounded by friends, to feeling abandoned and alone. Heavy silence pressed around her.

Slowly, she put away all the food the girls had left, wiped up the crumbs, and rinsed the glasses. Then she splashed a little citrus vodka and cranberry juice into her iced tea, and wandered back into the living room. She picked through one of the baskets from her friends. Some lotions and bath oils, Superberry tea, a book of inspirational quotes, and more chocolate. Very nice.

Claire picked up the small book of quotations, and opened it. As if on cue, the phone rang. It was still sitting on the counter in the kitchen. She glanced at it, wishing she could use "The Force" to snap it into her hands. Didn't work, so she let the answering machine pick up while she listened.

"Hello, Claire. Ray Gleason here. Just wanted to let you know I'm passing through town next Wednesday on my way to Paxton. I'd sure be happy to stop by and take a look at those plumbing problems you got. Gimme a call." He left his number, and the machine clicked off before Claire's brain engaged.

Was the man pursuing her? Before her divorce was even final? Surely he wasn't that excited about doing some odd plumbing jobs. Oh, but maybe he was. Maybe he needed the money. Now that she thought about it, he never said he'd do them as a favor. He certainly didn't owe her any.

She got up to retrieve the phone. No reason she couldn't throw him a bone. But then she remembered the appointment with Lauren Armstrong. Wednesday wouldn't work. She waited about an hour before calling back, so he wouldn't know she'd been sitting there listening when he'd called.

"Ray, this is Claire Stapleton returning your call."

"Well, hello, there. How are you?"

His voice came slow and easy, and again, Claire had the sense that he was a man with time on his hands, not someone desperate for work. Maybe he was just bored. She could understand that.

"I'm great, Ray, thanks. Listen, I really appreciate you thinking about me, but as it turns out, I have to be in Paxton Wednesday also for an appointment."

"Is that right? Well, I'll come by another time then."

"Sounds good," she said. No reason to argue with him.

"Hope everything goes well with your appointment."

She drew a shaky breath. "Yes. Me too."

"You don't sound so sure. Lemme guess. Visit with your lawyer?"

She took another sip of her iced tea then plastered on a smile, even though he couldn't see it. She would not be confiding in Ray Gleason. "You're right," she said. "But I expect it to be just fine. Really."

"Hey, Claire, I'm gonna be in Paxton most of the day. When you're done with your lawyer, let me buy you some lunch, or a drink or dinner. You might want to take a few minutes before heading back home. What do you say?"

She had no idea what to say, but it was kind of nice to hear a man want to spend some time with her. Willing to spend a little money, buy her dinner. Again. Not that she was the least bit interested in dating. Besides, technically, she was still married.

She hedged. "Well, my appointment is at three o'clock. That's not really lunch or dinner time. And I don't know how long it will last."

"Tell you what. You call me when you're done, and see how you feel. How's that sound?"

It was an out, and it would give her some time to think. "Perfect. Thanks, Ray. I'll talk to you next week then."

She ended the call, and wrote down the phone number and tucked it into her purse. When she reached for another cigarette, Reggie jumped into her lap. Absently, she scratched his chin and behind his ears. "I don't know, Reggie, babe. What do you think?" She stared out the window for a moment then looked him in the eye. "I think you might just be man enough for me right now."

Chapter Ten

The phone rang sharply, yanking Claire from the soothing warmth of a long, steamy shower, and forcing her into action. She wrapped a towel around her and stepped from the bath matt onto the cold tile of her bathroom. Someone sure had lousy timing. She could let it go, but Lauren said she'd call if something came up and she had to cancel their appointment.

Claire hoped that wasn't the case. She wasn't exactly looking forward to the meeting, but she was anxious to see what Stan and his lawyer were offering. And the appointment would at least get her out of the house and give her something to do.

She was padding down the hallway when the answering machine picked up.

"Hey, Mom. Just wanted to let you know I'm having a birthday party for Olivia. A mix of family and friends. At the zoo on the tenth. She'd like for you to come, so check your calendar, and let me know. You're welcome to stay here, of course. Maybe you could come early and help me with party favors or something. Give me a call when you get a chance."

Claire stopped and leaned against the bannister while she listened. Did she want to go to Wichita? She certainly had the time.

She wandered into the living room and lit a cigarette, mulling the possibility. It was the same old dilemma she had any time Elise invited her. Did she want to go, or was it simply an obligation? She couldn't smoke or enjoy a glass of wine. There was no privacy, but plenty of noise.

But Olivia wanted her to come? Claire inhaled, and blew the smoke out slowly. It was the right thing to do, of course. Play grandma. Babysit while Elise and Brian went out. That would be fine. She'd enjoyed Olivia on their last visit. Thinking back, she'd always enjoyed Olivia. Her granddaughter had been a darling toddler.

While she was there, she and Elise could cook, put a few meals away in the freezer. That actually had some appeal. She hadn't cooked a real meal in weeks.

The tenth Elise said? Claire lifted her calendar from the desk and opened it. The blank pages flashed at her like a neon vacancy sign, reminding her of the emptiness of her life. She drew a shaky breath, picked up a pen and wrote Olivia's party down in the empty box for July tenth. It was the only day with any notation. She slammed the calendar shut and hurried back to the bedroom. At least there was something to do today.

She pulled on a casual black skirt and a coral knit top. Then she tied a matching floral scarf around her neck. Scarves were her new favorite accessory. They were stylish, could be found to go with any outfit, and they hid the folds of her sagging neck and chin. Every woman over fifty should have a drawer full.

**

At noon Claire wolfed down a banana and some crackers, then climbed into the car. She'd have a little time to hit the shops in Paxton, and maybe have a quick drink to take the edge off before her meeting. She rolled her neck as she drove, trying to relieve some of the tension that had already crept in.

Forty-five minutes later, she parked in the garage between the shops and Lauren's office. If she bought anything, she could always run back by the car. Her first stop was Halston's Boutique where she'd bought

Olivia's sandals, to try and find an outfit to match for her birthday. Took about ten minutes to drop a hundred dollars there.

After that, Claire browsed the square, pretending it was just another day of recreational shopping. She drifted in and out of shops for about an hour before heading to the Gardenview Café. There, she slid into a cool booth and ordered a cosmopolitan.

When it arrived, Claire squeezed in extra lime juice and lifted the glass. Just what she needed. She'd avoided dwelling on the upcoming meeting with Lauren, but now anxiety tightened her chest. Why had Lauren insisted on a meeting rather than simply sending another email? Why did it seem so rushed? What was the hurry? Limbo Land, Jane had called it. Get it done with, and move on, the girls had told her. *But move on to what?*

She remembered her blank calendar, and nearly choked on the drink. What was she going to do with the rest of her summer? The rest of her life, for that matter? She toyed with the lime in her glass, but no answers came to her. Those questions were too big. And they'd have to wait. First things first. She gathered her courage with the last swallow of the cosmo and then gathered her things.

Claire arrived at the law firm's office with five minutes to spare. She took a seat, then picked up a magazine and leafed through it while she waited. Nothing caught her interest, though. It was just something to do with her hands. She glanced around, wishing she could have a cigarette, and found the only other occupant in the waiting area, a man, watching her. Probably guessing why she was there, knowing that she was being dumped for a newer model. Claire's throat constricted and she quickly looked back down at the magazine.

When Lauren opened the interior door a few moments later, Claire blew out her breath and quickly followed her attorney into the spacious, homey office.

The coffee table in the center of two chairs and a sofa was already set with two iced teas and an assortment of mints and cookies.

"Have a seat, and a drink," Lauren told Claire while she rummaged around at her desk.

Claire picked up a glass and sat back on the sofa. "This is lovely. Thank you."

Lauren shrugged out of her suit jacket and dropped into one of the chairs. She leveled a direct gaze at Claire.

"How are you?"

Claire looked way, and adjusted her scarf. "Oh, I'm fine."

They chatted for a few minutes then Lauren reached for a document from her desk and handed it to Claire.

"Here's where we stand. Stan seems to have no problem with you keeping the house. The only stumbling block I see is the lump-sum alimony."

Of course, Claire thought. The one thing she was adamant about. She twisted her hands together and waited for Lauren to continue.

"The thing is, Stan has a lot of money tied up in real estate and non-liquid investments. He doesn't have a lot of cash."

Cry me a friggin' river, Claire chanted to herself.

"Uh-huh. So what does he want?"

"Well, we could ask the judge for a sale. Or, you could accept some land or property as compensation and then sell it on your own. The problem is, both of those options would take some time."

"Problem? Why is that a problem? What's the big rush? I'm not in a hurry."

Claire didn't miss the flash of consternation across Lauren's face. Oh. Of course, she was being obtuse. *She* wasn't in a big hurry. But Stan was. He wanted to move on. And she stood in his way.

"I don't care if it doesn't move as fast as he wants," Claire said, her voice quivering. "I told you. That's the one thing that isn't negotiable."

"I know." Lauren paused a moment. "Claire, have you talked to a financial advisor about any of this?"

Oh, damn. She didn't want to talk to anyone else. Didn't want to air her entire life's affairs to yet another stranger. "No. I haven't. I don't think it's necessary."

"Are you sure you want that much cash rather than income-producing property?"

Claire stood then, bouncing a fist against her palm. "I don't want to be in business with Stan. I don't want any of his operations. I don't want any land that I have to pay taxes on and manage. I want to be free of it all."

"The judge isn't going to leave him with no cash, Claire. The man will have to have something to live on."

"Fine. Let him take out a loan. He could take out a mortgage"

"True," Lauren said, holding out a hand to Claire. "Come on, sit down. We'll work this out. Don't stress. You're going to be in good shape no matter what. I promise."

With tears threatening in her eyes, Claire sat down and took a long drink of tea. Why the hell was she supposed to care about what Stan wanted or needed?

"Claire. Do you know how much the bank stock is worth?"

"Of course. It's a nice chunk, and it should be enough to live on. But I'm not giving up the alimony." She deserved every cent.

"Of course not. You know that when the bank was bought out by National a couple of years ago the value of the stock nearly tripled, right?"

Claire sucked in her breath. She remembered Stan had been beside himself with glee, patting himself on the back for holding onto that stock for so long. But he'd never mentioned it tripling. Had never given her specific details. She shook her head. She'd trusted him.

Had been perfectly content to let him handle all their financial affairs. What an idiot.

"I, uh. No. I guess I didn't realize that." Now she remembered. The announcement had come shortly after Ben's funeral. She couldn't have cared less.

"Here's my suggestion, then. I say we ask for an increase in the bank stock, and we reduce the amount of alimony by whatever interest rate percentage Stan has to pay on a loan. What do you think about that?"

Her pulse raced. Could it be that simple? "I think it sounds reasonable," she said. "Perfect, in fact. Do you think the judge, or Stan, would agree to that?"

"Well, it's going to be the fastest resolution."

Claire's face flamed, and her voice went shrill. "And that's what he's looking for, right? He's in a big rush to dump the old and get on with the new. He'll probably be remarried the day the divorce is final."

Lauren reached out for Claire's hand. "I know it's hard, Claire. But try not to be bitter. I've seen this so many times. Try to look at it as a new opportunity. A new phase of your life with the freedom to do whatever you choose. Start a new career. Travel. Work for a cause. You might not think so now, but compared to a lot of women I see in this position, you're very lucky. You don't have to worry financially. You'll be a wealthy woman."

Claire's legs were heavy as she left the office, and she felt emotionally drained. As she expected. A wealthy woman, Lauren had called her. So, she'd have money. But she'd have to spend it alone. Great. She could eat out every meal – alone. She could travel the world – alone. She could buy expensive clothes but have nowhere to wear them.

Not only that, but if word got out, she'd be a target. She'd always have to wonder whether someone was trying to take advantage of her. One more thing to worry about.

As she approached the parking garage, she thought about her promise to call Ray Gleason. What was *his* motivation? Did he know anything of Stan's bank account? She couldn't imagine how he would, other than the obvious signs like Stan's trucks. His *stuff*.

Claire shook her head. No. She refused to believe that she could only attract the interest of a gold-digging sleazebag. Sure, her hair had grayed a little early but she was still an attractive woman with a decent figure. And despite the recent proof of her ignorance, she was an intelligent woman.

She fished Ray's number out of her purse and punched it into her cell phone. It was only four-thirty, but she'd had a light lunch. They could have a cocktail then an early dinner.

"Hello, Ray. It's Claire," she said when he picked up.

He cleared his throat. "Well, hello, there. I was hoping I'd hear from you today. How'd it go?"

Claire forced lightness into her voice. "Even better than I expected."

"All right, then," Ray drawled. "I'd say that calls for celebration. How does the Ranch House sound?"

Oh, my. The Ranch House was the nicest steakhouse in the region. Was he trying to impress her? But could he afford it? She shifted her weight, trying to think. She simply did not have his situation figured out.

"Ray, we don't have to do anything that fancy."

"I insist. Where are you?"

"In the downtown square."

"I'm ten minutes away, tops. Want me to pick you up or meet you at the restaurant?"

She always preferred to have her own car. It gave her a tiny bit of control and peace of mind knowing she could go whenever she felt like it.

"I'll meet you there in ten minutes."

**

97

Claire arrived before Ray and took the opportunity to visit the ladies room and freshen up. She fluffed her hair, applied fresh lipstick and adjusted her scarf, which had shifted to the side. Not half-bad, she decided. She straightened, smoothed the sweater over her stomach, and walked confidently out the door.

A smile on his face, Ray stepped forward, and greeted her with a pat on the shoulder. "Nice to see you, Claire."

"We can seat you now," the hostess told them.

They followed her to a small booth, and took the menus she handed them.

"Are you ready to eat dinner?" Ray asked.

"Oh, I don't know. Maybe I'll start with something to drink."

"Let's start with a drink and an appetizer."

"Perfect."

When the waitress arrived, Claire ordered a glass of Chardonnay. Ray ordered a beer and a sampler platter of appetizers.

"You sure don't look like someone who just met with a divorce lawyer," Ray said, leaning back in his chair and stretching an arm across the chair next to him. "Must've been a good meeting."

Claire smiled, but she'd prefer another topic of conversation. "Well, I think we're very close to a settlement. So, I guess that's good."

The waitress set drinks on the table. "Your sampler will be out in a few minutes."

Claire nodded and picked up her glass. But before she could take a sip, Ray picked up his beer and lifted it toward her.

"Here's to you, Claire. Hope you take the bastard to the cleaners."

Claire couldn't help but laugh out loud. It was the kind of comment she'd expect from Mary, but not from a casual acquaintance. It lightened her mood, and she clinked her glass against his mug. She wasn't exactly taking Stan to the cleaners, but she was getting what she wanted. And that was worth a toast for sure.

The waitress returned and set a platter of vegetables, onion strings and house chips with dip in the center of the table. Claire nibbled at a carrot, then, determined to focus on something other than her pending divorce, she picked up her wine glass and smiled across the table at Ray.

"So what brought you to Paxton today?"

"Just finished up an auction. Buddy of mine handles farm and estate auctions, calls me in for some extra help every once in a while."

"Ah. Anything interesting?" Her thoughts went to her mother-in-law, and she wondered if that's how Stan would dispose of her property.

Ray shrugged. "A few antiques, and an old T-Bird. That's about it."

"I think Stan's going to sell the contents of his mother's house when the divorce is final. You should have your friend contact him."

He nodded. "Huh. Maybe I'll do that. She got anything interesting?"

Claire laughed. "Well, not really. I think over the years Stan's moved just about anything of value over to our place. I imagine he'll hold onto the good stuff."

They talked for another twenty minutes until the waitress stopped again.

"You folks ready to order dinner?"

Claire picked up the menu. "Could you give us a couple more minutes?"

There was no way she could eat a heavy steak dinner now. Her eyes scanned the menu, and she had a sudden craving for her own roasted potatoes, the ones she seasoned and broiled in a hefty dose of butter. Maybe she'd do a little cooking and freeze some things for herself.

When the waitress returned, Claire ordered a steak salad and another glass of wine.

"A salad?" Ray asked when the waitress left.

"That's plenty," Claire said. "One thing I have to say for being on the divorce diet, I'm losing weight."

Ray chuckled. "And that's one thing you don't need."

"Oh, believe me, I'm not going to miss a few pounds. I do miss cooking, though." An idea popped into her head then, and she paused a moment, toying with it.

"You know, Ray, I haven't cooked a full meal in ages. At the risk of sounding vain, I can put together a pretty decent dinner."

"I have no doubt," he said.

She took a deep breath and blurted out the words. "Why don't you come for dinner?" She pushed on, put it out there before her nerves took over and she chickened out. "Are you busy this weekend?"

She saw surprise in his eyes. And maybe pleasure?

Ray leaned forward, tapping his fork on the table. "I'd love to, Claire. But damn, I already told Peggy I'd head over to Joplin this weekend to watch my grandson play a little baseball."

Claire forced a bright smile. "Oh, well, that sounds fun."

"I hear he's pretty darn good."

"So Grandpa should see him play. Another time then."

A slow smile spread across his face. "Now, Angel, I'm not inclined to turn down such a fine invitation. Any time next week works for me."

Claire's face warmed. "All right . . . let's see." Claire knew she didn't have any formal plans, but couldn't remember if she'd committed to getting together with any friends. "Why don't we say next Friday night, then. Would that work?"

"I'll look forward to it. And I'll bring my tools if you can stand the drips that long."

She smiled and held up her hands. "At this point, what's another week?"

Their meals arrived, and they finished eating with minimal conversation. Claire managed to finish most of the salad.

"Dessert folks?" the waitress asked.

"No, thank you," Claire said.

"I'll have a cup of coffee," Ray said.

The waitress turned to Claire. "Ma'am?"

"Oh, well, yes. Thank you."

It was just what Claire needed after all that food. It'd help her stay awake on the drive home. When the coffee arrived, Claire added a touch of cream and picked up the mug, inhaling the rich scent before taking a sip.

"So, Ray, tell me about this baseball-playing grandson of yours. How old is he?"

He flashed her a sheepish grin, and crossed a leg over his knee. "Uh-oh. Let me think about that one. I guess he'd have to be about ten now. Give or take a year. What about yours?"

"My oldest is a girl. She turns six next month. I'm supposed to go to Wichita for her birthday party."

"Wichita's not a bad drive."

"No, but they're so busy, I don't get over there all that often."

Ray nodded. "I know what you mean. Everyone's busy and scattered. Maybe you'll have time to go visit more often now."

Claire sighed, her mellow mood busted. Why did every comment, every thought, have something to do with her divorce? She could do without the constant reminders that she'd have more time on her hands than she knew what to do with.

She looked into her cup for a moment, then managed a shallow smile. "Yes. Maybe."

Chapter Eleven

"What? You're not bringing your world famous lemon bars? Did hell freeze over and nobody told me?"

Claire forced a laugh. "I'm pretty sure everyone will survive without them." But she knew her lemon bars, her secret recipe that she sweetened with a dribble of pineapple juice, were all-time favorites at the July Fourth picnic in the park. The Four-H kids always held a bake sale to raise money for trips, and Claire always made a contribution. They'd be missed.

"Are you kidding? You're going to break some hearts. So what's the deal?"

"Well, no one ever contacted me about it."

There was a beat of silence before Mary spoke, and when she did, Claire was surprised to hear an edge to her voice.

"Claire, you've been doing this forever. It's the exact same weekend every year. Why would someone need to contact you?"

"I just didn't think about it."

She heard the exasperated sigh on the other end.

"Why not? Come on, Claire. You've got to get back into life. Everybody misses you. When you didn't show up at the library board meeting, everyone asked about you. You didn't help set up for graduation. You haven't signed up to help with concessions this summer. God, you and I've been holding this town together for years. It's not the same without you."

Claire thought of the blank pages in her calendar, and all the community events she hadn't bothered to pencil in. All the things she used to do, the running around, organizing this and that, the volunteering. She used to be so busy.

"I guess I'm out of the loop."

"Well, get your butt back in it. You still have time to make the bars if you want to."

"No, I really don't. They take too much time." She used to make five or six batches, and it took three days.

"And don't you have too much of that on your hands right now?"

Claire took a deep breath. Time to spill the beans. "Not in the next couple of days. I'm making dinner for Ray Gleason tomorrow night."

"Who?"

"Ray Gleason. He lives over in Oakmont. You know, his family used to own the hardware store over there."

"Oh, yeah. Is he sick?"

Claire barked out a laugh. Boy, had things changed. Not so long ago her kitchen was practically a Meals on Wheels for every widow, invalid and tummy-ache in town. She shook her head. "No, dummy, I'm having him over for dinner."

"Why?"

"Because I wanted to cook dinner and have some company."

"You mean like a date?" Mary shrieked, her voice jumping a full octave.

Claire hoped no one was listening to Mary's side of the conversation.

"Sort of. He's bought me dinner a couple of times, and he offered to come over and fix some leaks around the house, so I'm reciprocating with a home-cooked meal."

103

"He's bought you dinner a couple of times? On what planet, and where the hell was I?"

"Remember, I ran into him the night I came back from the lake?"

"Oh, right. Okay, but then when?"

"He was in Paxton last week when I met with Lauren Armstrong. We had dinner at the Ranch House."

"And you failed to tell me this because . . . ?"

Claire squirmed in her chair, and reached for a cigarette. It was a fair question, but she didn't have a good answer. "I don't know. I felt funny about it."

"Uh-huh. Well, I want– Oh, damn, there's a delivery. Listen, I want to hear everything. You call me on Saturday. You're not going to back out on Sunday are you?"

"No, no. I'll be there. I promise."

"Okay. I'll see you then."

She'd told Mary she'd watch fireworks with her Sunday night. Since Grant was part of the volunteer crew that supplemented the county fire department, he helped with the shooting of fireworks nearly every July Fourth. She wasn't exactly looking forward to it. It'd be a huge public event. And everyone would be there.

**

Claire spent all evening dusting, wiping and sweeping the entire house. She dumped and washed all the ashtrays, and removed all the junk from under her bathroom sink and hid it inside her closet. Ray didn't need to see the menagerie of appliances, lotions and potions required for her to fight the battle against time and gravity.

The next morning, the faint chemical scent of cleaners still hung in the air. Claire grimaced as she padded down the hallway to the kitchen. She lit a vanilla-scented candle on the counter, and started coffee. Hopefully, once she started cooking, only the savory smells of steak and seasonings would fill the house. She intended to spend most of the day in the kitchen. First up, shortcake to go with the fresh strawberries and blackberries she'd bought yesterday.

Thirty minutes later, the aroma of fresh-baked shortbread escaped from the oven. Claire opened the door, and peeked inside. Oh, yeah. The top of the cakes had baked to a perfect golden-brown. With a sniff and a smile, she pulled the cakes from the oven and set them on the counter to cool.

At two o'clock, she poured herself a glass of the sangria she'd been keeping in the fridge. Humming along with the "new country" channel, she began scrubbing the vegetables. She expected Ray at four. He could look at the plumbing issues while she finished up the meal. It would give her something to do besides hover over him.

Her hand stilled against a potato. It would be so odd to have a man in the house. He'd have to walk through her bedroom to get to her bathroom. She tried not to think of the intimacy of that. At least the work would give them something to talk about. With any luck, the repairs would be quick and easy, and they could eat by six.

She'd just finished wrapping the filets in bacon when the phone rang. She wiped her hands as she checked the caller ID. When she saw that it was Elise, she picked up.

"Hello."

"Hey, Mom. How are you?"

"Fine. How's everyone there?"

"Good. Just wanted to check in since this'll be a busy week. You're still planning on coming down next Friday?"

"Yes. And I've got Olivia the cutest little outfit that matches her sandals. It's darling."

"I'm sure she'll love it. Hey, you know that zebra-striped serving tray you have?"

"Uh-huh."

"Could you bring it with you? It'd be perfect with the zoo theme."

"Of course." She reached for a pen and piece of paper. "Let me write that down now so I won't forget. I'm not sure where it is."

"I think it was under the counter downstairs the last time I saw it."

"Okay. I'll find it. Do you need anything else?"

"What would you think about doing some face painting? Do you still have that mask book that shows how to paint animal faces?"

"I'm sure it's here somewhere. I'll bring that, and why don't I pick up some things for the goodie bags? I can get some animal cookies and I've seen those gummy fruit snacks in animal shapes."

"That'd be great, Mom. And I've already got paints we can use."

"Perfect. This'll be fun." Had the potential, anyway. She hadn't done anything like this for a long time. She was looking forward to seeing what Olivia's friends were like. Maybe she'd toss in some nail polish and curlers for good measure. She'd make sure Olivia looked like the star of the show.

"Anything else going on?" Elise asked.

"Well, it's the big July Fourth celebration this weekend, so everyone's getting ready for that." *She* wasn't, but Elise didn't need to know that. No way would she mention her *date* with Ray to Elise.

"Right. So, you're going?"

"I'm watching fireworks Sunday night with Mary."

"Okay. Have fun, and we'll see you next weekend."

"Sounds good. Tell Olivia I can't wait."

Claire put the phone down, then placed the steaks in the refrigerator. Time to get herself put together.

She slipped into a deep rose-colored blouse and paired it with a rose-and-black patterned skirt that had a little tulle ruffle peeking out below the hem to give it just a touch of sass. Some low-heeled black sandals with shiny silver embellishments finished the ensemble – not dressy, but not everyday attire, either.

**

At three-fifty, Claire began pacing the living room. She couldn't sit still, but didn't want him to catch her checking the front window. By four-ten, her stomach was in knots. Could he have forgotten? Was he standing her up? She leaned against the sofa. Surely not. Not after all the cooking she'd done.

Calm down, Claire. You know you're the only person who's ever on time. The people around her always seemed to run at least ten minutes late. And he was a man. He probably left his house at four o'clock.

She took a few more sips of wine and wandered into the dining room, adjusting silverware as she walked around the table. She'd placed three small candles in the center of the table. They were cute and would add ambiance without looking romantic.

She jumped when a car door slammed outside. Scurrying into the entryway, she peeked outside. Oh, no! In one hand he carried a small toolbox and a shirt on a hanger, and in the other he held a bouquet of mixed flowers. Oh, Lord, if the neighbors saw that . . .

It was all she could do to keep from opening the door and yanking him inside. The man was strolling up the walk like he was out for a garden tour. She forced herself to wait a couple of beats after he finally rang the bell before opening the door.

"Hello, there," she said, stepping back to let him in.

"Evening, Claire." He handed her the flowers. "These are for you, of course."

"They're lovely. Thank you. Come on in, and I'll put these in a vase."

It was a nice gesture. She couldn't recall the last time Stan had given her flowers. She headed toward the kitchen with Ray following slightly behind. She looked

107

back, her eyes shifting to the shirt. "You brought extra clothes?"

He stopped and draped the shirt over the arm of a chair. "For dinner. Plumbing can be a messy job."

"Oh. Of course." That made sense. She just wished he'd had the sense to fold the shirt and bring it in a bag.

"Wow. Sure does smell good in here," he said.

She turned and flashed a smile. "Went out on a limb and guessed you might like steak and potatoes."

"A little bit."

Claire pulled a vase out of the cupboard and filled it with water, then arranged the colorful mix of sunflowers, daisies and snapdragons. "These are gorgeous, Ray."

"Glad you like them."

She moved past him and set them on the kitchen table. "Now, what can I get you to drink?"

"Oh, I don't need anything just yet. Probably ought to start on the plumbing, in case I have to step out and get to the hardware store."

"All right. The drippy faucet is in my bathroom. This way."

Twisting her hands, she led him down the hallway, and opened the door to her bedroom. She kept to his right side, hoping he'd look at her and refrain from even glancing toward the bed.

"In here," she said brightly, flipping on the bathroom light. She watched him give the room a once-over. It was a nice bathroom, with a granite countertop, a separate bath and shower, glass tiles and polished chrome fixtures.

"Pretty swanky," Ray commented, his brows raised.

"It wasn't always, believe me. We had it refinished a few years ago."

He moved to the farthest sink. "Looks like this is the problem."

"Yes. Why don't I get busy in the kitchen and let you deal with this. Just holler if you need anything."

"Will do."

Claire scooted out of the room and hurried back to the kitchen. But once she was there she couldn't help worrying about what was happening in the bathroom. She'd cleaned, and put personal items away, but would he open drawers and cupboards? Would he take a peek inside her medicine cabinet? There was nothing to hide, she supposed. Still, it made her uncomfortable.

Thirty minutes later, Ray emerged from the hallway. "Think I got that one taken care of. What's next?"

Claire let out a shaky laugh. "Oh, Ray, please have something to drink before you start the next one. I insist."

He glanced at his watch. "Yes, ma'am. Guess I'll take a beer then, if you've got it."

"Of course." She snapped the cap off a bottle and handed it to him.

"Thanks. Now, where to?"

She led him to the hall bathroom. "This is the toilet that wants to keep running. I have to jiggle the handle all the time."

He nodded. "Lemme see what I can do."

She left him to it. In the kitchen, Claire slid the potatoes into the oven, then stepped back into the hall. "What do you think?" she called. "Will you need a trip to the hardware store?"

"Don't think so."

Good. She calculated in her head. She'd start the steaks in a half hour. She really had nothing to do other than hover. "Do you have all the tools you need?" she asked.

"Sure do."

"Is there anything I can do to help?"

He chuckled and poked his head around the corner. "Claire, have yourself a drink and relax. You can keep me company, but that's about it. Okay?"

Keep him company? Really? Stan had always hated for her to watch him work. Made him self-conscious. Plus, if things took a turn for the worse, his temper flared, and it was best to stay out of the way of flying curse words and tools.

She did as Ray suggested and refilled her glass. As she poured the wine, she thought a moment. How many times had she refilled? She'd had a couple of glasses already. If she were going to make it through the evening and still be coherent, she'd have to pace herself. But she felt fine, and they were about to eat, anyway. She raised the glass and took a sip, then checked on the potatoes, and puttered in the kitchen, finishing up the small spinach salads.

Ray strolled into the kitchen a few minutes later. "Well, now, I think that about does it."

Claire turned and leaned against the counter. "Excellent. Thank you so much. Why don't you go ahead and clean up? We can have a drink and appetizers while the steaks grill."

He picked up his shirt and headed back to the bathroom, and Claire set out a tray of cut vegetables and some chips and dip at the bar.

When Ray returned, she pulled a frosted mug from the freezer and opened another beer. "Here, let me get you a cold one." She expertly poured the beer with about an inch of foam at the top, and handed it to him, noting that the fresh shirt was a definite improvement. It had either been to the cleaners or someone knew how to use an iron.

"You're good at this," he said, picking up the mug.

No, she really wasn't, but she murmured a polite "thank you." Here she was in her own house with a man who was almost a stranger, and she had no idea what to say or how to act. She'd have to concentrate on the food. Turning, she adjusted the flame on the grill, then placed the steaks on the rack.

110

After a few more minutes of light conversation, Claire took the salads out of the refrigerator. And realized she'd almost emptied her glass again.

Slow down, Claire. Why was she so uptight? It was just dinner, for heaven's sake. She took a deep breath and smiled at Ray. "You ready for a salad?"

He sauntered into the room, nearly colliding with her. "Whoops," he said, reaching out a hand to steady her. "Sorry about that."

She gave a shaky laugh and nodded to the warmly lit room across the hall. "In the dining room."

"Ah. After you," Ray said.

Claire set the salads on the two woven placemats that decorated the glass-topped table, wiped her clammy hands on a napkin, then retrieved the flowers he'd brought and set them in the center of the table. "Sit down, please." She'd positioned them on opposite sides of the corner, not quite facing, and not quite beside each other.

Ray stopped before he sat down. "Darlin' your glass is empty. Let me freshen that up for you." He picked up her glass and went back to the kitchen.

"Here you go," he said, taking his seat in the dining room. "This sure is a nice room. I'm guessing you've always cooked the holiday dinners, and put out quite a spread."

Claire nodded, stabbing a chunk of hard-boiled egg with her fork. "Pretty much. I enjoy cooking and setting a formal dinner in here for Christmas." Usually Christmas Eve was casual, and Christmas Day was a dress-up affair. Of course usual hadn't happened for a while. For that matter, it no longer existed. Maybe this year she'd go to Wichita, and she and Elise could cook together. Everything else had changed – why not Christmas, too?

"My wife wasn't much of a cook," Ray said, "but Peggy does okay. I seem to spend most holidays with her family."

111

Claire nodded. "So, tell me about the baseball game. How'd your grandson do?"

Ray swallowed, and took a drink before answering. "Did great. Boy, that was a lot of fun. They played a double-header, and won 'em both."

"Oh, very fun. Nice that you got to be there. Excuse me a moment. I'll check the steaks. Shouldn't be too long."

"Let me give you a hand."

He followed her into the kitchen, and leaned against the counter and watched while she arranged the potatoes and green beans and finished the steaks. "Medium all right with you?" she asked.

"Perfect."

She moved his to the side, and let hers cook a bit longer. In the awkward silence, she poured burgundy into a glass for Ray, and handed it to him. With the tongs, she fidgeted with her steak, turning it back and forth, willing it to hurry up and cook. When she figured it was done enough that she could eat it, Claire slid the meat onto her plate. Then she picked up both plates and cocked her head toward the bowl of potatoes. "Could you grab those, Ray?"

"Sure enough."

They moved back to the dining room. "I hope you don't mind, I'm being terribly gauche and sticking with my Chardonnay for dinner."

Ray leaned forward, an amused look on his face.

"You're entitled to drink whatever you want, Claire." His voice turned warm and low as the smile spread to a grin. "Break any rule you like. Not going to bother me one bit."

She liked the sound of that. She picked up her glass and held it up to his. "Here's to breaking the rules, then," she said with a little laugh.

"Hear, hear."

By the time dinner wound down, Claire's eyelids were growing heavy – the effect of multiple glasses of wine that had followed the sangria she'd had earlier. Maybe she'd better start coffee.

She lifted her plate, then reached for Ray's.

"Let me help you," he said, picking up silverware. He followed her into the kitchen. "That was the best dinner I've had in ages."

Claire smiled, her face warming. "Thank you. I'm glad you enjoyed it. But technically, it's not over. There's still dessert. Strawberry shortcake."

Ray shook his head, a hand going to the muffin top that edged over his waistband. "Damn that sounds good, but maybe we better wait a few minutes."

"I agree. How 'bout we sit on the patio for a bit?"

She took a cigarette from her case, and Ray stepped in and took the lighter from her. He flicked it open, inches from her face, and lit the cigarette for her. Her chest tightened as she caught a whiff of his cologne.

"Thank you," she murmured, flustered by his nearness. She opened the back door and stepped out, with Ray behind her. The evening had cooled, and was actually quite pleasant. She lit the citronella candle on the table, then took a deep drag on her cigarette and draped into a chair.

Claire closed her eyes, but quickly opened them again when a wave of lightheadedness washed over her. She stifled a yawn. Oh, yeah, the coffee. She'd forgotten about it.

"Sure is a nice night," Ray commented.

"Yes." How awkward, she thought. What in the world did they have to talk about? The weather? With effort, she racked her brain for conversation starters.

"Ray, did you put in a garden this year?"

"Always do."

Claire breathed a sigh of relief. "Anything producing yet?"

"Got some tomatoes and green beans already."

"Nice."

"I should've thought to bring you some."

113

"Oh, no. Not necessary. But that reminds me, how much do I owe you for the plumbing?"

"Not a darn penny."

"Ray, I would've had to pay someone else. No one works for free. How much?"

He leaned forward and met her eyes. "I'm not taking your money, Claire. It was a favor. Period."

"If you're sure . . ." If he needed the money, he'd at least hedge a little more, wouldn't he?

"Don't think any more about it."

"Well, thank you. I really appreciate it."

"You're welcome. And I appreciate a delicious home-cooked meal and the company of a lovely woman."

Without meeting his eyes, she gave a hesitant smile, and tapped out her cigarette. "Dessert?"

He stood and took her elbow. "Absolutely."

Claire cut chunks of shortbread, then added juicy sliced strawberries and a large scoop of whipped cream. Then she topped each dessert with a few blackberries.

"Couldn't get a creation like this in the finest restaurant," Ray said when she handed him a bowl. "I think I see a diet in my future."

Claire laughed. "Oh, now, look at all that fruit. It's a healthy dessert."

He took a couple of bites, and patted his gut. "Mighty tasty, Claire."

She jumped up from the table. "I keep forgetting to start the coffee. Would you like some?"

He caught her hand, and shook his head. "Don't worry about the coffee. I don't need any. Sit down, and relax."

Her stomach was so full, she didn't need it, either. "I suppose we can do without it, then."

At ten o'clock Claire stifled a yawn, and began to wonder how long Ray intended to stay. She was putting the last of the dishes into the dishwasher when he refilled her glass and handed it to her.

114

She took a couple of sips of the wine, then turned back to the counter to finish wiping it down. When he came up behind her, she stiffened. Alarm bells clanged in her head. Oh, God. Surely he wasn't expecting more than dinner. He put his hands on her shoulders, and her stomach fluttered. Oh, no.

She had to think. But the wine . . . his hands. Oh, his hands were firm and strong as they kneaded her shoulders.

"You're tense, Claire. Just relax."

She let her head fall forward, mesmerized by the motion. But when his hands slid under her blouse and splayed across her back, she stiffened again. Before she could object, the warmth moved from the small of her back to her shoulders, caressing her skin, sending shivers through her body.

His fingers resumed their kneading, working her muscles. Mmmm. It was very nice. When one hand dropped to her waist, Claire gripped the counter, hardly daring to breathe. "Ray?"

He leaned in, his breath warm on her neck.

"Hmmm?"

"I don't think I can do this," she whispered.

He nuzzled in, his lips brushing her neck. "Do what? Feel good?" He lifted his head and turned her around. A hand cupped her breast. "How long's it been since someone made you feel good, Claire?"

Unexpected tears burned her eyes, and she blinked them back. A long damn time, she thought. Forever.

His thumb played against her, making it impossible to think of anything other than the tingling sensations, the warmth that enveloped her.

"You're a beautiful woman," Ray said, an instant before his lips met hers.

She let out a soft whimper, just shy of a protest.

His body pressed against her. "Let me make you feel good," he whispered.

"It's not– Ray, I'm still married. I can't–"

"Shhh. Remember, you can break the rules, Claire."

Moments later, they were in her bedroom. She felt her blouse fall away, then her skirt. She shook her head. "I don't think–"

His hand slid between her thighs, and she gasped. Her hands clutched his arms, as the sensation that she was falling swept through her. His face blurred above her, and the bed spun.

"Oh, God."

**

Claire woke to the smell of fresh-brewed coffee. She started to sit up, but her head zinged, and forced her to flop back down. In the next instant, however, she bolted upright. Never mind her head. Where the hell were her clothes?

She tossed the covers aside, and scrambled out of the bed. What the–? Did he–? No . . . she . . . they. Memory flooded in. Bits of it, anyway. She remembered his hands. She saw her skirt and blouse on the floor. Along with her bra and panties. Heat shot through her, and she snatched them up. Claire clutched her middle. What was she thinking?

Her breath caught in her throat, and she sank onto the bed. How could she have? She jumped up again. He must still be here. He'd started the coffee. Oh, no. No! People would see his truck. They'd know it'd been there all night. Half the town might know already.

Quickly, she grabbed some clothes, dressed, and headed down the hall. She heard a car door slam outside. Maybe he was leaving. She pushed back a curtain and peered out the front window. On the walkway, Ray sauntered toward the house.

Claire dashed to the door, and yanked it open. "What are you doing?" she asked, her voice low and urgent.

Ray stopped, surprise on his face. "Well, good morning. How are ya?"

116

With a quick glance up and down the block, Claire motioned him inside. "What in the world are you doing out here? She hoped he hadn't talked to anyone.

"Just having a cup of coffee." He nodded toward his truck. "Went out to check and see if I'd left my wallet in the truck. Wasn't in my pocket this morning."

"Oh. Did you find it?"

"Sure did. No problem. Did you get yourself some coffee?"

She stepped back, avoiding his eyes. "Not yet."

"Well, let's take care of that," he said as he came back through the door.

Oh, Jesus. The last thing she wanted to do was sit and have a cup of coffee like this was a typical morning. She needed him to leave. About ten hours ago. If only she could crawl back into bed and forget that last night ever happened.

Chapter Twelve

Claire checked the number, and let the machine pick up. Why was he calling, anyway? He was supposed to go through her attorney.

Stan's angry voice barked into the quiet room. "Goddammit, Claire. Have you lost your mind? The things in that house aren't yours to give away or sell or whatever the hell you're doing. Ray Gleason's over in Missouri trying to sell my gun, and he's saying you gave it to him for doing some work around the house. You call me back, 'cause I'm coming over there to get the rest of them."

Claire stared at the machine, half-expecting it to explode. What on earth was he talking about? She didn't give anything to Ray. Her face flamed as she thought about that. Nothing he could sell, anyway. Mystified, she headed toward the basement. She hadn't even been near Stan's gun case since he left.

As she made her way down the stairs, though, dread churned her stomach. Hot shame swept through her veins. She'd let Ray stay at the house. What had he really been doing outside when she woke up? He said he was having coffee on the porch, but could he have been loading his truck with items from her house? She'd trusted him, but she hardly even knew the man.

Oh, please, no. Holding her stomach, she flipped on the light in the game room. One look, and her eyes clenched shut. Stan's gun case stood behind the pool table. And it was empty.

Doubled over, she slammed a fist against the green felt of the pool table. Damn it, damn it, damn it! How could she have been so stupid? So gullible. He hadn't wanted her company. He'd wanted inside her house. That's why he'd been so persistent about the plumbing.

Groaning, she forced herself to look around. What else? With heavy eyes she took visual inventory. Everything seemed to be in place. Wearily, she climbed back up the stairs. And a horrible thought struck her. Ben's room. She kept it locked, but the key was on the framework above the door. Easy to find. If he dared to touch Ben's things–. With her heart in her throat, she raced upstairs. Her hands shook as she fumbled with the key. When the door finally opened, Claire frantically surveyed the room. She yanked open the top drawer of his dresser. His watch was there. And his class ring. Scooping it up, she lifted it to her face. Thank God. She flopped onto the bed and let the tears flow, not caring that they ran down the side of her face and into her ears.

**

Claire had no idea how long she stayed in Ben's room. She only knew that when she tried to move, every bone in her body protested. And when she opened her eyes, memory of the nightmare flooded in.

Tears burned again, but this time anger flashed inside her. Why was this happening to her? Everything was so mixed up. She was an intelligent person. She'd been a good wife and mother. She did nice things for other people. And in return, she was being used and cheated. It didn't make sense. It wasn't fair.

Later, when she managed to get up and go through the motions of being alive, Claire poured a cup of coffee, and plodded through the house, checking cupboards and drawers, listlessly looking for missing objects. Not that she really cared.

She'd just opened the back closet when the doorbell rang. With a heavy sigh, she turned and trudged down the hall. Before she reached the entry, the bell pealed again, and a hard knock shook the door. She put one eye to the peephole, and gasped. A red-faced Stan stood on the porch, his fist pounding against the metal frame of the outside door. Even through the tiny window, she could feel his fury.

With great reluctance, Claire unlocked the door and pulled it open. But she stuck only her head out.

"You don't have permission to be here, Stan."

"I don't give a damn," he roared. "I'm getting the things that belong to me. If you don't let me in, I'll be back with the sheriff. I'll report a robbery. Some of those guns belonged to my dad, Claire. And I'm not having some low-life son-of-a-bitch like Ray Gleason make off with them."

"You're going to need to make that report anyway," Claire said, her voice hoarse, barely audible. "The guns are gone."

Stan's eyes bulged, and he pushed into the house. "Are you kidding me?" he yelled as he stormed toward the basement.

Claire stepped back. Didn't bother to stop him or follow him. She strolled into the living room, and fumbled for a cigarette. While Stan cursed and banged doors and cupboards downstairs, she leaned against the wall and waited, holding in the pain.

He returned moments later, his voice and his anger engulfing the room. "How could you be so stupid? You let him in here and then you passed out, didn't you? He probably went through the entire house while you were drunk out of your mind." Stan took a menacing step toward her, and shoved a finger within inches of her face. "I've never hit you, Claire, but by God, I've never been so tempted."

Claire straightened. "Go ahead," she challenged him. "I wonder what the judge would say if we added assault and battery to your list of indiscretions."

Stan's wild eyes darted around the room. "What else did he get? You don't even know, do you?"

"Nothing. I've looked. Just call the shop or whatever it was and buy the guns back. Take it out of my half."

He glared at her, the veins in his neck pulsating. "You think I'm going to track down my own guns and *pay* for them? That's not gonna happen. I'm going to the sheriff."

It dawned on her then, that if he did, there'd be a police report. A public record of her stupidity. No, she screamed inside. Oh, no. She couldn't let that happen. If Stan made trouble, would Ray tell? Would he tell people he'd been in her bed? Her face burned.

With a shaky breath, Claire pushed off from the wall, struggling to keep her own fury at bay. "Stan, please don't make a big stink about it," she pleaded. "Don't go to the sheriff. I'll handle it myself. I'll get the guns back. Just take what you want now. All of it. I don't want anything of yours left in the house that I have to be responsible for."

His eyes narrowed at her. "You protecting that asshole, Claire?"

That did it. The unfairness of the question, the whole situation, exploded inside her. "No, goddammit!" She clenched a fist against her chest. "I'm protecting *me*, okay? *Me*. For the love of God, can't you grant me this one thing?"

"The man's a dirty thief."

"Oh, bull." Her arms flailed in Stan's direction as she fought back threatening tears. "He saw an opportunity to get back at you for the things you've done, and he took it. And you know what? I don't care. Even if you go to the police, and they arrest him, I'm not pressing charges. I'm not going to be part of some public scandal. Jesus, haven't we given the entire town enough to talk about already? Your mother, the divorce, your mistress?"

"It's nobody's business."

Her voice shook. "Those guns were stolen from my house, and I *will not* press charges."

He studied her, and she saw the conflicting emotions pass across his face. She'd given him the opportunity to play the hero, put herself in his debt. Oh, how he loved that. As the seconds ticked, the anger turned to disgust and resignation. And then to pity. She didn't want his pity, but she'd take it this time. For self-preservation.

She looked away, but heard his heavy sigh. When she glanced back, his lips were pursed, both hands on his hips.

"Fine. You've got three days. If I don't see those guns by the end of the day Friday, I'm calling Howard."

Relief washed over her even as sweat pooled in her armpits and under her bra. Could she do it? Could she track down the low-life son-of-a-bitch and the guns? Could she keep her dignity intact? She had to. The alternative was unacceptable.

**

Of course he didn't pick up. No surprise there. But she'd leave a message. She'd call back. She'd call every five minutes and fill up his voicemail if that's what it took. She'd go to Oakmont and hunt him down. Good thing *she* didn't have a gun.

With a deep breath, she fought to keep any emotion out of her voice. "Ray, this is Claire. You know why I'm calling. I need those guns. I don't want to talk about it. I don't care why you took them, but I need them back. I'm willing to pay you whatever they're worth at an auction or a pawnshop. If I don't get them back, Stan's going to the police. Let's avoid that, shall we?"

Ten minutes later, she called again. She left the same message, but added an incentive. "Ray, please call and tell me how much you want for the guns. I'll get cash tomorrow. I'll have it ready for you when you bring the guns."

She hung up and paced the living room, trying to keep tears at bay. What the hell was she going to do if this didn't work? Every ten minutes, she called again. After an hour, unable to stand the feeling of being caught and bound any longer, she grabbed her cigarettes and went outside. At least the wind offered some relief from the suffocation she felt. She slumped into a chair, fighting nausea every time scenes from Friday night flashed through her mind.

Chapter Thirteen

The next morning, the sound of the doorbell chime jarred Claire from her numb perch on the couch. Her heart raced as she hurried to the door and peeked out. A truck from the city maintenance crew was parked at the curb, and a man with a clipboard stood on her porch. *Now what?*

She cracked the door open. Trust no one, she reminded herself.

"Yes? Can I help you?"

"Mrs. Stapleton?"

"Who wants to know?"

The man's brow furrowed, and he lowered the clipboard. "I'm from the city, ma'am. We've had a couple of complaints about your yard." He waved a finger behind him.

Confused, she looked past him. "My yard? What about it?"

"The grass, ma'am. It needs cut. You can take care of it, or the city will, but you'll be billed."

"What! Who complained?" Claire swung the door open, and glared at the man.

He took a step back. "I don't have that information, ma'am. If it's not taken care of in three days, the city will have it cut. You understand?"

Claire swallowed the bile that rose in her throat. A little grass? Really? With all the shit she had to deal with, who cared about the grass? Didn't people have more important things to worry about? Hysteria bubbled up inside her, but she fought it back. *Keep it together. Don't make a scene.*

She straightened, and pasted on a tight smile. "I'll take care of it. Thank you."

He handed her a clipboard. "This is a warning. I need your signature here. It just acknowledges that you received the information."

Claire yanked the notice out of his hands, scribbled her signature, then shoved it back at him.

"You have a nice day, ma'am."

A nice day. Right. She loved how people said that just after they ruined your day. Of course, her day had a long way to go. Things could always get worse.

By noon, she hadn't heard from Ray, and panic was setting in. She toyed with the idea of calling Mary. Maybe she could help her think it through. But the thought made her cringe. Mary knew just about everything there was to know about Claire. They'd shared tears and secrets for years. But for some reason, this was different. The embarrassment went too deep, hurt too much. She felt so raw and exposed already.

She traipsed into the kitchen and opened a box of crackers. But before she took a bite, the phone rang. Hardly daring to look at it, Claire held her breath as she peeked. It was him. No way would she pick up. She listened as his voice came on the line, fresh anger surging through her.

"Claire, it's Ray. I told you before, I don't want your money." He let out a low chuckle that made the hair on her arms stand up. "But I guess I wouldn't mind taking a little of Stan's. Tell you what, I'll trade his stuff for his money. Call me back."

She gaped at the machine for a full minute, then covered her face with her hands. No, she didn't want to call him back. Didn't want to talk to him. Why couldn't he just name his price and be done with it? Oh, how she'd like to shove one of those rifles up that man's ass. She wanted to bang her head against the wall. Instead, she opened a fresh bottle of her favorite Chardonnay, poured a full glass, and paced the floor like a caged animal. What was the next move?

It took another glass of wine and another couple of hours to gather the courage to call Ray back. She willed his voicemail to pick up. When it did, she breathed a sigh of relief, and started her plea.

"Ray, I need to know how much money to get. To tell Stan to get. Please–"

"Claire, it's Ray."

Oh, shit. Her hands shook as his voice came over the line.

"Guess that guy at the shop ratted me out, huh? Look, I don't mean any harm to you. I know–"

"No harm?" Claire screamed into the phone. "Are you kidding? Did you think he wouldn't notice?" Her voice quivered. "How could you? How could you do this to me?"

"He's threatened you somehow, hasn't he? The prick. I should've known."

There was a long pause and Claire wondered if he'd hung up. Until he cleared his throat.

"Listen, I just wanted to have a little fun with Stan."

"A little fun?" Claire said, her voice skyrocketing. "Are you crazy? Those guns are stolen goods, Ray. You could be in big trouble. If Stan goes to the police, you're going to be arrested." Was he really that stupid? She hadn't thought so. He probably figured he had more time. Months could've gone by before she would've noticed, that's for sure. If he hadn't been ratted out, maybe he could've sold them. She had no idea how easy it was to sell guns. Maybe his auction buddy could do it for him.

"All right, I'll bring the guns, but I'm not taking your money. This is between me and Stan."

Claire fought to stay calm, to hide her wounded pride. "He wants them by the end of the day Friday. When can you bring them?"

"Tell him to meet me at four o'clock Friday afternoon. In the parking lot at the Oakmont Post Office. And he better come alone. With two thousand. In cash."

Claire thought about it. Could the two of them settle this and leave her out of it? Oh, how she wished. But, no, she couldn't trust Stan not to show up with the sheriff if she wasn't there. If she hadn't begged, Ray could be in jail by now.

"No, Ray. It has to be here."

"Fine," he growled. "But he better be there himself. I want hundred dollar bills, and I want him to count it out for me." He gave a short chuckle. "I'll be looking forward to that."

She slammed down the phone, and sank to her knees.

**

In a rare stroke of luck, Michelle was busy with another customer, so Claire went to another teller window. She didn't recognize the girl working there. Her name badge said Kelly. Maybe she'd come over from the branch to fill in.

"You want this all in hundreds?" she asked.

Claire groaned inside, and felt the eyes of everyone at the teller counter on her.

The stupid girl may as well have made a friggin announcement. Claire gritted her teeth and looked straight ahead. "That's right."

She leaned an elbow on the counter, praying her knees wouldn't give out while she listened to Kelly count out twenty hundred dollar bills. It was an ugly mess of bills, and Claire's hands shook as she scooped them into her purse. "Thank you," she whispered.

With a tight smile, she turned and forced herself to walk calmly out the door. And not throw up.

The plan was for Stan to arrive a few minutes early. She'd give him the money, and he'd put it in his pocket. When Ray showed up, Stan would be the one to give it to him. He'd hate it. He'd be steaming mad, but she had to make him do it as quickly as possible, without goading Ray or causing a scene.

How she wished they'd do the deal somewhere else, just the two of them. But they'd probably kill each other. She'd have to supervise. And when it was done, she hoped to never lay eyes on either one of them again.

At home, she tossed her purse aside and swallowed a couple of Tylenol. She nibbled on a few crackers, then took the phone off the hook. For the rest of the day, she didn't want to hear from anyone. Didn't need the added stress of pretending that everything was okay. Mary told her she'd have a busy week helping with vacation bible school at the church, and so far, Claire hadn't heard from her. Another break. She could probably count on one hand the number of weeks that had gone by when she didn't talk to Mary every single day.

That night, Claire took a sleep aid, and went to bed early. Friday couldn't come soon enough. She just wanted it to all be over.

**

Claire tossed down a couple of pain pills, lit another cigarette, and paced the living room, her ears straining for the sound of Stan's truck in the driveway. When she heard the tires on the drive, and the door slam, she fought down a wave of panic.

She opened the door, avoiding his eyes.

"The money's on the table," she told him.

He was silent so long, she finally stole a glance at him. He stood staring at the bills, a snarl on his face.

128

"*Un*-believable." He rounded on her. "This is worth it to you? You'd rather pay him off than send his ass to jail?"

"He would've sold the guns, Stan."

"How the hell did you get mixed up with Ray?"

She shook her head, her hands up. "I'm not talking about it. Besides this is really more about you than me. You brought this on yourself."

"You think *I* did something? Is that what he told you?"

"He told me enough. Would it really have killed you to give his kid a job?"

"They're trash, Claire. And I was right. If I'd hired the kid he probably would've been stealing from me, too. Like father, like son."

"Whatever." She turned for another cigarette. She wasn't the least bit interested in debating their problem. The doorbell rang, and her lighter clattered to the floor. She picked it up and clenched it inside her sweaty fist.

Stan reached for the money.

Claire took several steps back, her pulse racing. When Stan opened the door, she looked away.

"Lemme see the guns, Gleason. Lay 'em all out here where I can see them."

Claire watched as Ray stepped inside and opened a large bag. He took out each gun and laid them on the floor.

"All six," he said.

Claire didn't look at his face, but she was certain she heard humor in his voice. Damn him. That would set Stan off for sure.

Stan knelt down and inspected each one.

When Ray's eyes settled on Claire, she took another step back, and gazed down the hallway.

"All right. That's my part of the bargain. Where's the money?" Ray said.

Stan straightened and pulled the bills from his pocket.

"You're scum, you know that, Gleason?"

"Well, I'm scum that's going to enjoy spending your money tonight, Stapleton. Don't worry, I'll buy a round in your honor."

Oh, God. Oh, God. Get these two out of my house, Claire chanted inside.

When Stan held the money out to Ray, he shook his head.

"Count it out. All of it."

Claire's eyes clenched shut as Stan slapped the money into Ray's hand.

"I don't think so, asshole."

Her head snapped up in time to see a smile spread across Ray's face. He folded the bills and shoved them into his pocket.

Then, he picked up the bag and took a step forward. Claire met his eyes then, sending a cool glare his direction.

Ray braced a hand against the wall in the entryway, his gray eyes shifting from Claire to Stan and back again. He leaned toward her, and with a wink, he said, "It's been a pleasure."

Claire's breath caught in her throat. In the same instant, Stan's fist connected with Ray's jaw. She let out a sharp scream and stepped out of the way. Ray lost his balance and stumbled into the side table sending the small studio lamp crashing to the floor.

Ray struggled to stand, and Stan loomed over him, arm raised. Oh, Jesus. Much more of this and they'd end up calling the police and an ambulance, causing the public report she'd hoped to avoid in the first place. Stupid, stupid. She grabbed the first thing she could get her hands on, one of the rifles, and attempted to wedge it between the two men. When that had little effect on the flailing bodies, she whacked them each on the shoulder.

"Stop! Stop it, you idiots. Both of you. Get out of my house. Now." Her voice shook, along with her entire body. "Dammit, Stan. Let him go. You just gave him a get-out-of-jail-free pass. If you try to press charges for theft, he can turn around and charge you with assault."

Good, she thought. Maybe that would keep them both from wagging their tongues.

With one hand extended to keep Ray back, Stan straightened and scowled at Claire. Then he wiped his mouth and turned back to his adversary. "Get the hell out of here. I don't even want to see you in Whitfield again. You got no business here, Gleason. None."

Claire burned inside when Ray's eyes shifted to her. He had the nerve to nod at her, as if this was some casual see-you-later. Without another word, he turned and sauntered out the door.

Claire couldn't face Stan. With blurred vision, she looked at her shoes. "Take your guns, and go," she whispered.

"You all right?"

She jumped when his hand touched her arm. She pulled away, wrapping her arms around her middle. "Don't act like you care now."

"Claire—"

"Please leave."

With gritted teeth, Claire waited while he gathered up the ridiculous heap of guns. His precious "stuff." As soon as he stepped onto the porch, she slammed the door with every ounce of energy she had left, taking small satisfaction in the rattling of the windows.

The scene played over and over in her head. Oh, God. Her stomach knotted. Claire dashed to the hallway bathroom and knelt in front of the toilet, heaving into the bowl. There was little to expel. She couldn't remember when she'd last eaten.

The thought of food turned her stomach. As did the rest of her thoughts. She dropped her head against her arms. She may never so much as speak to a man again. Her fists clenched, and she banged a hand against the toilet seat. Where was character and honor? Was this the life of a single woman in her fifties? Was she to assume that every man she came in contact with was a sleazy scumbag?

Chapter Fourteen

Elise glanced out the window again. The clouds had deepened to a purple-gray, and the sky was darker than it should've been at six-thirty.

Andy ran in front of her when she turned to reach for her phone again, and she nearly tripped over him. "Andy, don't do that," she scolded, her voice sharp.

"Mommy. I'm hungry. I want some crackers." He tugged at her shirt. "*Mommmyyyy!*"

"No. No crackers. We'll eat supper in a few minutes."

Brian stepped into the kitchen and scooped Andy up. "Babe, come on. We've got to go ahead and eat. We can fix something for your mom when she gets here. We gotta get the kids taken care of."

Elise let out a long sigh. She'd spent two evenings getting this meal ready, preparing the lasagna in advance. She knew her mother wasn't eating well, and she'd wanted to serve her a good dinner. Why did something always go wrong when her mother planned a visit?

"Fine. Come on, you guys. Wash your hands, and we'll eat." At least the lasagna could be easily reheated.

She shooed everyone to the table, then picked up her phone one more time and redialed her mother's cell. "Where the hell could she be?" Elise muttered under her breath. "You guys get started. I'm going to check the weather, and see if anything severe is happening down south."

Flashing red blotches on the screen indicated thunderstorms from Oklahoma up to the southwestern corner of Missouri. Looked like some rain had already moved through Whitfield.

After a few minutes, Elise joined the rest of her family at the kitchen table. She quickly downed her salad and a small slice of lasagna, trying to hide her worry from the kids. She could tell by the way Olivia was watching her, that she'd already sensed something was wrong.

After she cleared the table and got the kids settled with activities, Elise looked up the number to the hotel. Maybe her mother had got in early and decided to take a nap. With so many unknowns, Elise wasn't sure whether she should be annoyed or worried.

The clerk's cheery voice came on the line.

"Hello, I'm calling for Claire Stapleton," Elise told the man. "Can you tell me if she's checked in this evening, please?"

"One moment."

Elise listened to the click of fingers on a computer keypad and waited.

"No, ma'am. She's not arrived yet."

"And she hasn't cancelled the reservation?"

"No. We still have her booked for two nights."

Elise ended the call and glanced at her watch again. Almost eight o'clock. And with the storm brewing, it was getting dark. She imagined her mother off the side of the road in a ditch. Or maybe she was in an area that didn't have good cell reception, and she was stranded. Then another thought took her breath away. What if she'd been drinking? Elise leaned against the counter, rubbing her temples. No, no, no. Her mother wouldn't be that irresponsible. Surely the possibility of a DUI and public embarrassment would be enough to keep her sober.

But she wasn't right, hadn't been her normal self for months.

134

Brian came around the corner and stopped short. "What's the matter?"

Elise straightened, and glanced around to be sure little ears weren't listening. "She hasn't checked in at the hotel. She's not answering her cell phone or the house phone. Where the hell could she be?"

"When did you last talk to her?"

"Last Friday. Do you think I should call the highway patrol or Dad? Should I have someone go over to the house and check on her?"

Brian ran his hands up and down her arms. "Yeah, I'd say you probably should, but don't call your dad. What about Mary? Maybe she could run over there and at least see whether her car's in the garage."

Elise rested her head on Brian's chest for a moment. "I'm almost afraid to find out," she whispered.

He kissed the top of her head. "Don't freak out yet."

She pulled out of his arms and picked up the phone again. "I think I have Mary's number in my address book."

"Hi, Mary, this is Elise," she said when Mary's voice came on the line.

"Elise? Well, hi there, sweetie. How are you?"

"Fine thanks, but I'm a little worried about Mom. She was supposed to be here around five for Olivia's birthday party tomorrow, and she hasn't shown up. I've called a hundred times, but can't get her at home or on her cell."

"That's odd."

"Have you talked to her today?"

"I haven't, sweetie. This has been a crazy week for me. Listen, why don't I run over there."

"Thanks, Mary. If I at least knew she'd left, I could contact the highway patrol. I don't want to over-react, but something's not right."

"Don't call anyone yet. Let me check the house, and I'll give you a ring right back."

Elise ended the call, but for a moment wondered if she should confide her concerns to Mary, the woman who'd been like a second mom to Elise growing up. As her mom's closest friend, Mary knew her mother better than anyone else. But Elise knew Mary was fiercely loyal. She'd never betray her mother's trust.

**

Banging, banging. God, her head pounded. Who was making all that racket? Claire turned, and threw an arm over her ear.

Something hit her shoulder, and she turned again. More noise.

Someone was shouting at her. No. Just go away. Leave me alone.

"Claire! Wake up, Claire!"

She opened an eye. Someone stood over her. "Go away."

"No. Claire, come on. You have to wake up."

It was Mary, but why wouldn't she stop shaking her? Stop yelling at her? Claire stared at her friend as her face came into focus. "What are you doing?" she asked, her voice dry and raspy.

"Jesus, Claire, you were supposed to go to Wichita this afternoon. What's the matter?"

Claire lifted a hand to her throbbing head. "What?"

Mary put a hand under her shoulders. "Can you sit up?"

"I don't know. I need something to drink."

"I'll get you some water."

She watched Mary hurry to the bathroom, then flopped back onto the bed. Wichita? Her head was fuzzy. No, this afternoon was– Oh, no. Claire covered her face with her hands. Olivia's party.

"No, Claire! Sit up," Mary said, coming toward the bed.

She put a hand under Claire's back and pushed again.

"Okay, okay," Claire said. "What is your problem?"

Mary held out the glass. "*My* problem? My problem is I'm worried as hell about my best friend who seems to have gone out of her flipping mind."

Claire took a sip of the water, the liquid soothing her dry throat. Closing her eyes, she took a couple more sips. Then her stomach twisted. She threw back the sheet and pushed Mary out of the way, making it to the bathroom just in time.

Her shoulders tightened as she heaved into the toilet.

Mary was right behind her. "Oh, Claire. Honey, are you sick? What's going on?"

Mary pulled Claire's hair back from her face then got up and turned on the water. A moment later, a cool cloth soothed her forehead, and her friend's warm arms wrapped around her. Mary pulled her into a hug from behind and rocked her. "This is crazy. You're not taking care of yourself."

Tears rolled down Claire's cheeks, and sobs racked her body.

Mary stroked her hair as they rocked. "Shhh. Shhh. It's okay."

"No, it's not okay," Claire cried between sobs. "Nothing is okay. I don't understand why all this is happening to me."

"All what? Talk to me. What happened?"

She shook her head. "I can't," she whispered. "I can't tell anyone. It's awful. I'm so ashamed."

"Claire, you're scaring me. Let's go sit down and we can talk."

She didn't move. Couldn't. Her head was too foggy. She didn't want to talk, anyway. She wanted to sleep. To curl up and never talk to anyone again.

"Can you stand up?"

Claire shook her head. "Don't want to." She twisted out of Mary's arms and lay down on the floor, the tile cool against her arms.

"All right, look. I'm going to make you a cup of tea, and I have to check in with Elise. She's worried about you."

Elise snatched up her phone and moved to the kitchen.

"Mary?"

"Hi, honey. Listen, your mom is still at home. She's not going to make it. She's sick. I found her in bed when I got here."

"Sick? What does that mean?"

"Chills, throwing up. I gave her some water, and she couldn't even keep that down. I'm going to try some tea now."

"Well, for heaven's sake. Why didn't she call?"

"I think she's been sleeping. She probably meant to call, or thought she'd just rest a bit before she got on the road, and fell asleep. I'm going to stay here with her for a while, make sure I can get her hydrated. I'll touch base a little later, all right?"

"Yes. Thanks, Mary. I appreciate it."

Elise hung up, relieved, but still unsettled. Something didn't add up. To sleep through all those phone calls? There was a phone on her bedside table. Had she turned the ringer off?

She wandered back into the living room, and met the questioning eyes that turned toward her. "That was Mary. Mom's still at home." Elise ran her hand over the top of Olivia's hair. "Grammy's not going to make it, sweetie."

"How come?"

Elise saw the disappointment in her daughter's face. She'd been looking forward to having Grammy at her party. And Elise had been counting on her help, an extra set of hands to help corral the kids during the party. No Mom meant no fillers for the treat bags. No face painting book. Now, she'd have to make a trip to the store after the kids went to bed. One more thing to

138

do. And she'd have to muddle through the face-painting activity on her own.

"She doesn't feel good," Elise told Olivia.

"Ah-oh. Did she throw up?"

"Yes, I think so. We'll check in with her tomorrow after your party. She'll be fine, so don't worry. We'll still have a very fun time at the zoo."

Olivia nodded, and her big solemn eyes looked at Elise. "Maybe we should send her a card."

With a catch in her throat, Elise pulled Olivia into a hug. "That's a very nice idea, sweetie. If she's not better in a couple of days, we'll do that, okay? Now, since you're the birthday girl, we better get you cleaned up and into bed, so you'll be all rested for your big day."

After she kissed the kids goodnight, Elise glanced at her watch. She'd have to hurry. She turned to Brian. "I've got to run to the store. Mom was supposed to get some things for the treat bags, and I don't have enough without them."

"Babe, are you sure it's necessary? It's getting ready to storm out there."

"I know, but I won't have time in the morning."

He raked a hand through his hair, and Elise could tell he was losing patience with the whole birthday party. He already considered it an extravagance.

"Make me a list, and I'll go," he told her.

Elise shook her head. She appreciated his willingness to help, but the frustration in his voice didn't escape her. "It'll be easier for me. I know where everything is."

Quickly, she picked up her purse and headed for the door. A rumble of thunder met her as she pulled out of the garage, and lightning flashed behind her. She didn't love doing errands in the rain, but she sure wanted the storm to push on through and be gone before the party tomorrow. She could use a little cooperation.

As she drove, it weighed on her that she couldn't depend on her mother. She was the only grandmother her kids had, and Elise wanted her to be part of their lives. Okay, maybe she really was sick, but Elise couldn't help thinking that if Ben had lived to have children, her mother would've walked through fire to be at their events.

**

Claire shifted when Mary's hand gripped her arm.

"Come on, Claire. Try to get up."

While Mary pulled, Claire pushed off from the floor. They made it to the living room, and Claire sank onto the sofa. She rested her head in her hands, elbows on her knees.

"God, I feel awful."

Mary sat down beside her, and shoved a cup of tea at her.

"Here. Try to drink this."

It smelled good. Claire fumbled for the cup and took a sip.

"How long have you been sick? Why didn't you call someone?"

Claire shook her head. "I don't know," she whispered.

"Claire, is this the flu, or are you hung over? I smell alcohol. Honey, are you drinking?"

Tears welled in Claire's eyes again. "This has been the worst week of my life." No. She corrected herself. The second-worst week. Still, a week from hell.

Mary's arm went around her. "Then why didn't you call me?"

"I couldn't. Besides, I knew you were busy this week."

"Not *that* busy."

She rustled around, then held a cracker out to Claire. "Try to eat this."

Claire took it, and forced a nibble.

"Come on. When I left you Sunday night, you were fine. Tell me what happened."

Claire took another sip of tea, and closed her eyes. Then, wrapped in her friend's arms, she launched into the sordid story, her voice hoarse and broken.

When her eyes finally met Mary's, and she saw the tears running down her cheeks, Claire whispered, "It's so humiliating."

"Oh, Claire." Mary hugged her hard. "How awful. I'm so sorry."

They rocked on the sofa for several minutes, while Claire shuddered and sniffled. When Mary pulled back, she brushed Claire's hair from her face.

"You don't have anything to be ashamed of," Mary said. "You couldn't have known he'd turn out to be a snake. You had no reason to suspect anything. Stop beating yourself up."

She gave Claire a little shake. "Listen to me, you've got to take care of yourself. Eat. Exercise. Get back into life. You're wasting away over here all by yourself. Look at your house, Claire. In thirty years I've never seen it like this. It's a mess, and it stinks. That's not you. That's not the Claire Stapleton I know."

"I don't know how. I hate being alone, but I can't get the energy to do anything. I completely forgot about going to Wichita. When Ray said four o'clock on Friday, I said yes, and didn't think about anything else. How awful is that? I forgot about my granddaughter's birthday."

"Are you kidding? Who wouldn't? But, that's why I'm here. Elise called me. She was worried when you didn't show up. I told her you were sick. Let's just stick to that story, okay? You can make it up to Olivia later. Go up next weekend or something. Right now, we need to concentrate on getting you through this divorce, and back on your feet, girlfriend."

Claire closed her eyes. She'd be fine. If people would leave her alone, stop screwing up her life. It was

141

as if the world had become a giant game of ping-pong, and she was the ball being bounced and slammed around. Claire lifted the teacup.

"Oh, that'll be stone cold," Mary said, whisking the cup out of Claire's hands. "I'll warm it up. That cracker settled okay, what sounds good to eat?"

"Absolutely nothing."

Mary opened cupboards. 'Got any soup?"

"I have no idea."

"Here. Chicken and noodle. I'm heating this up."

Claire heard the water running, and knew she should get up, but stayed put. Every movement was a struggle. But when Mary came back and picked up the ashtray from the table, Claire grabbed her hand, spilling some of the ashes onto the carpet. "Just stop. You don't need to do that."

For heaven's sake, why was everyone so concerned about her yard and her house? What difference did it make? She'd get to it when she got to it.

Mary nudged her back down. "Claire. Take a seat, and don't argue with me. I'm your friend, and I'm going to help you." She screwed up her face. "Just don't think I'm making a habit of it."

Chapter Fifteen

When Lisa and Dana both called the next day, Claire knew it was Mary's doing. She'd sent out the Mayday, put Operation Rescue Claire into motion.

And Claire had played along, agreed to a couple of lunch dates – even wrote them on the calendar. Maybe she'd go.

But as she rocked in the glider on the patio, she couldn't imagine being in the mood. Lisa's words hammered in her brain. Kristen and her kids. *Her two boys*.

Lisa and Jack had been out to dinner and ran into Stan. Stan and his date – Kristen, the receptionist at the property management company in Paxton.

"She looked totally fake, and the boys looked about ten and twelve. Something like that," Lisa'd told her. "Jack had mentioned this Kristen gal before, but I didn't know she had kids. Bet she's looking for a daddy. A sugar-daddy anyway." Lisa laughed, and Claire had joined in, but it was hollow and forced.

Stan fit the bill as a provider, but Stan stepping in to help raise someone else's boys? He'd hardly helped raise his own kids. Sure, he and Ben had done the usual father-and-son activities. They played catch in the yard. Stan had coached their basketball team. He'd taught Ben to fish and handle a jet ski. But Claire had been the one to instill values, to dole out discipline, to help with homework, to nurse heart aches and tummy aches.

143

It was one more thing. One more lousy hit below the belt. He was replacing her, and replacing Ben, too. Was that how it worked for men? Just find another one? She couldn't fathom it.

She inhaled deeply on her cigarette, and looked out across the yard, the place where she'd raised her children and put down roots. A chill seeped through her. Only a few more days, and that chapter would be officially closed. On Thursday, she'd drive to Lauren Armstrong's office and sign the papers that would make her single once again.

**

Claire waited until late afternoon, when she knew the birthday party was over and things had calmed down to call Elise. Guilt gnawed at her, but she pushed it back, determined to sound normal.

Elise answered right away.

"Hey, Mom. How are you feeling?"

"Much better. I'm so sorry I missed the party, and wasn't there to help you get ready."

"What happened?"

"I don't know. It might've been something I ate, but I just felt sick, and I went in to lie down, and fell asleep."

"Did you turn the ringer off the phone?"

"I did."

"I wish you wouldn't do that, Mom. What if there was an emergency? I was really worried when I couldn't get hold of you."

Claire sighed. She heard the mix of irritation and hurt in Elise's voice. "I'm sorry you were worried. I didn't expect to sleep so long, or I would've called. Anyway, how was the party?"

"It was wonderful. Olivia had a great time. She had eight friends plus Brian's brother's two kids. And the weather was perfect. It's too bad you missed it."

"I know. I can't wait to see the pictures, and I absolutely have to make it up to Olivia. When can I come for a visit? Or when can you come here? Maybe we could meet somewhere and Olivia could spend a few days here with me."

She'd offered to have Olivia before, but Elise never took her up on it. Never mind that Claire had managed to raise two kids. Her daughter still didn't trust her with her own children.

"It'd really be easier for me if you could come here, Mom."

As usual. "That's fine," Claire said, her voice artificially sing-song. "Tell me when."

"Looks like any of the next few weekends would be all right."

"Why don't we say next weekend then. I'll be there when you get off work. Tell Olivia we'll do something fun, okay? Maybe I could take her to a movie, or back to the zoo and she could show me all the things they did."

"Sounds good. She'll love it. Why don't you plan to stay here instead of the hotel? They'll probably charge you for at least one night for this weekend since you didn't call and cancel."

Claire debated that. True, it was an unnecessary expense, but she much preferred her own space. Maybe just this once she'd stay at the house to make up for missing the party.

"I suppose that would work this time."

"We'll plan on it. I can put Olivia and Andy together, or keep Andy in with us. Let me know if anything changes."

"I will. See you then."

That was probably better timing, anyway, Claire thought, as she poured her first glass of wine of the day. It would give her something to do after the divorce became final – other than stew about being single after thirty-two years of marriage.

**

Claire lifted the document, but when the papers began to rattle in her shaking hands, she smoothed them flat against the table. She knew she should read every word, but she could hardly stand to even look at the decree. The flimsy piece of paper that would declare her unmarried. Divorced. Officially dumped. The Ex.

She closed her eyes for a moment, fighting the anxiety that could still take her breath away without warning. Lauren set a glass of water on the table in front of her, and rested a warm hand on her arm.

"Take your time, Claire. There's no rush."

Claire nodded, and gratefully sipped the water. Then with sweaty palms, she picked up the pen and flipped to the last page. She scribbled her signature and pushed the papers away.

Lauren placed more papers in front of her. "Just a few more things. I need your signature on these, then it'll all be done."

Claire bit her lip, and picked up the pen again. She signed the documents, sure the writing would bear no resemblance to her actual signature. She guzzled more water, though she could hardly swallow. When Claire met Lauren's eyes, she patted her hand.

"What are you doing when you leave here today?" Lauren asked.

Claire was surprised to see the sympathy on her attorney's face replaced with the hint of a smile.

"I brought a friend with me. We thought we might do some shopping."

The smile widened. "Good. Do something nice for yourself." She handed Claire another document. "Here's the whole list. The judge will sign it tomorrow morning, and this will all be yours. You'll get the alimony check in the mail, but you can splurge a little today, Claire. You deserve it."

Claire studied the list. Yes, she could splurge a little. Mary would certainly be a willing accomplice. But

146

Claire's emotions were all over the place. She didn't feel like celebrating, but she didn't feel sad, either. Events had caused her to accept that losing Stan wasn't such a bad thing. She understood it was a momentous day; she just wasn't sure exactly what that meant.

Tears welled and spilled over before she could stop them. She choked on a sob, and Lauren put an arm around her shoulder.

"This is completely natural, Claire. Even people who want a divorce have a certain amount of sadness. Because it's an ending. Just remember, it's a beginning, too. Be happy. Reinvent yourself."

Lauren handed her a tissue, and Claire sniffled into it. "Thank you, Lauren. For everything."

Claire tucked her copies of the papers into the large manila envelope Lauren gave her. Then she stepped into the reception area. She greeted Mary with a wan smile, and was immediately pulled into a fierce hug.

"There. You're a free woman."

Claire clung to Mary for a moment, half laughing, half crying.

"Let's get out of here," Mary whispered. "Time for a dose of fun, my friend."

**

Claire fingered the bright green silk of the simple jacket.

"Ooo-la-la," Mary crooned. "That's gorgeous. Try it on."

"I don't know. It's nice, but where the heck would I wear it? It's pretty fancy."

"Who cares? You can wear it to the grocery store as long as it makes you feel good. Besides, you never know who you'll meet in packaged goods."

Claire smiled, and pulled a jacket off the rack. She slipped it on and headed toward a full-length mirror.

"Hmm. That's too big," Mary said. "Let me get another size. What's that?"

"A ten."

"Really? Well, either they run big, or you've lost weight." She handed Claire the smaller jacket, and looked her over with a frown. "You've definitely lost weight."

Claire laughed. "Divorce diet. Don't be jealous."

"Well, unless you're planning to buy a whole new wardrobe, toots, you better get a little meat back on your bones."

With mock innocence, Claire turned wide eyes to Mary. "What's wrong with a new wardrobe? A whole size smaller? I'm all for that."

"Then spend away, my friend. And start with this jacket. It's fabulous."

They shopped for two hours, and Claire's bags were bulging with evidence of a spending spree. The new skirt and blouse would replace the ones she'd worn the night Ray was over for dinner. Those had found a new home in the landfill.

"Okay, we better put the brakes on, or I'll need one of those 'oversized load' signs for my car to haul all of this stuff home. Besides, I can't carry anything else," Claire said.

"And my feet are tired. And we need food," Mary told her. "What do you think? Gardenview or one of the other restaurants down here? What about the little Mexican place?"

"Sure. That sounds good."

A few minutes later, they dumped their bags into the extra chairs at their table, and dove into the basket of chips waiting for them.

"This is what I love about this place. Instant gratification," Mary said.

"Exactly."

Under the table, Claire eased her tired feet partway out of her sandals. Ahhh. Now all she needed was something for her parched throat.

The waitress stopped by with glasses of water. "What can I get you ladies to drink?"

Claire spoke first. "I'll have a house margarita on the rocks. With salt, please."

She glanced over at Mary and caught her frown.

The waitress turned to Mary. "Ma'am?"

"I'll have the same."

As soon as the waitress left, Claire pursed her lips, and set the menu down. Her eyes met Mary's.

"What?" Mary asked.

"You know what. I don't want to see that look every time I order a drink. We've been having wine with dinner, or drinks and appetizers forever. I can have one margarita, for heaven's sake."

Mary leaned forward, her brow furrowed. "But can you? Have just one? What about when you get home, Claire? What about the other night?"

Her throat constricted. Of all people, Mary should understand. "You know what happened the other night. It was awful, and I needed to go numb for a while. Jesus, can't you cut me a little slack on this?"

"Claire, I don't want to argue. I'm worried about you, that's all."

"I'm fine."

"All right, but if you're fine, why aren't you doing anything? Why don't you come help me with concessions at the baseball field next week?"

Claire shrugged. "I might. I'm not sure how long I'll be at Elise's or how worn out I'll be after that. I'll call you."

"When are you leaving?"

"Tomorrow after lunch."

"Want me to help you pack or anything?"

Claire rolled her eyes. "No, I do not need help packing, for heaven's sake."

"What are you doing with Reggie?"

149

"He's staying here. I'll put out extra food and water."

The drinks arrived, and they ordered dinner. Claire lifted the heavy margarita glass, and held it out toward Mary. "Well, that's that."

"To new beginnings," Mary said as she clinked her glass against Claire's.

Her attorney had said the same thing. A euphemism for starting over, Claire thought. Starting over at fifty-five. When she should be settled and comfortable. What was so great about starting over?

"Oh, hey," Mary said. "Since you'll have some down time while you're at the hotel this weekend, let's duck into the bookstore and pick you up a copy of the next read for book club." She started digging in her purse. "I've got the title written down somewhere. It sounds good. I think it was Jane's pick this time."

Claire's blood pressure spiked. Why was Mary pushing her? Another phase of Operation Rescue Claire? She'd been part of the book club with about ten women for years. Some had drifted in and out, but there was a core group of five who'd been the foundation, and she was one of them. But she'd attended sporadically in the last couple of years. For some reason, it irritated her that Mary assumed she'd want to go this month.

"I won't have much down time. I'm staying at Elise's place instead of the hotel this time. But, I guess I can take a look at it."

"What's that supposed to mean? You're picking and choosing now based on the book? That's not the way it works, and you know it."

"I just don't know if I'm up for book club this month," Claire snapped.

Mary stared at her for a long moment. "What are you going to do, Claire? You can't hole up in that house day after day. What about getting a part-time job? What about volunteering? You know how many organizations need volunteers. If you don't want to go back to the ones you've always helped with, change it up, choose some new ones. But do something, for —"

The waitress set steaming plates in front of them. "Here you go, ladies. Enjoy. Let me know if I can get you anything else."

Claire nodded, and waited for the woman to step away. Then she looked across the table at Mary. "What am I going to do? I'm going to eat dinner, then I'm going home. I'll get up tomorrow and go to Wichita, and that's as far as I can see in my crystal ball right now."

Chapter Sixteen

Claire dumped an extra scoop of coffee into the filter. Today would require extra-strength caffeine. She debated calling the hotel. Again. It'd be so nice to get to Wichita early and take a quick nap rather than heading straight to the commotion of Elise's house. Really, wouldn't it be easier on everyone?

She let out a long sigh. Not if Elise and Brian wanted to go out. In that case, Claire would need to be at the house to put the kids to bed and stay until Elise and Brian got home, which would probably be late. She filled her cup and took a couple of sips. Fine. She'd try to stick it out this once.

She glanced at her watch. If she left around one, she could get there at four and run into the grocery store before arriving at Elise's. She certainly didn't want to show up before Elise did and have to make idle chit-chat with Brian.

At twelve-thirty, Mary called.

"Hey," Claire said.

"Hey. You getting ready to head out?"

"Yeah. I'm all packed. Got about an hour."

There was a slight pause before Mary answered. "Oh, really? If you're ready, why not go ahead and go?"

"Don't want to be early. Elise won't get home from work until five-thirty."

"Okay, just don't decide to take a nap."

Claire heard the light chuckle from Mary's end, but it sounded like a fake nervous laugh. And it struck a nerve. Claire's face warmed. Mary was calling to check up on her.

"I'll take a nap if I feel like it. But don't worry, it's not in the plan."

"Now, don't get testy. Where's your sense of humor?"

"I'll laugh when it's funny."

"All right, then, grumpy. Be sure to give Elise a buzz before you leave, so she'll know you're on your way."

Were Mary and Elise in cahoots now? Keeping track of her every move? She'd have to nip that in the bud.

"I don't think that's necessary, but you can call and tell her if you like."

There was a beat of silence. "Claire, you're being bitchy. What's going on?"

"Nothing. I don't need someone constantly checking up on me, that's all."

"You know, you don't make any sense. One day you say you don't like being alone. The next, you don't like people calling you."

"I don't like the reason you're calling today. You called to make sure I was up and getting ready to leave for Wichita. Would you like me to wear an ankle bracelet so you can track me?"

"Hey, you're taking out your anger or bad mood or whatever it is on me, and I'm just trying to help. Let me know when you get back in town. And don't forget to put out extra food and water for Reggie. Have a good trip."

The line went dead, and Claire snapped the phone back into its holder.

She filled a thermos to take on the road then marched to the mudroom and sliced open a fresh bag of food for Reggie. There now, she muttered, that should take care of it. She was not an animal abuser and was not going to forget to feed her pet. She filled an extra water bowl, knowing full well that Reggie could always get a drink out of any of the toilets if he needed it. She often caught the lazy beast lapping from hers.

She leaned against the counter, and let her head fall to her chest. Should she call Mary back or let her cool down for a few days? They'd had minor tiffs before, usually over something stupid. They'd laugh about it and move on, no big apologies or drama necessary. But things were so different now. And Mary was acting more like an overbearing mother than a friend. Maybe a cooling-off period was best.

**

Claire turned on the television for background noise, and forced herself to putter around the house. She suddenly wished she'd left in the morning, with the caffeine from the coffee buoying her energy level. She could feel it waning, and as it did, a glass of wine and a nap sounded more and more appealing.

But she *would not* prove them right. Instead, she reached for her cigarette case then began loading the car. As she tossed in the shopping bag that held Olivia's beautifully wrapped but tardy birthday gift, she wondered if she should take the bag of snacks she'd bought for the party favors. She'd never eat them, but would they be a reminder that she'd screwed up? That was one thing she didn't need. Maybe she could give them to Mary for the concession stand.

Claire left fifteen minutes early. She couldn't stand any more waiting around.

As it turned out, the grocery shopping ate up the extra time. The store closest to Elise's house must've been the size of a football field, and the layout was a maze, complete with illogical twists and turns and dead ends. By the time Claire made it to the checkout line, she felt as though she'd finished a 10K run. Tired, sweaty and frazzled. And parched.

She thought of the thermos in the car. She'd hoped to save that for later, but she needed something now. Her hands were unsteady as she wrote a check and gave it to the cashier. Outside, she shaded her eyes and looked around the strip center as she led the kid carrying her groceries to the car. Maybe there was a restaurant close by where she could slip in for a few minutes to cool off and have something to drink.

Hmm. There was a Chinese place. She started the car and drove slowly through the parking lot. On the corner was some kind of sports bar. That'd do. She climbed out of the car and hurried to the door. She was trying to decide between something frozen and something on ice when the cold air inside the restaurant hit her skin. Then Claire remembered she'd just loaded nearly two hundred dollar's worth of food into her car. And it was sitting in the blazing sun. For a moment, she sagged against the bar. She'd have to dip into the sangria after all.

She left the restaurant and went back to her car. After she started the engine and flipped the air conditioning to full blast, she poured herself a cup of sangria and sat back against the leather seat. A few more minutes wouldn't make any difference.

The cup was almost empty when her cell phone buzzed. She dug it out of her purse. A text from Elise. *'I'm home. Are you close?'* Checking up. Trying to help? Claire swallowed the last few drops then put the cup back on the thermos and tightened it. To the people around her, she'd become unreliable, untrustworthy. Well, what do you know, here she was. Right. On. Time. She texted back, *'be there in five.'*

Claire pulled into the driveway, noting that Brian's old Saab sat at the curb. That was a nice gesture, she conceded. She popped a mint into her mouth, and stuffed the thermos into her cosmetic case. With a bag of groceries in her arm, she headed up the front steps of the small Cape Cod-style house. A faded welcome mat and a flag with a huge sunflower and ladybug greeted her.

She rang the bell, and heard a band of footsteps jump into motion.

Elise flung the door open. "Hey, Mom. Come on in."

She stepped inside and handed the bag to Elise. "This is just the first one."

Brian stepped forward and gave Claire a brief hug. "Hi, Claire. Good to see you. You go on in, and I'll get the rest."

"Thank you."

She started to follow Elise inside, but stopped short when Olivia flew from behind Elise and wrapped her arms around Claire's waist.

"Hi, Grammy. Do you feel better now?"

Claire reached for the wall to steady herself, then bent down, patting Olivia's back. "Oh, sweetie. I sure do. I'm so sorry I missed your party. I want to hear all about it." She straightened and looked around for Andy. He appeared to be bolted to the floor in the middle of the living room.

Claire's heart caught in her throat. For an instant, Andy reminded her of Ben. How was that possible? The kid looked nothing like Ben. Would she ever be able to look at a little boy and not see her own son, not feel a jolt of emotion?

"Hello, Andy," she managed.

He looked at the floor and mumbled, "hi."

Claire put her hand on Olivia's shoulder and steered her out of the way when Brian came through the door with more groceries.

"Come on. Let's help your mom get all this stuff put away."

"Wow, Mom. Is there anything left at the grocery store?" Elise said, already pulling items from the paper bags.

"Oh, a couple of things. That place is so huge it could feed all of China for a month. I practically got lost."

Olivia grabbed her hand. "It's okay, Grammy. I got lost in there one time, too."

Claire glanced at Elise. That would've been a tense moment. "I can imagine. How scary."

She stepped farther into the tiny galley kitchen. "Want to put me to work, or shall I just stay out of the way?"

"You can visit with Olivia, and I'll deal with all of this."

"Are we cooking or going out tonight? Or do you and Brian want to go out tonight while I watch the kids?"

Elise tucked a loose strand of hair behind her ear, and gave a nervous laugh. "Mom, we didn't invite you up to babysit. We're perfectly fine staying here. We can all go out together one night."

"Elise, I'm happy to sit with the kids one evening while you and Brian have a date. You should go out."

"Well, we'll see."

Elise studied her mother. She seemed fine. Her face was a bit red and splotchy. From crying? Lack of sleep? Hard to say. Was alcohol a factor? As usual, she put on a good front, but Elise had the feeling her mother was distracted, simply going through the motions. The way she'd been after Ben died.

The divorce had set her back, for sure. If only she'd gotten some therapy after Ben died, maybe she could handle the divorce easier. But going to a doctor for mental health was against her mother's religion. The commandments her mother lived by included, 'Thou Shalt Keep Proper Appearances at All Times.'

Psychiatrists were for crazy people. And word might get out.

As she folded the grocery bags, Elise considered her mother's offer to babysit. It might be nice to go on a date, but she and Brian weren't desperate to go out. They had a few trusted and reliable people they called occasionally. It was mostly a matter of time. And convenience. It was a lot of work to have the kids ready and to write out all the instructions for a sitter. Easier to stay home. And she simply didn't know whether her mom was up to the task.

At the kitchen table, Olivia had wrangled Grammy into an endless game of tic-tac-toe on a wipe-off board. Elise couldn't help but notice that the wand shook in her mother's hand. She moved a little closer and looked at the board. Her mother's marks were distinctly unsteady.

"Mom, your hands are shaky. Do you need something to eat? We could go ahead and get supper started."

Her mother glanced up, and squeezed her fists a moment. "I had a lot of caffeine today. Wanted to make sure I didn't get sleepy this afternoon. So, yes, I should probably eat something pretty soon."

Hmm. A lot of caffeine sometimes made her jittery, too. Okay, Elise, stop looking for problems.

She started to turn back toward the kitchen but caught a curious expression from Olivia who looked from Elise to Grammy, then blurted out, "Grammy are you thirsty? Mommy said you might want to have a drink."

Oh, shit. Elise groaned inside. Why did the kids have to pick up on every word she said? At least every word she didn't want repeated.

Her mother's eyes were on her in a flash. And a knowing smirk played around her lips.

"Paybacks . . ." she said softly.

Elise tossed a glare in her daughter's direction then pasted on a tight smile. "Mom, would you like a glass of iced tea?"

Her mother looked at Olivia, and grinned. "No, thank you. I'm not thirsty right now."

"All right then. Decision time. Eating in or out?" Hopefully that awkward moment would pass and not be revisited.

Her mother stood up. "I vote for out. Let me take you all to dinner tonight, then tomorrow you and I can start cooking. I'd rather leave all this food for you."

They ended up at Olive Garden, which was a little silly since an Italian meal was one of the easiest to throw together at home. But Elise claimed it was one of the kids' favorites, so that tipped the scales. It was on the noisy side for Claire's comfort, but at least it was perfectly acceptable to have a glass of wine with dinner there. In fact, they encouraged it. And Claire wasn't driving, so Elise wouldn't have to get in a snit about that.

Claire considered it a small victory. She picked up her glass and sat back, happy to let the parents keep Andy occupied while she smiled at Olivia and let her thoughts drift.

Should she tell Elise the divorce was final, that her lousy dad was liable to be remarried any day now? Would she care? This wasn't the time or place, but maybe tomorrow they'd have a few minutes alone. Of course, it was possible that Elise already knew. Maybe she'd been keeping in touch with her dad. A shudder ran through Claire. Maybe they'd go to the wedding.

**

Finally alone in their bedroom, Brian locked his arms around Elise's waist and nuzzled her neck. "Hey, did I hear your mother mention the possibility of a date?"

159

Elise met his eyes in the mirror. "You did. What do you think about it?"

He stared at her. "Hell, yes. We need a break. Olivia seems to enjoy her, and holy Christ it's nice having someone else to read with her. I don't think I can read a single page of Little House in the Big Woods ever again."

Elise laughed, and turned in his arms. "Very true. But does Mom seem okay to you?"

Brian let out a long sigh. "This might be the new normal, babe. Your mom is probably changed forever, or at least for a long time. Seems like she's only about half here sometimes, but you don't think she's a danger, do you?"

"I honestly don't know."

"Maybe spending a few days here will be good for her. It'd be great if she'd bond with the kids now that they're a little older," he said.

"It would. She's good with Olivia, but she acts like Andy doesn't even exist. She shows no interest in him at all. Never touches him, and hardly ever looks at him. It's strange. I thought she might latch on to him after Ben died, but it's been the exact opposite."

"Reminds her too much of what she lost."

"I know I'd be a zombie, too, if we lost Andy or Olivia, but people do lose sons to war. I don't know how to help her move forward. I wish she'd see a therapist or join a support group, but she won't even discuss it."

Brian tipped her chin up and pressed a light kiss to her lips. "Let's go out and let her spend a little one-on-one time with them. It'll be okay."

Chapter Seventeen

Claire tucked the blanket around Andy then smoothed his hair, letting her hand linger a moment.

"Nighty-night," she whispered.

Before heading downstairs she slipped into Andy's room, which was her room for the weekend. Earlier, she'd managed to add some ice and a small bottle of wine to the sangria left in her thermos. She twisted open the thermos and poured a cup then sat on the bed and sipped it. Nothing wrong with taking a few minutes for herself before she joined Olivia for a movie or games.

From the doorway she called down, "Olivia, did you decide?"

"Movie, Grammy. Are you ready?"

"I'll be right down, sweetie. You pick one out."

She finished the wine, and replaced the cap on the thermos.

∗∗

Claire woke with a start. Disoriented. Had she fallen asleep? The static blaring from the television shouted yes. She sat up, and her brain engaged. Oh, right, she'd been watching a movie with Olivia. Guess it was over. Standing, she stretched and turned off the TV then glanced around for her granddaughter.

"Olivia?" she called.

When she didn't get an answer, Claire climbed the stairs and peeked inside Olivia's pink and purple room. "Olivia?"

No sign of her. Well, for heaven's sake. Where did she go? Andy, thank goodness, was sound asleep in his parents' bed.

"Olivia. Where are you?" Maybe she'd gone to Claire's room. She opened the door, and turned on the light, and gave the room a quick search. Nothing. With a twinge of concern, Claire started back downstairs.

Where could she be? Claire leaned against the wall in the hallway, and rubbed her temples, wracking her brain. She simply couldn't remember. Had they started a game of hide-and-seek, and she'd fallen asleep? They'd played earlier before Andy went to bed. Good grief, how long would she wait to be found?

Claire retraced her steps, more quickly this time, opening closets and looking under beds. She checked the showers.

"Olivia. I give up. You can come out now."

She shook her head, trying to think. Oh, God, Elise would kill her if anything happened to Olivia. But she was six years old, old enough to know danger and keep herself out of it. Did she have a friend in the neighborhood she'd go play with? Maybe she phoned Elise and got permission. No. Elise would've wanted to talk to Claire about anything like that. She remembered Elise telling Olivia not to wake her the last time they were at her house and Claire had accidentally swatted at her.

She checked her watch. It was ten o'clock, and she'd spent nearly thirty minutes searching the house. Panic swept through her, and her voice sharpened. "Olivia, answer me! The game is over."

She went through the house again, shoving aside clothes in closets and looking in ridiculous places like under the bathroom sinks. Her pulse escalated with each step. She groaned at the thought of waking Andy. But would he know Olivia's favorite hiding places?

Back in the kitchen, Claire considered her options. Give her a little more time? Text Elise? She glanced at the kitchen window. Surely Olivia wouldn't go outside. It was pitch dark out. But a quick check of the back door showed it was unlocked. Claire yanked open the heavy door and stepped onto the deck.

Olivia looked up at her. "Hi, Grammy."

Claire blanched. Oh, sweet Jesus. Olivia was sitting at the patio table twirling a lighter. Claire's lighter.

Her heart pounding, Claire hurried to the table and snatched the lighter out of Olivia's hands.

"Olivia, what are you doing? Don't ever pick one of those up! It's not a toy. It could be very dangerous." Her voice was shrill, and she saw Olivia's lips quiver.

"I know, Grammy. I was going to give it to you. I didn't want Mommy or Andy to find it."

"Where did you get it?"

"I found it out here."

Claire's chest heaved. She must've left it out there last night. Thank God Andy hadn't found it.

"And what are you doing out here? I've been calling for you, young lady. I've searched all over the house. You scared me half to death."

"I was waiting for you to wake up. The movie's over." Her voice was soft, but her eyes were huge in her face.

Claire took a deep breath, and gripped the table to stop her hands from shaking. Okay. She's all right. Calm down.

She rolled her neck a moment, then perched on Olivia's chair, and pulled her into a tight hug, patting her back. "You're a good girl, Olivia. I'm sorry I yelled at you. It scared me when I couldn't find you, that's all. I wouldn't want anything bad to happen to you, sweetheart."

163

Claire cringed inside. She'd been so careful. The lighter had to have fallen out of her case. She did *not* leave that lighter on the table. She knew she didn't. Her head pounded now that the adrenaline rush was over.

Claire took Olivia's hand. "You know what, honey? Grammy's tired. Do you think it's about bed time for you?"

Olivia nodded and slipped out of the chair. "I'll go brush my teeth."

Claire smiled and kissed the top of her head. "You do that. But be really quiet so you don't wake up Andy." With all the yelling and banging of doors she'd done looking for Olivia, Claire was amazed the kid hadn't already woken up. That was the last thing she needed.

She slumped in the chair a moment. What she did need was a drink and a cigarette. But did she dare? Her fist closed around the lighter that had betrayed her. For tonight, maybe she'd take a couple of aspirin and have a glass of wine, but skip the cigarette. She'd try, anyway.

**

The following day, Claire was cautious as she joined the rest of the family in the kitchen.

"Morning, Mom," Elise said, handing Claire a cup of coffee.

"Thanks." Claire took it and watched Elise, but didn't detect anything out of the ordinary. She glanced at Olivia, busy mashing the cereal in her bowl. Could she trust her not to tell her mother that Grammy had fallen asleep during the movie or left a lighter on the deck? She hadn't specifically told her not to tell. It wouldn't be right to ask a child to keep a secret from her mother. That'd backfire for sure.

"Did you two have a nice time last night?" she asked, hoping her voice didn't give her away.

"It was great, Mom. Thanks. What did you guys do?"

164

Claire spoke up quickly before Olivia could get a word out. "Movie and games. Lots of fun."

Elise smiled, and as breakfast wound down, Claire breathed a sigh of relief. Apparently Olivia had sensed it would be best to keep information about last night to herself, and she was not going to be found out.

She let herself relax, and switched gears. "Okay, why don't we get breakfast cleaned up and start on the next meal?"

Claire and Elise spent a couple of hours in the kitchen finishing up some seasoned chicken breasts and meatloaf to put in the freezer.

"Let's save the fried chicken for tonight," Elise said. "A Sunday dinner tradition."

Claire turned sharply, her eyes widening. Of course. She'd forgotten. When the kids were growing up, she'd made fried chicken and mashed potatoes nearly every Sunday night. It was one of Ben's favorite meals. The gravy, especially.

She smiled at the memory. "Remember how Ben used to drown all of his food in a pool of gravy?"

Elise nodded.

"His plate would be a huge mess, and you couldn't tell one food from the other." Her voice softened and trailed off, and Elise touched her arm.

"You know, Mom. I miss him, too," she said.

Claire looked at her daughter, and saw the sorrow in her eyes.

"Maybe you didn't realize it, but Ben and I were pretty close, much closer than you and Uncle David."

Elise leaned against the counter, facing Claire. "We used to talk about how the two of us one day would have to be there for each other, to look after you and Dad, make decisions about elder care. We talked about our kids being cousins *and* friends. I really would've liked that."

Claire studied Elise a moment. That was a bond they shared. Sure, Ben's friends missed him, but they went on with their lives. Elise was the one other person whose life had changed as a result of Ben's death. One day she'd be alone. No parents. No siblings. So unfair. Her lips trembled.

"Let's have chicken dinner in Ben's honor, then," Claire whispered, swallowing past the lump in her throat. "Is that what you do on Sundays still?"

Elise shook her head with a wry smile. "Are you kidding? I can't replicate your fried chicken, Mom. This'll be a treat. Wait 'til I tell Brian. He'll be in here salivating the minute we start."

Claire blinked hard, and turned back to her task. Memories had a way of knocking the wind out of her when she least expected it.

By the time they finished cooking, Elise easily had a couple of weeks' worth of meals stored away. Claire smoothed a label on the chicken, and handed it to Elise.

"Thanks, Mom. This is fantastic. Oh, my gosh, this is going to help so much. Want to come back in two weeks?"

Claire smiled. She knew Elise was kidding, but it lifted her spirits to be appreciated. "I should go home and do the same thing," Claire said.

"Absolutely. You should."

"I might. But right now, I want to spend a little time with Olivia. I think she's got her heart set on that dolphin movie. That all right with you?"

"Sure."

"Okay, then. We'll be back in a couple of hours or so."

They arrived back home at four-thirty, both tired, and not the least bit hungry.

"I think we ate too much popcorn," Claire said. "Mind if we wait a while before we start cooking again?"

"No. That's fine," Elise said. "How was the movie?"

When Olivia hopped in front of Elise, and launched into an excited play-by-play of the movie, Claire took a step back. "You tell your mom all about it, sweetheart. I think I'll go lie down a while."

She'd had a nice time with her granddaughter, but Claire was ready for a break. She took a glass from the cupboard and filled it with ice and water, then headed to her room. In the bathroom upstairs, she poured the water from the glass. Then she closed the bedroom door behind her, and replaced the water with Chardonnay. She propped a pillow against the headboard, and leaned back, enjoying the quiet.

Over dinner, she decided she'd leave the next morning when Brian and Elise left for work. Turned out Olivia didn't want to miss the activities at the day camp, and Claire had no desire to hang out at Elise's house all day.

"I'll just head on home," she said. "I've had a fun time, but you all have your regular routines. It's fine."

She helped with the dishes, then climbed the stairs to start packing up.

**

"Mother!"

Claire jumped, and her head snapped around at the sound of Elise's shrill voice in the bedroom. "What?"

Her eyes followed her daughter's gaze.

Oh. Her suitcase was open on the bed. And the small bottles of wine she'd tucked in between her socks and underwear were clearly visible through the mesh pouch.

Elise stared at her, a stricken look on her face.

"What's the matter?"

"Mom. Oh, my God. You had to bring wine. You're hiding it in here?"

Her daughter's voice bordered on hysterical, but Claire tried to remain calm. It wasn't a big deal.

"Obviously I'm not hiding it. You can see it."

167

Elise shook her head. "I can't believe this. We left you with our kids last night. We trusted you with our kids!"

"And look at that, they survived, didn't they? They're perfectly fine."

Brian poked his head into the room, eyebrows raised. "Hey, is everything okay? Kids are up here."

Claire crossed her arms, but said nothing.

"Can you take them downstairs or outside for a little while, hon?" Elise asked.

He hesitated a moment, then gave a quiet, "oooookay."

As soon as he left, Elise whirled back to Claire, hands on her hips.

"Mom, you have a problem."

Claire struggled to maintain a cool composure, though the censure in her daughter's eyes irritated her. Elise had no idea what Claire had been through, the memories and thoughts that bombarded her constantly, the grief that punched her in the gut without a moment's notice. "Yes. I have a problem sleeping. A glass of wine before bed helps. I'd rather have a glass of wine than take sleeping pills."

Elise gave her a hard glare. "Really. One glass before bed. That's all?"

"Would you like to count them?" Claire asked. Good thing she'd stuffed the empty bottles in her cosmetic case. She'd have to be more careful next time.

Like hell. Next time she'd be at the hotel for sure. In fact, a hotel would be better than this hostility. She considered whether it might be best to pack up her things and go. Immediately.

Elise rubbed a hand across her brow, visibly struggling for words. "No, I don't want to count them. But I want to know how much you're drinking. We left our kids with you last night. Did you have a drink while we weren't here?"

168

"I had a glass of wine before I went to bed, after the kids were both asleep." It wasn't the whole truth, but it wasn't a lie, either. Claire fumed inside. She should not have to put up with this kind of grilling from her daughter.

"That's not acceptable, Mom. You know how dangerous it is to drink and smoke."

"I wasn't smoking."

"Are you drinking when you're home alone? Jesus, Mom, do you need to get some help?"

That did it. Claire threw up her hands. "Some help? What does that mean?" she shouted. "Is someone going to turn back time and *help* me get my son back, make my husband love me? Can someone help make sense of any of this? I don't think so."

"Counselors and psychologists can help you with your feelings, Mom. The anger and depression. You know that. Having someone to talk to might make you feel better, stronger."

"I just need some time," Claire ground out. "And a little understanding would be nice, too. If that's not too much to ask." She folded a pair of pants and slapped them into the suitcase. With one hand on her hip, she scanned the room for a moment. Then her eyes rested on Elise again. "It's over. I signed the papers before I came up. And the judge signed them Friday morning, so it's official."

Elise slumped against the dresser with an audible sigh. "Wow. That was fast."

"Yes. Your dad was in a real big hurry."

"I'm sorry. I wish you'd told me earlier."

"I didn't want to bother you with all the ugly details."

"Mom. Come on, that's a pretty big deal."

"So you haven't talked to your dad? You didn't know?"

"No." Elise pushed a hand through her hair. "How did . . . are you going to be all right? You have enough money?"

"I'll be fine. I'm staying in the house. I have no idea what he'll do." That was a big fat lie, of course. She knew exactly what he'd do.

Elise straightened and took a step forward, resting a hand on Claire's arm. "Come on, let's go sit down, and we can talk. I'll make some coffee. I have decaf."

"Fine." Claire said, blinking back tears that burned in her eyes. She followed Elise out of the room and into the kitchen dabbing at her eyes. *She would not cry.*

"You sure you want to stay in the house, Mom?" Elise asked while she put the coffee on. "It might be easier for you if you started over someplace new. Without all the memories."

Claire shook her head and dropped into a chair at the table. "It's too soon," she whispered. She simply couldn't leave Ben's room. "I may do some redecorating. Change things up a bit."

"Yeah. That would keep you busy for a while. But you should probably think about a part-time job or a volunteer program to give you something to do with your time. You need to *do* something."

Claire winced. If she got a part-time job everyone would assume she needed the money, that her standard of living had fallen as a result of the divorce. No. She wouldn't do that. Not right now, anyway.

"We'll see. I can't imagine what kind of job I'd get in Whitfield. So many people are commuting to Paxton to find work. And I wouldn't want to take a job away from someone who really needed it."

Elise handed her a cup of coffee. "Mom, *you* might need it. If not for the money, then to be productive, to be around people and feel useful." She paused, drumming her fingers on the table. "You should start a catering business. You're a great cook, and you enjoy it."

170

Elise's face lit up. She was clearly enthused about the idea. "What do you think about that?"

Claire's thoughts skipped to her last attempt at cooking for someone else. What a disaster that had been. "Catering?" she echoed. "I doubt there'd be a high demand for that in Whitfield." She held up her hand. "It's too soon for me to think about it right now. If something interesting comes up, I'll consider it."

She could operate a bakery or cater dinners or desserts. But that would make her the help. Instead of attending events, she'd be behind the scenes setting up and cleaning up. Not where she wanted to be at all. Besides, she wasn't licensed. The details that would go into starting up and operating a business seemed overwhelming. No. She wasn't ready for that. Nor did she want the regimented schedule that operating a business would entail. Everyone kept telling her she was free. Well, what was wrong with having a little freedom, then? Why were they pushing her into a life of routine and work?

Chapter Eighteen

It took two more weeks. That was the only surprise.

Claire and Dana were watching a movie and enjoying the bottle of Chardonnay Dana had brought with her, when the phone rang.

Claire shoved the popcorn bowl aside and checked the caller ID. Elise. It'd be rude to pick up, but guilt reared its head. With an apologetic glance at Dana, Claire answered the call.

"Hello, Elise."

"Hey, Mom. How are you?"

"Oh, fine. Watching a movie. What's going on there?"

"Just put the kids to bed."

"Is Andy's cold better?"

"Yes. He went to his regular daycare today."

"Good."

There was an awkward pause. Elise rarely called just to chat, so Claire shifted, and waited, wondering if there was a specific reason for the call.

Oh, yes. There was.

"Mom, Dad's getting married."

Claire nearly laughed at the hesitancy in her daughter's voice. She looked at Dana while she spoke.

"Of course he's getting married, Elise. Did you think he was divorcing me so that he could be a bachelor? Honestly, who would cook his meals and do the laundry? Do you think he could manage that? Do you think he'd go without sex or clean clothes? No, honey, the only surprise is that it's taken him so long to get around to it."

"Her name is Kristen. Do you know her?"

Claire closed her eyes, and an unwelcome visual came to mind of her husband's mistress – the big boobs, bottle-blonde hair and ultra-whitened teeth. Embarrassing. Claire was actually embarrassed for Stan. Making such an ass of himself.

"I know who she is," Claire answered the question finally. "And I really don't care to know anything more."

"I'm surprised," Elise said. "I didn't expect it so soon. I mean . . . you were right. He's obviously been seeing this woman."

Claire let out a sigh. She supposed on some level Elise had still idolized her daddy. They'd been such a typical family. Elise was closer to Stan, and Ben was closer to Claire.

"Yes." She swallowed hard then blurted out a question. "Does he want you to attend?"

"No. He didn't ask. And I didn't ask for details."

"Good. That's just as well. You don't want to be in the middle of all that."

"I suppose I'll meet her, sometime. I mean, at holidays, maybe. I'm sure he'll still want to see the kids."

Claire rubbed her temples. Oh, this naïve girl. Did she really think so? Good grief. No man with a wife that age wants to be a grandpa.

"And holidays will be more trouble now. We'll have to divide our time."

Her stomach rolled. *Holidays.* As far as she was concerned this could be another year without them.

They hadn't celebrated in the last couple of years. Those months after Ben's death were a blur. She'd barely been functioning then. She couldn't remember if she'd even bought gifts for the grandkids last year. The robot probably had. God, her mind was blank. She honestly couldn't remember.

"Yes. More complicated, I imagine," she said. But she didn't really believe it. Stan's holidays would be focused on Kristen's kids without a doubt.

"Well, I just wanted to make sure you knew before you heard it through the rumor mill. I know you expected it, so I hope you're not upset."

Upset? Claire thought about that. No. She no longer thought of Stan as her husband. It was all so surreal. The man she'd married and shared a life with for all of her adult years was nothing to her anymore. Only the father of her children.

She spoke brightly into the phone. "I'm fine. I'm glad you called, though."

There was a long pause. "Are you alone?"

"No. Actually, Dana's here with me."

"Oh, good. Well, I hope . . . Don't let this make you drink, Mom. Okay? You can handle this."

Claire's gaze shifted to the wine glasses on the table. They'd finished the bottle Dana brought in record time, and she was about to open a second. Yeah. They were gonna need that second one.

"You don't need to worry, honey. I'm fine."

"Okay, I'll talk to you later."

As soon as she hung up, Dana moved toward her, a worried frown on her face.

"You okay?"

Claire drew a shaky breath. "Wonder what took him so long?"

Dana threw her arm around Claire's shoulder. "Listen, I know it isn't much consolation, but be glad the kids weren't in the mix. You don't have to deal with them playing you against each other, and visitation schedules. And that bitch won't have a hand in raising your kids."

Dana picked up the bottle of wine and filled both glasses, then she handed Claire her glass. "Thank God you got the lump-sum alimony. I hear she knows how to blow through the cash."

"Lot of maintenance goes into that piece of work," Claire said. She closed her eyes and took a drink. "Out with the old, in with the new."

She felt Dana's arm around her again.

"Screw him. He doesn't deserve you."

Claire choked out a laugh, and lifted the glass to her lips again. No, he didn't. She wanted to believe that she'd be better off in the end, and he'd get the comeuppance he deserved. But her confidence was thin. Things didn't always work the way they were supposed to.

**

Claire sat on the patio in the morning sun with her coffee and newspaper. She didn't much care what was going on in the world, but she enjoyed her routine. One thing that hadn't changed.

Just for curiosity's sake, she opened the paper to the classified ads and perused the job listings. *Great.* Looked like auto mechanics were in high demand. And nurses. And most everything was located in Paxton. It'd be ridiculous to drive forty-five minutes to and from a part-time job.

She drummed her fingers on the table. Maybe she could get creative and think of something to do from home. She could write. Or start a book exchange. Operate a used bookstore. One with limited hours, of course.

Sipping her coffee, she stared across the yard. A bookstore might be fun, but that would compete with the library. She couldn't do that – it was struggling enough already.

If she'd finished her degree, it would've been in Journalism. Surely three years of higher education plus fifty-five years of life experience was worth something. A newspaper column? Would anyone hire her? The local weekly always seemed desperate for material. Maybe they'd be interested. She could write about raising kids. And losing one.

The familiar lump formed in her throat. Could she? So many things she could say about Ben. But would anyone else care? For several minutes she contemplated the idea. Lou, the owner of the Whitfield Weekly, would probably give her a chance, at least.

As the sun intensified, she closed her eyes, still bleary from the late night. Dana had stayed past midnight.

Claire remembered that all the dirty dishes still sat in the living room waiting for her. But she wasn't ready to face those yet. With a heavy sigh, she turned the page of the newspaper, and the travel section caught her attention. Travel. Go see the world, Lauren had told her. Have some fun. That was another option. But where would she go, and with whom?

Dana was her only single friend, so she had the fewest family constraints. Unfortunately, she also had limited time off from work. Skilled nurses were hard to come by in Whitfield, and Dana was the highest-ranking nurse the hospital had. Besides that, she was always strapped for cash even though she made a decent salary. Her loser husband had gotten them so far into debt that she'd worked for years just to pay off their credit cards. Her alimony was pitiful, and child support had been sporadic. In the last ten years, she'd spent every spare cent she earned on her kids. Nothing left for herself. The woman certainly deserved a vacation, but it probably wasn't in her budget. Claire could help out, of course, but she knew Dana well enough to know she wouldn't accept charity.

**

As she dumped out ashtrays and rinsed dishes, Claire's thoughts returned to the possibility of writing a newspaper column. Ideas bounced around in her head.

She rejected some, but others stuck around. She wiped her hands and reached for a pen and paper. After making a few notes, she picked up a cloth to wipe down the coffee table. But before she'd started, another idea popped into her head, and she dashed back to the kitchen for the pad of paper. This could be kind of fun.

Quickly, she shoved the movie selections back into the cupboard without bothering to put them all back in their proper cases, then headed to the office for her laptop.

At the kitchen table, Claire swirled the wine in her glass as she stared at the blank Word document, wondering if she could put her jumbled thoughts into some kind of order. Even if she came up with ideas, could she produce the necessary words and finished piece?

Her stomach fluttered.

Okay, first things first. She set the glass down and began typing. Adrenalin flowed through her, and in less than an hour she'd sketched out ideas for a dozen articles. She read back through each one, and made some adjustments, added a few notes. She'd concentrate on the lighter ones first. They'd be easiest. The ones about Ben would be more poignant, deeper, but also harder and more gut wrenching to write.

The one about Olivia's flip-flops and painted toes made her smile. She started there, tapping out a few ideas until she'd composed about ten paragraphs. By five o'clock she'd drafted two articles. Her writing was rusty, and she knew from past experience, she'd need to put the stories away for a bit then come back to edit and re-write with fresh eyes.

With a sense of accomplishment, she finished her wine then headed to her bedroom to pick out something fun to wear to book club.

Chapter Nineteen

Claire licked the excess frosting from her finger then picked up the phone.

"Hey."

"Hey, yourself," Mary said. "What are you doing?"

"Cutting lemon squares."

There was a pause before Mary answered. "Really? Dare I hope that means you're coming to book club tonight?"

"It's a possibility."

"I'll pick you up."

"It's three blocks away. I think I can manage to get there."

"I know, but you could also manage not to. I really want you to come. So does everyone else."

Claire considered it. If she wasn't driving, she wouldn't have to give any thought to the number of times her wine glass was refilled. That was appealing.

"Fine. Pick me up at ten 'til. But I didn't read the book. Hell, I don't even remember the title."

"Doesn't matter. You know we'll spend more time catching up than talking about the book, anyway. It'll be good for you."

At seven o'clock Mary pushed through the door of Jane's house in front of Claire. She latched onto Claire's arm and sang out, "Look who I've got. And she's not even handcuffed."

A chorus of greetings rang through the room, and several women crowded around to give Claire a hug.

"It's about time," Jane said. "Let me have that stuff, and I'll grab you a glass."

Claire relinquished the bottle of wine, but followed Jane into the kitchen with the tray.

"Just set those on the table," Jane said. "But then come back here for a minute."

Annie Jennings sidled up to the table. "Oh, my gosh. I finally get to taste the famous lemon bars I've heard so much about."

She was the newest member of the group, and the one Claire knew the least.

Claire smiled and offered the tray before she set it down. She watched Annie snatch up a square and take a bite.

"Oh, yum. This is wonderful."

"Help yourselves," Claire called out, turning back to the kitchen.

Jane gave her a quick squeeze. "So glad you're here. And you've been baking. Guess it's our lucky night."

"Figured I'd better show up with something since I didn't bother to do any reading."

"Honey, you show up with goodies and booze, and nobody gives a damn about a book." Jane handed her a glass of wine. "Here you go. And speaking of books, here's to a new chapter in yours." She raised her glass and tapped it against Claire's. Then she leaned in close. "I heard the latest. You doing all right?"

Claire nodded. "It's exactly what I expected."

"I know, but still . . . Come on. Grab some snacks and find a seat."

Claire rearranged a pillow and settled into a cushy armchair. It was a good crowd tonight, with all the regulars plus a few others. She sipped her wine and listened to the multiple conversations going in the room – kids, grandkids, home repairs. The usual.

179

It took only a few minutes for the conversation to turn to Stan.

"Boy, is he going to have his hands full," Kelly said.

"Yeah, and his pockets empty," Dana added with a laugh.

"Good thing her kids don't go to school in Whitfield. I hear she's Miss PTA over in Paxton, wants to run every little thing. Or at least have a hand in it."

"Yes, for sure. We don't want her over here. Paxton can keep that white trash."

Annie gave a little laugh. "Oh, come on. Being involved in PTA, even if it's a little over the top, doesn't make her white trash."

Eight sets of eyes, including Claire's, stared at her.

"But sleeping with the boss knowing full well he's a married man, certainly does," Claire said evenly.

"Not to mention being a home-wrecker," Dana added. "Definite trash."

"Yeah, now we know how she manages to get all that time off for PTA and school events," Kelly said. "Special favors."

Susie picked up her book from the coffee table. "I think that's my cue to get started. I did some research on the author. Sounds like an ordinary gal. She could've been one of us."

While the others began discussing the book, Claire's thoughts remained firmly fixed on the earlier conversation. Stan's mistress. Was she trash or just another mom trying to be involved in her kids' lives and education? Just like the rest of them had been. As a single mom, maybe she was over-compensating.

She wondered if Annie knew her personally. Of course the woman would have friends. Not everyone would dislike her. Even Claire hadn't disliked her when they first met during the hiring process, back when Claire had some involvement in the business. She hadn't been Claire's first choice, but she'd been Stan's for sure.

He thought she was more friendly and would establish better rapport with the tenants than the other candidate they'd considered.

Had he been attracted to her even then? Claire couldn't excuse the fact that Kristen had allowed herself to be the other woman, had obviously made sure Stan knew she was available, but a home wrecker? Had she wrecked their marriage, or had it already been coming apart? It'd been damaged by Ben's death, without question. But as she thought back, Claire admitted there'd been distance between she and Stan even before. Stan had been spending more time working, less time at home. Less time with her. Kristen had worked for Stan for six years. Their affair could've been going on much longer than Claire originally thought. But she hadn't been paying attention. Never imagined it was necessary.

Claire looked up when Jane appeared in front of her. "Thanks," she whispered as her friend refilled her glass. Claire saw the nervous glances that flickered her direction. They were probably all afraid she was going to crack. With effort, she smiled and stood, and made her way to the dining room for munchies. While she filled her plate, Mary nudged her.

"You okay?"

Claire popped an olive into her mouth and nodded. "I'm perfectly fine. Stop worrying." A giggle bubbled up, and Claire leaned into Mary. "I bet Annie thought she was about to be burned at the stake there for a minute."

"I would've lighted the match," Mary whispered.

Claire grinned.

When the conversation about the book started to wind down, Claire sat forward and clapped her hands together. "Okay, ladies, I have a proposition."

All heads snapped her direction.

"Who's up for a little vacation? I need to get out of here, and I need a buddy or two to go with. Anybody up for a girls' getaway?"

She took a sip of wine and cast her gaze around the circle of women. There were a few nods, but several frowns and shaking heads.

"Oh, man, that's a great idea. I'd love to," Kelly said. "But my summer is totally booked."

"Same," Susie said. "And we just had to replace our air conditioning, so I know Carl's not going to want to spend any more money."

"What were you thinking? End of summer?" Jane asked.

"I'm thinking anytime, anyplace. Next week, next month . . . overseas, a cruise, Hawaii. My only requirement is that I get to relax and be waited on."

"Amen, to that," Susie said.

Jane gave a rueful smile. "It's probably too late for this year, hon, but we could look into planning something for next summer. We've talked for years about doing something after all the kids were out of school, and we never got around to it."

Claire smiled, but her spirits fell. "Boy, that's a lot of buts," she said, managing a short laugh.

"No time, no money," Dana said, a wistfulness to her voice.

Guilt washed over Claire. Maybe she should've contacted people individually. She'd suspected from the beginning that Dana wouldn't be able to do anything. Still, Dana wouldn't have wanted to be excluded from the invitation, either.

"All right, let's think about next year, then," Claire said, trying to sound upbeat. "Dana, maybe that'll give you time to save up, and you can get your vacation request in early."

"Do we need to make a pact?" Mary asked. "What's it gonna be? Spit, blood, first born?"

They all laughed and joked at that, but a wave of sadness hit Claire. She loved these women, but she might have to find some new friends. Friends who were available, who had a similar lifestyle. Similar issues. She and Stan had taken vacations with Grant and Mary several times. They'd been camping together, and had gone to the lake regularly. They'd been to Hawaii together. Now, Grant and Mary would go by themselves, or find another couple. She was the odd one out.

Summer was more than half over and she hadn't been invited to one dinner party or cocktail party by the pool. She didn't fit in anymore.

Her thoughts drifted to the lake. Lena could introduce her to more of the locals. The people out there generally had time on their hands. Elise had suggested she host a get-together. Maybe she could make a few friends that way.

Mary interrupted her thoughts. "You ready?"

Claire picked up her purse. "Sure." She waved at the group, and gave Jane a hug.

She sank into Mary's car with a sigh.

"So you're thinking you want to go someplace besides the lake?" Mary asked.

Claire turned. "The lake house isn't really a getaway for me anymore, Mare. It might as well be haunted."

"Listen, I want to go somewhere, as soon as I find four or five days in a row when someone doesn't need me for something."

"That's the difference, of course."

"Okay, stop right there. I know you have a million and one reasons to feel down, Claire. But none of them are a reason to feel bad about yourself. Did you have any fun tonight?"

"Sure." A little.

"All right, then. You need to focus on that. And getting out more. Doing things. What are you doing tomorrow?"

"No big plans."

"Let's go have lunch. It's been a while. In fact, I'm working at the food pantry ten to noon. Why don't you come with me, then we can have lunch after that?"

Out and about two days in a row? Could she even be presentable by ten in the morning these days? Doubtful.

But lunch would give her a chance to bounce her idea off of Mary.

"All right. I have something I want your opinion on anyway. But let's decide on lunch. If I feel like it, I may come to the church. Otherwise, I'll meet you at twelve fifteen. And don't call me. I don't want to be hassled."

"God, you're testy these days. Fine. Want to say Hannah's? I think they're doing that cherry cream pie you like this month. You know, you ought to sell desserts to them."

Claire rolled her eyes. Everyone had an idea what she *ought* to do.

Mary pulled the car into the driveway. "Meet me tomorrow, at least for lunch. It's not good for you to spend so much time home alone. I bet you'll feel better and have more energy if you start doing more."

"Easier said than done. I still gotta find the energy to do the stuff."

"Well, if it wears you out to have lunch, you can always go home and take a nap afterward, you know."

"That's right," Claire said as she got out of the car. "Lucky me. I can do whatever I want." She snapped the door shut with a toss of her hip.

Chapter Twenty

At eleven o'clock Claire pushed through the back door of the church and made her way to the food pantry the Presbyterians operated there. Penny, the long-time director, looked up from her desk.

"Well, Claire Stapleton. If you aren't a sight for sore eyes. Mary mentioned you might be in this morning. It's good to see you, honey."

"Not too late to put me to work, I hope."

Penny's loud cackle rang out. "Lordy, that'll be the day. Get on in here, and I'll find you a job. Mary's with a client right now."

Claire stocked shelves until Mary hustled into the backroom. "Hey, you. I'm impressed. Dressed and everything."

Claire shooed her away when she pretended to look her up and down.

"Earrings, too? I might faint."

"Yeah, yeah. Get over it."

Mary laughed, and gave Claire's arm a squeeze. "Glad you're here."

They worked together for a few minutes until Penny poked her head in the doorway. "Who wants a customer?" she whispered.

Mary nodded at Claire. "Why don't you go?"

Penny handed Claire a clipboard, and she greeted the pregnant mother, Danita, who stood just inside the doors with a toddler on a hip, and a young girl hanging onto her hand.

She checked Danita in and grabbed a cart, then waited while the young woman wrestled the toddler into the seat at the front of the cart. He wore only a pair of shorts. No shirt, and no shoes. The girl walked shyly behind her mom, sucking her thumb as they moved down the aisles. Claire smiled, but didn't try to cajole the kids with silly talk. Instead, she picked up two boxes of animal crackers and held them out to the children. Danita gave her a grateful smile, and prompted the children to say "thank you."

Claire couldn't help wondering about the family as they strolled among the shelves of food. Danita wore no wedding ring, but maybe they simply couldn't afford one. Was her husband, or the father of her children, around? Did he work and try to provide for them, or had he taken off and left them to fend for themselves? Did she work? Multiple jobs? Claire couldn't ask, of course. She nodded politely when Danita made her selections, and put a box of cereal into the cart.

For just a moment, Claire's own struggles seemed small and distant. Her children hadn't been hungry a day in their lives. They'd had more than they needed. Yes, she'd been humiliated during the ordeal with Ray, but it was over and done with. She didn't have the bi-weekly embarrassment of visits to the food pantry. She wasn't living day to day wondering how she could scrape by.

And Danita wasn't the only one. The food pantry didn't lack customers. Claire thought about that for a minute. Maybe there was a story there, something she could write about in one of her columns.

She helped Danita load the groceries into small bags, then with a quick glance around, she grabbed her wallet from her purse under the desk before helping the young woman to her car. While Danita dealt with the kids, Claire quickly fished a couple of bills out of her wallet. When Danita turned and mumbled a soft "thank you," Claire pressed the bills into her hand.

Danita looked down, then quickly back at Claire, her eyes wide. "Oh, no, ma'am, I can't take this." She shook her head, but Claire saw the tears welling in the girl's eyes.

She took her hand, and closed it around the bills. "It's yours. I'm not taking it back. Please. Take the kids out for pizza, or go to a movie. Whatever you want. It's a gift."

Claire turned and hurried back inside before Danita could object any further.

**

Claire and Mary settled into a small booth at Hannah's Café, a quaint Main Street restaurant that was nearly as old as the town itself, and decorated with old photographs and framed newspaper clippings to prove it. Named for its original owner and chef, Hannah's was like a miniature Whitfield museum.

These days, the third generation ran the restaurant, and the menu offered more contemporary fare with a bent toward healthy eating, which suited Claire. But the cakes and pies remained its most valuable asset, and even folks from neighboring towns came regularly to pay homage.

Claire twisted in her seat to glance at the specials board. Sure enough, cherry cream pie with walnuts made the list. She'd definitely be indulging.

She turned back and looked at Mary. "What are you grinning about?"

"You," Mary said. "You're practically drooling."

"Am not."

Mary laughed. "I'm glad you came today. I know it takes effort, but it's good to see you out." She leaned forward. "You're starting to look like yourself."

"I'm assuming that's a compliment," Claire drawled.

187

"It is, and you know how stingy I am with those."

They ordered drinks and salads, and when the waitress left, Mary pounced.

"Okay, what's this idea you wanted to bounce off of me?"

Claire sucked in her breath. "This is just between you and me, okay?"

"Okay, I promise. What?"

Her words came out in a rush. "I'm thinking about calling Lou at the Weekly and seeing if he'll publish some articles, like a column."

Mary's forehead crinkled. "What kind of articles?"

"Stories about this and that. Raising kids, grandkids, small town life."

"You mean you want to write for the newspaper?"

Claire picked up the glass the waitress had just left, and took a gulp of iced tea. "Yes. I've made a list of ideas, and I wrote two articles. Will you look at them?"

"Of course," Mary practically screeched. "Oh, my gosh. You've already written two articles? Do you have them with you?"

While the waitress set their salads in front of them, Claire turned to her purse and pulled out the papers she'd printed.

With flutters in her stomach, she handed them to Mary.

Claire picked up her fork, and bit off a cucumber, but Mary unfolded the papers. "You don't have to read them right now," Claire told her.

"I want to. I can eat and read at the same time."

So much for conversation. Claire gave the salad her full attention, trying not to wonder what was going through Mary's mind while she read what Claire had written.

Her head snapped up, though, when Mary burst out laughing.

"Claire, this is hilarious. I mean it. You're good at this."

188

Claire smiled, and breathed a sigh of relief. Of course Mary was her friend, and would never tell her the writing stunk, but she knew Mary's laugh, and that one was for real. A warm glow settled over her. Maybe she could do this.

Mary finished the first article, and took a couple of bites of her salad, then started on the second page. Claire watched her eyes scan the paper, saw Mary's smile.

"Aww. This one is really sweet," Mary said after a few more minutes. "I like them both, and they show a nice range. The one about the uses for kitchen utensils other than cooking is funny, and the one about Olivia's toenails and flip-flops is adorable."

"You think anyone would read them?"

"Absolutely. And they'll talk about them, and that'll sell newspapers, which will make Lou money, and make him happy. You've got to do this, Claire." She flailed her hands in the air. "Call him today. As soon as you get home. No. Better yet, skip the nap, and go straight over to his office."

"Jeez, would you take a breath? You know, I appreciate your enthusiasm, but I wish you weren't quite so desperately excited. I'm not even sure I can do it long-term. I mean, these two came together pretty easily, but the well could dry up after a couple of months, you know."

"And I could get run over by a truck when I leave the restaurant, but that doesn't mean I'm staying here forever. Come on. You've got to give it a shot. What harm could it do?"

✳✳

The following week, Claire nearly pushed Mary through the door of Hannah's. Her hands shook, and she could hardly keep a straight face.

"What is your rush?" Mary asked.

"I have something to show you."

She tossed her purse on a chair, then turned to the waitress. "We'll both have your house Chardonnay."

"You're ordering me a drink?"

"That's right. I am. We're celebrating."

"Uh-huh. Want to let me in on the secret?"

Claire grinned, and pulled a sheet of newspaper from her bag. She leaned forward and glanced around at the nearby tables. "This is hot off the press," she whispered, handing the paper to Mary. "It'll be out tomorrow."

Mary shot her a questioning look, and slipped on her reading glasses. It was only a second before she gasped, and her mouth dropped open.

"Oh, my gosh. Claire! I know you said he wanted them, but already? This is so exciting."

Claire laughed. "Can you believe it? Lou was dying for some new material. After I went to see him, he practically begged me to go home and write a dozen more."

Mary jumped up from her chair and pulled Claire into a hug, half laughing, half crying. "I'm so proud of you for doing this. I mean it. Good for you."

The waitress delivered their wine, and they both lifted their glass in the air.

"To my friend, the columnist and celebrity," Mary said.

Claire clinked her glass. "All right, now. Don't get carried away."

"It's a great picture of you. Who took that?"

"Lou took it right there in his office."

"Have you told Elise?"

"No. It all happened so fast. I thought I'd wait and send her a copy of the paper."

"Oh, she'll love it. You should throw a party, Claire. I mean it. Let's have some fun."

Chapter Twenty-One

Claire read through her notes while her fingers hovered above the keyboard. Now that the articles were expected, nerves knotted her stomach when she sat down to write. Each time, she had to convince herself to relax and let the thoughts and words flow. It always took a few minutes for that to happen.

Both of the columns published so far had been well-received, and had put Claire in the spotlight. She didn't exactly love that, but at least it gave people something to talk about other than her divorce. Something good, for a change.

She took a sip of wine as her cell phone rang through the silence. She dug it out of her purse and checked the number. Mary.

"Hi there."

"Hey, where are you?"

Claire turned her full attention to the call, a little bump in her heart rate. Something in Mary's voice . . . "I'm home. What's up?"

"I have some news. Are you sitting down?"

"Mary, just tell me. What's going on?"

"I heard Stan's looking at houses."

Claire frowned. So what? The less she knew about his new home and life, the better. She wedged the phone between her ear and shoulder while she picked up her notes.

"Hmmm. Well, I suppose they'll need a place to live."

"But here? Really. I expected him to have more decency."

Claire's blood ran cold, and she slapped the papers onto the table. "What do you mean?"

"They're looking at the Henderson place."

Her friend's voice sounded distant, and Claire strained against the phone. She could hardly breathe.

"Mary, what are you talking about?"

"I heard they're thinking about buying Henderson's old place."

Dizziness roared through her head, and Claire grabbed the table to steady herself. "Just a minute," Claire croaked.

She dropped the phone and doubled over as Mary's words sank in. This couldn't be happening. No, no, no. Not now. She was just starting to feel almost normal again. Trying to put some kind of life together.

Her stomach rolled, and she clutched the chair, sinking to her knees while sobs shuddered through her. Old place? "Old place?" she screamed into the emptiness. The Henderson place was the newest, biggest house in town. By the time the Hendersons had finished it, the economy had tanked, and they couldn't afford it. Never even lived in the house.

Oh, God, she could see the roof and chimneys from her back patio. That bastard. *The nerve.*

She beat her fist against the chair for a few moments before she remembered she'd left Mary dangling on the line. Of course the line was dead by the time she picked up again. She pushed herself upright and went to the kitchen for ice water. Wiping her mouth, she started to call back, but the doorbell interrupted her.

"Claire? Claire, are you all right? Open up. It's me." The door rattled under Mary's assault.

192

With weariness in every muscle, Claire opened the door, and leaned against it.

"You want in, or what?"

"Claire, you scared the hell out of me. Are you okay?"

"Of course I'm okay. Why wouldn't I be?"

Mary threw her arm around Claire's shoulder. "Listen, woman. Don't let that son of a bitch get you down. We'll get through it."

"We? Look, Mary, you don't have to babysit me. You've got your own life to deal with without adding me to into the mix."

"Hey, I'm in this boat with you, and I'm not gonna let it sink. Come on, sit down. You got any iced tea made?"

Claire shook her head, and followed Mary into the living room. "No. I need something a little stronger than iced tea these days."

Mary turned sharply. "Claire, you are not going to let that bastard get the best of you."

Claire snorted. "Too late. He already did. Gave him the best years of my life. For nothing." She slumped onto the sofa while Mary banged around in the kitchen.

"Here," Mary said, shoving a wine glass at her. "This'll work for now, but I'm brewing you some tea. Maybe a little caffeine will get you revved up."

Claire sipped the wine and ran a hand through her hair. Confused, she looked at her friend. "Why in the world would I need to get revved up?"

"So you can fight back, of course. Come on, Claire. What are you going to do? We can't let him and that floozy move into the neighborhood. What in God's name are they thinking?"

Slowly, Claire shook her head. "I can't imagine. But there's nothing I can do about it. If they've got the money, they can buy whatever house they choose. The question is why would they want to move here? If he wants a new life, why would he want to be so close to me? It doesn't make sense."

"It's downright mean and heartless," Mary said. "What he needs is a good kick in the ass, and the first chance I get, I'm telling him so."

Like a bolt of lightning, realization blasted Claire in the face. She fought for breath, feeling as if something, or someone, was squeezing the life out of her. *Oh, my God. It made perfect sense.*

Claire raised heavy eyes to her friend. "He wants to run me off. To force me out. It's his town, you know." She'd moved there for him. Whitfield was his hometown, not hers. Many of their friends started out as his buddies. She shook her head. Should've seen it coming.

"I can't stay here," she whispered. "Can you imagine? I'll run into them everywhere . . . the Post Office, the bank, the grocery store." She choked on a sob. "Oh, God."

Mary grabbed her hand. "You cannot let them run you out of your home. This is *your* home, too. *Your* town."

She shook her head, tears burning her eyes as it all became clear. "So I got the house. A house I can't live in. That's why he gave it to me so easily. He made the judge think he was being kind and generous, but he knew all along. He knew I couldn't stay here if he moved in with his mistress."

Her friend's face twisted, and she brushed away her own tears. "What about Wichita? Elise is there. You'd get to see the kids more often."

Claire rolled her eyes. "Mary Logan, it's me you're talking to. You know very well my daughter doesn't want me following her around."

She took a long sip of her wine, leaning back against the sofa. She didn't understand the malice of Stan's actions. Was he trying to get back at her for the

194

thing with Ray? Was it something from years ago? How could a man who'd once loved her be so hateful?

A thousand memories flashed through her mind. Their wedding, vacations, playing with kids in the backyard. They'd had happy times. Lots of them, in fact. So much history . . . gone.

"I can't fight them, Mary. I just don't have the strength. Is it for sure? Who'd you hear it from?"

"Susie called me. I guess they're working with another realtor in her office. Said the guy was beside himself ecstatic over it, and telling everyone."

"I'm sure. That thing's been on the market more than a year."

"I do not want to see that bitch move into this town," Mary said, slamming a fist into her hand.

Claire sat up, and put a hand on Mary's shoulder. "I don't either, but I'd bet my last dollar it's going to happen. I can see it now."

With a heavy heart, she got up and poured Mary a glass of wine. "Here. You might need this."

**

The next day, the news appeared to be official. Susie called, speaking in hushed tones. "Claire, I'm so sorry. I did everything I could think of to steer Hal to some other properties. I guess they were adamant about being in Whitfield. If it hadn't happened so fast, we could've unleashed an army of termites over there or something."

Claire laughed. "That's an excellent idea, Susie. It's not too late, you know. Mechanical inspections, and all. What's the penalty for arson these days?"

But she knew as she spoke and tears welled in her eyes that the jig was up. Her time in Whitfield had come to a close.

She ended the call, but kept her hand clenched around the phone. It was all she could do to keep from picking up her computer and smashing it to the floor.

195

No way could she write her column now. Of course she could write from a distance. From anywhere, really. But she could not bare her soul and tell her stories in front of Stan's new wife. Couldn't share her thoughts and recipes and memories with that woman. Absolutely not.

"Damn them," she screamed. "What the hell am I supposed to do?" Doubled over, she rested her arms and head against the table. "I don't know what to do."

**

The lake house was the only solution. And she had to get there fast – before Stan's moving van came rolling into town. She'd seen one of the inspectors on the roof of the new house yesterday morning while she sat on the patio having coffee. Heard them yelling at each other. So, that's how it would be. If she stayed, she'd be able to hear the kids out in the yard, hear parties and music. That was unacceptable.

On autopilot Claire snatched clothes from hangers and filled her suitcases. This time, she packed for an extended stay.

Mary folded clothes as Claire tossed them to her. They hardly spoke at all. Claire knew she'd break down if she talked about it.

"What about valuables, Claire? Are you taking your jewelry? Putting it in a safe deposit box? Do you want me to keep anything?"

"There's no point putting things in a safe deposit box in a town I don't live in. I'll take it with me."

"Okay," Mary said, her voice cracking.

Claire looked at her friend. "I'll be back to visit, you know."

"Why don't you wait, Claire? Next weekend is Labor Day, and you hate to be at the lake then."

"I know, but I don't want to be here when they move in. I just can't. I'll go down to the lake and see what it's like. If I can't stand it, I can always come back for the holiday. I could stop in Oakmont for food and not have to leave the house."

"You could stay with me."

Claire met Mary's eyes then, and hot tears welled.

"I hate, hate, hate this," Mary wailed.

"Don't start," Claire said, dragging a laundry basket full of clothes out of the closet.

"Are you going to leave all the utilities on?"

"For now, I'm leaving everything on. I'll have to come back to finish moving or put the house up for sale, but I can't deal with all of that right now. Just drive by every once in a while, would you?"

"Sure. I'll keep an eye on it."

Claire turned away, unable to respond around the lump in her throat. What did it matter? She couldn't live in the house anymore, but would she ever be able to part with it?

197

Chapter Twenty-Two

When a loud boat cruised by for the third time, its motor belching into the air, Claire snapped her book shut. *Enough.*

She made up her mind. While other people headed to the lake in droves for a final fling, Claire would flee back to Whitfield. She'd only been at the lake for a few days, but even around her area, the traffic was bad both on the roads and on the water. Boats and people screamed by at all hours of the day and night.

Labor Day weekend was hands-down the worst weekend at the lake. People got plain stupid on that last weekend of summer. The traffic and noise escalated, and there were always accidents.

She chewed her lip a moment before dragging the suitcase out of the closet. Surely if she went back for the holiday weekend, she could avoid seeing Stan and his new family. She hadn't made any plans for selling the house, but she knew it was only a matter of time. Whitfield simply wasn't big enough for three Mrs. Stapletons.

**

"Here we go again, Reg," Claire said, loading the car for the return trip. "Next time we'll stay put for a while, I promise."

Even though she drove against the swell of traffic, it took thirty minutes longer than usual to get to

Whitfield. Claire glanced toward Stan's new place, but didn't drive down the street. Her news reports had confirmed a moving van had already been there. So. They should be getting settled in.

And she'd be holing up at home with Mary and any other friends who might be available. Grant had graciously agreed to give Mary the night off from any responsibilities.

Claire fixed chicken salad on a bed of spinach for the two of them for dinner.

"That was delicious," Mary said. "I can't believe you just whipped that up this afternoon."

"Didn't have anything else to do."

"What's for dessert?"

"Whatever you brought," Claire said.

"Oh, come on. No dessert?"

Claire shook her head. "Jeez, do I have to do everything?"

"Let's go get some ice cream."

"I don't need dessert."

"Of course not, but deep down inside you desperately want it. Come on, I'm buying."

Claire buckled her seatbelt then remembered she'd pledged to avoid the grocery store this weekend. "Where are we going?"

"The store, of course."

She sucked in her breath, and reached for the door handle. "No. I'd rather not. Why don't you go and pick something out? I'll stay here."

But Mary was already backing the car out of the driveway. "Claire, come on. It'll just take a minute. And we might see some other junk we need for movie night."

**

"Which one has more fat?" Mary asked.

199

Claire rolled her eyes then pretended to read the labels. "Let's see, one is bad for you and the other is even worse. Take your pick.

"Oh, what the hell." She dumped both caramel swirl and chocolate almond ice cream into the cart, startled when she heard a shriek down the aisle.

"Grammy!"

Automatically, she turned. And saw Olivia running toward her. Behind Olivia, Stan's wife stood frozen like the box of Popsicles in her hands.

Claire's face flashed white hot. What in the world was her granddaughter doing there? With Kristen? What the hell? A sharp pang hit her in the stomach, and she clutched at the shopping cart. Elise had left Olivia in the care of Stan's new wife?

She hugged Olivia to her for a moment, while she caught her breath and tried to speak calmly. "Olivia, honey. What are you doing here?"

"Visiting Grandpa."

She glared in Kristen's direction. "Where's your mom, sweetie?"

"Ar-kan-sas," Olivia said, enunciating each syllable in a silly voice.

"Where's Andy?"

"In the car."

Claire gasped and her gaze snapped to Kristen, still standing at the other end of the aisle, watching. "You left your brother in the car alone?" She took Olivia's hand and began marching down the aisle. "Are you crazy?" The last question was directed at the idiot woman her ex-husband had married. Who would leave a three-year-old in the car?

Kristen took a step forward, but avoided making eye contact with Claire. "He's waiting in the car with my son." She held her hand out toward Olivia. "Come on, Olivia. We'd better go. Remember, we were supposed to hurry."

200

Olivia hesitated. "Grammy, can I come to your house?"

Claire smiled with trembling lips. *Thank you, Olivia.* She wanted to snatch her granddaughter up and twirl her around. She swallowed hard, hoping her voice would sound steady. "Of course you can, sweetie. I'd love it. Just tell Grandpa, okay?" But she knew the request would fall on deaf ears.

"Okay."

Claire squeezed Olivia in a hug then sent Kristen a cool glare.

"Bye, Grammy." Olivia waved then followed behind Kristen, the woman's streaked blonde hair, cut-off jeans and too-tight tank top labeling her the trashy bitch she was.

Claire burned inside. She could hardly breathe.

Mary moved in close. "It's okay, Claire. Keep it together."

Claire shook her head as tears threatened.

Mary grabbed the cart and Claire's arm, steering her in the opposite direction. "Come on. This is enough junk. Let's get out of here."

"Yes," Claire's voice rose, and she didn't care if it carried to the checkout lanes. In fact, she hoped it did. "Lots of junk in this place. And an awful lot of trash, too."

In the car, Claire stared out the window, her thoughts assaulting her. Stan had only been remarried a matter of weeks, and already Elise had the kids staying with them. How was that possible? And why? What the hell were they doing in Arkansas?

"Your place or mine?" Mary asked, interrupting Claire's mental diatribe.

She shook her head. "Take me home. I need to call Elise."

Mary reached over and placed a hand on Claire's arm. "Claire, maybe you should wait until you've calmed down a bit. You don't know the circumstances."

Claire pulled her arm away. "Which is exactly why I need to call. I want to know what the hell is going on."

"But you're angry and hurt. That's not a recipe for a good conversation."

Claire's voice broke. "I don't care. God, how could she? How could she leave the kids with them?" She turned toward Mary, and hollered in disbelief. "I just ran into my granddaughter with my husband's mistress."

"I know, honey. I know. But maybe it was a last-minute thing, Claire. I'm sure there's some reason. Listen, let's go to your place and have some ice cream then you can give her a call."

Inside the house, Claire threw her bag on the counter and pulled two wine glasses out of the cupboard. She filled them both and handed one to Mary, then snatched the phone from its cradle.

"Claire!" Mary's voice was sharp. "Can't you wait five damn minutes?"

"No." With a clenched jaw, she punched in Elise's cell number.

"Hey, Mom," Elise's voice came on the line.

"Hi. What's going on? I hear you're in Arkansas."

Silence filled the air for several seconds. Claire ground her teeth while she waited.

"Um, yeah. We are. What are you up to?"

"What am I up to? I'm trying to recover from what I just witnessed at the grocery store, hoping you've got a good explanation."

"Mom, what are you talking about?"

"I ran into Olivia at the grocery store with your father's whore. You want to explain that to me?"

"What? I thought you were at the lake . . ."

"So you thought if I was at the lake it'd be all right to leave your kids with that bitch? You never want to leave the kids with me, but you'll leave them with an adulteress and a cheat? I cannot believe you. And for your information, she left Andy in the car. What are you doing in Arkansas, anyway?"

She heard the deep intake of breath before Elise answered.

"Brian and I are in Eureka Springs. We decided to take a little get-away for our anniversary. It was a last-minute thing. Dad and Kristen were up last weekend, and they offered, so–"

"Why didn't you call me?"

"I don't get it, Mom. Why would I need to call you?"

"To stay with the kids!"

"Mother, we've been through this before. I don't feel comfortable leaving the kids with you, not when you're smoking. And possibly drinking. I can't do it."

"And you couldn't have warned me? Do you have any idea what a shock it was for me to run into them in town? I can't believe you'd do this to me."

"I wasn't trying to do anything to you, Mom." Elise's voice rose. "I thought you were at the lake. And I told you at the very beginning of this I wasn't taking sides. Did you think I'd never see Dad again?"

"Well, I can't imagine why you'd want your children around him. Not exactly a stellar role model. You know, Olivia asked if she could come to my house."

"That's fine. On Monday before we head back we could stop by for a little while."

"I'm not interested in being an obligatory stop you have to make, Elise."

"That is not what I said, Mom. If we'd known you were there, we would've planned to see you in advance. But if you're going to be mad and unreasonable, we'll skip it. I don't need to expose the kids to that, either."

"Fine, then maybe you shouldn't bother."

Claire disconnected and tossed back a gulp of wine, then met Mary's eyes.

"Oh, Claire. That didn't sound good."

"Stan and Kristen were in Wichita last weekend, I guess making introductions. Get that. A week later, and they're leaving my grandkids with them." Claire's voice shook. "She's so particular about everything when it comes to her kids, but she'll leave them with people like that. Makes no sense."

"No, it doesn't, so don't beat yourself up trying to figure it out. It's obvious Olivia would rather be with you. Her face lit up when she saw you in the store, you know."

Claire reached for a cigarette. "Damn right."

Her chest heaving, she whirled back into the kitchen and pulled the ice cream they'd bought out of the freezer. "Some of each?" she asked Mary.

"And plenty of it."

The ice cream helped, and so did spending five hours with her best friend. But Mary left at midnight, and then a heavy silence pressed around Claire. She dropped to the floor and let the tears roll, sobbing as resentment and desolation flooded through her.

Chapter Twenty-Three

For the second time Elise listened to her mother's story of the deer on the dock and the fox on the deck. She listened again to how Reggie had come face to face with a squirrel in the window, and how the two had yacked at each other for a full ten minutes.

"That's cute, Mom," she said, indulging her, but cringing inside. Her mother had refused to talk of anything significant since her blow-up over Labor Day. She'd simply withdrawn behind a façade of pretense. "You should take some pictures. Sounds like you've had some great wildlife encounters this year."

When Elise finally ended the call, she cradled the phone against her chest for a moment.

"Now what?" Brian asked, coming into the kitchen.

She shook her head. "Mom. She's getting worse. I'm sure she's drinking. Her words were slurred, and she kept repeating herself."

Brian folded his arms and leaned against the counter, regarding her. "You know, at some point you might have to intervene."

The words hit Elise like a punch in the gut. "What does that mean? Try to force her into therapy?" Her mother would never forgive her. "I can't do that. God, I'm tired of dealing with this. It's so frustrating. On one hand, I want to yank her up and tell her to get some big-girl panties on, but on the other hand, I understand she's suffering, and I'd like to help her. It's exhausting."

"Do you need to go down there?"

Elise held up her hands. "I really don't want to. I don't want her to be dependent on me, or think that every time she's down and starts drinking, I'm going to drop everything and run to her rescue. I can't do that."

Once again, she wished her brother were there to help. Their mother would listen to him. She'd snap out of it for him. Of course the truth was, she never would've gone so far over the edge in the first place if Ben were still there.

"Have you guys talked about Thanksgiving?" Brian asked. "The invite from Derek and Meredith included your mom, you know."

"Oh, boy. I don't know about that. Not sure I want to expose your family to my mother right now. And I doubt Mom would go, anyway." It'd be more fun for the kids if they got together with Brian's brother and his family, but more noise and commotion, which her mother wouldn't like. It was also possible she'd go to Whitfield to see friends instead.

"It's only a couple of weeks away. We'll need to give them an answer pretty soon."

And that would require another conversation with her mother. At a time when she was lucid and listening. Elise would have to call her from work mid-morning.

"Yeah. I'll talk to her about it."

**

Thanksgiving Day arrived cool and gray. But it was her mother's arrival that concerned Elise – and the fact that she was thirty minutes past her estimated target time. Surely she wouldn't pull another no-show. Not on Thanksgiving.

Brian's brother expected them around noon, with a plan to have dinner about one o'clock. She'd assigned her mother to bring some pop and a pie – things they could live without if she changed her mind at the last

206

minute. It'd taken three phone calls to convince her to come at all.

Elise brushed out her hair, and left it down, with just a headband to keep it back from her face. For her mother's benefit, she put on some make-up. One less thing for her to be grumpy about. The dinner was casual, but Elise knew her mother would be dressed up, so she put on a denim skirt with boots and an autumn-red sweater.

When a car door slammed outside, Elise hollered to the kids. "Okay, guys, Grammy's here, so we'll leave in a few minutes. Come say hello."

She opened the door, and stepped onto the porch. "Mom, do you need help with anything?" Her mother had refused to stay at the house, choosing to book a hotel room instead, so she wouldn't need to unload her suitcases.

Why was she walking in slow motion? "Mom?" Elise went down the steps to greet her. And stopped short. What the–? This was not right. Her mother looked as though she'd aged ten years in the last few months. Her hair was flat, and her eyes were dull. The pasty gray color of her skin matched the gloomy sky around her.

She took hold of her mother's arm. "What in the world is the matter, Mom? Are you sick?"

Her mother pursed her lips. "Of course I'm not sick. It's a long drive."

Elise caught a whiff of mint as her mother spoke. She'd obviously put a mint in her mouth as soon as she arrived to help clear her breath. From what? Cigarette smoke? Alcohol? Elise groaned inside. How could she take her mother to her in-laws' house in this condition? In her entire life, she'd never seen her mother so unkempt and weak. Instead of her usual stylish pumps or boots, she wore a pair of basic loafers, and her normal confident gait had been replaced by an unsteady shuffle.

Elise helped her up the stairs and into the house. "Do you need to freshen up before we go?"

"Yes."

Elise let go of her. "Okay, you do that, and I'll gather everyone up."

Oh, shit. Oh, shit. As Brian came down the stairs, Elise grabbed his arm and pulled him aside. "Mom looks like hell, and she's acting like she can hardly move. This is not going to be good."

He peered down the hall. "You think she should stay here?"

"I can't leave her by herself."

"Look, we gotta go. It'll be fine. All she has to do is sit around and eat."

"Why don't you go ahead and get the kids in the car, and pull into the driveway so she doesn't have to maneuver through the garage."

Five minutes later, when her mother still hadn't emerged from the bathroom, Elise knocked on the door. "Mom, you doing all right?"

"I'll be right out," came the raspy response.

She leaned against the wall, and rubbed her temples. This was so much worse than she expected.

An eternity later, the door opened, and her mother stepped out. She'd tried to fluff her hair up a bit, and was standing a little taller. A slight improvement. Elise put on a smile. "Okay, you ready? Where's your jacket?"

"Oh, let me get that."

She retrieved the leather jacket from the bathroom, then Elise helped her put it back on. It was like having another child.

"Come on. We're running late."

Elise held her mother's arm while she climbed into the car, then shook her head at Olivia, who watched wide-eyed. She knew her daughter was old enough and sharp enough to see that her grandmother was not herself.

208

"Oh, wait," her mother put a hand on the car door. "I need to get the pie."

Brian opened his door. "I'll get it."

"In the back seat," her mother said.

Elise shut the door then hurried to her mother's car with Brian. "I don't think I'd trust anything she made," she said.

Brian lifted a grocery bag from the floor of the backseat. "Looks like it's all store-bought."

"Good. Let's go."

Elise twisted her hands in her lap, and stared out the window, trying to keep tears of frustration in check.

"Grammy, do you want to read?"

Elise turned when Olivia spoke, and she watched her mother's glazed eyes settle on Olivia. She gave a half-hearted smile and patted Olivia's knee.

"Not right now, sweetie."

Olivia's eyes met Elise's, and Elise shot her what she hoped was a reassuring smile. "We won't be in the car very long, Livvy."

"Will they have coffee, or should we stop for some?" her mother asked suddenly.

"If they don't have any made, we can make a pot when we get there." And fast, Elise thought.

Elise hadn't briefed Derek and Meredith on the situation with her mother, and she saw the surprise register on their faces when everyone bustled into the house. They'd met before at weddings and funerals, and other family functions through the years, so even though they didn't know about the drinking, they knew something was wrong. Both of them turned worried frowns on Elise.

She ignored them, and steered her mother to the living room. "Here, Mom, why don't you have a seat, and I'll get some coffee started." She headed for the kitchen, with Meredith on her tail.

"Hey, would you mind making some coffee for Mom?" Elise whispered.

209

"Not at all." Meredith touched her arm. "Elise, is everything okay?"

Elise put up her hand. "No, but I can't talk about it right now. I'm sorry. I had no idea Mom was in such bad shape."

"Don't be sorry. Just tell us how we can help."

"I think some coffee will help. And just try to act normal."

But the day was far from normal. Her mother contributed nothing to the conversation through dinner, and barely interacted with anyone, including Olivia. Olivia had tried to engage her grandmother a couple of times, until Elise couldn't stand to see her rebuffed anymore. Finally, she pulled Olivia aside.

"Liv, leave Grammy alone for a little while. She's not feeling good today."

As soon as they'd all gathered around the table, they held hands while Derek said grace. Elise bit her lip until she tasted blood on her tongue. She wanted to shout and scream for God to intervene, to do something about her mother. But like her mother, she sat down to eat as if nothing was wrong.

Elise watched her mother pick at her food, lifting an occasional shaky forkful to her mouth. She'd taken only a small portion of turkey and potatoes and a little fruit salad. Hardly enough to keep anyone alive. How had it gotten so bad? Elise wondered if Mary knew. When was the last time her mother had interacted with anyone? Did Nathan ever check in on her?

Living by herself at the lake house obviously wasn't working. Elise would have to make some phone calls.

She refilled her mother's coffee mug, leaving plenty of room at the top for sloshing. "Mom, did you get enough to eat? Can I get you anything else?"

Dull eyes looked up at her. Her mother shook her head, then turned to their hostess. "It was a lovely dinner. Thank you."

210

Polite, dutiful and automatic. She said the right words, but Elise knew her mother was simply going through the motions. The rote words were delivered in monotone. Fear swept through her. She was losing her mother. Elise hurried back to the kitchen with the coffee pot, and swiped at the tears that escaped as she braced her arms against the sink, trying to catch her breath. A few moments later, Brian's strong hands squeezed her shoulders.

"Hey. Take it easy, hon."

"My mom is gone, Brian," Elise whispered, hands at her mouth. "She's completely lost it."

He pulled her into his arms, warm hands circling over her back. "Shhh. It'll be okay. Let's just get through another hour or so, then we can leave."

For the next two hours, they all pretended everything was perfectly fine. Her mother was the elephant in the living room, and they all danced around her. Derek built a fire in the fireplace, and turned the television on to one of the football games. That's what they did on Thanksgiving Day.

Elise watched in disbelief as her mother smoothed the crease in her slacks, drank coffee, and stared into space.

**

"Well, I think it's about time for a nap," her mother said when they were settled in the car.

"No! Don't want a nap," Andy wailed.

Elise turned. "Not you, silly boy. Grammy wants a nap." Although naps all around sounded like a fabulous idea.

"Why don't we drop you at the hotel, then we can swing back by to get you for supper later."

"No. I'll need my bags," her mother said.

"Okay, well, let's get the kids home, then I can take you over."

"I'll drive myself."

Elise decided not to push the issue in front of everyone else, but when Brian pulled into the garage, she helped her mother out, and scooted the kids on into the house.

Her mother headed straight for her car.

"Mom, wait. I'll take you."

"No. I want my own car."

"Why?"

"Because I don't want you to have to cart me back and forth, and I want to come and go when I please. I may not feel like having supper later."

"Mom, you didn't eat enough at lunch. Of course you'll need something else later."

"I have some snacks."

"That's not the same," her voice sharpened, and she clutched her mother's arm. "Did you bring alcohol? Is that why you want to stay at the hotel by yourself? So you can drink?"

Her mother yanked her arm away. "I told you why."

It was the most life she'd exhibited all day, and that in itself annoyed Elise. "I don't think you should be driving, Mom."

"You're being ridiculous. It's cold out here, and I want to go lie down."

Elise stared helplessly as her mother started the car and backed down the driveway. Then she marched inside the house and picked up the phone.

"What are you doing?" Brian asked.

"Calling Mary."

Brian reached out and closed his hand over hers, phone and all. "Babe, not now. Let's don't ruin someone else's holiday."

"I want to know how long it's been since she's seen Mom. And I want to know if she knows how bad it's gotten. Wouldn't you think she'd call me?"

"Not if she's protecting your mom."

"Protecting her from what?"

212

"From embarrassment. From your anger."

"Well, that's crazy. If somebody doesn't do something, Mom's going to get herself killed. It's a miracle she even made it here. And now she's going over to that hotel, and she's going to have a cigarette and start drinking. And if she passes out with a lighted cigarette, she could burn the whole place down. God, I cannot understand why she'd rather have a drink than a life."

Chapter Twenty-Four

Four hours was surely enough time for a nap, or a drink, or whatever kind of break her mother needed. Elise wandered away from the kitchen to place the call. But after she hung up, she slapped the phone onto the counter a little harder than she intended, and all eyes shifted to her.

"She's refusing to come over, and doesn't want us to pick her up."

"Maybe you should go anyway. Your mom kind of likes to be coaxed," Brian said.

"What am I supposed to do? Go over there and drag her out? I don't even know what room she's in, and hotels aren't allowed to give out that information. They'll call her room, but that's it."

"I bet she'd let you in, though, if they called and told her you were in the lobby. You know how she hates a scene."

Elise almost laughed at that. It used to be true, but these days she wasn't so sure. She doubted her mom would even bother to answer the phone.

With a resigned sigh, she lifted Andy to her hip. "Let's eat without her. We can have the leftovers Meredith gave us from this afternoon, then we can watch a movie."

"What about tomorrow? Think you guys'll go shopping?"

"Are you kidding? It's Black Friday. The way Mom's moving, we'd be trampled."

"Do you need to go? You usually get some good deals."

Elise shook her head. "I'm really not up for it. I don't think there are any deals out there I can't live without this year." The kids didn't need a thing, and would be happy with small gifts. She and Brian had already agreed to purchase a joint gift for the house, and she had an idea for her mother that would involve more time than money, and would only require a trip to a craft shop.

"Okay, well, I'd like to hit the gym for a while."

"Sure. That's fine. Let's see how Mom feels about brunch or lunch."

She reheated the food and set the table. Normally she asked Olivia to help set the table, but this evening she preferred the quiet of doing it herself. Worrying about her mother had sapped her energy. Only seven o'clock and she was already exhausted.

After dinner, she reached for the coffee pot. "Hey, hon, would you drink some coffee if I made it? I'm about to fall asleep."

"Nah, I don't need any. Just make some for yourself."

As Elise poured the water, an idea formed. Maybe she could go over to the hotel and convince her mom to come down to the lobby to have a cup of coffee. All of those hotels had free coffee available. Would she agree to talk one-on-one?

Once again, she lifted the phone and punched in her mother's cell number. It went to voicemail, so she tried again. On the fourth ring, her mother picked up.

"Hello, Elise."

She tried to make her voice upbeat, even though she heard the impatience in her mother's tone. "Hey, Mom. Had an idea. Want to meet me in the lobby for a cup of coffee?"

Her mother coughed. "No. I'm already in my pajamas. I'm not going out again."

"Well, I could bring a thermos. We could sit in your room and chat."

"You want to get in my room, is that it?"

Elise gasped, and her face warmed. "No, Mom. That isn't it. I'm worried about you."

"I'm perfectly fine. Now, I'm going to curl up with the book I brought until I fall asleep, and–"

"Don't turn off your phone, okay?"

"I'll leave it on, if you stop calling. For heaven's sake, you'll have the neighbors complaining."

Elise swallowed hard. Why had she even bothered? "Fine. I'll talk to you tomorrow."

An hour later, Elise cuddled up with Olivia, and held on a little tighter and a little longer than usual, stroking her soft curls while her thoughts strayed to her own mother. So many ups and downs and bumps along the way in their relationship. How would her relationship with Olivia evolve? She couldn't imagine having the same fights and tension that she had with her own mother.

Seemed they'd been in and out of sync forever, but things had taken a turn for the worse after she got married and had kids. Elise's life just didn't comply with her mother's vision and expectations. Her mother saw work as a dirty word, a sign that she didn't have the money to stay home with her kids. She didn't understand that Elise wanted a career. She enjoyed her job and even though it meant less time with the kids, it balanced her life.

"Mommy?"

"Hmmm?"

"Is Grammy going to die?"

Elise's heart slammed against her ribs. She sat up, and rested a hand against her daughter's cheek. "Oh, sweetie. I'm sorry you're worried about Grammy. No, I don't think she's going to die, but she's sick. She's having a hard time right now."

"Because Grandpa married Kristen?"

Elise sucked in her breath. Oh, boy. How to explain this? "That's part of it. But it's also because Uncle Ben died and she misses him, and because she moved away from her friends, and she's lonely. She's not taking good care of herself."

"Smoking is bad."

"Yes, and there are other things. She's not eating enough good food."

"Will she get better?"

Elise pulled Olivia into her arms. "I hope so."

"Do you miss Uncle Ben?"

That did it. Elise choked on a sob, and tears spilled from her eyes. "Yes, I do. Very much. He was a good guy. A lot of fun to be around." She paused a moment, catching her breath. "He was my little brother, just like Andy's your little brother."

Olivia nodded. Elise smiled as she swiped at the tears. At her age, Olivia probably couldn't imagine actually missing her younger brother.

"Try to go to sleep now, okay? We'll see Grammy again tomorrow and maybe she'll feel like reading or playing games with you."

Elise turned out the lamp, and closed the door, but instead of going back downstairs, she went to her room and flopped onto the bed. Would they really see her mother tomorrow, and was there any chance she'd be better?

**

The next morning, Elise waited until nine o'clock and after a full cup of strong Italian bold to call her mother.

"Hi, Mom, did you sleep well?"

Her mother cleared her throat and gave a cough. "Oh, fine."

"We're thinking about going out for brunch. Do you want to come over here or meet us someplace?" She wasn't even going to bother offering to pick her up. Waste of breath.

Her mother coughed another moment before responding. "I suppose that would be fine. What about that copper place? It's close, isn't it?"

"The Copper Kitchen? Yeah, it's right down the street from the hotel. Let's do that. Want to come over to the house for coffee first?"

"Oh, no. I'll need to get ready. I'll see you there."

"What time?

"Let's say eleven."

Really? Two hours to get ready? Elise shook her head as she agreed then ended the call. "I guess it *would* take that long if you moved in slow motion," she muttered.

She puttered around the kitchen and spent some time looking at the mountain of retail ads from the newspaper, forcing herself to wait until ten to call Mary.

Her mother's friend picked up right away.

"Hi, Mary, it's Elise."

"Oh, honey, is something wrong?"

Elise's breath caught in her throat. It spoke volumes that Mary's first reaction was to assume there was a problem.

"Something is very wrong, Mary." She couldn't keep the quiver from her voice. "Mom's here for the holiday, and I hardly even recognize her. She's like a zombie."

She heard the heavy sigh from Mary.

"I don't know what to tell you, Elise. This move to the lake has been hard on her."

"Well, what can we do about it? Do you have any idea what she's doing? Does she see anyone? Is she just holing up there all by herself every day?" Elise took a deep breath, and spoke the words she'd been afraid to say. "Mary, you realize Mom's drinking, right?"

218

The question hung in the air between them.

"It helps dull the pain," Mary said, finally. "Honestly, honey, the person you need to be talking to is your dad. Your mother was doing so much better, really starting to come around. She was excited about writing for the newspaper, then your dad got married and moved back to town, and ruined everything for her."

Accusation hardened Mary's words. Of course she'd taken sides against Dad. Elise waited a moment before answering.

"Mary, I understand. That wasn't ideal. But Dad's not making Mom drink. He's not the one buying the alcohol. No one's forcing that on her."

"But he's the one who told her she wasn't good enough anymore. He's the one who ran her out of her home and out of town."

"She didn't have to leave Whitfield. That was her choice."

Mary's voice rose. "Elise, I don't want to argue with you, but I'm telling you, your father has been mean and selfish. Moving into one of the fanciest houses in town practically in your mother's back yard, flaunting a new, younger wife. He's got two boys now. And your mom has none. Think about how much all of that hurts her. This is a small town, Elise. It's too small for both of them."

"Even if all that's true, she didn't have to move to the lake so far away from everyone."

It was another long pause before Mary spoke again.

"Well, honey, when I suggested she move to Wichita so she could be closer to you and the kids, she told me you wouldn't want her there."

Elise gasped. "What? That is not true. She never even mentioned it to me."

"Because she already felt she wouldn't be welcome. Maybe she's wrong. Mixed up. I'm just telling you what she told me."

Elise squeezed her eyes shut, guilt weighing on her. It was true. She preferred her mother to be at a safe distance. Close enough to visit for a weekend, but not so that she was in their day-to-day business. Her preference for Ben, and later, her attitude toward Brian, had put emotional distance between them, and that had led to a physical distance as well. But if her mom could get her act together and really take an interest in the kids, she could live in Wichita. It was a big enough city that she could make friends and develop her own interests.

"Do you think she'd move here if I suggested it? We could find a little patio home or condo with maintenance included for her. But does she need more than that? I really don't know if that's enough, Mary. I think she needs professional help."

"It couldn't hurt to let her know you'd like to have her closer, Elise. Your mom is feeling very alone. I talk to her almost every day, hon."

"And you think she's okay?"

"No. I don't. But all I can do is be here for her. I can't make her do something or not do something. And if I pressure her too much, she'll push me away. Believe me, I'm just as frustrated as you are." Mary's voice dropped to a whisper laced with sadness. "I miss my friend."

**

Elise waited until they'd received their drinks and ordered lunch to broach the topic with her mother. She tiptoed in cautiously. "Mom, are there many people living at the lake year round these days?"

Her mother turned to her and lifted her coffee cup before answering. "In our area, a few folks stay all year."

"So, you've met some people?"

"I know most everyone around me."

She answered the question, but only that and no more. No extending the conversation. Elise sighed, and pushed on. "Seems like it could get lonely out there in the winter. What would you think about getting a little place around Wichita? Maybe something outside of town if you don't want to deal with city traffic."

Her mother's eyes narrowed, and a guarded expression replaced the blankness on her face. "I don't want to be responsible for three houses. Until I sell the house in Whitfield, I'll stay at the lake."

"Have you put it on the market?" Brian spoke up.

"No. I'm not ready to do that."

"It's not good for a house to sit empty," Elise said. "Things rust. Pipes break." A weight settled on her shoulders. In her current state, how could her mother possibly get a house ready to sell? As far as Elise could tell, her dad's departure from the house hadn't left many empty shelves and closets. The place bulged with a lifetime of possessions, plus odds and ends of heirlooms and leftovers from her grandparents' lives as well.

Her mother needed to downsize. What in the world would she do with all the material possessions?

Her mother sat back in her chair with her cup. "I'm not ready."

Elise flicked a quick glance at Brian and gave a tiny shake of her head, hoping he'd understand not to push it.

"That's fine. But when you're ready, think about coming up here and leaving the lake house as a summer place." Mary's words rang in her head, and Elise forced herself to sound cheerful and sincere. "We'd love to have you closer, Mom."

Her mother stared into space a moment. "We'll see."

No commitment. No discussion. Feeling as though she were floundering from one dark abyss to another, Elise moved to the next topic they needed to tackle. "We should probably make a plan for Christmas. It'll be here before we know it. What are you thinking? Would you want to come back up here? We'd like for the kids to be home on Christmas morning."

Her mother shook her head. "You all plan your own holiday. I'm not doing Christmas this year."

They all stared at her.

"Grammy, you don't want Christmas this year?"

She patted Olivia's hand. "I want *you* to have Christmas, sweetheart."

"But, Mom, half the fun of Christmas is watching the kids open their presents," Elise said. She saw her mother's eyes glaze over, and her heart sank. Her mother was withdrawing from life. She couldn't get past her sadness or whatever it was to experience someone else's joy. A bitter taste settled in Elise's mouth. Why couldn't her mother make the transition from mother to grandmother? Why couldn't she take joy in her grandchildren? Because they were Elise's and not Ben's? Or because they were the children of a lowly school teacher rather than some wealthy executive? As unpleasant thoughts bombarded her, Elise's temper flared.

She pushed the thoughts back, fighting to keep calm. She refilled her mug before responding. "What will you do then?"

Her mother shrugged. "Stay home."

"Oh, Mom, we don't want you to be alone on Christmas Day. Is there someone at the lake you could invite to have dinner with you?"

Her mother looked at her as if she were a dense child. "I *want* to be alone."

Elise's blood ran cold. No one wanted to be alone on Christmas. There was no question, whether she was wallowing in self-pity, truly depressed or still suffering the effects of grief, her mother needed professional help. How the hell was Elise going to make that happen? With two kids and a full-time job, she had no spare time already.

222

Brian would be off work for almost two weeks for Christmas break. Maybe he could spend some extra time with the kids while she did some investigating. But even as she thought about it, resentment gnawed at her. It was ridiculous. Here was a woman with nothing but time, and plenty of money at her disposal . . .

Chapter Twenty-Five

This was the last time she'd try to convince her mother to join them for Christmas, Elise told herself as she punched in her mother's number. She simply couldn't beg or cajole any more. If her own kids were going to have Christmas, she'd have to spend some time focusing on that. The days were slipping fast. She'd done very little shopping. And no wrapping. The embroidered felt skirt around the Christmas tree was empty and bare.

While she waited for her mother to pick up, Elise's eyes shifted to the haphazard Scotch pine they'd installed in the living room two weeks ago. They'd managed to string the lights and attach a smattering of ornaments, but Elise had to admit, though she was no Martha Stewart, the finished product was sub-standard, even for her.

"Hello, Elise," her mother's muffled voice came on the line.

"Hi, Mom. Did I catch you napping?"

Her mother coughed a moment. "No."

Elise waited a beat, but her mother didn't offer any additional information. What *was* she doing?

"How's the weather there?"

"Not too bad. Had some snow."

"Really? How much?"

"Oh, I don't know. A little."

Elise cringed at her mother's vague answer. Could she really not make an estimate? Or could she not get up and look out the window?

"I called to see if you'd made a plan for Christmas Day. The offer to come and get you still stands."

"Oh, yes. I'm spending the day with Lena, the woman who knew Grandmother, remember?"

Relief swept through Elise. "That's great. She's close by, right?"

"Down the street."

Good, Elise whispered. At least she wouldn't be alone. And it wouldn't require any significant driving. She felt as though a weight had been lifted from her shoulders. Maybe she could enjoy the holiday rather than spend it worrying about her mother.

"All right. We'll miss you, but I'm glad you have someone to be with. I think I'll wait to give you your gift. It's kind of large and bulky for mailing."

"That's fine."

Absolutely no interest or curiosity. Elise groaned inside. Her mother was wasting away. Not even participating in life. No mention of sending gifts for the kids or wishing them a merry Christmas. Was that really too much to ask? She was their only grandmother. Hell, even her dad's bimbo of a wife had called to ask what the kids would like for Christmas. And a large box had already arrived.

For a second, Elise wondered if she should mention that. Would it snap her mother into action? Or give her a reason to pour another glass of wine?

She couldn't risk it. "What are you taking for the dinner?" Elise asked instead.

There was a long pause.

"Mother?"

"Hmmm?"

"Aren't you providing something for the dinner at Lena's?"

"I suppose I'll take a salad or something."

225

Her mother's voice was dull and distant. Elise closed her eyes as she remembered how her mother used to cook and bake for days before Christmas – the endless cookies, fudge and peanut brittle, breads and pies. Sadness washed over her as she was reminded once again that the woman she recognized as her mother had disappeared.

A lump formed in her throat. She had to end the call, or she'd be caught bawling by one of the kids. "Okay, Mom. I've got to go. We'll talk to you on Christmas."

Chapter Twenty-Six

Elise scooped the coffee and started the brewing with one hand while she held onto Andy to keep him from attacking the Christmas tree or the bulging stockings that hung from the mantel.

He jumped up and down, tugging on her arm.

"Okay, okay. I'm coming." Laughing, she snatched him up and ran to the living room. Olivia bounced on the sofa, her eyes huge.

Brian lit a fire, then peeked out the front window. "I'm pretty sure we're the first ones up. It's really dark out there."

"Oh, well. We can take naps later," Elise said. This was one day she didn't mind getting up early. She loved Christmas morning, the frenzy and commotion, snuggling up with a cup of coffee and watching the kids play with their new toys. She especially loved staying home and tuning out the rest of the world for a few hours. And that's exactly what she intended to do.

Even though the coffee maker hadn't completed its gurgling, Brian handed Elise a steaming mug. "Ready or not . . ."

She flashed him a smile, and slid an arm around his waist. "Thanks, hon." She allowed herself one quick sip of coffee, then set it down and unfastened the stockings. "Okay, let's do this."

As soon as she set Andy's stocking in his lap, she grabbed the camera. While Olivia would savor her packages, and inspect each one, time was short with Andy. He'd rip his apart in seconds.

Elise snapped several photos, then picked up her mug and curled into a chair. She didn't want to watch the entire episode through a tiny viewfinder.

While Elise took in the scene, Christmases past flooded her memory. As kids and young adults, they'd had some great Christmases. Ben used to entertain everyone. Always had a joke ready, and did spot-on imitations of various movie stars and politicians. Grandma used to be there, and in earlier days, her other grandparents also. Uncle David rarely went to Whitfield, and never on Christmas.

Sometimes it had bothered her that Ben garnered so much attention and hogged the spotlight. But when her mother had tried to force her to play the piano and sing carols, Elise discovered she had neither the talent nor the personality for holding center stage. Poor Mom, she thought, taking a sip of coffee. She'd wanted to find some trait or talent in Elise that she could be proud of. And show off. As far as Elise could tell, that still hadn't happened.

But her mother had never skimped on Christmas. They'd had mountains of gifts and treats – enough candy and cookies to make them alternately hyper and sluggish. A lump formed in Elise's throat. Oh, the elaborate gingerbread houses they used to make. That would've been such a great tradition to continue, something that her mother and Olivia could've enjoyed doing together. Unfortunately, by the time Olivia was old enough to make a reasonable effort, Ben had died, and so had the Stapleton Christmas.

There was no turning back time. Elise could buy the candy, but it was expensive, and she didn't have the creative flair her mother had. She wished she'd thought of the gingerbread houses earlier. Maybe that would've convinced her mother to be part of Christmas this year.

Elise glanced at the clock. Probably too early to call Mom yet. She waited until the kids were cleaned up and dressed, then picked up the phone. Ten-fifteen, and no answer. She had no idea what time her mother was expected at Lena's.

Brian's brother and his family arrived at eleven, and by one o'clock, all the food was put away, and the kids were busy playing. The adults hung out at the kitchen table with coffee and Bailey's Irish Crème.

Elise folded her legs underneath her and sipped the coffee, determined to enjoy the day and push worries about her mother to the back burner. Her mother was spending the day the way she'd chosen.

Still, Elise tensed when the phone rang.

Brian handed her the phone, and she looked at the caller ID. Her dad.

Elise excused herself, and spoke to her father for a few minutes. While she did, a single thought kept running through her mind. This is normal, the way it should be. Family members calling to say Merry Christmas, touching base. Maybe her mom would call.

When Elise sat back down at the table, Meredith turned toward her, concern in her eyes. "How's your mother doing, Elise? Is she coming later?"

Elise shook her head, not wanting to lie, but not ready to air the family's dirty laundry, either. She couldn't quite bring herself to label her mother an alcoholic. Even thinking those words caused a disconnect in her brain. It just didn't compute.

"She's staying at the lake house for the holiday. Didn't feel like driving, or celebrating. It's been a tough year for her."

Meredith nodded sympathetically.

Elise studied her mug. Clearly she wasn't going to be able to escape thoughts of her mother today.

**

By five o'clock, Elise wanted to scream. She'd called the lake house and her mother's cell phone at least five times, only to be greeted by a stiff and formal recording suggesting that she leave a message or try again later. Neither option had proven successful.

She ran a hand over her face and fiddled with her bangs.

"El, you know she did say she wanted to be alone today," Brian reminded her.

Elise threw up her hands. "But it's crazy. Who wants to be alone on Christmas?" She shook her head and wandered to the window, fighting the uneasiness that stole over her. "I just wanted to tell her Merry Christmas." She turned back to Brian. "What if something's wrong?"

"I don't know, sweetheart."

"Why wouldn't she want to talk to the kids? To tell Olivia Merry Christmas?" *Or me?* Christmas had always been her mother's favorite holiday. A family day. Elise pushed off from the wall. "I don't get it."

She picked up one of Olivia's new books, and leafed through it. That took about two minutes, then she pulled a deck of cards from the drawer in the side table. But before she could suggest kicking Brian's butt in a game of gin rummy, Andy scrambled into his lap. Instead, Elise shuffled the cards and started a game of solitaire.

Big mistake. All she could think of was her mother alone at the lake house on Christmas.

"I'm calling Nathan." She stood up, tears burning her eyes. She found the number then went upstairs to place the call.

"Hi, Nathan. This is Elise Keaton, Claire Stapleton's daughter. I'm sorry to bother you, but I've been trying to get hold of my mother all day, and haven't been able to reach her. I know this is a huge imposition, but I wonder if you could run over there and check on her."

230

"I sure would, Elise, but I'm in St. Louis right now, visiting my folks."

"Oh, I'm so sorry to bother you. Hope you're having a good Christmas."

"Not a problem. Honestly, I thought your mom was visiting you for the holiday."

Elise sucked in her breath. "Really? Did she tell you that?"

"I believe so."

"She told me she was having dinner with a woman named Lena who lives not far from her."

"Huh. I could sure call Mrs. Bishop for you."

"Would you? I hate to impose, but I'd really like to make sure she's all right."

"No problem. Give me a few minutes, and I'll call you back."

A few minutes later, the call came, and Elise snatched up the phone.

"Nathan here, Mrs. Keaton. Listen, I spoke with Mrs. Bishop, and she said she hasn't seen your mom for several days. Your mother told her she was going to Wichita for the holiday. I sure am sorry. I don't know where the mix up happened."

But Elise knew. Her mother had deliberately deceived them.

"Nathan, how often do you see my mother?"

"Not too much this time of year. I stop by occasionally."

Occasionally. What did that mean? She wanted to ask so much more, but it was Christmas. She couldn't unload on the poor guy.

"I wonder . . . if the weather's not bad, do you suppose Mrs. Bishop could run over to Mom's place and see if she's there?"

She heard Nathan's heavy sigh.

"Unfortunately, they're not at the lake, either, Mrs. Keaton. We could call the police and have someone check on her if you think there's something wrong."

Elise groaned.

"No. I don't want to drag someone out on Christmas if there's no need." Sending a friend out was one thing, but calling the cops was totally different. She'd have to go herself. "Thanks for your help, Nathan. I really appreciate it."

Elise made one more call, to Mary, and confirmed that her mother hadn't gone to Whitfield, either. She hung up the phone and hurried back downstairs. She stared at Brian. "I've got to go to the lake."

His eyes widened. "What? Honey, wait a minute. Are you—"

Elise held up her hands. She'd made up her mind. "I have to, Brian. I won't be able to sleep tonight if I don't check on her."

"El, that's a six-hour drive. Why don't you call the police? Tell them it's not an emergency, but you'd like someone to stop by."

Elise shook her head. She had to be the one. If something was wrong, if her mother was passed out or sick – she refused to think of anything worse – then Elise wanted to get there first. Not the police. Her mother wouldn't want that. In fact, she'd be mortified.

For a moment, she hesitated, leaning against the stair rail. If she called the police, would it be a wake-up call for her mother? Would it be enough to get her attention? No, she'd just be furious with Elise. Her mother would never forgive her for the humiliation of that. Protecting her mother from embarrassment was automatic, second nature. It'd been drilled into her head from a very young age. The worst indiscretions were the ones that reflected badly on Mom and the image of her family.

Elise threw some clothes and toiletries into a bag while Brian brewed another pot of coffee. As soon as it was ready, she filled a thermos, gave the kids hugs, and headed for the door.

"Call me as soon as you get there," Brian said, pulling her into his arms. "And call me if you get sleepy. I'll talk you through it."

"I will. Don't worry."

Chapter Twenty-Seven

Elise kept the heat on low, and the CD volume on high, willing herself to stay alert. A misty fog had developed as she got closer to the lake. And on Christmas night, the roads were eerily deserted. It'd been a good thirty minutes since she'd passed another driver. No surprise there. Everyone should be home, sitting by a warm fire with family and friends. Five hours into the drive and she was still trying to convince herself that making the trip was the right thing to do.

As she approached the house, Elise saw her mother's car in the driveway. A tiny bit of hope flamed inside her. At least she wasn't out on the streets. But as Elise drove closer, her heart thumped. The car wasn't in the drive at all, but halfway in the ditch off to the side. Her mother had obviously missed the driveway and slid off the road, bumping against the mailbox.

Oh, God. Elise gasped. When had it happened? It was freezing outside. If her mother had been in the car all evening . . .

Her pulse pounding, Elise brought the minivan to an abrupt stop and ran to her mother's car. She yanked open the door. "Mother? Mom?"

The car was empty. That was good, Elise told herself. She'd made it inside. Oh, please let her be in the house. She sprinted back to her van and grabbed her purse, groping for the key to the lake house. Where the hell was it? Elise pounded on the door, yelling. When there was no answer, she dug through her purse again. Her hands shook as she grasped the cold metal and fumbled to get it into the slot.

Finally, the lock turned, and Elise pushed the door open. As she stepped inside, the overwhelming stench of cigarette smoke and cat urine assaulted her senses, and she nearly gagged.

With a cry, Reggie leapt from a table. Elise screamed and dropped her purse. Reggie wound through her legs.

"Oh, my God." Covering her mouth and nose, Elise stepped farther into the house nudging the cat from under her feet. Stunned, she took in the chaotic scene. The place was strewn with dirty glasses and overflowing ashtrays. Cigarette butts littered the floor around the coffee table. A sweater hung on the back of the new leather recliner, and a crumpled blanket dangled from the sofa.

"Mother?" Elise swiveled as panic hit her. "Mom!" She ran toward her mother's bedroom, jumping over the coat in the middle of the hallway floor.

The door was open, and her mother, fully clothed, lay sprawled across the bed. "Mom!" she screamed. Elise turned her over, shaking her. "Mom, wake up!"

Elise felt for a pulse, hardly able to hear anything over her own blood pounding in her ears. "Oh, God. Oh, God." She reached for the phone and dialed nine-one-one.

With fear and anger warring inside her, Elise answered question after question from the paramedics. She answered as best she could, but her information was woefully inadequate. She didn't know how long her mother had been in that condition, or when she'd last eaten, or how much alcohol she may have consumed, or what her doctor's name was or what kind of prescription drugs she took. She shook her head. She knew so little.

235

While the paramedics loaded her mother onto a stretcher, Elise found food for Reggie. There was no time to do anything else. And what did it matter if he did his business a few more times on the floor? The inside of that house was ruined. It'd have to be practically gutted before it could be lived in again.

Somehow, she'd have to convince her mother not to go back, not to be so far away from friends and family. Clearly she needed a support network.

Elise followed the ambulance in her car, talking to Brian on the way. It was a forty-five minute drive to the nearest hospital.

"Listen, El. Don't forget you're running on empty, babe. We were up at six o'clock this morning."

"I know. And believe me, I'm feeling it. I'll spend the night at the hospital and call you in the morning."

"Yeah. Don't drive back to her place."

"Don't worry. I won't. I couldn't stay there, anyway. The house was awful. I can't believe she's been living like that." Her voice dropped to a whisper. "I can't believe this is my mom."

**

Her mother lay unconscious when a nurse ushered Elise into her room. Oxygen tubes ran into her nose. Saline dripped from a needle in her arm, and a dialysis machine wheezed in steady intervals as it pumped toxins from her kidneys.

Biting back tears, Elise spent twenty minutes talking with the doctor. She grew more chilled with every sentence out of the man's mouth.

"I won't lie to you," he said. "Your mother won't live much longer in this condition."

Talk of little blue pills, nausea, withdrawal, alcohol poisoning, long-term care, and treatment facilities hammered in her brain. Lose her mother at just fifty-five? She should have so many good years left. Elise clenched her eyes shut. How could this be happening?

236

She'd already lost her only sibling, and her dad was drifting away, busy with a new family.

And dammit, she needed a mom. Even though her mother wasn't always the easiest to deal with, Elise wanted her in her kids' lives. She had such potential to be a wonderful grandmother. Elise's eyes strayed behind the doctor to the figure lying in the bed, while scenarios ran through her head. She couldn't imagine losing her mother. It was too soon. She'd have to find a way to put some things on hold and get her mother well again. She refused to consider the alternative.

**

Elise spent an uncomfortable night on a sofa, and woke to unfamiliar sounds. When she swung her legs to the side and sat up, memory flooded in. A nurse leaned in close and touched her shoulder.

"Your mother's awake, hon."

Elise scrambled up, but stepped aside while a nurse wheeled the dialysis machine away. The other nurse gave her an encouraging smile, then turned to speak to her mother. She spoke in soft, gentle tones, the way you would to a sick child.

Elise hovered out of the way for a few moments, then approached the bed. Her mother's eyes turned toward her, but Elise wasn't sure they held any recognition.

She lifted her mother's hand. "Hey, Mom. How are you feeling?"

Her mother's eyelids fluttered, then opened wide. "What's going on? Why are you here?" Her voice was unnaturally low and thick.

The nurse interrupted, "The doctor will be in later this morning to talk to both of you."

Elise nodded. Good. It'd have more impact coming from a doctor. "I'm here Mom, because you needed medical attention. You have some serious problems."

Her mother frowned. "What are you talking about? Did I fall? Was I sick?"

Elise gripped the bed rail to keep from screaming. The denial had to stop. "No, Mom." She spoke softly, but firmly. "It's the drinking. You're here because you had alcohol poisoning. I had to call an ambulance last night."

When her mother started to protest, Elise cut her off. "We're not denying it anymore. You need help."

Her mother's lips pursed, and she glanced at the nurse. "I don't feel well."

In one quick movement, the nurse produced a plastic tray, then turned to Elise. "Maybe this would be a good time for you to get some coffee."

Elise nodded and headed for the door on wobbly legs. She needed coffee. The stronger, the better.

When she returned to the room, the nurse, Karen, took her arm and, to her surprise, steered her back into the hallway. Karen nodded vigorously as she faced Elise. "You're doing the right thing. Talk to her straight. You have to be strong and firm and honest. The doctor will talk to you about her physical condition and her treatment options, but I'm telling you I've been through this before. Don't let her get away with anything, or she'll end up right back here like this again. And next time she might not be so lucky."

By the time the woman took a breath, Elise's lips trembled. "I understand," she said, nodding like a girl getting a scolding from the school principal.

Karen shook her index finger. "She'll give you all kinds of reasons why she needs it. She'll swear it'll only be one glass. But don't you believe it. She'll cry. She'll scream. And you'll feel sorry for her when she's puking and shaking and begging for it. But you can't give in. Is that clear?"

Yeah, pretty much, Elise thought. How could it not be? She took a tiny step back and swallowed hard. "Yes. Thank you. I understand."

238

Karen's face softened, and her lips almost formed a smile. "All right, then. We'll do everything we can for her while she's here, but I'm afraid the worst is yet to come."

On that note, the nurse left Elise standing in the hallway not at all sure she was up to the task. Part of her wanted to run to her car and drive as fast as she could back home where things made sense. Away from all of this. But she couldn't do that. She had to get through to her mom, make her care. Find a way to make her want to live again.

**

As Karen predicted, the following day was worse. The anti-nausea pills kept her from getting sick, but still, her mother was irritable and irrational. No matter how many times Elise brought her water or orange juice or iced tea, she still complained of being thirsty.

"Here, Mom. Let me get you some more ice chips."

Elise held the plastic cup out to her mother. With shaking hands, she nearly jerked it from Elise, and fished a few cubes out. She crunched them for a moment, then moaned, shoving the cup at Elise. "Take this. It's not helping. I'm tired. Get the nurse and tell her I need something to help me sleep."

"Mom, are you sure you need something? Just close your eyes. I'll dim the lights. Maybe that'll help."

An hour later, when her mother drifted to sleep, Elise took time to make a few phone calls. She had to do it before she chickened out. She wouldn't cover it up, and she wouldn't sugarcoat or spin the story. Like it or not, people would know her mother's condition. Maybe a little mortification would be good for her.

Elise started with Nathan, since he already knew something of the situation, and gave him a condensed version of the events.

Next, she called her uncle. She hadn't seen nor spoken to him since Ben's funeral. And even that had been brief. She had few memories of the man, but still, he was her mom's only other family besides a few cousins scattered across the country.

"Hi, Uncle David. This is Elise. Can you talk for a minute?"

Her uncle cleared his throat. "Sure, Elise. How are you?"

"Not so good, actually. I'm calling about Mom. You know she and dad are divorced now, right?" She heard the heavy sigh from the other end.

"She emailed me about the divorce a while back."

"Well, I'll skip over the graphic details, but Dad's already remarried. Mom moved to the lake house, and she's been drinking. I had to bring her into the hospital last night."

"Really? That surprises me. Honestly, she didn't seem too emotional about it in her email."

"That figures. You know Mom can be pretty good at hiding her emotions. And it's not just the divorce. It's losing Ben. It's moving away from her home and friends and spending so much time alone."

"Does she need money?"

What? It took a moment for that question to register. "Oh, gosh, no. Financially, she's fine. I . . . I just thought you'd like to know. Maybe it would help if you'd talk to her. I can't seem to make her understand that she's loved and needed, and she still has a lot of good years left to live. There's no reason to be wasting away like this."

"So, that's the situation, huh? Drowning her pain and sorrows in alcohol. That's a tough one, Elise. Tell you the truth, it's gotta come from her. We can talk to her 'til cows lay eggs, doll, but that's not going to do any good. I've seen this before."

Briefly, Elise wondered about his experience with this. But she didn't really care. She heard his reluctance

240

to get involved, and her temper rose. He couldn't be bothered to help save his only sister? What a schmuck.

"Listen, Uncle David, you're probably right. I'm sorry to have bothered you."

"Now, honey, it's not a bother." His voice turned apologetic. "I'd be happy to give it a shot if you honestly think she'd listen to me."

"Yeah. Let's see how she does in the next couple of days."

"Sounds good. You keep me posted, all right?"

As politely as she could manage, she said, "Of course. I'll talk to you soon."

What on earth was wrong with this family, anyway? Elise clenched the phone in her fist for a long moment. Then she called Mary.

Choking on tears, Elise could hardly get the words out. "Mary, it's about Mom. She's in the hospital. I found her passed out last night." Elise shuddered, and her voice caught. "Alcohol poisoning. Mary, she's drinking herself to death."

"Oh, honey. Tell me where. I'll be there as soon as I can."

"The hospital in Branson. She's hardly been awake, and not making any sense. She acts like she doesn't even know what happened. Or refusing to admit it." The more she talked, the harder the tears came.

"Okay, Elise. Calm down. She'll get help there. That's the most important thing. Tell me what she needs."

"She needs to stop drinking!" Elise practically screamed into the phone. "You have to tell everyone. Let all her friends know. Dana, the book club, the people at the liquor store. Everyone. I mean it. They all need to know."

"Elise, I can't announce to the whole town that your mother has a drinking problem."

Elise couldn't help but wonder how many of them suspected already. The words of the nurse ran through her brain. *Don't let her get away with anything.* "But you've got to let all of her friends know. Make sure no one brings her a bottle of wine, or suggests happy hour or anything like that. She can't have any alcohol whatsoever. It's going to take everyone working together to get her out of this."

"We'll have to deal with that later. How long will she be in the hospital?"

Elise bent over and flopped her arms onto her knees. "Not sure. Maybe a couple of days, but she can't go back to the lake house. It's filthy and nasty. She wasn't taking care of Reggie."

"Oh, Lord. So, you're taking her to Wichita?"

Elise swiped at the tears. "I don't know yet. I know she won't want to stay at our house. But she can't stay by herself."

"Why don't I come and help clean up the lake house?"

Buying some time, Elise sniffled into a tissue while she debated Mary's offer. How could she let anyone into the house? But then how could she care for her mother and at the same time do something about the house? If anyone would help protect her mother's dignity, it was Mary.

"I don't know, Mary. It's really a mess. The carpet is going to have to go, and maybe some furniture."

"Elise. You take care of your mother, I'll deal with the house. Maybe Grant can get away and come with me."

Another person? Elise groaned inside. She hated to allow anyone in the house, friends or strangers, but she didn't have many options.

She blinked back fresh tears. "Sure. Whatever you can do would be great."

**

Elise didn't know whether to laugh or cry when she saw Mary charging down the hallway, her arms loaded with flowers, a huge tote bag and a bright throw blanket that looked like a field of poppies had exploded on it. She did a little of both as Mary swept her into a tight hug, bags and all.

Mary rocked her a moment. "Oh, sweetie, it's gonna be all right," she said, her voice soft and soothing.

Elise shuddered, finally able to exhale. For the first time in more than forty-eight hours, she felt a sense of relief. She wasn't alone. Mary would help. Maybe it really would be all right. When Elise pulled back, Mary rested a hand on her cheek. "Your mom is lucky to have you, sweetie. I know this has been hard for you. It's gone too far."

With a lump in her throat, Elise could only nod. Then Mary squeezed her hand. "Come on, kiddo. Where is she?"

Elise hung back while Mary bustled into the room. Mary turned and handed her the bouquet of flowers and simply dropped everything else. In only a second, Mary reached the bed and pulled her mother into her arms.

As far as Elise could tell, no words were exchanged. But the release of emotion between her mother and her friend was palpable.

Several minutes later, Mary tossed the poppy blanket onto the bed, and tucked it around her friend. Then she dug into the bags she'd brought and spread a few magazines in her mother's lap. Elise gaped when Mary next pulled out a brush and began brushing her mother's hair. Why hadn't she thought of that?

"Oh, stop, you fool," her mother said in a raspy voice, almost laughing. "I can brush my own hair."

"Well, do it, for heaven's sake," Mary said. "Hey, it's not the Ritz, but you know the better you look, the better service you'll get."

Elise watched her mother make a feeble attempt to brush her hair, but her hands shook, and her arms were weak. The brush slipped from her fingers and clattered to the floor. In seconds, Mary'd retrieved it, brushed back her mother's hair and inserted a large jeweled clip. Her mother's face, and the whole room, seemed transformed.

Elise shook her head, and managed a grateful smile for her mother's best friend. "Mary, you're amazing."

It wasn't the first time she'd witnessed the incredible bond between these two women, but it was the first time she'd been thankful for it.

Flopping onto the small sofa, Elise thought of her own girlfriends with a sense of melancholy. Sure, she had friends, but no one who she'd compare to Mary. Elise kept in touch with a couple of friends from high school and college, and since Olivia had started school, she'd met some other moms. Her best friend from college had moved to Portland, Oregon. She couldn't remember the last time she'd had a girls' night out. Their lives were so busy and hectic. How could she possibly have time to nurture friendships? Maybe it was one of the trade-offs for having a career.

Watching her mother and her friend made her envious, though. They shared something special. Elise had Brian, of course, truly her best friend, but it'd be nice to have a close girlfriend, too. Maybe when she got home and things settled, she could work on that. Make more of an effort Maybe it'd be her New Year's resolution. Unfortunately, finding the time would require nothing short of wizardry. And she had no magic wand.

Chapter Twenty-Eight

Holding onto her mother, Elise pushed the car door shut with her foot, grateful that the temperatures had warmed over the last couple of days, and all traces of snow and ice had disappeared. Slowly, they made their way to the porch and up the front steps.

With some trepidation, she unlocked the door, and helped her mother inside. Nathan and Grant had removed the carpeting and put down temporary rugs, and aired out the house. They'd cleaned up trash and put the house back in some kind of order. It was far from finished, but at least it smelled better.

"Here, Mom. Why don't you sit down and I'll get some tea started. Are you cold?"

Her mother shook her head. "Where's Reggie?"

Elise crouched down, touching her mother's arm. "Remember? I sent him home with Mary. She'll take good care of him. I think she has a soft spot for that cat."

Elise filled the teakettle and reached into the cupboard for mugs. She pushed aside a stack of plates, and froze. Just behind the cups was a bottle of vodka. Holy crap. Quickly she swiveled around to look at her mother. Oh, God. She'd have to go through every cupboard. Why hadn't she thought to ask Mary to do that? No telling how much booze her mom had stashed around the place. With a tight knot in her stomach, Elise yanked open the refrigerator. She breathed a sigh of relief. Nothing but good fresh food and juice. Another gift from Mary. But she'd bet her mother had other places, a stockpile somewhere. The closest liquor store was at least thirty minutes away, not exactly convenient. She'd have to deal with that while her mother napped.

She glanced out the kitchen window. It was so nice out, maybe they should go outside. In fact, that was an excellent idea. After being cooped up in the hospital, a little fresh air would probably do her mom a world of good.

"Hey, Mom, what do you think about going outside and sitting on the deck for a few minutes? Getting a little fresh air? We could wrap up in some blankets."

A memory floated in as spoke those words. Smiling, she touched her mom's hand. "Remember that year we came out after Christmas because Dad was afraid the pipes had frozen, and Ben and I wanted to make s'mores?"

Her mother's eyes were blank. "We started a fire in the little grill, and Dad got mad?" Surely she'd remember that. Their dad was unusually grumpy from the drive. He'd been the fun-sucker that day, while their mom had laughed at the cold and joined in the antics. When their dad told them they couldn't have the fire on the wooden deck, they'd moved it out to the grass, but it was too windy, so they'd taken it around to the front. But the driveway was too exposed, and they moved to the porch. The three of them huddled there in the cold, wrapped in blankets, and ate s'mores. And practically froze their butts off.

"That was so much fun. Wasn't that the time Ben got sick?" Elise laughed out loud, nudging her mom. "Remember? When we were done with the s'mores, he ate the rest of the marshmallows. The whole bag." She clapped her hands together. "I think he threw up later that night."

246

A shadow of a smile turned her mother's lips.

"Remember the next day, Dad was mad because the fire left that black mark on the porch? And we couldn't clean it up because the water would freeze."

Her mother did smile then. "I remember."

Still chuckling, Elise stood. "Come on. Let's go outside, just for a little while."

But her mother shook her head. "You go ahead. I think I'll lie down. I'm tired."

Elise slumped onto the sofa. For a minute, there'd been a tiny spark of life. "Okay. Sofa or the bedroom?"

"Help me to my room."

They shuffled down the hall. Inside the bedroom, Mary's touch was obvious. A new bedspread covered the bed. All the clothes had been picked up, and a vase of fresh sunflowers sat on the side table. Elise pulled back the covers on the bed. "Here you go, Mom. Do you need anything else?"

Her eyes were already closing. Elise pulled the blanket around her. "I'll keep the door open, okay?" She leaned against the doorframe a moment, her heart aching.

At least this would give her time to work on the house. She retreated to the kitchen, reheated her tea, then faced the reality of the monumental task left for her. Her mother still hovered on the brink of disaster, and there were still so many details to deal with.

Without bothering to put on a jacket, Elise headed back out to the car for the bag of cleaning supplies she'd bought. She opened a couple of windows in the main living area, lit some vanilla-scented candles, then sprayed disinfectant on all of the curtains and upholstery.

After that, she began her treasure hunt.

**

Two hours later, standing at the kitchen sink, she emptied every bottle she'd found. And she'd found plenty.

247

Pouring money literally down the drain, she fumed. What a flipping waste. A waste of money, and a waste of her mother's life. She glanced over at the sickly woman she barely recognized as her mother, as she sat, hands shaking, watching her and puffing on a filthy cigarette. They were going cold turkey on the alcohol, with the help of some drugs the doctor had prescribed, but agreed that she could continue to smoke, for now.

Her stomach rolled. Jesus, wasn't that vice enough? Elise couldn't help wondering – again – where the hell her mother was. Not this glassy-eyed shell of a woman, but the woman who'd put delicious meals on the table every night, who'd kept an immaculate house, attended countless school events and volunteered untold hours at the church and in the community. How could she just disappear?

And *why*, in God's name, couldn't she see that drinking, not a divorce, was ruining her life?

The more she thought about it, the more frustrated she got. She slammed the wine bottle into the recycling bin and it clanged against another one.

Her mother was unfazed. "You're upset," she said.

Elise nearly laughed as she stared at her mother. Instead, she took a deep breath and forced herself to get her emotions under control. Anger wouldn't help the situation. She poured a cup of coffee and set it in front of her mother.

She tried to speak calmly. "You know, Mom, we have to make some plans. I can't stay here any longer. I've got to get back to work."

"It's such a shame you have to work so much. You work all day then come home and do all the housework."

Elise had taken the time off under the Family Leave policy, but the days were unpaid. They needed her paycheck. And her mother knew it. Besides, she missed her kids and her husband.

"We're not having that conversation again, Mother. Brian and I both work. It's just the way it is for us. Period." Her mother could never resist an opportunity to point out that Brian couldn't support his family on his teacher's salary. They both thought she'd get over it once she got to know him better. She never did. For that matter, Elise thought, she never really put any effort into getting to know him, either.

Brian was her rock. Sure, he got impatient and frustrated with the hectic lifestyle occasionally. So did she. Sometimes he lost his temper, and she had to remind him not to shout in front of the kids, but he never wavered in his support. He put up with all the turmoil of her family, and her mother's obvious disappointment and criticism. Most of the time, he let it roll off his shoulders. And he was nice to her.

Elise wiped her hands on the offensively cheery lemon-yellow kitchen towel, and headed to the table. She picked up the pile of brochures, and spread them in front of her mother. "You need to choose one of these, or I'll have Dr. Schwartz choose one for you."

Turning, she picked up the towel again and began wiping down the counter.

Her mother was silent for a few moments, and Elise stole a sideways glance at her. She appeared to be looking at the materials from the treatment facilities the hospital had recommended. Elise didn't care which one she went to, but she was going even if it meant locking her in a room and standing guard. At least three weeks of serious detox and treatment. She couldn't handle another episode like this.

Her mother pushed the brochures around on the table.

"They all look lovely," she said, finally. "I suppose some rest and a change of scenery will do me good."

Elise groaned inside. Her mother was so far into denial she truly wondered if there was still hope. She turned and stared at her mother until she met her eyes.

"This isn't a vacation, Mom. You do realize that, don't you?"

She pulled out a chair and sat down, her elbows resting on the table, looking straight into her eyes. "These are treatment facilities. There are doctors and psychiatrists and pastors on staff. They want you to analyze your life."

"That doesn't sound too difficult."

"Yeah? One of the exercises is writing your obituary. You ready to do that? And you get to write an essay on why you're committing suicide."

"Suicide," her mother scoffed. "That's ridiculous."

"Is it? What else would you call it? You're slowly killing yourself. It might not be the same as putting a gun to your head and pulling the trigger, but the end result is the same. The alcohol's just taking longer."

Her mother gasped. "You have a cruel streak, Elise Keaton."

Elise stood up again. "Right. Here I am cleaning up your filthy gross house, taking time away from my family, trying to help you. Such cruelty."

Her mother nursed the cigarette, and made no response. She also stopped looking at the brochures. Elise let out a heavy sigh, and leaned against the counter.

"Mom. These places will help you. You've got to pull yourself together and get a life. As far as I can tell, you've done absolutely nothing in the three months you've been out here. No work. No volunteering. No socializing. You smoke, and drink, sometimes go shopping. What kind of life is that, Mom? What's the point?"

The point. Hmmmm. What *was* the point? Claire had no idea. But she was tired of hearing about the problems. Everything she was doing wrong. Everything that was wrong with her. She hadn't caused any of it. Resentment exploded inside her.

250

"What's the point? You tell me!" Claire yelled. "What's the point of getting married if your husband can walk away and screw it all up? What's the point of having kids if the Army is going to take them and kill them? What's the point of that?"

There is no point, she thought bitterly. To any of it. You just put in your time. You bounce around and see where you land.

Suddenly, Elise knelt in front of her, her hands tight on Claire's arms.

"The Army didn't kill all of your kids, Mom. You still have a kid. I'm still here. You know, I could use a mom. A little help. That last time you came down and we cooked together, that was really great. It was fun, and it made a huge difference. It was so wonderful to come home and have dinner almost done. We could do more of that. Hell, you could do it as a business."

Claire pulled her arms away. "Stop it. That hurts."

Elise stood, but kept her face down low. "And you know what else? My kids could use a grandmother. Someone else to give a damn about them. You could do that, Mom. You've got the time and the money. And you're just wasting it. You're wasting your life."

"It's my life," Claire said softly. "I can do with it what I want." She looked away. Ha. What a joke. "But I don't get to, do I? Because someone else always thinks they know what I should do. Someone else always changes things, and what I want gets killed or destroyed or taken away." Her voice rose as she clenched her fist against her chest. "Then I'm supposed to pick up the pieces and put everything back together. Well, I can't!" She shook her head, tears spilling from her eyes. "I know a thing or two about a wasted life."

"I know you're thinking about Ben, Mom. Yes, his death was a huge loss. His life was cut short, but don't call it a waste. Look at the impact he had on the people around him. I wish you'd think about Ben a little more.

Would you want him to see you like this? What would he say? What would he want?"

"Don't lecture me," Claire bit out.

"I'm sorry I can't replace him or bring him back or fill his shoes." Elise said. "I'm sorry all you have left is me."

Oh, she could be such a martyr, Claire thought. With shaking hands, she took a drink of the coffee in front of her, but it turned her stomach. She set the mug down hard on the table and looked at Elise. "You know, what I'm hearing is that it's all about you. What I can do for *you*. What *you* need."

She stood up and flung the coffee mug across the room, brown liquid sloshing through the air.

Elise gave a sharp gasp. "Mother!"

Clutching the table, Claire rounded on her. "Nothing bad has ever happened to you," Claire screamed at her daughter. "You have no idea what it's like. You've always had everything you wanted."

Sobbing, she turned toward the bedroom on unsteady legs, away from Elise's outstretched arm.

"Mom. Stop."

"Leave me alone."

Shaken, Elise let her go. She slumped back into the chair, and stared at the ceiling for a long moment, wondering why everything she said got twisted around in her mother's mind.

She couldn't keep the tears at bay. Elise pulled her knees up, and with her head resting against her arms, she sobbed, despair and exhaustion seeping through her entire body. None of this made sense, and she'd never felt so alone. She missed the smiles and warm hugs of her kids and her husband. She missed her brother's goofy jokes and teasing grin.

Several minutes later, Elise forced herself upright. With slow movements, she retrieved the mug from the floor, and dabbed at the cheap rug with a damp rag.

252

Then she poured herself a fresh cup of coffee and picked up the brochures. For more than an hour, she studied the pamphlets and the corresponding websites. Then she chose the one.

Chapter Twenty-Nine

Claire pulled her jacket closer, and gazed out the window at the tree-lined drive leading to Lakeview Village, the place she'd call home for the next four weeks. Where she'd be trapped without a car, baring her soul to total strangers. Classified as an alcoholic. A danger to herself and others.

Snow-splattered trees shone against a sharp winter-blue sky. At least it was pretty.

She glanced at Elise, who'd been chatty early in the trip, but had gone silent. What was left to say? Elise planned to stay long enough for a meeting with Claire's case manager, then head home. They'd have a joint meeting, and Elise would have a private consultation as well. How Claire would love to be a fly on the wall for that one.

It was standard procedure, they'd told them, for family members to be involved. While she realized that Elise was making a sacrifice staying with her for so long, Claire was ready for her to go. It was too uncomfortable to talk in front of Elise. How could she talk about the void Ben's death had left in her life or what a son-of-a-bitch Elise's father had turned out to be? Sounded too much like a Dr. Phil episode for Claire's liking. Besides, Elise would be hurt and defensive. What good would that do?

Writing assignments, Elise had said. Well, she could write. She could write about Ben. Claire mulled over the possibilities. Maybe that's how she'd spend her time in confinement, writing the articles she might've written for the Whitfield newspaper. All the memories of Ben, the shattered hopes and dreams. She dabbed at her misting eyes.

"Mom? You okay?" Elise asked.

Claire's resolve gave way. She turned to Elise. "Let's turn around. I don't want to be here."

"Oh, Mom. We can't do that. Come on. Look at it – the grounds are beautiful." She pulled the car into the parking lot and stopped. Without turning the car off, she turned toward Claire. "We're here. It's only four weeks, and like you said, it'll be good for you to have a change of scenery."

Claire rubbed her temples. When did she say that?

"Well, I'm not hugging anyone."

Elise gave a little laugh and stared at her. "What is that supposed to mean?"

Claire waved her arm. "Oh, you know, group therapy. Everybody giving everybody a hug. Ugh. I don't want strangers touching me."

Elise chuckled. "Mom, I think you've been watching too much daytime TV. And I really don't think anyone's going to make you do something you don't want to do. They're here to help you."

Claire grimaced and shook her head. "I need a Tylenol."

"Okay. You have some, don't you?"

Claire dug through her purse for the small bottle, and shook a couple of tablets into her palm. She hadn't had a drink in a week, but she couldn't begin to count the number of pills she'd taken.

Inside the lobby of the complex, a fire glowed in the seating area, and Claire moved toward it, leaving Elise to handle the check-in. The lobby had the feel of a lodge or clubhouse, with cozy pockets of seating, and nice window views. Claire sat down in a denim blue chair near the fire and twisted her hands, waiting for

Marjorie, her chaperone or shepherd or whatever they called her, to appear.

A few minutes later, a woman with short silver-blond hair approached Claire. The woman wore a black pantsuit, and looked more like an accountant than a doctor. Claire stood, and the woman smiled.

"Hello, Claire. It's so nice to meet you. I'm Marjorie. Welcome to Lakeview." Then she took another step forward and wrapped her arms around Claire.

While Marjorie patted her back, Claire flashed Elise an I-told-you so look. Her daughter's eyes were wide, and her hand covered her mouth, but it didn't hide the amusement on her face. When their eyes met, Claire almost laughed at their shared joke.

Marjorie ushered them into her office, which had a desk, but also featured a small sitting area with sofa and chairs. Once they were seated, Marjorie began talking about the center, and the program.

"You're free to move about the facility at any time, but we ask that you remain on campus for the duration of the program."

To Claire's ears, the words were distant, foreign, meant for someone else. She detached as her thoughts drifted. Her eyes settled on the small white nametag fastened to Marjorie's lapel.

She wondered if the woman knew how funny it was that her last name was Collins. Was she married to Tom? Claire bit back a smile. Hmmm. A Marjorie Collins, now what flavor would that be? Something fruity? Vodka with a citrus twist, perhaps?

Marjorie raised her eyebrows and gazed Claire's direction. No, probably something dry. Very dry.

**

Claire had to admit the center made their inmates feel comfortable. Her suite was beautifully decorated in neutral greens and tans. Tasteful artwork and mirrors

256

hung on the walls. While no flowers were blooming, Claire's patio window offered views of boxwood and evergreen, tall ornamental grasses, and a low stone wall with tile accents.

Her eyes swept through the kitchen. Interesting. The small nook provided a sink and microwave, but no refrigerator. Of course. No cold beverages. She stole a glance at Elise, who probably hadn't even noticed. Or maybe she'd been briefed beforehand.

Elise moved toward her and rested a hand lightly on her shoulder. "It's really pretty, Mom. You should be comfortable. I think I could crawl into that bed right now."

Claire managed a wan smile. So could she. And stay there for about four weeks. Even though she'd slept off and on during the ten-hour drive, she couldn't seem to shake the heaviness in her limbs and the sleepiness. Probably the drugs.

"Well, I'll leave you two to get settled," Marjorie told them, inching toward the door. "Feel free to set out photos and other personal items. We want you to feel at home, Claire. I'll see you at dinner."

When they walked into the dining hall two hours later, Claire's throat tightened. She glanced around for Marjorie, careful to make eye contact with no one. She could see heads swivel, felt the curious eyes on her. Elise took her arm and steered her through the room filled with large round tables toward a small room to the left. And there was Marjorie.

"In here," she said, smiling. "First night, you order off the menu, and the staff serves you."

Claire's lips trembled, so she simply nodded, and snatched up one of the glasses of water on the table. Marjorie handed her a menu.

"The food is excellent," she said. "It's a top priority. We believe healthy eating is the first step toward recovery. Your body needs the nutrients and energy."

257

Oh, great, Claire groaned inside. All she needed was to gain twenty pounds by the time she got out of there.

When Marjorie gave a short laugh, Claire's eyes snapped to hers.

Marjorie patted her hand. "I know what you're thinking. At our age, food equals fat. Don't worry. We're not trying to fatten you up. We want you fit and trim. It's all about healthy habits."

All about healthy habits. Claire was wondering how many times she'd hear that phrase over the next few weeks when an outrageously handsome young man walked into the room and pulled up a chair at the table. He wore a white lab coat and a wide, friendly smile.

Claire's mouth dropped open. Who in the world was this delightful hunk, and what was his role? Did they just sprinkle in a little eye candy to help keep the patients' spirits up?

He extended his hand to Claire and gave a deep, "Hello, Claire. I'm Dr. Gannon, one of the staff doctors who'll be working with you during your stay. Good to meet you."

"Oh, my." Taking his hand, Claire let out a light chuckle, and received a nudge under the table from her daughter.

**

Standing in the lobby near the front door, Elise pasted on a smile. The time had come . . .

"Hey, since I'm not a stranger, can I give you a hug?" she whispered.

Her mother's eyes had already filled with tears. This was harder than she thought it would be. She put her arms around her mother and held onto her a moment. She seemed so thin, as though she might snap if Elise squeezed too hard. "Love you. Call me whenever you want."

Her mother nodded. "Bye."

"Mom?" She searched her mother's eyes. She wanted her to take this seriously, but couldn't be sure she would. Would she make an effort? Would she open up once Elise was gone? Or would she drift away as she had several times during their meeting that morning, or spend her time practically flirting with the cute doctor? Elise took a deep breath, and touched her mother's hand one last time. "Get well, okay? Let them help you."

Elise started the ten-hour drive ahead of her with blurred vision. Marjorie's words during their joint session kept running through her brain.

"You're here because your daughter loves you," Marjorie had told her mother. "She cares about you, and she wants you around for a lot more years, Claire. Do this for yourself, but also for your daughter, and your grandchildren. You have so much to live for. So much to live for."

Her mother had pursed her lips and looked right past her. In her heart, Elise wasn't sure her mother believed it, or that it truly mattered to her. When she'd used similar words, her mother had accused her of being selfish. She leaned against the window, one hand on the steering wheel, the other supporting her head. What more could she do?

First on the agenda would be finding her mother a place to live in Wichita. Something small, with maintenance included, but large enough for Mary and other friends to visit.

And they'd have to sell the house in Whitfield. Somehow, she'd have to pry her mother away from Ben's room. It wouldn't be easy. Elise set a tentative agenda in her mind. Then her thoughts turned to her husband, and her kids. She couldn't wait to see them.

Even though it was past bedtime when Elise pulled into the drive, she knew immediately that the kids were still up, waiting to see her. Light blazed from every window in the house. She dashed to the door without

259

bothering to gather anything from the car. She could deal with that later.

She nearly fell inside when the door opened just as she was about to push.

"Mommy!" Olivia and Andy shrieked.

Brian leaned against the wall, a huge smile on his face, waiting his turn. Despite the smile, she saw the questions and concern in his eyes.

On her knees, Elise hugged the kids to her, laughing and kissing their faces.

"You were gone a long time, Mommy," Olivia said.

"I know, sweetie. I missed you."

Brian pushed off from the wall, and pulled her into his arms. "Too long," he whispered.

Chapter Thirty

Claire zipped one suitcase, then began gathering up miscellaneous belongings for the other one. She tossed in the magazines and books she'd brought, and wrapped the photo of her and the kids in some bubble wrap. She paused by the table a moment before lifting the bright red folder the center had given her – her *packet*.

With a heavy sigh, Claire sat down, keeping the folder in her lap. She supposed she had to take it with her. It was her link to Lakeview, and included all of the campaign materials designed to help her jump-start her life. She ran her hand over the top of the packet. There were other things inside as well – the exercises from therapy sessions, and all the essays she'd written, including the one Marjorie had forced her to write about Elise. And, of course, her obituary. Why would she ever want to look at that again? She was supposed to give it to Elise, her next-of-kin. Claire's throat tightened. Not. Happening.

She glanced at her watch. Elise would be there any minute. To take her away from Lakeview. Claire looked around the room with a sense of ambivalence. She hadn't wanted to be there in the first place. Now she worried that she couldn't manage without it, without the support, the constant encouragement and pep talks.

She could see why they didn't want patients staying any longer. The place was like a cocoon, protecting those inside from the harsh environment outside. You got used to it.

"Knock-knock."

A soft voice broke Claire from her thoughts. She shoved the folder into her bag and stood.

Marjorie smiled, and glanced around the room. "Looks like you're about ready. I brought you a cart." She wheeled a luggage cart into the room. "This one ready to go?"

Claire nodded. She retrieved her cosmetic bag from the bathroom and placed it beside the other suitcase. Then she added the second bag.

"You packed lightly," Marjorie commented.

"Uh-huh."

It was so awkward. The light, nervous chatter after so many gut-wrenching and tearful conversations. She'd told this woman things she'd never told anyone. And it was quite possible she'd never see her again.

Marjorie reached out and touched Claire's arm. "You doing okay?"

Claire attempted a smile. "This is a crazy thing to say, but I think I'm going to miss this place."

"No. It's completely natural. And we'll miss you, Claire. But I'm so excited to see you go, so hopeful for you, and what lies ahead." She squeezed her hand. "I want you to stay in touch."

Did she really, Claire wondered. Did she keep in touch with all the patients who came and went through the doors of Lakeview? It seemed unlikely. After all, the whole idea of the program was to catch and release.

With a slight nod, Claire hitched her purse over her shoulder then took hold of the cart. She'd meet Elise in the lobby.

Elise was already there, standing by the fire. She turned when Claire and Marjorie clattered into the room with the cart. With a hesitant smile on her face, Elise moved toward her.

"Hey, Mom."

262

"Hi, honey."

Elise opened her arms, and Claire pulled her into a hug.

When she stood back, Elise looked her up and down, inspecting her, probably looking for signs of change. Claire had no idea whether she looked changed or not. She'd fixed her hair, anyway. And she knew she'd put on a few pounds. She could tell that by the way her clothes fit a little tighter than they had four weeks ago.

Elise's smile widened. "You look good, Mom." She gave a quick laugh. "You do."

"Hello, Elise." Marjorie stepped forward and gave Elise a brief hug, then she beamed at Claire. "She does look good, doesn't she? And now we give her back to you."

Claire nearly rolled her eyes. They were talking as if she wasn't there, or as if she were some household object that had been borrowed and returned.

"You ready, Mom?"

"Yes. I guess so." She turned to Marjorie. "Thank you. For everything."

Marjorie wrapped Claire in her arms. "Be well, my friend. Remember, we're all cheering you on."

Blinking back the tears, Claire followed Elise out to the van.

"How's everyone at home?" Claire asked after they turned onto the highway.

"Good. Can't wait to see you."

"I appreciate the cards they sent."

Elise reached over and touched her hand. "Everyone wants to see you better, Mom."

Claire wondered who 'everyone' was. Had Elise been in contact with Mary? Or Nathan? Her defenses rose automatically, and Claire had to remind herself that her family and friends were her support group now. If they were collaborating, it was in her interest. They were for her, not against her. Why was that so hard to remember and accept?

"I've got three appointments set up in the next couple of days to look at condos," Elise told her. "And Marjorie said you had people in Wichita to contact, so we should probably get some kind of schedule figured out. I'll work Wednesday and Thursday, then take Friday off so we can have all weekend in Whitfield."

"Well, I don't have to contact anyone right away. Let's see how the houses work out first." She wasn't committing to moving to Wichita just yet, so there was no reason to contact the local AA group or the other support people in the area. But she had to come up with a living arrangement soon. She certainly couldn't stay with Elise for long.

A giggle bubbled up inside her. Here she was, a woman with two houses, and no home. Apparently she'd really hit bottom. She'd become a homeless person.

**

"I like this one," Claire said.

It was the newest of the places they'd looked at over the past two days. The light, open feel of it appealed to her, and the fact that the homes sat in small clusters with landscaped courtyards in between – neighbors close by, but not right on top of each other. Just the way she liked them.

With three bedrooms and two baths, the size was perfect. Claire ran her hand over the smooth granite countertop of the kitchen island. Could she visualize herself there?

"Visualize where you want to be, who you want to be," Dr. Gannon had urged. "Visualize it, and get there. Be the person you want others to see in you."

It was one of the many pep talks he'd given. Some had felt a little too scripted, bordering on cheesy. But this one had struck a chord. He'd pushed, and Claire would've sworn he'd been speaking directly to her.

"How do you want others to see you?" he asked. "As a down-and-out loser? Somebody who doesn't give a damn? Or someone who's out there trying to give it a go? Someone who's picking up the pieces and still has something to share with the world?"

She'd had trouble with her vision. But she remembered his words. "Practice it, and after a while you won't have to work so hard at it. It'll be the person you are."

Well, she might not know what person she wanted to be exactly, but she could see herself in this place. All new and clean. Full of possibilities. Seemed like a good place for a fresh start.

Claire turned to Elise, and caught the uneasy look on her daughter's face.

"What's the matter?"

"It's nice," Elise said. "But, Mom, this is the one that isn't available until May first. Remember? All of the units in phase one are filled, and phase two isn't ready yet."

Claire sighed. Damn. Three months. What could she do for three months? Stay with friends? Travel? A cruise, perhaps? She mulled the possibilities, but then reality crashed in. She swallowed hard. No. Travel was out of the question. That would inevitably lead to dining out . . . happy hour . . . cocktails. She wasn't ready to face that situation, to be the one standing around with her tonic water while everyone else sipped fine wine.

"Well, I could rent one of those long-term hotels that are like small apartments. Is there anything close by you?"

"I'm sure there's something, but that would be awfully expensive. What about staying with Mary?"

"For three months?" Claire screeched. "I'd probably kill her. Besides, I don't want to be around someone else's husband that long."

"Okay, ladies, what do you think?" the real estate agent entered the kitchen and flashed them a bright smile.

"I'll sign today if they'll sell this one," Claire told the woman.

Elise gasped. "Mother! Slow down. That's a little brash."

"No. It's decisive." She wanted to be decisive. Not wishy-washy.

The woman faltered. "Oh, well. I– I can ask, but I seriously doubt they'd do it. This is their show unit. They're trying to get twelve units sold based on showing this one."

Claire ignored the agitation on Elise's face. "See what you can do. I'm not in a position to wait three months."

They thanked the agent, and Elise steered her mother back toward the van, shaking her head as she went. But by the time they got there, her laughter spilled out. Elise hadn't been able to get much information out of her mom about her treatment at Lakeview. She'd been very stingy with the details. Something must've clicked, though, because Elise just got the first real glimpse of her mother. Relief washed through her. Her mom was back.

Her mother turned puzzled eyes to her when they stopped at the car. "What is so funny?"

Elise hugged her arm. "You. And I mean that in a good way."

Chapter Thirty-One

The closer they got to Whitfield, the harder Claire fought to stay calm. She twisted her hands in her lap and tried to focus on the familiar landscape out the window, the bare trees and dormant fields that were winter in Whitfield. No matter how many times she told herself she'd be surrounded by friends, she envisioned being stared at and talked about. She imagined phones ringing all over town as news made the rounds. The alcoholic was back in town.

And what would she do? Hide in her house? Hide behind her daughter and her friends? Dr. Gannon's words rang in her head once more. Be the person you want others to see. God, she wanted to be confident and carefree, but could she pull it off?

Just breathe, she told herself.

She shifted in her seat. "I cannot wait to get out of these boots," she said. "And to change my clothes. I'm so sick of all these winter clothes." She hadn't taken much to the center with her, which meant she'd worn the same clothes over and over for four weeks.

"Aren't most of your clothes at the lake?" Elise asked.

"Yes, but I didn't take everything. There's still a decent variety here."

"Well, I hate to tell you, but you're in Kansas, and it's still winter."

"I don't care. I want to wear some high heels, something fun."

"You do?"

Claire heard the quick intake of breath, and turned sharply to look at Elise. "What is that supposed to mean? Why wouldn't I?"

To Claire's surprise, Elise swiped at her eye. What in the–? She studied Elise a moment. Oh. She figured she could guess the reason for her daughter's erratic mood swings.

"Elise. Are you pregnant?"

Her head snapped around, eyes wide. "What? Why would you think that?"

"Elise, really. I've never seen you so weepy."

Elise laughed then, a funny cross between a choke and a snort. "I'm not pregnant, Mom. I'm just– I don't know, happy, I guess. It's so nice to hear you sound like yourself."

Claire gaped at her.

Elise sniffled. "I knew things were bad at Thanksgiving. Not just because you seemed weak and out of it, but because you weren't dressed up. Those plain old flat loafers you wore were a dead giveaway." She looked over and smiled. "My mom wears heels. And she always dresses up for holidays."

Tears pricked Claire's eyes. At this rate they'd both be a mess by the time they got to Whitfield. "Did you bring anything dressy?" she asked.

"Not really. I threw in a black skirt."

"Heels?"

"Boots with heels. Does that count?"

"Probably. I think we should get Mary and all the girls we can round up and go out tomorrow night."

"Sure. Sounds fun. But don't forget, we've got a lot of work to do."

Claire heaved a sigh. Yes, she remembered. She wished she'd just hired someone to come in and pack up the house. What in the hell was she going to do with

268

all the stuff in that house? And if she couldn't move for three months, did it really make sense to pack up everything? If she wanted the all-new Maple Grove condo, she might have to endure a little more time in Whitfield after all.

**

They made a quick stop for a sandwich, then hit the first traffic light in Whitfield at two-o'clock. Claire felt detached as they drove through town. Nothing had changed. The streets and shops were all the same. The tall bell tower of First Methodist Church shone white against the blue sky, welcoming them, like always. The neighborhoods were familiar. Yet, everything was different. She'd been gone only five months, but there was no escaping the truth – Whitfield was no longer home. She felt like a visitor.

Mary's car sat at the curb when Elise pulled the van into the driveway. She had a key, of course. Claire and Elise went in through the garage, and Mary stood just inside, holding Reggie in her arms.

"Awww. Reggie, babe," Claire crooned. She hugged Mary with one arm and reached for Reggie at the same time. "How's my kitty?"

"Kitty?" Mary hooted. "More like leopard. I think that cat could eat a small child."

Reggie nuzzled his nose into Claire's neck, and she indulged him for a moment, scratching behind his ears. "Thanks, Mare," she said softly as she moved ahead of her.

In the kitchen, she put Reggie down then turned back to Mary. "What is *that*?" she asked, pointing to the table.

Mary shot her a grin. "Flowers."

In the middle of the table sat a bouquet of mixed flowers in a miniature toy wagon. Claire stared, trying to decide whether it was amusing or offensive.

269

"Now don't be testy," Mary said, nudging Claire. "Just having a little fun."

Finally, Claire shook her head and smiled. "Okay, it's a little bit funny. And the flowers are nice."

"I've got wagon-wheel pasta salad in the fridge."

"What?" Claire marched to the fridge. "Are you serious?" Sure enough, a large bowl of pasta salad in the shape of wheels took up the better part of a shelf inside.

Mary sidled up beside her, and gave her shoulders a squeeze. "There's a glass canister on the counter with the rest of the pasta. Just a little reminder, my friend. I hope they help."

Claire thought of all the reminders tucked inside her packet from Lakeview. Nothing nearly as clever. There was the list of all the positive aspects of her life. That one was short. Then there was the list of all her positive traits and skills. That one had gagged her to write, the flagrant bragging and tooting her own horn. She considered restraint, modesty and class among her more positive attributes, and she'd written those at the very top. She well remembered the cool stare Dr. Gannon had shot her way when he read her list. The group leader had collected those and made laminated copies. Now they were supposed to tape them up around their houses, on mirrors and refrigerators where they could read them every day.

"Oh, and here's something else you'll like," Mary said, interrupting Claire's thoughts.

She shook a small dish on the counter filled with colorful candy. "There's more in the cupboard. Any time you feel like you need a drink, pop in one of these jelly beans. There's peach bellini, pina colada, margarita, strawberry daiquiri. I have to admit, I tried them all, and they're pretty tasty."

Claire laughed. "If you ever need a job, you should consider running a group therapy session at a rehab center."

270

Mary's eyes turned serious. "Uh-uh. Don't ever want to have anything to do with one of those places again."

Claire got the drift. Time to change the subject. "Were you able to find us some boxes?"

"Tons," Mary said. "You'll probably need more, but these should get you started. I took a load upstairs, too."

"Thanks, Mary," Elise spoke up, wandering into the living room. "These are great."

"So you girls ready to start? Did you already eat lunch?"

"We stopped for lunch. Let me get my bags out of the car, and take a minute to get settled. I hardly even remember what's here. Oh, and Susie's coming by at four to look at the house and talk about getting it listed."

"Mom, I'll get the stuff out of the car," Elise said.

"And I'll pour us all a glass of iced tea," Mary said. "Already made. It's passion fruit, and it's delish."

Claire studied the living room a moment, then headed back to her room. On first glance her bathroom was the only room that didn't still look lived-in. Though she'd left an entire wardrobe at the lake house, her closet was far from empty. Even with Mary's help, they'd never get everything packed up in a weekend.

She remembered Mary's iced tea and turned back toward the front room, but stopped before she got there. In the kitchen, Elise and Mary had their heads together, and were speaking in hushed tones. "I'm ready for that iced tea," Claire sang out, alerting them to her presence.

Elise picked up a glass and held it out to Claire. But before she took a sip, Mary swung her glass in the air.

"To your health and happiness, my dear friend."

The three of them drank the tea, and shuffled a few boxes around while they talked, but made little progress by four o'clock when the doorbell rang.

271

"Okay, I'm outta here," Mary said. "By the way, I've got roast in the oven for dinner. After I get Grant situated, I'll be back."

"Oh, Mary. That sounds wonderful," Elise said. "Thank you."

"No problem, sweetie. See you in a few."

But Claire couldn't help feeling that Mary was going overboard. They'd imposed on her enough.

"Mary, really, that's not necessary. We can—"

"Claire, it's a done deal. Don't argue."

With that, Mary opened the door, said a quick hello to Susie, and practically ran down the porch steps, leaving Claire no choice but to let her go while she ushered Susie inside.

"Claire!" Susie threw her arms around Claire. "Oh, it's so good to see you. You look great."

Susie looked past Claire and waved to Elise. "Hey, Elise." Then she clutched at Claire, and lowered her voice. "Are you sure about this? You're ready?"

Claire stepped back, and gave her a wry smile. "Well, the house is far from ready, but yes, I want to start the process." She spread her hands. "So, do your thing, girlfriend. It was appraised in the divorce, of course, but I need to know whether it can be sold as-is, and how fast you think it could move."

"I'll take a look."

Claire hovered behind, answering questions and watching as Susie meandered through the house, opening closets and taking notes.

"Where do you want me to start, Mom?" Elise called.

Claire joined her in the living room. Good question. She pushed her hair back, and surveyed the room. Every shelf and cupboard there and throughout the house was crammed full. Some she hardly dared to open.

"Start packing up anything personal," Susie hollered from down the hall. She poked her head

272

around the doorway. "Leave a few decorative items, but pack up any family photos. We need to get rid of clutter. It needs to be clean and simple for potential buyers."

Claire braced herself against the sofa, Susie's words ringing in her ears. Anything personal? Wasn't it all personal? Didn't every single item in the house represent something personal, right down to the movies in the television cupboard? After all, they only bought their favorites.

In that second Claire wondered if Elise had disposed of all the wine in the collection downstairs. Couldn't be called a wine cellar, but a rack down in the coolest part of the basement. It had always been stocked with some of their favorites. And a few special ones, as well. Bottles they'd picked up on vacations or to celebrate anniversaries and birthdays. Personal.

Even in the fog she'd been in after the disaster with Ray Gleason, she hadn't dipped into the good stuff. Now would it go to waste? She knew Elise wouldn't want it, and she damned sure wouldn't give it to Stan. Guess she'd be giving wine to all of her friends this year – if it hadn't all been poured down the drain. Remembering her daughter's anger, how she'd poured out every drop of alcohol at the lake house, Claire refrained from mentioning it. She'd go downstairs and see for herself.

"Mom, what do you think?"

Claire shook her head. "We can't just pack everything up. We're going to have to divide up what can be sold or given away from what I might keep."

Elise shot her a familiar 'well-duh' look.

"Yeah. So that means you're going to have to make a lot of decisions."

Oh, boy. Decisive again. "All right. Guess we'll have to work together, but it'll slow us down. Let's start on these cupboards. I'll hand you stuff to box up. Set up a box for yourself, too, and holler if there's anything you want." As the thought occurred to her, though, Claire knew Elise wouldn't want much. Even if she did, she simply wouldn't have room in her house. No, ready or not, it was time to purge the possessions of her old life.

**

They worked until Susie joined them again.

"Hey, Claire? You want to talk for a few minutes?"

At the kitchen table, Susie slid a piece of paper in front of Claire. "This is the standard checklist we use. I've rated your house where I think it falls based on the market and other homes in the neighborhood. Your house is in pretty good shape, but there are some areas that should probably be addressed to maximize sales potential."

Claire nodded, her eyes scanning the form. "Any big things?"

"Well, I'm going to have John from our office come out and look at the exterior." She handed Claire another form. "I need you to fill this out. Buyers will want to know how old the appliances are, and big-ticket items like the furnace and the roof. Can you get me all of that?"

"Sure." It would just take time. Like everything else.

"I'd love to be able to list it at the end of March."

"End of March?" Claire echoed. "That's almost two months."

"Yes. It'll have the most curb appeal in spring, and that'll give you time to make any necessary improvements."

Two months. Plus projects. She glanced back to the living room where Elise was still clearing out cupboards. Looked like Claire would be stuck in Whitfield until May, anyway. And God only knew how long it'd take to actually sell the house. People weren't exactly clamoring to move to Whitfield these days.

**

At midnight, Elise finally heard the door to Ben's room snap shut. She waited a few more minutes, until her mother's footsteps retreated down the stairs and toward her own bedroom.

Then Elise tossed back the blankets and tiptoed across to Ben's room. She switched on the bedside lamp, and sagged against the wall. All of the boxes were still stacked neatly at the foot of the bed. And the room looked as though her brother still lived there. Her mother hadn't packed a single thing. Would she ever be able to?

Elise was tempted to do it herself, to just quickly throw everything into the boxes and seal them up, but she didn't dare. She didn't want to be responsible for setting her mother off, or sending her into a tailspin. She fingered the items on the dresser wondering if she could get away with taking a few more mementos for her project. But she wasn't sure whether her mother would notice if they went missing.

As she inspected the room, she spotted the red folder on the side table. Without thinking, she flipped it open, then gasped as she realized what it was. Gingerly, Elise leafed through several pages in her mother's handwriting. Her chest tightened as she uncovered the one titled 'Obituary of Claire Stapleton.' Her hand snapped back as though scalded. She didn't want to read that.

Elise knew she should put the papers back and close the folder, but she couldn't. Instead, she hurried to the door, and quietly turned the lock.

It took only a moment of scanning the pages to see they were mostly about Ben. "Little Boy Ben," and "The Day Ben Died." Elise swallowed past the lump in her throat. At the next-to-the-last paper, her hands stilled. The one-word title at the top of the page was, "Elise."

With flutters in her stomach, Elise pulled the paper out and smoothed it against the bed. Right or wrong, she needed to read this. She desperately wanted to know her mother's feelings. She turned the paper over. Her mother's writing covered both sides of it. Taking a deep breath, Elise sat back against a pillow and started reading.

Tears formed at the very first sentence. *"My daughter has always been the more difficult of my children . . . more defiant, more contrary . . .*

"Of course I love my daughter. I always have. She was my first born. In fact, my only for five years. Those early years were precious. We had fun. I remember how we used to dance around the house. She loved to snuggle up and read with me. We walked to the park and I'd watch her slide, watch her climb, push her in the swing. It seemed like we did that for hours . . . As she got older and I had Ben, Elise tested me more and more. Looking for attention, I suppose.

"The problem is, as the kids got older, Elise became more attached to her father, and Ben was more attached to me. Frankly, I enjoyed Ben more. He was a happy, agreeable kid at the time Elise headed into adolescence and became more difficult and argumentative. Maybe it was the timing and the five years separating them.

"I don't know, but even after she grew up, we never seemed to find a common bond again. She had such a low opinion of me and the things I did. It was as if she wanted to do everything completely the opposite from me – from what she wore to how she raised her children. It was exhausting.

"She got married, tied herself down to a husband and house and job. And she immediately started having kids. And now it's even more difficult to enjoy her. I had visions of the two of us taking adult trips. Sipping martinis by the pool, reading and shopping. We've never taken an adult trip together. I think that's sad. By the time she has any free time, I'll be too old to do anything. Or I'll be dead. She wants me to be Grandma, and I could have some fun with that. But she wants to tell me how to do everything. She has so many rules. They make my head spin. She makes me feel inept . . .

"And then Ben died. I know she thinks I wish she'd died instead of Ben. She thinks if I had to choose, I'd save Ben and let

her die. It's not true. I could never wish that. I only wish I had them both. And I wish we liked each other more."

Elise clutched the paper against her chest, trying to keep it from getting wet as tears spilled from her eyes. Inept, really? She made her mother feel inept? Unbelievable.

She put her head in her hands, trying to think it all through. She read the pages again. And again. So much of this was ancient history. She could hardly be held responsible for her behavior as a kid. At least it was a relief to know her mother wouldn't sacrifice her for Ben. Elise knew her mom was frustrated that she didn't have time for trips and travel, but they'd never really talked about why. She had no idea her mother saw that as a way to *enjoy* her. All Elise felt was the pressure. And criticism.

Sniffling onto her sleeve, Elise flopped back against the pillow. They had to talk more. It didn't have to be this difficult.

She closed her eyes and remembered dancing through the house with her mom. They'd made up routines – everything from silly marches to waltzes and pretend ballet movements. They'd staged pretend shows, and held tea parties, and made craft projects. Until Ben was born.

Elise hadn't realized just how much her life had been defined by her little brother. Before Ben. With Ben. After Ben.

Chapter Thirty-Two

"Well, it's official," Claire told Elise the next morning, handing her a cup of coffee.

"What?"

"They won't budge. The management company says May first. Period."

Elise studied her mug a moment then lifted guarded eyes to Claire's.

"So what are you going to do?"

"Looks like I'm staying put for a while. I have plenty to do here, that's for sure."

"We could look at some other places, Mom. It's doesn't have to be Maple Grove."

Claire gazed out the window, the one that offered a view of the back side of Stan's new place. She wanted a nice place, too. Something different, modern, new. She shook her head at Elise. "No. I like that one. I'll wait."

"Did they ask for a deposit?"

She snorted. "Of course. They're sending a contract. I'll have Susie take a look at it before I sign."

Elise let out a heavy sigh. "Okay. At least you have people to do things with here. But, Mom?"

Elise's voice held doubt. She obviously wasn't convinced that Claire was well enough to live alone.

"If you aren't going to be in Wichita for three months, maybe you should contact a support group here. Or in Paxton. I bet there's an AA group in Paxton. Do you want me to call Marjorie and get some names?"

Claire blanched. No way. She absolutely would not be going to an AA meeting where she might bump into someone she knew.

"No. If I decide I need to talk to someone, I'll call Marjorie myself. I'd rather wait until I get settled so that I'm not just popping in for a few meetings then gone again. In such a short amount of time, I wouldn't even get to know anyone. Besides, like you say, I've got plenty of friends here. Stop worrying."

Claire wondered, though, if word would get to Marjorie if she didn't show up at a meeting in Wichita. Did they keep tabs on people that way? She wasn't entirely sure how much surveillance she was really under.

They worked on the hallway closets until two, when Elise stood and stretched.

"Hey, Mom. Do you mind if I take a little break? I'd like to go over and see Grandma."

Claire swiveled on the ladder. Great idea. She could use some time alone. Time to sit and think and smoke a cigarette. And to investigate the basement.

"Sure, honey. That's fine. I could use a break myself. Don't rush. This mess isn't going anywhere."

"Think I'll stop at the store and get her some flowers. You need anything?"

"Don't think so. But why don't you take her a stack of those magazines in the living room? I'd love to get rid of some."

"Oh, sure. That's a good idea. I'll be back in an hour or so."

Claire locked the door behind Elise, then headed for the basement. She wiped her hands on her jeans, and opened the door to the storage room. Holding her breath as she went around the corner, she flipped on the light. The case was there. And it wasn't empty. Claire quickly estimated twenty dusty bottles of wine in the rack. Her pulse raced as her thoughts jumbled.

She lifted one bottle with a familiar label from the wooden groove. Five of those. A few bottles of champagne. She could give those as gifts. The burgundy could go, she mused. In fact, all of the reds could go to Mary and Grant.

What should she do? Haul them all up now? Hide them? Or wait and let Elise stumble across them?

It was possible they could start on the basement tomorrow . . . Claire looked around. Was any place safe from Elise's watchful eyes? Could she put a few in her bedroom? Just for safekeeping? She hated to waste it or give it all away. She damned sure wouldn't pour it down the drain.

The attic, maybe? Claire sank onto a box and twisted her hair up off of her neck. Oh, Jeez, she hadn't even thought about the attic. She should've required Stan to help with all of this. It was overwhelming.

She sat for a moment, then remembered she didn't have much time. She chose two bottles, and stuffed them inside a box marked Christmas decorations. No one would need to look at those any time soon. Then she grabbed two more and carried them upstairs to her bedroom. No reason for Elise to look inside her luggage, either. Claire wrapped the bottles in towels and slid them into the suitcase.

The rest of it could wait. If Elise found it, they could deal with it then.

**

Perched back on the ladder, Claire started and nearly lost her balance when the doorbell rang. She climbed down and hurried to the door, wishing she'd thought to unlock it before Elise got back. No need to invite suspicion.

But when she pulled the door open, Mary, not Elise, stood on the porch.

"I'm baaaack," she said, holding up a grocery bag. "And I've got munchies."

"Jesus, Mare. More food?"

"How else do you think you get a job done?" Her face pulled into a frown. "What's wrong? You look flushed."

Good grief. Was she that transparent? She gave a little laugh. "Well, I ran to the door so you wouldn't be standing out here in the cold."

"My fingers thank you," Mary said, wiggling her gloveless hands. "So, you girls still up for a night on the town?" Mary asked.

Claire swallowed hard. It'd been her idea, but . . . would she end up being the wet blanket that dampened the evening for everyone else. Keeping the others from enjoying a cocktail? Maybe they should scrap the idea. She wasn't nearly as far along in packing as she'd planned. And not sure she was in the mood to get dressed up after all. The temperature had dropped throughout the day.

"I don't know, Mary. Maybe we should just go out to dinner here in town and leave it at that."

Mary stood in front of her, fiddling with her necklace as she looked Claire up and down. "I know what you're thinking, Claire. Come on, just because you can't have a drink doesn't mean you can't have some fun. We could go to a movie, if you'd rather."

Elise pushed through the door, interrupting the conversation.

"Hey, Mary."

Mary crossed her arms. "Hi, sweetie. Want to help me convince your mom we're going out tonight?"

Elise spun around, her eyes wide. "I sure do. Mom, you were looking forward to this yesterday."

"I know, but it's colder, and we've been working all day—"

"That's exactly why we need to go out," Elise said.

"So wear a fur," Mary added. "I've already made reservations at Bentley's. You know that big table by the fire? It's ours."

"Mother, think how many times you've wanted me to come down by myself so that we could do something together. No kids." Elise pressed harder. "Come on. This is our chance. And we deserve a little fun."

It was true. Claire couldn't remember the last time she had her daughter to herself with no obligations, no children, and no husband. The last time she came to Whitfield alone they'd gone to a wedding and reception, and Elise had left immediately afterward.

**

At six o'clock Dana and Jane arrived, and they all piled into Elise's van with enough hats, coats, boots, gloves and scarves to outfit a small boutique.

Mary practically shoved Dana into the back row. "You're smaller. You crawl back there."

"I'm working on it. Get your hands off my ass."

"Check out my new muffs," Jane said, twisting as she snapped the seatbelt. "Aren't they cute?" Furry pom-poms in a bright blue-and-black leopard print covered her ears and matched the scarf tied around her neck.

"Yeah, I had a pair just like that when I was eight," Mary said.

"Bitch," Jane muttered while the others laughed.

In the front seat, Claire glanced at Elise, wondering if the noise and commotion would bother her while she was driving. But when she saw the grin on Elise's face, she settled into her seat, letting herself relax and enjoy the friendly banter.

As promised, the table by the fire at Bentley's was waiting for them. So was Mary's daughter, Annie. Claire watched as Mary and Annie greeted each other. Mary, dressed in a long sweater belted at the waist with skirt and tights, and her signature chunky necklace, hardly looked ten years older than her daughter. Sure, her eyes crinkled with lines as she smiled, but her whole face lit up when she pulled Annie into a big hug. Even when she stepped back, Mary kept her hand on Annie's shoulder, patting and caressing.

Claire swallowed hard, and glanced at Elise. Had she noticed the easy affection between the two? She couldn't be sure because in the next second, Annie moved toward Claire, her arms outstretched.

"Hi, Annie. It's so nice to see you, honey. Glad you could come."

"Oh, my gosh, me too. This is great. How are you?"

"I'm just fine, but I want to hear all about *you*. I hear you've met someone."

Annie laughed, and sent her mom a playful glare. "Figures. We'll get to that later."

With a sharp squeal, Annie skipped over to Elise. The two girls hugged, nearly jumping up and down. Almost a year older, Annie hadn't been in Elise's grade, but the two of them had been close. They had no choice, their mothers always said. They'd been thrown together, forced into each other's company, from the day Elise was born. The friendship had waxed and waned over the years as they each pursued their own interests, but that early bond had stuck. Claire smiled, happy that Elise could enjoy some girl time.

It took a couple of minutes for the group to get settled into chairs and the chatter to die down. When the waitress approached the table and asked for drink orders, Claire plastered a tight smile on her face. She could almost see the unspoken message zig-zagging across the table from one set of eyes to the next.

"Ladies, please. Order whatever you'd like to drink," Claire said. Without making eye contact with anyone, she spoke to the waitress. "I'll have an iced tea, please."

"Why don't you go ahead and bring us a pitcher of iced tea and a pitcher of Diet Coke?" Jane suggested.

They all agreed, nodding and murmuring. The awkwardness lasted only a moment, and then the conversation and chatter resumed. Claire chimed in, but she also kept an eye on Elise. She rarely had the opportunity to see her daughter in a social setting, and for some reason had the idea she was a bit of a wallflower.

But tonight she seemed perfectly at ease, talking with Annie, but also with Claire's friends. Nothing stiff or forced. When Elise looked up and caught Claire watching her, she grinned.

"Mom, I love your friends," she shouted across the table.

Beside her, Dana gave Elise a squeeze, but spoke to Claire. "Tell her you're not going anywhere, and she has to move back."

In that moment, Claire realized she was about ten years behind. Her relationship with Elise needed to evolve. Sure, she'd always be the mom, but Elise was a grown woman. They should be friends. She swallowed back the lump in her throat, and smiled at Dana. "Nope. It's all set. I've got a place picked out with two guest rooms. We'll have regular pajama parties."

"Count on it," Jane said. Then she nodded at Dana. "Don't turn around, but I think there's someone at the bar you should check out."

Dana turned around.

A man with a beer in his hands sat alone at the bar, and was clearly focused on their table.

Jane groaned. "Nice. Could you be any more obvious?"

Mary laughed. "Yeah, she could get up and join him."

"Good idea," Jane said. "Why don't you go to the ladies room by way of the bar and have a look-see?" She nudged Claire. "Hey, you ought to go with her."

A warm flush spread over Claire's face. She wasn't the least bit interested in checking out a man, and certainly not in the vicinity of the bar. But Dana was on her feet.

"An excellent idea," she said, motioning to Claire. "Come on."

Claire shook her head, her eyes darting toward Elise. She really didn't want to behave like a silly teenager in front of her daughter. But Dana was game, and the rest of them were relentless, on the verge of making a ridiculous scene. Against her better judgment, Claire pushed back her chair and joined Dana. Together they walked slowly past several tables and the end of the bar. Claire let her eyes briefly wander in that direction, and found the man's eyes following them.

She sucked in her breath. *How embarrassing.* When they got to the restroom, she leaned against the wall, laughing. "That guy was so checking you out," she told Dana.

"Or you," Dana said, grinning.

Claire doubted that. Not only did Dana look younger, she dressed it, too. Her black blouse with large mother-of-pearl buttons down the front offered a rather generous view of cleavage.

"So now what?"

Dana shrugged. "Who cares? It's just part of the stupid game."

They waited a couple of minutes, then headed back toward the table. The man at the bar was standing, and turned toward them. With one hand in his pocket, and the other holding a beer, he smiled and nodded. As they went past, he turned – and plowed straight into a waitress, sloshing beer into the air, and nearly upsetting her tray of dirty dishes.

Dana grabbed Claire, her nails digging into Claire's arm, as they hurried to the table.

Dana collapsed into her chair practically convulsing with laughter, but Claire squirmed, feeling vaguely sorry for the guy.

"Oh, my God, that was hilarious," Dana managed. "I think I'm gonna pee my pants."

"Jeez, Dana, that's the second time you've said that tonight," Jane said. "Are you having a little bladder control issue? Maybe you need to see a doctor."

"You're a nurse," Claire added. "Haven't you heard of Kegels?"

"Oh, believe me, I'm quite familiar with Kegels," Dana said. She paused, then leaned in with an exaggerated grimace on her face. "It's the only stimulation I get down there."

The younger girls blushed, but the rest of them hooted, and Claire knew Mary was right. Alcohol wasn't necessary. They were having a ton of fun without it.

Chapter Thirty-Three

Claire slumped against the counter, resting her head in her hands, and kicking at the floor. At least two additional weeks before she could take possession of the condo in Wichita. Now they were a full month behind. Another month in limbo. How was she supposed to start a new life when she couldn't escape the old one? She'd rescheduled the movers twice, sold easily half of her belongings in the sale, had two storage units sitting in her driveway, and just wanted to get on with it. Now that spring had arrived, people would be outside, and there'd be more pressure for her to get involved in activities in Whitfield. And that was one thing she couldn't do. She was leaving.

At this point, she might as well go out and open the lake house and retrieve all the clothes and things she'd left there. At the very least, she needed to get new carpet installed. But she knew Mary and Elise would have a fit if she even mentioned it.

Claire gave a little laugh. Why mention it? Why not go and tell them once she got there? Truth was, she was stir-crazy. Tired of being a puppy on a leash. Tired of being watched and monitored. She'd been two and a half months without a drink.

She swallowed hard, admitting to herself it was getting harder, not easier. She had too much time on her hands. At least if she went to the lake she'd have something to do. Whitfield was getting on her nerves, and the best thing for her frazzled nerves was a glass of wine. God, she had to stop thinking about it.

She shoved the stack of magazine clippings she'd been reviewing into a tote bag, and glanced out the window. Good, the rain had stopped. She grabbed her cigarettes and went outside, still mulling the idea.

She'd go. After tomorrow, she'd go if she wanted to. Well, she might have to wait a day or two, because people would be checking on her tomorrow. If they remembered the date. She shivered in the chilly air. Would anyone remember? Surely Elise and Mary would. Thoughts of the anniversary of her son's death turned to thoughts of the wine she'd hidden in her closet. One glass wouldn't hurt.

Of course she knew the statistics. They'd been drilled into her head at Lakeview. But that was for alcoholics. People who were addicted to alcohol. Claire had never had a drinking problem before her life imploded. She'd been a social drinker, and had handled an occasional drink just fine. Now that she was back on track, why assume she couldn't be the same person she'd been before? Without the trauma and upheaval, she'd have no need to rely on alcohol to blur the days or help her sleep.

**

The next morning, Claire forced herself out of bed, though it was tempting to stay there all day. The memories would haunt her, but even so, she wouldn't miss visiting the cemetery.

She stopped at Millie's and picked up two-dozen red tulips, and for some reason she couldn't explain, was disappointed that Millie wasn't there. The girl behind the counter didn't know Claire. And didn't ask if there was an occasion for the flowers. No reason to mention her son. With heavy legs, Claire climbed back into the car, and headed west to the small Whitfield cemetery.

288

An old limestone wall ran the length of the cemetery along the front side, while a tall wrought iron fence, and dozens of large maple trees marked the other boundaries. Whitfield had done it right. While other small towns placed their cemeteries right on the highway in plain view, Whitfield's set back from the main road, tucked into the landscape, and surrounded by trees, giving it a serene, private feel.

One dusty road ran around the perimeter of the place, and only a couple of interior roads crossed through. Visitors parked their cars as close as possible, then walked to the gravesite. Claire pulled the car through the main gates. Thankfully, no other cars were present and she didn't see Dan, the caretaker, out. Good. She wanted to be alone with her son without the chatter of trimmers or mowers or useless conversation.

She parked and climbed out, clutching the tulips. There was no way to get there without walking on other graves. Even so, she tried to step lightly, sensitive to the fact that she was crossing over someone else's son or daughter or mother or . . . Of course no one else would be coming to the grave. The day held no great significance for anyone else. Not even the boy's father. Briefly, Claire wondered if he even remembered the date.

Claire lowered herself to the damp ground and placed the tulips gently at the base of the headstone. Then she reached out and traced the engraving of her son's name with her fingers. Tears spilled from her eyes, as she knew they would. She poured a cup of coffee from the thermos she'd brought with her, and sipped it in the silence while memories of her son floated through her brain.

His adorable baby face smiled at her, and his cocky teenaged grin. But somehow, she didn't feel his presence the way she did in his room at the house. It was just as well, she supposed. Better to think of him in his favorite places. Maybe next year, instead of coming to the grave, she'd go to some of his regular hang-outs. Or maybe she'd visit some of the places he used to talk about. After all, she wouldn't be living in Whitfield this time next year. With any luck.

Claire stayed until her coffee was cold and she could no longer feel her legs. When she stood to go, she saw another car come to a stop along the road. Quickly, she put her things back into her bag and murmured one last good-bye, then turned stiff legs toward her car.

"Mrs. Stapleton?"

Shading her eyes with her hand, she stopped as the stranger approached. It took only another couple of steps for her to recognize one of Ben's best friends.

She held out her hand. "Dylan. How are you? It's so nice to see you."

He leaned in and dropped a peck on her cheek, then rested his hands on her shoulders.

"I'm okay. I'm sure this is a hard day for you."

Claire nodded. "The worst."

Dylan glanced toward the grave, then back at Claire. "I sure do miss him."

Claire choked on a sob. "Thank you for coming. It's nice to know he's not forgotten."

He shot her a lopsided smile then. "He'll never be forgotten, Mrs. Stapleton. You can be sure of that. Seems like most of the good times I can remember had something to do with Ben. The guys . . ." He shrugged. "Well, we talk about him an awful lot. Sometimes it's like he's still with us."

Claire swiped at the tears, then reached out and took Dylan's hand. "Thank you, honey. That's the nicest thing I've heard in a very long time."

She let go of his hand, and whispered, "You go ahead and visit now."

All the way back to her car, Claire berated herself. She hadn't done enough to keep Ben's memory alive. She'd checked out, barely able to function after his death. Why hadn't she invited his close friends to

290

dinner, or at least kept in touch with them? She'd never gotten around to setting up a memorial – something public such as a scholarship or a fundraiser in his honor, something to trigger a memory of her son.

She climbed into the car and started back to the entrance, lifting her hand in a brief wave to Dylan as she passed. It wasn't too late. She could still do something. Maybe Elise would help. She checked that thought. Probably not. Elise wouldn't have time. But maybe she could contribute some ideas.

"Jesus, Claire," she muttered. "You can do this." She'd run school fundraisers, building campaigns and community events. Why was it so difficult to put together a memorial for her own son?

She slumped into her seat. Because it had to be perfect. Anything less was unacceptable.

Should it be a college scholarship? A memorial at the high school or the college? An annual event? Music . . . basketball . . . leadership? With Ben, there were so many things to choose from.

Did she dare contact Stan? Would he provide half of the start-up money? It was the least he could do. Chances were slim, though. The new missus probably controlled his finances now.

Claire pulled the car onto Cedar Drive, and slammed on the brakes. There, through the scattered trees, she saw a dirty gold pick-up turn onto the highway. She sucked in her breath. What in the hell was he doing in town? If Stan saw him . . .

She banged her fist on the steering wheel. Stan. Ray. As if this day wasn't torture enough already. That was it. She had to get out of there – before she saw either of them, or they saw her. The sooner, the better.

Back at home Claire once again dragged her suitcase out of the closet, and carefully opened it. She unwrapped the two bottles of wine, and set them on the dresser, where they presided over her packing. She imagined the two bottles testing her, talking to each other, placing a bet, perhaps. Would she, or wouldn't she?

Problem was, if she was leaving tomorrow, she couldn't open a bottle tonight. No way could she leave an open bottle of wine in the fridge. Nor could she take one on the road. She wrapped them back up and tucked them in the center of the suitcase, surrounded by clothes.

**

Claire shook off her guilt as she hit open road and accelerated. It felt good to do something spontaneous. Something that hadn't been discussed, analyzed or cleared by her guards.

This trip would be so different. She was better now. Not recovering from an unexpected bomb that had shaken her entire life. She had a purpose. It was earlier in the season than she'd ever been out, and she enjoyed the spring scenery, had never realized how much forsythia lined the property along the highway, or grew unchecked in the ditches.

Thirty minutes from the lake, her phone rang. She dug it out of her purse, and groaned. Mary. Claire considered letting it go to voicemail, but that would raise a red flag. Mary had probably tried the house already, and if Claire didn't answer, she'd go charging over there to check on her.

With a heavy sigh, Claire picked up, and tried to sound normal.

"Hey," she said.

"Hi. It's me. Are you busy? I need a favor."

Oh, shit. "Well, I'm not home. What do you need?"

"Can you come over and wait for the appliance guy? They said between noon and four, and I can't just sit here all day. Sally went home with a migraine, so Grant needs me up at the office."

Of all days. God knew she owed Mary a favor or two. Not only could she not do it, she was busted.

"Oh, Mare. I wish I could. But I'm not in Whitfield."

"Where are you?"

The question hung in silence for a long moment. Claire swallowed hard. She wouldn't lie. "I'm almost to the lake house."

"What?" Mary screeched. "What are you doing?"

"I needed to get away from Whitfield. And I want to get the carpet replaced out here before summer."

"So you just up and left without bothering to tell anyone?"

"I'm sorry. I didn't want to have to explain or justify or cause any drama, okay?"

"Right. Like sneaking off without telling anyone isn't drama in itself." She paused a beat. "Claire. Tell me the truth. Are you all right? I know yesterday was tough, but you got through it."

"I got through it, and then had nothing to do but dwell on it, Mare. And the agent for the condo in Wichita called, and they've pushed my move-in date back again. I feel like I'm trapped. Like I got sucked into one of those black holes and I can't get out."

"Which is why you shouldn't be going off to the lake by yourself."

Claire heard the unspoken accusation, the mistrust, and irritation crept into her voice. "Well, I had to do something."

"Did you take any alcohol?"

The question hit Claire like a slap in the face. "What? I haven't had any alcohol since Christmas. You know that."

"But that's not what I asked. Dammit, I should've spent the night at your place last night to help you through it."

"No, Mary. You're not my keeper."

"Does Elise know?"

"Know what?"

"Come on Claire, don't play dumb. Does she know you've gone to the lake?"

Claire exploded. "No, she doesn't! Remember, I'm sneaking off by myself. Are you going to call her and tell on me?"

"Okay, look, I don't have time for this. I've got to find someone who can help me out."

The line went dead, and a cold sweat dampened her neck as guilt washed over her.

At least she hadn't lied.

**

As she turned the car into the drive, Claire had an awful thought. What if Elise had told Nathan to shut the place down and turn everything off? Nathan usually opened the house back up for the summer. But she'd been there for a good part of winter, and hadn't given any directions when they left for the center after Christmas. It could be cold, and dark, and without running water. Most of the bills came directly out of her bank account, but she should've double-checked.

She held her breath, and punched the remote for the garage door. Thankfully, after another try, the door lifted. At least there was electricity. Still, it was cold inside. Someone must've turned the thermostat down. Claire cranked it up then went to the bedroom for a sweater. She tugged it on and immediately opened her suitcase.

The two bottles were intact, snug inside her clothes. She yanked them out and headed to the kitchen. For a second, she considered going outside and smashing them. But what was the point of saving them, hauling them all the way out here with her? She put them in the refrigerator, then opened the door that held miscellaneous kitchen tools, including her corkscrew. A little slip-up on the part of her daughter. She'd poured

294

out every last drop of alcohol, but had forgotten about the accessories. There it was.

Claire pulled it out and drummed it against the counter, arguing with herself. What was she doing? She didn't need a glass of wine. Especially not in the middle of the day. But that was the point. She didn't *need* it. She'd simply like to enjoy a glass of wine like a normal person. Like the normal person she was.

Finally, she set it down and finished unloading the car. Then she pulled her computer out of her bag. She knew the internet was still on because she'd paid that bill recently. It only took a couple of minutes to find the two places in town that sold carpeting. Tomorrow, she'd visit them both and get that taken care of. Something neutral and durable shouldn't be hard to find.

Next on her agenda was going through her closet and all the winter clothes she'd left there. When she went into town tomorrow, she'd take what she didn't want to keep and drop them off at the donation center. She expected to have a couple of trash bags full.

Before she tossed the first sweater into a bag, her phone rang. Didn't need three guesses to figure out who that might be. She let the sweater drop, and picked up the phone. Might as well get it over with.

She'd barely said hello when Elise's urgent voice came on the line.

"Mom. What's going on?"

"You already know, right? I'm at the lake."

Claire only half-listened to Elise. She let her vent. And didn't bother defending herself.

"Mom. Are you there?"

"Of course. Are you done? Here's the deal. I'm getting things in order here so when I get to Wichita, I can focus on the new place. And the lake house will be ready if Mary and I want to come out, or if you and Brian want to come out this year. I'm going into town tomorrow. I'm picking out carpet, and getting rid of old clothes. I'll probably come to Wichita a little early and stay in a hotel until I can move in. At least I can go ahead and get some things bought. I'm not moving everything from Whitfield, you know."

"Well, I don't understand why you couldn't have told someone," Elise grumbled.

"I'm a big girl, Elise. I live alone now, remember?"

"Yeah. I remember. And I remember what happened the last time you were living by yourself at the lake, Mom. And it wasn't good."

Claire tamped down an angry retort. "You're right. But I wasn't myself then. I'm perfectly fine, so stop worrying."

"Mom. If you're going to be there for even a week, I think you need to find a group or an AA chapter. It's been too long. Marjorie said–"

"Elise, I'm well-aware of everything Marjorie said. I've got audios and videos and reminders. I'm not likely to forget."

"If you feel down or lonely or anything, promise me you'll call someone, okay?"

"All right. I'll talk to you later."

Claire ended the call, and resumed her purging. With satisfaction, she hauled the over-stuffed bags into the living room, and decided it was supper time.

Humming to herself, she pulled out the spinach salad she'd made yesterday and opened a box of sesame wheat crackers. Then she took one of the bottles of wine out of the refrigerator. With a firm grasp, she twisted the corkscrew and popped open the bottle.

Chapter Thirty-Four

Her phone pealed inside her purse. "Oh, shut up," Claire muttered. She didn't need to talk to anyone. And wasn't the least bit interested in playing twenty questions with Elise or Mary.

Ten minutes later, it rang again. She blew the smoke from her cigarette into the air and watched it waft and curl until it dispersed. Whatever they wanted could wait.

She pulled the baggy sweater tighter to ward off the chill of the morning's damp, cool air. There were signs of spring all around the lake, but the weather hadn't committed to the new season yet. Fine with her. Claire liked the silence of these misty mornings, unbroken by the noise of boats and people.

But her stomach was unsettled this morning, and her head ached. She closed her eyes and drifted in and out of sleep, aware that for most lake residents, life was about to swell with familiar busy-ness and activity, but not for her. She was supposed to leave familiar behind and start a new life . . .

Footsteps woke her, but it took a moment for Claire to recognize the sound and then Nathan's voice.

"Claire? Mrs. Stapleton?"

His hand tapped her arm.

She opened her eyes and found his tanned face close to hers. She struggled to sit up. "What? What's the matter?"

"Hi, Claire. Sorry to wake you."

"It's okay. Is something wrong?"

"I'm afraid so. Your friend Mary called me–"

"Mary?" Did she still have a friend Mary, and how the hell would she get hold of Nathan? And why?

"Yes. She's been trying to call, I guess. She's on her way now to pick you up."

Claire shook her throbbing head. Nathan wasn't making sense.

"What are you talking about? Why would Mary pick me up?"

Nathan took her hand. "There were some big storms last night in Kansas. A tornado went through your town, and your daughter was in an accident."

"Oh, but my daughter doesn't live in my town anymore."

"I know, but there were storms in Wichita, too. There was a car wreck, and your daughter's in the hospital."

Claire stood slowly, the fog in her brain clouding her thoughts. "No, I'm sure her husband would've called me."

"They've been trying to call you since early this morning."

She pushed around Nathan, stumbling forward. He caught her arm. "Why don't you sit down and take a minute, okay?"

"No. I've got to go. They'll need me to watch the kids."

"Your friend said the kids were with family, and your son-in-law is at the hospital."

"Fine. I'll head straight to the hospital."

Nathan steered her to a chair, and she dropped down and rested her head on the table.

"Just give me a minute, then I'll go."

"Mrs. Stapleton, you can't drive. Wait for Mary to come. Please."

298

No. She wasn't asking Mary to come to her rescue again. Absolutely not. Claire started to get up again, but nausea churned her stomach. "I feel sick." She almost made it to the side of the deck, but not quite. "Oh, God. Oh, God. I'm sorry. You can go now. I'll wait. Just go."

"No. I'll wait here with you."

She leaned against the rail, limp and spent. Moments later, Nathan climbed the steps with the hose.

He took her arm and moved her back to the chair. "I'm going to take care of this. You rest a minute."

With her head in her hands, she watched him hose down the deck, clearing her mess away. Shame swept over her. Why wouldn't he go away?

**

Mary helped Claire into the car, but neither of them spoke. Claire rested her head against her arm along the edge of the window.

When they crossed into Kansas, Mary broke the silence.

"We're going to the hospital, Claire. Are you feeling okay?"

"I'll be fine." She looked out the window. Away from Mary.

"Did Nathan tell you what happened?"

"He said Elise was in an accident and in the hospital."

"That's right. She's got some internal injuries, a few broken ribs, and honey, she's in a coma."

Claire's head snapped around. "What?"

Mary reached over and took Claire's hand, squeezing it tight. Claire felt as though she was squeezing the air from her lungs. "What are you talking about?"

"She's in a coma, Claire. And Stan's there."

Claire pulled her hand away. "I don't want to see him."

"Dammit, Claire!" Mary shouted. "This is not about you. Your daughter is in a coma. Do you hear me?"

The car swerved then came to an abrupt stop, the seatbelt cinching tight against Claire's chest. She yelped and reached for the armrest.

But she froze when Mary turned toward her, fury contorting her face.

"God, I want to shake the living hell out of you, Claire. What's it going to take, huh?" Tears streamed down Mary's face. "Your little girl needs you. It's Elise. Sweet Elise. Oh, Claire."

Mary was sobbing now. Shock jolted through Claire. She stared at her friend. She opened her mouth to speak, but Mary shook a finger in her face.

"And before you start in on Stan, let me tell you this, he might be the world's biggest ass, but he got the gaping hole in your roof covered, and he's already contacted the insurance company."

Claire frowned. Mary was a blubbering mess and making no sense.

"Mary, what the hell are you talking about?" she whispered.

"You don't even know, do you? Unbelievable." She shook her head as she pulled a tissue out of her purse. "There was a tornado last night, Claire. Half the town was wiped out. Do you get what I'm saying? People died. People are missing. Houses were blown away. Dana's house is a pile of sticks. And the library is gone. Can you understand that?"

Mary's words finally began to sink in. Nathan had said there was a tornado. Oh, no.

"Who died?"

Mary sniffled. Two teenagers. Looked like they tried to stay in their car. And Heather Emerly's parents. But there could be more. "I've got to get you to Wichita, then I have to get back to Whitfield. The cleanup is going to be a nightmare, and I have to help."

300

She pushed her face close to Claire's, digging her fingers into Claire's arm. "And you have to help Elise. The kids will need you, and so will her husband. They need you Claire, and it's time for you to be there for them."

Slowly, Claire nodded. She reached for Mary's hand, and in a second, her friend's arms were around her, and both of them were crying.

"Do you want me to drive?" Claire whispered.

Mary choked, and gave her a tight squeeze. "No. I'm the designated driver. Let's go."

**

With Mary at her side, Claire hurried down the hallway of the Wichita Medical Center. When she pushed the door open wider, Brian motioned her in.

Claire saw Stan, but looked past him to the bed, and ignored the look of disgust on his face. Up his. It wasn't about him, either. She took in the tubes and needles and machines all around Elise, and saw the fear in Brian's eyes.

She rested her hand on his arm for a moment as she walked past him to the bed. Claire gazed at her daughter's face, and smoothed her thick hair. Bruising was already evident around her eyes and cheekbones, and her skin was paler than usual.

Tears burned her eyes. Oh, God. Oh, God. She couldn't lose Elise, too. They'd been through so much. Somehow, they'd survived. Surely they could survive this, too.

Claire reached out and touched Elise's cheek. They weren't very touchy, the two of them. She probably hadn't touched her daughter's cheek since she was a little girl, when it was smooth and round. As she'd gotten older, they'd become less affectionate. She wasn't sure why.

The memories were hazy, but thoughts tumbled through Claire's mind. She knew her daughter wanted more from her. Wanted Claire to be proud of her. She could've been. If Elise hadn't married a man with such low ambitions. If she hadn't done exactly what Claire warned her not to do. At only twenty-three, right out of college, Elise had gotten married, and then pregnant only a year later. So headstrong. Difficult. Always testing her, pushing the boundaries.

Now she worked full time. Had two children, whom other people raised, a mortgage, and a husband who had no hope of ever fully supporting them.

Turning, Claire glanced at Brian and saw the raw emotion in his face. She drew a sharp breath, and turned back to Elise. *It had been her choice, Claire. She married the man she loved, and you gave her no support. She chose a different lifestyle and all you did was criticize.* Regret washed over her.

Brian moved to her side and leaned against the bed rail. "They did tests this morning. The doctors say her brain is fine, full range of activity. She should come out of it." His voice wavered. "It's got to re-start itself."

Mary also moved up to the bed, and hugged Claire's arm. "You okay?" she whispered.

Claire nodded. She couldn't speak.

"Why don't we go down and get some coffee?"

"I don't want to leave."

"I'll go," Stan said from behind them. "What do you want?"

Mary turned and spoke to Stan, but Claire couldn't make out the conversation. She only knew that Stan left the room. Thank God.

He returned a few minutes later, and handed a cup of coffee to each of them. Claire took it, wondering if he'd added anything other than a little cream to hers. Minutes later, nurses bustled in like a swarm of bees, and shooed them all out of the way. Claire stood back and watched for a moment before she gave into the pressure of Mary's fingers on her arm.

They moved to a small waiting area, and Claire sank gratefully into a chair. Mary shoved a sandwich at her.

"At least take a couple of bites of this," she whispered. "You need to eat."

Nodding, she took it. She felt Stan's eyes on her, but she refused to look his direction.

When Mary's cell phone rang, she stepped away to take the call.

Claire chewed a bit of the turkey sandwich and sipped her coffee. She didn't raise her eyes until Mary sat back down beside her.

"They found Jack Hunter's body in the rubble," Mary said. "His house just blew apart."

Claire's eyes squeezed shut. Jack was a good guy. He'd gone a little daft in later years, but he'd been a good teacher. Students liked him, respected him. And he'd been a major proponent of upgrades to the schools and library.

With a heavy heart, Claire pushed the food aside. "Tell me about Whitfield."

"That was Dana on the phone. Her house is destroyed, but she's okay. She was working last night. Half of the business area was hit, and all the neighborhoods close by. Thankfully the hospital and manor are okay. The little Shawnee grade school is gone. They think everyone is accounted for now, but it's a huge mess. And power's down. They've got the high school gym set up as a temporary shelter."

Claire was aware that Stan was watching them, but she didn't care. She reached into her purse and removed her house key from her key ring. With shaking fingers, she pressed it into Mary's hand. "When you go back, give this to Dana. Tell her to stay at my house. She can take the guest room upstairs. I'll let Susie know."

Mary had mentioned the roof. Hopefully that was the extent of the damage. Dammit, she'd just got that house ready for showing – and, hopefully, selling. She did not want to start over. Of course, a new roof would appeal to potential buyers. Might make the house easier to sell. Even as she thought it, guilt swept through her. It might, but it wouldn't be right to benefit from such a tragedy.

At nine Stan finally left. He'd gotten a hotel room. The rest of them squeezed back into Elise's room.

"What do you want to do?" Mary asked Claire. "Stay here or get a room?"

What she really wanted was something to drink. Her head throbbed, and her whole body ached. She needed a glass of wine. Just one. If she could escape Mary's watchful eyes for a few minutes . . .

Claire glanced at Brian.

He nodded at her. "You go get some sleep. I'll stay here. I'll call you if there's any change."

Claire smoothed a strand of hair back from her daughter's face, and couldn't help but think how peaceful she looked. No trace of the worried frown she'd seen so often recently. The fear and worry over her, Claire realized. She sagged against the bed. Get some rest, she whispered silently to Elise. Maybe she just needed a little time out.

"Brian, can we get you anything before we leave?" Mary asked.

"No, thanks, Mary. I'm fine."

Summoning her courage, Claire turned and patted Brian on the shoulder. To her surprise, he stood and pulled her into a hug. Then he hugged Mary, too. "See you in the morning."

They started out the door, then with a quick look back at the bed, Claire saw Brian lift Elise's hand to his lips. The tenderness of the moment cemented itself in Claire's brain.

**

"Claire, let's move. I've got to get home. I'll be praying for Elise every minute. And I'll check in with

304

you." Mary took her hand. "You going to be all right?"

"I'm going to need a car," Claire said, her voice low and terse.

Mary heaved a dramatic sigh, and studied her a moment.

"All right, Claire, I'll take you to rent a car, but you have to promise me you won't have one drop of alcohol. Absolutely none."

Claire crossed her arms. "You're being a bitch."

"No. I'm saving your ass from a DUI or worse."

"I can't live at the hospital, and if I go to a hotel or Elise's house, I won't have a way up to get back up there."

"You can take a cab."

"A cab? Are you crazy? You think this is New York City with a taxi on every corner? Get real."

Mary gave her a cool stare. "Do you have any in your purse?"

Claire shot out of her chair and dumped the contents of her purse on the bed in their hotel room. "No, I do not." Her voice shook with anger. She hadn't had a drop of anything since Mary had picked her up at the lake house. Last night she'd almost left the hotel room, but she was exhausted and managed to fall asleep first. Why had Mary mentioned it, anyway? Now it'd be on her mind.

"Fine," she ground out, glaring at Mary. "I'll try."

"Not good enough. I can't do it, Claire. I'm sorry. You need to be here for Elise, and your grandkids, and you need to be sober. Period. I told you before. I won't be your enabler. Put all that junk back in your purse, and let's go."

The hotel was only a few minutes from the hospital, and Claire sat in stony silence while Mary drove. But she noticed, and hoped Mary hadn't, that only a half-block from the hospital entrance was a car rental shop.

"Claire. I love you. I'll call you."

Swallowing hard, she nodded, and gave Mary a quick hug. Then she watched from inside as Mary's car turned out of the parking lot and blended into traffic.

Thirty minutes later, Claire pulled into the parking lot in a rented Chevrolet. She hurried up to Elise's room. Brian hadn't called, so nothing had happened overnight.

Elise was stable. That was good news. But still comatose, Brian told her. Stan had been there and gone already.

"He's going to run to Whitfield then come back up this evening," Brian said.

Good. Claire stood beside the bed and looked at Elise. "Her color's better."

"Yeah."

"Brian, what about the kids? Should I go get them?"

"They're fine. My sister-in-law's getting them to school and day care. I think it's probably best to keep things the way they are for now. I may leave for a few minutes tonight and go see them."

"Yes, that's a good idea." The kids were probably confused. Andy wouldn't know any better, but Olivia was sharp, and probably scared.

She sat down, and picked up the newspaper again, the images from the tornado's path hard to put out of her mind. "I can't believe this one storm did so much damage," Claire said. "All the destruction in Whitfield and clear up here. The rain causing accidents on the highway."

Brian stared at her, and his face hardened. "The storm didn't cause the accident, Claire. It was a shit-for-brains drunk out on an all-night drinking binge. Elise was on the road at four a.m. because everyone in I.T. got called in to help get the systems back up and running."

Claire's mouth dropped open as she took in Brian's words. A shit-for-brains drunk. A drunk driver had hit

306

Elise. Her blood turned to ice. She'd just rented a car. And she was thinking about finding a liquor store close by.

Panic swept through Claire, and her entire body began to shake. Her mind reeling, she snatched up her purse and ran for the door. She heard Brian call out to her, but she didn't stop running until she found the car. Inside, she banged on the steering wheel, screaming. No. No. No! She ignored the curious looks, the people who stopped and outright gawked. They had no idea. Claire gasped. She couldn't breathe.

Frantically, she dug into her purse. It was there somewhere. Tears blurred her vision, and she could hardly see. Finally, her fingers found it. Claire pulled out the paper, and her cell phone.

"Hello?" a woman's soft voice came on the line.

Claire could hardly get a word out. "Marjorie?" she croaked.

"Yes, who's this?"

Claire heard the instant concern in Marjorie's voice.

"It's Claire Stapleton. Do you rem–"

"Of course, Claire. What's wrong? Are you all right? Do you need help?"

"Oh, God. Oh, God."

"I'm here, Claire. Take a minute. Whenever you're ready, tell me what happened. But first, I need to know if you need medical help. Is this an emergency? Do I need to call nine-one-one?"

Claire swallowed, trying to get enough air to speak. "No. I'm at a hospital right now. Well, in a car. My daughter . . . She's– My daughter's in the hospital. She's in a coma. Hurt. A drunk driver hit her."

"Oh, Claire. I'm so sorry. Are you in Wichita?"

"Yes," she squeaked.

"Do you still have the phone numbers I gave you?"

"Yes."

"But you haven't called any of them?"

"No."

"Have you had a drink since you left the center?"

Guilt and shame surged through her, churning her stomach. She rocked harder, clenching her fists. "Yes," she whispered into the phone.

"Oh, Claire. All right. I'm going to call Stella. She'll find you, and she'll help you. If you let her, Claire. You have to let her help you. She knows about alcoholism. She's lived with it. She also knows what it's like to lose a child. I'm going to have her call you, okay? Promise me you'll talk to her."

"Yes, yes. Okay," Claire cried. "I will."

"I'll check back with you soon."

Five minutes later, Claire jumped when the phone rang in her shaking hand.

"Hello," she said, her voice hoarse and raw.

"Claire, this is Stella Jennings. Can you tell me where you are?"

"Wichita Medical Center."

"I'll be there in ten minutes. Can you wait in the lobby for me at the main entrance?"

Claire glanced around. Where the hell was that? Oh, right. The doors she'd gone in originally. "Yes. I can get there."

"I'm wearing a yellow shirt, and I have red hair. I'll find you."

Claire stayed in the car for a few more minutes, her body quivering. She knew she must look a complete mess, but she didn't care. She got out of the car and made her way back to the hospital, again ignoring the stares coming her direction. She shuddered a deep breath. Didn't matter. Those stares were for a woman who no longer existed. As of this day, that pathetic excuse for a living person was gone. *Be the person you want to be.*

She didn't want to be that person anymore.

Claire dropped into a chair in the lobby, trying to collect herself, but the tears wouldn't stop. Several people stopped and offered help, but she waved them away.

"I'm fine, really."

When she saw a tall redhead rush through the automatic doors, her face etched with concern, Claire stood. The instant she met Stella's eyes, the woman bolted forward, arms outstretched. The yellow shirt burst toward her like a bright sunny day, full of hope and warmth.

This woman Claire had never seen in her life, wrapped Claire in a fierce hug, and squeezed, rocking her back and forth.

Chapter Thirty-Five

Four days later, Claire helped Olivia strap into the car, then handed her a vase of flowers. "Hold them tight, so they don't spill, okay?"

Olivia nodded, and Claire climbed into the driver's seat.

Her eyes met Olivia's in the rearview mirror. "Let's go home," she said softly. She pulled the car around to the circle drive and waited while Brian helped Elise into his car ahead of them. Before ducking into the car, Elise looked their direction, smiled and gave a little wave.

Claire's chest tightened, and she blinked back the flash-flood of tears. Seeing her daughter upright, walking normally, was almost like watching her take her first steps again. With a silent prayer of thanks, Claire pulled the car away from the curb.

Elise was on the mend, but still moving slowly, with pain around her ribcage. No lifting, the doctor had ordered. Claire didn't let her lift more than a book and a coffee mug. Unable to raise her arms for long, Elise needed help in the shower, and washing her hair. For two weeks, Claire stayed with Elise. She ran errands, did laundry, picked the kids up from school, got them to their activities, and looked after her daughter.

Her thoughts often turned to Whitfield and the devastation there. She wanted to help, but she couldn't leave Elise and the kids. She kept up with the progress through Mary and Dana. Thankfully, the damage to

Claire's house had been minimal, only some shingles missing from the roof. She'd been one of the lucky ones. At least she could help by letting Dana and her son stay at her house. Susie had agreed not to show the house for a few weeks.

"But we can't take it off the market," Susie told Claire. "Let's let things settle a bit and see what happens. Most people tend to rebuild after this sort of thing. At least, they do if they have insurance. But they'll need temporary housing. You might want to consider renting it for a year or so."

"That's fine," Claire told her. "But I want Dana to be able to stay there until she gets her bearings and figures out what to do."

She'd go back as soon as she could but right now her plate was full. Looking after Elise and the kids kept Claire busy, and each night she fell into an exhausted sleep. No sleeping pills, and no alcohol. Every day she talked with Stella or Marjorie. Sometimes both. Sometimes more than once. Not because she craved alcohol, but because without warning, anxiety rushed through her. Fear of failing again. She couldn't ever let that happen.

With Stella by her side, Claire attended her first AA meeting. And another. Then, with a tiny sense of confidence, she attended two more on her own. And a germ of an idea started to grow. She planned to set up a desk in her new house, with a view of the courtyard, and she'd start writing again. Not for the newspaper, but for a collection of essays. She could write all the same articles she would've written before, just with a different purpose. Maybe she could find a publisher.

But first she had to get moved in then get to Whitfield. She wasn't a resident anymore, but her friends were. And they needed her. The town would need everyone working together to rebuild and recover. Perhaps from the rubble of the tragedy a stronger community would grow and prosper. She couldn't let the library be forgotten.

When Elise was stronger, Claire rented a hotel room for two weeks, still helping with errands, but giving Elise time to reconnect with her family for a few days before she started back to work.

Finally the new house was ready.

Twenty minutes away from Elise seemed much longer now, but Claire knew the daily visits would end eventually.

Claire couldn't contain the grin on her face as she finished up the paperwork and picked up the keys at the management office.

"Oh, Mrs. Stapleton, you've already had a couple of deliveries. They're in your unit."

"Deliveries?" Claire echoed. She hadn't ordered anything to the new place – yet.

But she had friends. Amazing, wonderful, thoughtful friends. And Claire suspected they were up to something. With flutters in her stomach, she turned the key, and crossed the threshold of her new home.

The grin returned. A large twisted ficus tree stood near the patio window in the front room. And on the kitchen island sat a vase of flowers and a large basket wrapped in cellophane and a big yellow bow. Claire picked up the card. The flowers were from the Maple Grove Realty Company, and the basket of goodies was from her friends.

Claire twirled around the empty space. She still loved it. The pearl-white walls beckoned to her like a blank canvas, just waiting for her brush strokes. She picked up the card tied to the potted plant. *"This tree is like us, dear friend, lots of individual branches going every which way, but with deep roots, and a trunk that's a little bit twisted, but fused together forever." – Much love, Mary, Dana and Jane*

Claire's eyes welled, and she scanned the counter. They should've known to send a box of tissues along with a gift like that. She dug one out of her purse and sat down on the soft pile carpeting beside the plant, gazing at her new view, reflecting on her new life. It wouldn't all be new. She'd never give up those women who'd helped her in so many ways over and over. Who'd saved her life.

After a few more minutes of quiet, Claire initiated the chaos. She called the moving company, then each of her friends while she hauled in the first load of new linens.

**

That evening after dinner, Elise called Claire into the family room.

"Be there in a sec," Claire said. She finished wiping down the table, then switched off the kitchen light.

"What do you need, honey?"

"Nothing. I have something for you." She pointed toward the fireplace.

Claire looked from her daughter to the fireplace.

"What in the world is that?"

"Your Christmas present."

Claire's mouth dropped open, and tears welled in her eyes. Leaning against the hearth was a large wooden box frame with varying sizes of dividers and shelves. Probably three by three, she guessed. The present she would've received had she been functioning at Christmas.

Claire crossed the room to stand in front of the frame. On the left side, Ben's I'm-ready-for-anything grin beamed at her. With his thick hair tousled from the wind, and laughter in his eyes, it was one of Claire's all-time favorite photos. So Ben.

Claire reached out and touched the photo. She could almost hear him, his last words to her before he left for his tour. "It's gonna be okay, Mom." *It's gonna be okay.*

One by one, she examined the objects in the display. One box held a couple of guitar picks. Another

313

held military pins and medals. The tassels from high school and college graduations hung from a peg. Ben's childhood artwork that she'd saved decorated the back of several cubbies.

Another photo dominated the center of the right side – a photo of Ben and Elise arm-in-arm. Ben was about two. And flat-out adorable. Elise was squeezing him to her side, and they were both smiling. Both happy.

"Nothing is glued down except the photos, and they're just copies of the originals," Elise said. "Everything else is pinned, or held in place with Velcro."

Claire couldn't speak. Finally, she let out a choked laugh, and once again touched the life-size photo of the face she dearly loved. "That's him."

Elise nodded beside her. "Yes. That's how we should remember him."

Elise reached over and removed a small box from the mantel. "There's one more thing." She lifted the lid and held up a silver necklace. A square locket hung from the chain, with several small tokens dangling underneath.

Claire took it, her fingers grazing the small trinkets . . . a silver heart, a key, some beads. Then she opened the locket and saw a miniature version of the photo on one side, Ben's name and birthdate engraved on the other. She squeezed it to her chest, and met Elise's eyes.

Elise pulled a second locket from the box. "I had one made for me, too. They match."

"Oh, honey. Thank you. They're beautiful. Let's put them on."

Claire's fingers fumbled with the clasp, but they shook too much to make it work. Elise took it from her and fastened the clasp behind her neck. Then she put on her own.

"You had them made?" Claire asked, her voice quivering with emotion.

314

"Yes. I met a woman at an art fair who created personalized jewelry. That's what gave me the idea. I talked to her about it, and she said she'd do it. These are plated with white gold, so they won't tarnish. One of the beads is a Topaz, Ben's birthstone. The blue Lapis stands for healing and peace."

"Oh, Elise. These had to be expensive. I want to pay for them."

Elise shot her a grin. "You did, actually. You know the money you gave me after the divorce was final? I used it to pay for these."

"Well, for heaven's sake. You were supposed to buy yourself something, spruce up the house."

"It was plenty for both. And this is what I wanted to do. You're not upset that I took Ben's things and put them in here, are you?"

"Of course not. I love it. And I love that I can still take them out and touch them. It's very thoughtful, Elise."

She swallowed hard, and took Elise's hand. "This has been a tough year for both of us. I know I put you through some bad times. I'm sorry for that."

When tears spilled down Elise's cheeks, Claire wiped them away, Ben's words echoing in her ears again. *It's gonna be okay.* "No more tears," she whispered. She gathered her daughter into her arms. "I love you, honey."

"Love you, too, Mom." Though Elise's words were muffled, Claire understood each one.

Chapter Thirty-Six

Claire sensed something was wrong even before Olivia climbed into the car. Her steps were slow, and her happy smile was missing.

"Hey, sweetie. How was dance today?" Claire glanced over, and Olivia shrugged.

"Okay."

"Are those papers for your mom?" She saw that Olivia clutched a couple of sheets of paper in her hand.

"Yes. She has to sign them," Olivia said in a small voice.

"Okay. We'll give them to her when we get home. Is there something you want to talk about?"

"She has to give permission for me to be in the recital."

"I don't see any problem with that."

"She has to promise I'll be at all the rehearsals."

Oh. Olivia was a little behind in her dance lessons. While her mother was hospitalized and recovering, Claire had tried to step in and get her to ballet, but some days were too short and too busy. Some were too rainy. And some days all Olivia wanted to do was curl up beside her mother or grandmother and read a book.

No one pushed.

Claire blew out her breath and reached across to squeeze Olivia's soft hand. "It's up to you, sweetie."

Olivia didn't answer, but the subject came up again at dinner that night.

"Hey, Princess, Mom says you have a dance recital coming up," Brian said after they'd all sat down and said grace.

Olivia looked at Elise.

"I won't be as good as the other girls," she said into her plate. "I might mess up."

Claire heard the fear in Olivia's voice. She'd fallen behind, and had lost her confidence. Was she hoping Elise would tell her she didn't have to participate? Claire didn't want that to happen.

"Olivia. The other girls didn't have moms in the hospital. Maybe they didn't miss any classes or rehearsals. It doesn't matter. All you have to do is give your best effort, and you'll be great. It's just a chance to get dressed up and show what you've learned. And to have fun. You can do that, can't you?"

"I guess so." Olivia's wide eyes stared at her. "Will you come, Grammy?"

Once upon a time Claire thought she'd been to enough music programs and dance recitals and baseball games and plays to last a lifetime. The thought of enduring those things had lost all appeal. But as she looked at Olivia's hopeful expression, her heart swelled. There was no place else she'd rather be.

She gave Olivia an encouraging smile. "Of course, I'll come. I wouldn't miss it."

**

On impulse, Claire stopped at the grocery store. Inside, she headed for the floral department. She'd become quite familiar with the nooks and crannies of the place in the last several weeks. She wandered the boutique, and fingered some bright Gerbera daisies and sunflowers, trying to decide what would be best. Tradition, she supposed, was to give a ballerina roses.

317

She peeked inside the refrigerated case. There were plenty to choose from.

"I'll take the light pink roses," she told the girl at the counter.

"How many would you like?"

Claire thought for a moment, and glanced at the girl's nametag. Ashley. What would be appropriate without being over the top?

"Three, please. With greenery, wrapped in tissue."

The sales girl nodded and pulled three stems from the cooler. "What's the occasion?"

"My granddaughter's dance recital." Claire couldn't contain the hint of pride in her voice, and her pleasure that Ashley had asked.

Ashley stopped and turned toward Claire. "Oh! How old is she? I have some fun sparkly swirls I could add."

Sparkly swirls? She wasn't familiar with such a thing.

The girl reached under the counter, then held up a spiral stick covered in a heavy layer of pink glitter.

Pink glitter. Claire reached out for the stick, watching it twinkle as she turned it.

A memory crashed in, and she was reminded of her own daughter dressed as a princess for Halloween when she was about five, and wearing a glittering tiara in her hair. Elise had worn the tiara in the bathtub, and to bed that night. Refused to take it off. She'd loved the way it sparkled.

Claire smiled at the girl, and handed her the pink stick. "Perfect."

THE END

Acknowledgments

Many thanks to my critique partners, Michelle Grey and Janice Richards, and other advanced readers/ editors, Sandra, Paula and Toni, who put in hours of time reading and improving The Storm Within.

I'm grateful for the many websites that offered information on alcoholism and treatment.

Special thanks to all of my friends, fans and family who have supported me along my writing and publishing journey.

I hope you enjoyed meeting Claire and her friends. They'll be back in Book Two as Dana literally picks up the pieces of her life following the tornado that devastates Whitfield.

Darlene Deluca writes contemporary romance and women's fiction from her suburban home in the Midwest. The Storm Within is the first book of her small town trilogy, Women of Whitfield.

Darlene would love to connect with readers. You can visit her author pages at Facebook, Amazon or Goodreads.

www.threewritersofromance.com

Made in the USA
Charleston, SC
08 August 2013